'A poignant story ... moral choices'
– **Nick Rennison,** *Sunday Times*

'A wartime thriller about two women connected by their love for
an enigmatic Polish airman with a daring plan to expose Soviet
atrocities' – **Robbie Millen,** *Times Best Books of 2020*

'Driven by two strong female characters, each of whom could
sustain a novel on her own, connected by the more ambiguous
figure of Stefan, *When We Fall* was inspired by the Katyn
massacre of 1940 and explores the emotional toll of war and
the indelible marks left on people's lives by tragedy and human
wickedness' – **Alastair Mabbott,** *Herald Scotland*

'It's a tale of tragedy and brutality, with characters that are so
well-drawn they practically get up and walk from the page...
I simply wanted to pick up when I had finished and start
over again' – **Jenny Quintana**

Memorably descriptive prose... Carolyn Kirby is a past-mistress
of the little twist, the soupcon of uncertainty that creates an
atmosphere of tension' – **Gaynor Arnold**

'An example of this genre at its finest' – **Howard Linskey**

'An engaging and elegantly written novel on the grim realities of
war, and the moral choices that can result. Highly recommended'
– **Roger Moorhouse**

'A meticulously researched novel of love, intrigue and betrayal...
reveals how in war truth so often falls victim to expediency.
In a story where loyalties are called into question, she kept me
guessing to the final page. Carolyn's writing is so vivid and so well
researched – I was sitting in the cockpit with Vee and walking the
streets of Poznan with Ewa!' – **Anita Frank**

'Such a skilfully constructed novel about one of the less well
trodden events of the war peopled by complex, sympathetic
characters. Compelling and moving – it's a wonderful read which
often sends the pulse rate into overdrive. I loved it'
– **Annie Murray**

Also by Carolyn Kirby

The Conviction of Cora Burns

WHEN WE FALL

CAROLYN KIRBY

NO EXIT PRESS

This edition published in 2021,
first published in 2020 by No Exit Press,
an imprint of Oldcastle Books Ltd,
Harpenden, UK
noexit.co.uk

© Carolyn Kirby, 2020

This is a work of fiction. Names, characters, places, and incidents either
are the product of the author's imagination or are used fictitiously, and any
resemblance to actual persons, living or dead, businesses, companies, events or
locales is entirely coincidental.

ISBN
978-0-85730-397-4 (print)
978-0-85730-396-7 (epub)

2 4 6 8 10 9 7 5 3 1

Typeset in 10.5pt Minion Pro
by Avocet Typeset, Bideford, Devon, EX39 2BP
Printed and bound by CPI Group (UK) Ltd, Croydon, CRO 4YY

For more information about Crime Fiction go to @crimetimeuk

'Scores of senior Polish figures including President Kaczyński have died in a plane crash in Russia.

Polish and Russian officials said that no one survived after the plane hit trees as it approached Smolensk airport in thick fog.

Poland's army chief, central bank governor, MPs and leading historians were among at least 90 passengers who died.

Prime Minister Donald Tusk said that the crash was the most tragic event in the country's post-war history.

The Polish delegation was flying from Warsaw to mark the 70th anniversary of the Katyn massacre of more than 20,000 Polish officers by Soviet forces during the Second World War...'

BBC News
10 April 2010

10 April 2010

Air

Bournemouth, England
Saturday 10 April 2010

The radio-voice stumbles over the names of the dead. Foreign syllables are tripping her up, like bodies strewn through wreckage. And at the sound of one of the mispronounced surnames my heart buckles. Did she just mention you? But, no. A lifetime has passed since I last heard anyone say your name. Then the announcer utters a Russian word without hesitation. *Katyn*. The place in the forest. A sick-taste of guilt rises and I flick the off-switch.

Outside through the kitchen window, high cloud films the sky like a girl's well-brushed hair. Those gauzy cirrus clouds are so far away from us that their turbulence seems slight. But if you take your eyes off them for more than a moment, their icy formations will have altered forever.

You told me this as we stood on a wide grassy airfield that morning you first took me up. *Look!* you said, your rolled shirt sleeve falling back as you pointed at the clouds, *they are moving faster than anything in the sky*. In a leather flying-helmet and men's slacks, I tapped sceptical fingers on my forearm. *I don't believe you*, I said, *they're not moving at all*. Your grin was still boyish as you squinted into the sunlight. *All right then. Let me take you for a closer look*.

And so you did. Up, up went the old bi-plane in a climb so fast and so vertical that it could not last. At the top of the loop, the engine slowed then coughed into silence. We sat suspended in air. Then we began to fall; slowly at first, then faster, faster, into a gut-churning plunge. I forced my eyes to stay open. A farmhouse loomed below, white sheets waving on a washing line. *Hang on,*

I thought, *maybe this isn't a joke.* The white sheets grew, filling my goggles. I pictured myself slamming into the farmhouse's orange roof, saw white lilies on my coffin and tears rolling into my father's moustache. But then, when there was nowhere left to fall, the engine hiccupped and the plane, as you knew it would, swooped back up into the crisp air.

You had to help me out of the open cockpit. I couldn't walk. *Did you not like it?* you asked, smirking. *Quite a thrill, I suppose,* I replied, cool as you like.

You raised an eyebrow, fixing me with your pale blue stare. *Then I'll have to think of something even more exciting.* My gaze, always bold, did not waver from yours. And I let my fingertip rise to touch the V of tanned skin inside your unbuttoned collar.

No photograph of you exists anywhere on the planet. I used to think that I could not bear to stay on earth either unless I could see, just once more, your face squinting up at cirrus clouds. But here, implausibly, I still am. Along with the only relic of you that remains.

I drag the chair from the kitchen table and climb somehow on to the seat. But even on tip-toes, I seem no longer able to reach the back of the top cupboard. My fingers pat around unseen knick-knacks and forgotten paperwork; a tight wad of thirty-year-old tax records for The South Coast School of English; the crinkle of an aerogram with a West German stamp. My ring taps against the smooth glass curves of a lighthouse filled with multi-coloured sand. Mine is not much of a wedding ring; the plain copper is dull and worn, and it is on the wrong hand. But it tells me, even if it lies, that you loved me more than the foreign girl.

Reaching into the sandwich of paper, I edge my thumb and forefinger around the logbook and gain some purchase on the grainy cover. Inside, your writing still bounds across the page, through flying times and aircraft types, with such youthful elegance it is as good as a portrait of your face.

I pull harder and the logbook slides forward. Then suddenly it pops free. The release uncorks a shower of long-paid bills and unanswered letters that rocks me back on to my heels. And then forward. Slowly at first, but inescapably, I lose my connection to the chair and start to fall. I become as free and untethered from the earth as that girl in the bi-plane, although this time the ground hits me and with a force that could have come from a thousand feet instead of two.

Tiles are cool under my cheek. Black spots dance across my eyes. Then the spots start swelling, joining, almost blotting out the paperwork that is scattered across the kitchen floor. But, just before blackness closes in, something glints at me through broken glass and sherbet sand. For there, on the faded blue cover of a Royal Air Force logbook, are your initials, *SB*, in still-shining gold.

Spring 1943

Stratus

Low blankets of dense grey cloud with clear air above.
If very low-lying, stratus becomes mist or fog.

Essex, England
Wednesday 31 March

The Tiger's yellow wings slice over sodden fields. Vee glances down then double-checks the map but all appears as it should. Printed red roads still match the pattern of snaking grey macadam on the ground. Ten more minutes and RAF Birch should be in sight.

But to the east, the air is murky; sea, sky and shore are merging. As Vee squints into the propeller haze, whiteness begins to blank out the earth. Her pulse quickens. Perhaps she should have taken the advice of that watch officer at Stradishall to give Birch a miss. But how would that have looked on her training record? They would think her slack or spineless. Not quite up to scratch.

Then, through a sudden clear hole, spidery roads sprout from the fat body of a village and Vee's eyes jerk back to the map. Halstead perhaps? But the mist, damn it, has already shifted, swallowing the village up. Cloud tightens around the cockpit and Vee shoves the useless map under the seat. Now that she is flying blind, there is nothing left to see.

Sweat trickles into her brassiere and a corner of Vee's brain enjoys the rush of adrenalin – the tightening of focus, the heightening of her senses. This is what she craved, after all, during those dull afternoons staring at a criss-cross of vapour trails through the factory office skylight. And the heat building inside her flying suit comes less from fear than from irritation; irritation with the watch officer whose warning of low cloud near the coast was not forceful enough to make her change course, and irritation with Captain Mills for tutting when she had asked, only last week, whether there would be any training to fly on instruments. *Oh no,* he had chided, *we won't be worrying your heads with that. You'll be too busy keeping one eye on the ground and the other on the motoring map on your knee.* It was hardly even a motoring map that she'd been given today – more like something that before the war would have come free with a Sunday newspaper. But any map would be useless now.

The engine drones on, oblivious to danger. Vee's face, goggles and fleece collar are all soaking. Inside a clammy glove, one hand grips the control stick, trying to keep it motionless and perfectly upright as the other raises her goggles. But it is no better. The ground could be anywhere. Watery air coats Vee's eyelids but her mouth is dry.

How long since she last saw the ground? A minute, or three? She has read somewhere that time is the most important thing to keep track of when flying blind, although she has no idea what comes next. She checks the altimeter. *500 ft.* Too low. But going up is off limits. Captain Mills had pointed, smugly, at the instruction written in capitals into the ATA rule book: *DO NOT, UNDER ANY CIRCUMSTANCES, TRY TO FIND YOUR WAY OUT OF MURK BY GOING OVER THE TOP.* Because sunlight may lie just above this layer of cotton-wool cloud, but Vee knows that without reliable instruments or training in how to use them, the seductive prospect of clear air is a deathtrap. Fuel can so easily run out before the cloud that hides the ground ever does.

But does she dare go down? Her heart beats double time at the thought. Clear air may be only a few feet below the Tiger's wheels. Or fog may drape right into the corduroy soil. Vee glances at the small wooden instrument panel even though she knows that at this height, the Tiger's gauges cannot be trusted. She takes a proper breath. Fifty feet down is worth a try.

With her eyes on the altimeter, Vee pushes the control stick gently forward and feels the familiar downward lurch in her stomach. The needle descends. Five hundred; four fifty. The fog is dense with moisture. Black spots crowd across her vision as her eyes strain into the glare. Is something there, dark and shifting, not far below the plane? Is there? Good grief. Vapour suddenly clears and furrowed black earth looms up. The plane is not at four fifty. Nowhere near. Two hundred feet she'd guess, or less. Instinctively, she pulls back on the stick and the Tiger jumps up, top wings cutting at rags of cloud. But she rights the stick and the plane levels. Just above the telegraph poles will have to do.

Except that there are no telegraph poles here; there's not much of anything. Ploughed fields give way to squashy-looking marshland, and then, across a line of listless surf, land turns into sea. The Tiger gives a cough as if to enquire, politely, if this is really the way that she wants to go. Sweat accumulates in Vee's armpits and behind her knees.

Here comes land again, dull green and curlicued with marshy channels, and beyond it, another expanse of dark water. Vee's eyes cast around for the horizon. Water. Marshland. Water again. And in the distance, embedded in a shroud of mist, an eerie green light. She blinks. The glow becomes more solid and more definitely green. It reflects vaguely in the approaching expanse of open water. Something must be illuminated out at sea. But what vessel would be lit up like a target practice for the Luftwaffe? Then the eerie light lengthens to a rectangle of green dots. A flare path. And inside it sits a dead-straight strip of concrete with a squat control tower to one side.

Vee feels a wave of hot relief pass through her. This is not Birch; too close to the coast for that, but any landing ground is better than a turnip field. Pressing a boot on to the rudder pedal, she banks the Tiger on to a low circuit around the aerodrome. The limp yellow windsock rises in a sluggish salute as she levels down towards the strip. She pulls up the nose into the faint headwind. Wheels skim clean concrete. There is a bump of touchdown but the rest of the run-in is satisfyingly smooth.

Vee steers the Tiger to a stop but lets the engine purr. On

the roof of the control tower, inside a glass observation box, binoculars glint. They cannot, surely, object to her landing here. Anyone can get caught out by fog. She reaches down for the map and scans the jigsaw of green and blue for an aerodrome.

Then the Tiger rocks drunkenly to one side. An airman wearing a deflated life-vest has put his foot on the lower wing, weighing it down. His hand slices across his throat in a signal for Vee to cut the engine, but he is smiling. She reaches out to the switch beside the half-windscreen and flicks off the ignition. As the engine stutters into silence, she looks at the airman, and when his icily pale blue eyes meet hers, his smile collapses.

'Mein Gott!'

Colour washes from him.

Vee tenses and unease needles the back of her neck. That last stretch of water… it could not possibly have been the North Sea, could it? And that bomber beside the runway is surely a Bristol Blenheim, not a Junckers 88… Her eyes search around for a familiar red and blue roundel. And, of course, the RAF symbol is there on the Blenheim's fuselage. How could she be anywhere except England?

She turns back to the airman and realises how long she has been all but holding her breath. Her voice comes out clipped and shrill.

'Where is this?'

Shakily, the airman's smile returns. 'You don't know?'

'No.'

'Really?'

'Why bother lighting a flare path unless you're expecting people to become lost?'

'Yes.' His smile strengthens. 'You are right.'

'And if you hadn't told me to switch off the engine, you could have simply pointed me in the right direction and I would have got out of your way.'

'But the sea fog is too heavy now for take-off.'

15

His accent is not strong but there is one, and she cannot quite place it. Could it really, somehow, be German? She hears her voice become brittle.

'You seem rather reluctant to reveal our location.'

'Classified information.'

'What?'

He laughs. The sound is reassuring as well as infuriating.

'No, no, I am sorry, a joke. Bradwell. This is RAF Bradwell Bay.'

'Thank you.'

She looks back at the map and feels hotness in her face even though he can have no idea that she just imagined herself to have flown into Nazi-occupied Belgium. She hopes the airman might go away but he leans over her and points with a clean white finger. He must be a pilot; they can never resist a map.

'We are here, see. Bradwell. Where did you come from?'

'Sorry. Classified information.'

He nods sheepishly to one side indicating that they are even, now. But as she tries to look back at the map his eyes hold her. A dark ring around their paleness gives him a striking, foreign look. His smile grows warmer.

'No, I am sorry. And I must give you something to make up for my bad joke. Tea, maybe?'

'No need.'

'Please, just wait here for a short time. Believe me, half of one hour will change everything.'

'With the vis, you mean?'

He nods. 'Cloud will soon disappear.'

Vee taps a finger on the buckle at her waist. He is probably right. And it would not be sensible to get even colder by sitting out here for half an hour.

'All right.'

She snaps open the harness straps. The airman stretches to help her from the cockpit but she ignores his hand, hauling

16

out the parachute and overnight bag behind her. She will not risk leaving them. Anything might happen to an unattended aeroplane, especially this close to enemy shores.

Only when Vee steps down on to the concrete does she realise that her feet are numb. The airman raises his arm, indicating the way and she tries not to let her legs collapse as she follows him. He seems to have thought better of offering to carry anything for her. Vee feels vaguely guilty for her sharpness.

'Stradishall,' she says.

'Excuse me?'

'That's where I've come from, RAF Stradishall. Or at least, that's where I last touched down. I set off on my cross-country this morning from Luton.'

He slides her a glance. 'So what... what are you?'

'A pilot.'

He winces and again she senses that she is being too sharp.

'I'm Vee.'

His eyebrows exaggerate a frown. 'Like V for victory?'

'V for Valerie.'

'Valerie.' His tongue rolls around the syllables.

'Vee,' she corrects.

'Please, excuse me. I must make an introduction.' He gives a sharp nod and raps his heels together. 'Flight Sergeant Stefan Bergel, 302 Squadron. How do you do?'

Vee tries not to laugh. 'Pleased to meet you. Vee Katchatourian.'

She walks on and gives him a sideways look as he catches up. He is tall, even for a pilot. Every movement inside his baggy overalls has a hint of coiled energy. His face has an eager look.

'You are Armenian, Vee?'

She does not miss a beat. 'No. I'm English.'

Her voice has sharpened but actually she is impressed. She cannot remember the last time anyone got it right. And it is a perfectly fair question; a good many of the other cadets are from abroad. It is just that her senses are always primed for the usual reaction to her surname; the slight frown of incomprehension, the wince of embarrassment at her foreignness even though, despite her olive skin and hazel eyes, Vee is as English as anyone she knows.

She blinks sideways at Stefan Bergel. 'But you're not. English, that is.'

'No, no, no!' He chuckles and inclines his shoulder towards her, lifting the flattened yellow edge of the life-vest. '*POLAND*' is embroidered on to the shoulder of his overalls.

'I see.'

So, what he said before must have been in Polish, or perhaps it had just been *My God*, with that accent of his.

Grey fog swirls around the green flares. In the control tower, shadowy figures move around behind big windows criss-crossed with tape. Stefan raises a thumb in their direction then leads the way to a blackened wooden hut that even inside smells of creosote.

In the corner of the uncertainly furnished room, an urn steams on a ring-stained bench. An airman slumped in a saggy armchair snores. Vee drops her parachute pack to the floor and sits at a scuffed card table. She takes a gulp from the cup that Stefan puts down in front of her. Despite the steam, the tea is not very hot.

Stefan leans back and in his chair. 'So. What do you think of our mess?'

'Messy.'

'We need more ladies to visit.'

'To do the tidying?'

He laughs and his dark hair, wet from the fog, falls forward on to his brow. But beneath the smile, his pale eyes are fixed, unblinking, on Vee. This makes her feel awkward but also faintly excited. Luckily, the hut is too cold for her to have any urge to undo the collar of her Sidcot, or even take off her leather helmet. She must not be tempted to stay too long. Given that she hasn't made her scheduled touchdown at Birch, Captain Mills might already be wondering where she and the Tiger have gone.

Stefan leans across the card table, half whispering. 'Okay. I give in. I know you are not WAAF, so tell me what you are? Coastal command or civil aviation of some sort...?'

'Of some sort, yes. Air Transport Auxiliary.'

'Oh, yes. You deliver our new planes and take the knackered ones out of our way.'

She laughs. His English is good, but eccentric. 'That's right.'

'And Luton is your base?'

Vee shakes her head. 'White Waltham.'

'Ah yes, near Northolt.' He nods as he takes a sip of tea. 'And giving radios to ATA pilots would make their navigation too easy?'

'It would rather take the fun out of it, I suppose.'

'Seriously?'

She laughs. 'Of course not seriously.'

He looks a little hurt and again guilt folds through her. She cannot remember a man ever being so alert to what she has to say. It makes her feel older than him although clearly she is not. She takes a sip of cool tea then puts the saucerless cup on to the felt tabletop. A few dark hairs on Stefan's wrist seem trapped in the steel links of his watch. It is all she can do not to run her finger around the rim of the strap and free them. She blinks the thought away. Her wits must be addled by the fog. She keeps a grip on the teacup with both hands.

'There's lots of reasons we don't have radios. ATA often have to fly brand-new planes from the factory to maintenance units for the radios to be fitted there. So we have to learn to fly contact with the ground and not rely on wireless signals. And anyway, the channels have to be kept clear for you lot.'

'So if sea fog comes down they don't mind to lose a Tiger Moth and a lady pilot?'

'They haven't lost me, have they? I'm here.'

'And I am most glad that you are.'

She thinks for a mortifying instant that he is going to take hold of her wrist just as she had imagined taking his. But instead he smoothes back the wet hair from his brow.

Across the room, the airman in the armchair farts noisily as his head flops on to his shoulder. Stefan picks up a flattened cushion and throws it at him, barking out a swoosh of syllables. Grunting, the airman shifts and opens his eyes, then he sees Vee and jumps to his feet. Without a word, he steps forward and takes hold of her hand pressing it to his lips before Vee can resist. Then he makes the same Germanic head bowing and clicking of heels as Stefan but with more flourish.

He says something unintelligible and then, 'I delight to meet you, madam.'

Vee frees her hand and grins. 'Hello.'

Stefan raises his chin and then his voice at the airman, who immediately does the same then torrents of words swish back and forth across the room. Vee sees that she was wrong; Polish sounds nothing like German. This language glides and cracks in an unfamiliar, incomprehensible stream. Not a single word resembles anything English.

'He is trying to tell you that his name is Piotr Drzewiecki. But everyone here now calls him Double Whiskey and he must get used to it.'

'Must he? Why?'

'Because we try to make things easy for our English hosts.'

'Not everyone can have a name that is idiot-proof.'

Stefan turns back to face her as he realises what she means. He blinks slowly. 'Your name…'

'…is Armenian. You were right. My father came to England as a very young man and then he met my mother. Katchatourian might be a mouthful but my father kept the name because it is all that he has left from his homeland.'

'Which is now in… the Soviet Union?'

'The town where he was born is in Turkey, I believe. But he

washed his hands of the place long ago. People with names like his were treated horribly there.'

Vee surprises herself by how much she has said. Usually, she throws down her surname like a challenge, refusing to excuse or explain, and is ready to pounce when anyone gets it wrong.

Stefan is staring at her with an intensity that is disconcerting. She picks up her cup, draining the tepid tea. Then she looks at her watch but Stefan is quicker.

'A quarter to two.'

'Yes.'

'You have been here only twenty-five minutes. And vis is not much better.'

'Actually, I'd say that it seems much improved.'

But the window is too misted and dirty to tell whether the weather is getting better or worse.

'Why not stay here? You have your things.' Stefan nods at her overnight bag.

'That's only in case of real emergencies.'

'Perhaps if you stay here you will avoid a real emergency. Piotr says no routine take-offs will be allowed for the rest of today.'

Is that what they'd been talking about? There seemed more passion to it than a conversation about the weather. Vee summons her most crystal-cut English voice.

'Well, ATA authorises me to make my own decisions. So I'll leave now and get back whilst there's enough light.' With a scraping of wood, she stands up. 'Better not let the engine get too cold.'

Stefan stays seated with his arms on the table and begins to make some other argument for her staying here, but Vee is out of the door before he catches her up.

The mist is most definitely lighter now and Vee enjoys a shiver of smugness that she was right. Her pace slows as she senses Stefan's broad shadow behind her.

'Please don't trouble yourself to come with me.'

'But you need someone to turn the airscrew.'

'Do you not have ground staff?'

'I am very happy to do it myself.'

And perhaps, now she thinks of it, that would be for the best. Someone else here might demand official clearances and maybe even telephone Captain Mills. Which could make things tricky. All being well, she will not have to mention this forced landing at all, just say that she gave Birch a miss due to the nearby sea-fret. That should keep her cross-country record in the clear.

The haze has lightened enough for Vee to see the row of Hurricanes and Spitfires on the far side of the runway. She cannot stop herself asking.

'You fly fighters?'

Stefan nods. 'You too?'

'Oh no. Not yet, at least. I have to get my Wings first.'

'Soon, then.'

'Maybe not, after today.'

'Ach! All pilots get lost in cloud. What do ATA expect, if you have no radio?'

She smiles. He seems so indignant on her behalf.

'Do you think anyone will tell ATA that I was here?'

'It is better for you if they do not?'

'Well, a forced landing doesn't look very good, does it?'

'In that case I will make sure there was no Tiger Moth landing here today.'

'Will you? Thanks awfully.'

Stefan shrugs with one shoulder. 'It is nothing.'

Briefly, his hand touches her sleeve. 'Please, stand there a moment.'

He steps closer, scrutinising her face. Vee smells the cinnamon edge of his soap and the leather of his flying jacket beneath the overalls. Her pulse quickens as he pulls a perfectly white handkerchief from his pocket.

'There is grease. Close your eyes.'

Without thinking, she does as he says and puts her face up to him like a child. Her eyes close. Soft fabric strokes, again and again, at the same spot just below her eyebrow.

'There.'

Her eyes open and she feels a tug of air as he steps away. His expression has changed; it is serious, embarrassingly so, and there is something in his gaze that seems desperately sad.

She smiles awkwardly. 'Is it really so perplexing for you to see a woman in a cockpit?'

'No. Why?'

'You look at me so oddly, and when you first saw me you seemed...'

'What?'

'Shocked.'

'No. You are wrong. I have nothing against women pilots. The very opposite, in fact...' She sees his throat move as he swallows. 'In fact, I...'

He opens his mouth as if to say more but then shakes his head. His skin instantly has a greyish tinge.

Suddenly self-conscious, Vee puts a hand to her forehead to peer down the runway.

'I think the cloud base has lifted above a thousand now.'

He sighs. 'You are right.'

They go to the Tiger and Stefan stands beside the cockpit. Vee lowers the parachute pack into the hole in the seat before settling herself on top of it. She takes out the map and once again Stefan leans over it, pointing.

'Keep dead east until you see the railway track. Then, if the vis is still bad, follow the track north to Rivenhall and land there, see?'

'Thank you.' Another unscheduled landing? She would do no such thing. Vee flips the ignition switch. 'Now, if you wouldn't mind? The screw?'

Stefan nods and moves off towards the nose.

'Throttle set.'

'Throttle set. Contact!'

He pulls the blade with both hands and the propeller blast throws his hair across his eyes. The Tiger's engine blurts into its sewing-machine patter and Stefan steps back, waiting as Vee tightens the strap across her lap and pulls on her gloves. He is still there, hands in pockets and a twisted look on his face, as she tests the flaps and checks the dials whilst the engine warms.

Perhaps she reminds him of someone he used to know. Maybe someone in Poland. Maybe even another female pilot. A chap that good-looking will have had lots of girls. Although something about Stefan's drained expression suggests that he does not much want to think about whoever it is that Vee has brought to mind.

Vee gives him a polite wave before steering the Tiger on to the concrete. She throws a final furtive glance as she pushes the throttle lever forward. He does not wave back. The windsock lumbers up in the slight breeze from the sea and the Tiger hops easily, as it always does, into the air.

Almost as soon as the wheels are released from the pull of the ground, the atmosphere around the bi-plane dilutes into weak sunlight. Vee circles on to an easterly bearing by crossing and re-crossing the stripe of listless waves along the estuary's edge. As she gains height, a slice of clear air opens between the ground fog and a high ceiling of cloud. To the east, a railway track scores through drab fields. Ahead on the horizon is the brown smudge of London. Then as Vee looks back at the receding aerodrome her heart jumps. Illuminated by the flare path, Stefan is still there, hands in pockets, shoulders hunched. And he is still looking her way.

Posen, Greater German Reich
Thursday 1 April

Ewa can tell by the way her father is frying eggs that he is in a bad mood. The fat is too hot and it spits grease over the stove top, burning black bubbles into the egg-whites. He looks over his shoulder at her, glowering. Beer froth flecks his grey moustache.

'Lie-in?'

'Hardly.'

'You know how much there is to do. And another Schutzstaffel officer is arriving this morning.'

'Without any notice? They've got a nerve.'

Her father's eyes dart. 'Keep it down, Maus.'

Ewa clatters dried-up dishes in the sink and bangs the half-full coffee pot back on to the stove. 'Where will we put him? In the gable room?'

'No, he is an SS-Obersturmführer. He should go in the oak-bed room.'

Ewa nods. At least the attic room next to her own will stay empty a little longer. Panic sometimes waves through her when she thinks of those few thin centimetres of plaster and wood that separate her secret drawer from the head of a snoring officer of the Reich.

Overcooked eggs bounce as her father tips them on to a cracked plate. He balances it on a pile of papers on the dresser and, still standing, chops the rubbery eggs with a spoon. Ewa leans the base of her spine against the sink and folds her arms.

'And will we charge extra for the bigger room?'

Her father shakes his head as he pokes a slice of stale black bread into the hardened yolk. 'A flat rate was agreed. Let's just be glad of the business.'

'And the extra work?'

'Yes, why not? A new lodger will make up for the empty dining room.'

'What else did you expect, Papa, when we put the "*Germans Only*" sign on the front door?'

His hand with the black bread halts mid-air as he glares. Ewa has gone too far. She knows that he feels uneasy at the extent of their collaboration with the occupiers. But whereas Ewa can justify her own politeness to the lodgers as a cover for her secret resistance, her father, Oskar, must make himself believe that he has no alternative. The German invasion was inevitable, he argues, because the Republic of Poland was so weak. The country existed only for twenty years before dissolving again inside the borders of its mighty neighbours. How can he be a traitor to a state so flimsy and one that is no more?

Ewa suspects that her father was, in part, relieved when the Wehrmacht marched into Poznań and promptly changed all of the town signs to *Posen*. The city immediately began to look and feel a bit more like it did in Oskar Hartman's youth. And no longer did he feel a twinge of embarrassment about his German name, or have to sing his favourite Christmas carols in private.

Although he would never admit it to her, Ewa wonders if her father prefers to be an actual German rather than a German-speaking Pole. But Oskar was born and raised in the city when it was part of Germany and he even fought unswervingly for the Kaiser throughout the World War. Ewa suspects that her father does not himself know where his loyalties really lie and she cannot help picking at his discomfort like a half-healed scab.

'Enough, Eva.'

The sound of the wrong name in his mouth, with its hard German *E*, makes Ewa want to rip the scab right off.

'We should never have gone on the DV List.'

'Not again, Eva. And quietly.'

'I'm not Eva. I'm sick of that name.'

But in order to secure their place in Category One of the

Deutsche Volksliste and so be allowed to continue their business in the guest house after the occupiers arrived, Herr Hartman had sworn that the name on his daughter's birth certificate was not his choice. In 1919, when she was born, the newly appointed Polish officials who filled out her birth certificate had automatically changed her German name *Eva* into the Polish *Ewa*. But at home, Oskar insisted convincingly to the sympathetic SS-Scharführer, his daughter was always called *Eva*.

Oskar brings his empty plate to the sink and hisses. 'If you were still *Ewa* we would not be living in this guest house any more. Some smug settler would be standing where I am, cooking herrings for every meal and speaking German with a Russian accent. Imagine that!'

She shrugs with one shoulder but knows he is right. They had no real choice about the Volksliste. Their life, if they had been categorised as Poles then evicted and perhaps sent west to the Alt Reich as forced labourers, is unimaginable. And how could she be any use to the Polish underground army, the AK, if she were slaving in a German factory somewhere wearing a purple star with a *P* on it?

Ewa pours half-warm coffee and raises the bowl to her lips to hide her defeat. It is pitiful really, to be arguing like this with her father. She sounds as if she is fifteen not twenty-three. But there is comfort in a bad temper; it stops her thinking about the life she might have had without the war.

'I am sorry, Papa. I will put the best sheets on the oak-bed.'

'Good, Maus.' He turns on the tap. 'I know it is hard for you to be running everything, especially with the guests we now have…' He puts his hand over hers and squeezes it. 'I could not manage to keep the guest house going without you.'

She feels an unexpected prickling at the back of her nose and leans herself against her father's warm bulk. His cheek bristles against her forehead.

'I'm glad to do it, Papa. And they do not give me any trouble really.'

She stands back and pulls a speck of yolk from the tail of his moustache.

He nods and keeps his voice low. 'At least I am too old to be called up, unlike some who chose the DV List. You will not have to worry about being here on your own.'

In the yard, a door bangs and Ewa's heart jumps. Could that be the new lodger? She was not telling her father the entire truth about the officers. Most of them, if not polite, at least keep their hands to themselves. But a few do not. An aloof officer in the oak-room would be a godsend. She peers through the net curtain into the yard. But it is just Scharführer Feldman pulling his braces over his vest as he comes out of the guest house's toilet block.

'I know, Papa. I shall go and clear the breakfast things. They have all finished now, I think.'

And when Ewa gets to the dining room with her tray, she sees that the officers have indeed all left, apart from one. His back is to her. It is the same grey-green jacket that they all wear but she knows instantly that she has not seen this one before.

She has learnt to speak first. 'Heil Hitler!'

He turns. His hair, dark blond, is slicked back as though wet through. He smiles and Ewa sees that he is quite extraordinarily good-looking.

'Good morning, Fräulein Hartman.' He stubs out his cigarette and stands, giving only a quick nod of the head. 'SS-Obersturmführer Beck. Delighted to meet you.'

It is good of him to spare her the full *Heil Hitler* rigmarole.

'Thank you, Obersturmführer. You are our new guest, I take it?'

'I am.'

'So sorry I have kept you waiting. You should have rung the bell for me or for my father.'

'The front door was open and I did not like to trouble you in the kitchen.'

His smile is friendly and he does not seem to have the striding confidence that oozes from most of the others. Ewa always has to fight her instinct to be cool and sullen towards the occupiers because she knows that friendliness is the insurgent's best disguise. And she tries not to actually like any of them. But she can see that with this one that could be hard.

'Thank you, Obersturmführer, you are very kind. Would you like breakfast now? I have not quite finished preparing your room.'

'Just a coffee, if you please.'

'Certainly. I have made a fresh pot.'

In fact, the dregs from the coffee pot have been stewing on the stove for a good while but Ewa pours them into one of the best Rosenthal cups. She blinks as she remembers Beck greeting her by her name. How did he know that she wasn't just a girl who had come in to help with the breakfasts? And the way he had slipped straight into the dining room from the street seemed, if not fishy, then at least a little surprising. But if he has been sent here with a purpose, to watch her, he would surely have been more careful with his instant greeting. Perhaps he simply recognised her from descriptions given him by the other lodgers.

Ewa puts the cup with its pale pink roses and muddy coffee on the tablecloth in front of Beck. He has unbuttoned his jacket. The beige shirt beneath seems to cling to his skin as if damp. Ewa tries not to look as she clears the other tables. Some of the checked napkins are already tightly rolled inside their individual rings and stacked beneath the mirror on the side-board. Other linen squares have been left crumpled on the tables with a high-handed assumption that Ewa will know to which officer's ring each belongs. She certainly knows the rudest officers by the way that they leave their napkins.

29

Obersturmführer Beck sips from the porcelain cup. 'Thank you for this, Fräulein. Such an improvement on barracks' coffee.'

Ewa keeps a clear smile even though she knows he is lying. 'You have been staying at the Castle?'

'Yes. And I'm delighted that my request to move here has been approved.'

'You requested us specially?'

'Oh yes, everyone says that this is the most superior guest house in the city.'

Now he is definitely lying but Ewa's smile broadens. 'You flatter us, Obersturmführer.'

'So please forgive me for arriving at breakfast-time, but after rising early for my swim, I could not quite face crossing town again to go back to the bunk-room.'

Ewa stacks the remaining rolled napkins on the side-board. A swimmer. That would account for his wet hair, and perhaps, his muscled shoulders.

'You like to swim, Obersturmführer?'

'Indeed.'

'At the new pool?'

'You know it? An excellent amenity for the city. Have you swum there yourself?'

Her smile does not waver as she shakes her head. 'Not yet, but I hear it is very fine.'

In fact, the thought of swimming at the indoor pool turns her stomach. For although the pool is new, the building that houses it is not. Who is to say that St Adalbert's might not be next to go the same way? A church could be turned into a gymnasium as easily as the city's grand synagogue has become an Olympic-sized swimming pool.

Beck clinks cup to saucer. 'It is such a modern sports facility. The water is kept at a perfect temperature for athletic swimming but the air is always warm. If you wish, I could arrange for you to swim there privately, after public hours.'

His finger strokes the delicate handle of the cup as he looks at her and warmth rises in Ewa's neck. For once, the heat does not come from the effort of suppressing her resentment to the occupiers.

'That would be delightful, Obersturmführer, as soon as I have some time to spare. Do you swim often?'

'Every day, if I can. The pool is so convenient for the library.'

'The library?'

'Indeed. That is where I am working.' He pauses and runs a hand over his wet hair, smiling at her confusion. He taps a yellow packet on the tablecloth. 'Do you mind?'

Ewa indicates for him to go ahead and smoke. Then he holds the cigarette pack out and her heart skips. Mokri Extra Strength – the same type that Stefan always had in his pocket.

Beck gestures to the chair beside him at the table. 'Do you have time now, for a smoke?'

'All right. Thank you.' She makes herself smile as she goes forward to take a cigarette. Why not be friendly to this new one? At least, at first.

Beck clicks his lighter and holds the tall flame to her face.

Ewa sucks on the smoke and hitches up her skirt a little as she sits. 'So, you are a scholar, Obersturmführer?'

He sits back and rests an elbow on the table, a curl of smoke rising from the cigarette in his hand.

'Ah, before the war that was my dream. But at least my linguistics work now has a practical application.'

Ewa blows out a plume of nicotine fumes and tries not to seem over-interested. 'How so?'

'I have been placed in charge of the re-naming project.'

She smiles and puts her head to one side. 'Changing the street names, do you mean?'

'Not just streets: I have been charged with finding the proper German name for every place on the map of the whole of the Warthe region, even down to the lowliest hamlets and narrowest alleyways.'

'Goodness! That sounds like a big job.'

'It is. I could spend every night in the library and still not get through all of the research that should be done.'

The cigarette hovers close to Ewa's lips. She fixes a steady gaze on his light grey eyes. 'It can't be easy to find the old German name for every place.'

'As long as I have sufficient time with the antique maps and land documents I shall do it. Although not all of the old names are appropriate.'

'Really?'

'The street that leads to the new swimming pool, for example.'

Zydowka Street, he means.

Ewa taps the cigarette against the ash tray. 'I am too young to remember what it was called when our city was part of Prussia.'

'Indeed! But the name was the same. Jüden Strasse. So we couldn't have that name back, could we?'

'No. I should think not!'

She laughs and tries not to sound awkward.

He smiles. 'I think that the new name, *Becken Strasse*, suggests the proximity of an engineered water feature. A pure coincidence that my own name will form part of the new street sign.'

He winks but seems to poke fun at himself and Ewa laughs without having to fake it.

'What a fascinating and important job!'

He pulls out his chair at an angle from the table and stretches out his legs, one ankle crossed over the other.

'Oh, it can sometimes be tedious. I have only been working here for a month but already there are disagreements between the army and the Post Office about maps and addresses.'

Ewa takes a long drag on her cigarette and tries to place his origins from his voice but his German is accentless. She realises, as she listens to him talk, how gentle and melodious the language can sound.

32

'Where are you from, Obersturmführer?'

'Where do you think?'

'Somewhere with a very pure dialect.' She shrugs. 'Hanover, perhaps?'

'Good try.' He nods, grinning. 'Do you want to guess again?'

'Erm… Dortmund?'

'Let us not end the game too quickly. Why not have one guess on each day that I am here in your lovely guest house? But I doubt that you will get it right.'

Ewa's foot bounces as she crosses her legs. 'I might surprise you!'

With a jolt, she realises that her guard has fallen. For a few moments she has been talking to Beck without any thought to his uniform, or to the threat he might pose.

'Well, Obersturmführer, I look forward to my daily quiz, and to providing you with Hartman hospitality.'

She stands and goes to the side-board for the spare napkin rings from the drawer then places them on the table in front of Beck. Golden hairs bristle on the back of his neck above his jacket's velvety green collar.

'Would you like to choose one? We launder the napkins weekly so each officer keeps his own in a personal ring.'

There are three distinctive designs; one made from horn and carved with stags' heads, one painted with mountain flowers, the other an unadorned pewter band. Beck surprises her by picking the plainest.

'Good choice, Obersturmführer.'

'Plain as a wedding band.'

He smiles and holds Ewa's gaze as she rolls a pink linen napkin. Only the pat of her heartbeat tells her that she is holding her breath.

As she turns away to replace the unused rings in the drawer, Ewa composes her face. On a few occasions, she has had to make an effort of will not to take a fancy to one of the officers billeted in the guest house. Her friendly, sometimes flirty, act must not become real feeling or her cover could be compromised entirely. Besides, although she may not dislike every officer who stays under her roof, she detests what they stand for.

But her instincts have never before been tested quite like this. Because at this moment, Ewa can think of nothing she would like better than to be inside the former synagogue on Becken Strasse watching Obersturmführer Beck climb, dripping, out of the pool.

She sets her face into a tight smile before she turns. 'Could I get you another coffee whilst I prepare your room?'

'No, thank you. And please do not go to any great trouble.'

'Oh, it is no trouble, just a little dusting and fresh sheets.'

She nods, as brisk and airy as she can manage then leaves the room.

But as she creaks up the stairs, a dull, familiar wash of guilt tugs at each step. She passes the door to the oak-bedroom and continues to the next flight of stairs up to her low-ceilinged bedroom amongst the eaves. She locks the door behind her then sinks down on to the rug.

It is not fair. Why can she not admire a good-looking man without the pleasant sensation of lust being doused by guilt? Saints in heaven, it has been three years since she last heard from Stefan. Three of her best years, wasted. It would be better if she knew for sure that he is definitely dead. Because, as it is, the whole of the rest of her life might have to be lived in the shadow of a Stefan-shaped question mark.

Is the rest of her youth to slip by without any sort of love? She cannot save herself for a ghost. If things had been the other way around, Stefan would have found himself another lover by now. For all Ewa knows, he maybe already has. She sits unmoving on the floor, willing herself to imagine Stefan with an imaginary girl in another country. But tears prickle her sinuses. She shakes her head. Three years is long enough, damn it. Somehow, she must rid him from her heart.

Ewa sniffs and then pushes herself softly on to the glossy, uneven floorboards. With her face pressed against the wardrobe, she reaches both hands beneath it until she can feel the two clips. Bracing her arms to catch the weight, she swivels the clips and lowers out a square tray a little bigger than a shoe box. Soundlessly, she carries the secret drawer to her bed and places it on the eiderdown.

The few bits of old underwear on the top would fool no one but she cannot bring herself to leave the contents entirely undisguised. She lifts the noiseless typewriter on to the bed along with the sheaf of closely typed papers – numbers, words, dots and dashes that she has copied from the agents' scribbled notes and blurry photographs without a clear understanding of what any of it means. The sheaf is growing. She must let the liaison girl know that she needs to make a drop.

Beneath the typing is a little pile of opened brown envelopes. The sight of his handwriting always makes her catch her breath, as if Stefan himself has been hiding beneath the wardrobe. She does not really need to conceal his letters so closely. Even in the Reich, it is not a crime to have had a fiancé who served in the armed forces of the extinct Republic of Poland. It is just that until now, Ewa has not been able to bear the thought of anyone else reading Stefan's words of love.

But the words are fading. And although Ewa can recall her emotions from the time when the letters arrived, she no longer feels them very much. She pulls the letter from the bottom of the pile. It is the one that came just before the first Christmas of the war when she had not seen nor heard from Stefan since the sultry summer morning on which he had boarded a Warsaw train crammed with troops in brown uniforms. Their last kiss had been so fierce that it left a bruise inside her lip.

And so, the first sight of an envelope with her name written in his hand threw Ewa into a swirl of emotions. As she tore it open, joy washed through her. Stefan was alive, and entirely himself;

his words proved that. '*I have to admit,*' he wrote, '*that the Karas crashed on our very first sortie against the Soviets, and it was brought down embarrassingly, not by an enemy bullet but by a slight mechanical malfunction. Then, I and my co-pilot walked in so completely the wrong direction that we soon bumped into a charming Red Army captain who seemed rather embarrassed to lock us up.*' Even now, Ewa hears his voice in the words and cannot help but smile.

Stefan made the prisoner of war camp sound bearable, impressive, even. The ancient monastery citadel where he was kept is so vivid in Ewa's mind that she sometimes forgets that she has never actually seen the towering perimeter walls or the bunks piled six high inside the magnificent domed church. Stefan told her that he slept in the best spot at the very top of the bunk-stack with a clear view of the coloured frescoes of the saints. This position also spared him, as he says: '*…the unpleasantness endured by those on the lower bunks who are dampened by a constant trickle down the walls of moisture from the breath of hundreds of men (as well as the moisture created by those men unwilling to climb down to the bucket during the night!).*'

Perhaps Stefan knew that after her initial relief, Ewa would be terrified about what lay in store for him during the Russian winter and he was trying to reassure her. But the details he related had the ring of truth – that his breakfast porridge stayed warm in a wooden bowl, that the prisoners were provided with chess pieces and harmonicas, that there was a cinema hut in the camp and entertainment from the wireless: '*…we have constant enjoyment of Radio Moscow played through loudspeakers in every part of the walled compound, even the latrines.*' The censor must not have noticed Stefan's sarcasm. Even the address provided for her reply, '*Gorki Rest Home, Moscow, PO Box 12*', helped to soothe Ewa's anxiety. She imagined the prisoners receiving therapeutic massages from stout Russians in white coats.

Ewa's eyes move, warily, down the page to the most affecting part of that first letter. *'My darling Ewa... your photograph stays inside the flap of my jerkin pressed against my heart... and when I remember the curve of your shoulder or the smell of your hair I find myself in a daze...'* She finds, annoyingly, that her nose still prickles as she reads.

But what follows is, most definitely, beginning to annoy her. How could Stefan have been naïve enough, in December 1939, to imagine that he would soon be released? His letters from Russia continued through that first winter, one every few weeks or so, until the spring of 1940. And then nothing. But the words in Ewa's hands are adamant, not only will Stefan soon be free, but he and Ewa will soon be married. *'The vision of our spring wedding keeps me warm,'* he writes. *'Do not scoff, Ewa, for I see you clearly sometimes, standing in front of a photographer, radiant in the sunshine with a garland of cherry blossom in your hair.'*

Dry-eyed, Ewa folds the letter back into the box. How wrong he was. This is the fourth spring since he wrote those words, and still the only ring on Ewa's finger is the paste stone that Stefan had bought hastily on Zydowka Street when his deployment orders arrived.

With each passing season, Stefan's once endearing faith in the future reads more like arrogance. Yes, arrogant. That's what Stefan Bergel was. And he is no more. Ewa grips the silky eiderdown with both fists as irritation with her absent lover sharpens. And this time, her vexation is almost fierce enough to set her free.

White Waltham, England
Sunday 11 April

Cold air gusts in with each slam of the door but the corridor still reeks of overcooked bacon. Vee leans a shoulder to the wall as Marjorie Hyde-Barker and Freddie Dunne pass by, chits in hand and voices raised: *What's yours?... Hurricane to Hullavington... Jammy!*

Oh yes, very jammy. They have had a head start in this game, arriving with air licences and plenty of logbook hours paid for by Daddy, no doubt. As soon as she has her Wings, Vee will be as much a pilot as they are, but it seems to be taking her longer than the other new cadets. And since that business at Bradwell Bay nothing has gone quite right. Landings have been heavy and navigation inaccurate; too much trim at Debden, a completely wrong bearing for Ratcliffe. Even her written marks have dropped. And there is no good reason for any of it, except that she finds herself looking out, all of the time, for fighters from 302 Squadron.

Another cold blast and Sonia appears from the doorway; hair intricately rolled, lipstick like shellac and the belt of her new jacket pulled a fraction tighter than it needs to be. Gold wings gleam above the breast pocket.

'Sonia! Your uniform! That came quick.'

Vee does her best to maintain a congratulatory smile as Sonia joins her in the queue, trying not to beam.

'Yes, didn't it?'

'From Blackstones?'

Sonia picks a loose thread from the dark blue slacks that fall in effortless folds. 'No. From town, actually. Managed to persuade my father's tailor to do it.'

Vee knows that Sonia doesn't mean to sound superior, she just can't help it.

'Buck up, Vee, you'll get yours soon.'

Vee nods but knows her smile is unconvincing.

'Next!'

The shout from the Ops office lets her look down at her overnight bag and kick it along the floor as the queue moves forward.

'Do you know where you are off to today, Vee?'

'Another cross-country, I suppose.' Vee shrugs and smiles at Sonia. She keeps her voice neutral. 'What have you had since you qualified?'

'Only an Albacore, and Tigers, of course. But I'm training on a Master now.'

'For fighters?'

Sonia nods and does not even seem smug. How splendid she will look in her stylish navy jacket, lowering herself into the cockpit of a Spitfire. Vee can imagine Sonia pulling back the Perspex hood as if it is the driver's door of her father's Bentley.

They edge into the Ops office where the air is toffeed with tobacco smoke. Sonia takes a slip of paper with her name on it from a woman in a tweed suit. Another woman scratches chalk on to the movements board and a telephone trills through the clatter of typewriters. Vee puts an elbow on the high counter and listens to Captain Mills bark into the receiver.

'A Halifax... and four Hurricanes? You must be joking. I shall have to ring you back.'

Then he slams the receiver down and returns the pipe-stem to the corner of his mouth. Staring at the paperwork in his hand, he comes back to the counter.

'Next!'

Still he does not look up and Vee stares at the spot of white light on his high forehead. 'Sir.'

'Yes? Katchatourian, is it?' The name is pronounced with an odd emphasis on the last syllable which makes Vee want to both laugh and wince. But she keeps her face blank as he glances, at last, over the top of his round-rimmed spectacles.

'I've got something here...'

Papers shuffle on the counter. There is a flash of gold; embroidered feathers encircle the shining letters *ATA*.

Vee's stomach flips. 'For me?'

'No. For the gentleman behind you.'

'Oh.'

'Do get your brain in gear. Of course they're for you. And I've got this for you as well...' An authorisation card comes towards Vee with her own monochrome face looking a little too pleased with itself. 'And this...'

The white paper slip, a blue copy sheet underneath, is indented with black type. A chit. Her first.

Pilot: Katchatourian, V,
Swordfish P.4532,
Gosport to White Waltham.

Jesus Christ. A Swordfish. She has never seen one but she knows that they are big. Bigger than a Walrus, even. Captain Mills is still shuffling paper.

'Are you sure, sir... I mean, will someone at Gosport go over the Swordfish with me?'

'Go over it? What on earth do you mean?'

'I haven't...'

'You've got your *Ferry Pilots Notes* with you?'

'Yes.'

'Well, you should not need to be told that those are all you need. Read the page which is clearly marked *Fairey Swordfish* and get on with it.'

'Yes, sir.'

'Except that you might not be able to get on with it just yet.'

'Why not, sir?'

40

'You're a qualified pilot now. You tell me.'

'Erm...'

'What sorts of things might prevent you from flying today?'

'A problem with the taxi plane?'

'No...'

He taps the pipe-stem against his teeth.

'Or enemy action on the route? If I check with Maps and Signals...'

'Or, Third Officer Katchatourian, you could simply look out of the window?'

She slides a glance through the cross-hatch of tape on glass. It is true that the vis today is a bit iffy. Mist rises above patches of melting snow on the landing ground. But the spire of Shottesbrooke church is more or less visible through the murk.

'I can see the church all right. Sir.'

'So, in your judgement, you would take off in this, would you?'

'Erm...'

'Well?'

'Yes, sir.'

'And that, Katchatourian, is why it has taken you a little longer than most to get these Wings.' He is talking with the pipe-stem in the corner of his mouth but if Vee can hear what he is saying, Sonia might too. She will not give him the satisfaction of looking round to check. 'There is a fine line, you know, between courage and recklessness. Make sure you stay on the right side of that line.'

Vee is stung. She stiffens. 'Yes, sir.'

'Good.' Captain Mills gives her a long unblinking look. 'I'm glad that is clear. So I would find yourself a ladies' magazine or a bridge partner for now. And hope the sky perks up soon.'

She cannot bring herself to reply. A nod will have to do. She clutches her Wings, chit and authorisation card then turns her back.

Sonia is waiting in the corridor. 'I say, Vee! Congratulations!'

'Thanks.'

'Aren't you thrilled?'

Vee nods and stuffs the scrap of fabric and gold thread inside her coat pocket. She is smarting too much to be thrilled. Achieving this goal has had her entire focus since she first saw the advert for ATA cadets in *Flight* magazine. But success has simply left a bad taste in her mouth.

Vee swallows. 'I'd be rather more thrilled if there was a bit more blue sky.'

She is getting the hang of making light of everything, no matter what emotions are seething below the surface, as all the proper pilots seem to do.

Sonia picks up her bag. 'Quite! I've got a Walrus from Whitchurch today, as well as a lesson in the Master. I'll be lucky to get either of them done in this sky.'

Vee follows her into the high-ceilinged mess room where pilots sit on the unmatched chairs to shuffle cards or flap at newspapers or lean over outspread maps. The tea trolley, pushed apparently by a schoolgirl, clinks around the furniture.

Sonia takes the threadbare settee in the alcove and Vee perches on the wooden arm, tapping her foot against the floor. Across the room, the chief instructor, Captain McKay and an Australian pilot are bent over a tiny backgammon board, grey heads almost touching. They are not even keeping half an eye on the weather. Perhaps they do not expect to fly at all today and it is only a quarter to ten.

Glossy pages squeak as Sonia flicks through *Country Life* but she is not looking at the magazine.

'What is he like then, your Polish chap?'

Vee snorts but her foot taps faster. 'He's not my chap. I only met him once.'

'Yes, but you must have liked the look of him or you wouldn't have mentioned it.'

Vee's face wobbles into a stupid smile. 'Oh, you know.'

She can't even begin to put it into words without sounding

soppy. But the truth is that every time she thinks of Stefan, she imagines the horizons of her world widening just as they do when she leaves the ground and takes flight.

Sonia pats Vee's hand and drops her voice to a whisper. 'I don't blame you, darling. RAF pilots are so much sexier than this ATA lot.'

'But Tony is one of "this lot".'

'Well, he's an exception.' Sonia stretches her nails, which are precisely the same shade of red as her lips, across a photograph of a wood-panelled drawing room. There is a diamond flash from her left hand. 'Do you think Mr 302 fancies you?'

'Goodness! How should I know?'

Vee tries to tame the muscles in her face but her smile will not stop wavering.

'Oh Vee! Don't be a prig. You must be used to men looking you over. Very used to it, in fact. And you must have gone a bit further with some of them than just moony looks.'

The mess, apart from their embarrassingly loud conversation, seems suddenly quiet.

Vee stands up. 'Tea?'

'All right. Two sugars.'

As she goes to the trolley, Vee realises that just the mention of Stefan spoken out loud has made him seem more real in her mind. She can no longer pretend to herself about the strength of her longing to see him again.

Sonia cannot be convinced that Vee has had no love life to speak of, but moony looks have been about as far as she has got. It is not as if she has never fancied men before. That was just it, they were men; chaps with moustaches and sports cars who, like her, used to hang around Hanworth aerodrome. But they never looked twice at the serious girl with the peculiar name. And Vee suspected that if she ever got close enough to one of her heroes to speak, she would not like him all that much. It was just that those aerodrome men gave off an aura of knowledge about the world, and a promise of grown-up excitement that was lacking in the boys who sometimes tailed after her.

Yet Stefan already seems to her so much more intriguing and exotic than the Hanworth men. The thought of him gives her that same queasy lilt of excitement and he did not even have a moustache. Miraculously, Stefan seemed interested in her too, although the oddness of the way he had looked at her meant that she is not entirely sure why.

She hands the teacup to Sonia.

'So come on, Vee, spill the beans. What is he like, this Pole?'

The idiotic smile returns. 'Don't go on, Sonia. I don't know if he even liked me much. He kept giving me funny looks.'

'Funny looks? Well, that's a sure sign.'

'Of what?'

'That he was mentally undressing you out of your flying overalls.'

Vee splutters her tea from the rim of the cup. 'Shhh!'

'Seriously. Getting those things off is a bloody nightmare.'

Vee laughs too loud and the room looks round. She takes a long drink of tea but Sonia will not let up.

'Why don't you track him down and find out for sure?'

'How can I?'

'Well, it wouldn't be too hard to check 302's movements. I know a few people who could help with that.'

'I couldn't possibly.'

'Why not? Don't want to look too keen?'

'No! Well… yes.'

'Listen, darling, the time for all of that Victorian nonsense is long gone. We none of us know what might be around the corner. So if you see something that you really want, you must grab it.'

Vee has a sudden apparition of herself pulling Stefan Bergel to her and wrapping herself around him, pressing her mouth against his. She tries to laugh but for a second she can't quite breathe. Sonia might just be right.

Vee rolls her shoulders and catches sight of her watch. Ten twenty-five. The chit for the Swordfish seems to pulse in her pocket. For something to do she takes the empty cups to the trolley and as she puts them down, the piled crockery tinkles. But the tinkling does not seem to stop, and it is soon swallowed by a vibration of air that builds to a low rumble. Metal window frames rattle.

Vee goes to the bay window and wipes a hole in the condensation on the glass. Freddie Dunne is there too, leaning both hands on the cill as he peers up at the cloud.

Vee follows his gaze. 'Is that the taxi plane do you think?'

Freddie does not look at her as he shakes his head. 'Bigger than that.' He shouts over at Captain McKay who has glanced up from his backgammon. 'Not Jerry is it?'

Captain McKay snorts. 'That's a Lanc. Can't you tell? We're expecting one in from Sherburn.'

The rumble deepens to a roar and Vee's ribcage judders. The Lancaster bomber must be circling, as low as the pilot dares, looking for a way through the cloud. But then the aeroplane growl lightens and fades. The pilot, whoever it is, has thought better of it.

Captain McKay is pressing fresh tobacco into his pipe. 'Must look even worse from up there than it does from down here.'

Freddie crosses his arms. His face is unusually red for a youngish man and he has a slight limp which, Vee assumes, is why he flies for ATA rather than the RAF.

He turns to face Captain McKay. 'I say, do you think I should go up and have a closer look? I mean I know the cloud base seems damn low, but I hear that it is pretty clear over at Langley. Perhaps if I take the Tiger up for circuit it would give us all a better idea of the actuals.'

Captain McKay does not reply. Then he gives a quick nod. 'Go and see what Ops say.'

A few other pilots wander over to the window. There is muttering amongst the dark uniforms – men and women, young and older, British and foreign. Vee feels a hot flush of anger. If she was to suggest making a test circuit, would it be taken as proof of her recklessness? She presses her nails into her palm at the realisation that any decision she now makes as a pilot will be inhibited by Captain Mills' 'fine line'. Perhaps that is what he intended. Irritation makes her restless and she goes back to the alcove but cannot bear to sit down.

Then, Freddie Dunne comes back into the mess with a parachute pack hanging from his shoulder and goggles already over his eyes. As he picks up his gloves, he shouts out, to no one in particular.

'Captain Mills thinks it a capital idea.'

Vee folds her arms as vexation pulses through her. Capital? Does he, indeed? Clearly, Freddie fits into the pilot-shaped template in Captain Mills' estimation better than Vee ever can.

'Bon voyage, Freddie!' Sonia calls over to him as she stands to adjust her jacket. 'Why don't we all go outside and cheer him on?'

Vee shrugs but follows Sonia into the raw breeze. Several other pilots are bored enough to come with them and at the edge of the paved roadway, Vee steps up on to the long, low wall alongside a couple of South African pilots and Frank Spratley who before the war worked in a car showroom in Birmingham. They all want to know how Freddie will get on, and they are all, Vee thinks, annoyed with themselves for not making the same suggestion first.

She puts her hands in her trouser pockets and hunches her shoulders as she looks at the sky. A brooding cloud flows into the distance. Grey rain drapes the horizon and patches of melting snow give off spectral yellowy light. Nothing looks quite real.

Just across the holding bay, a mechanic tugs again at a Tiger's blade. The engine stutters but does not take. There is a whiff of coal smoke as well as petrol in the breeze. Vee shivers on to her toes and wishes she could be strapped into that cockpit with everyone watching. She would make sure to get it right.

Finally, puffs of black smoke belch from the Tiger's nose and the plane bumps over the grass, skirting the grid of chocked aircraft. But then it idles so long at the head of the strip that Frank Spratley takes his cigarette out of his mouth.

'What ho? Has he changed his mind?'

The South African first officer shrugs theatrically. 'Perhaps three feet off the ground is as high as he dares!'

But their laughter is buried by a thin wail as the Tiger sets off then rises into the jaundiced air. Vee follows its slow corkscrew towards the ceiling of cloud.

Spratley's cig goes back into his mouth. 'Rather him than me.'

The engine's thrum fades as the plane arcs away and for a moment Vee can't tell if there is an echo. But then she realises that there is another engine in the sky, one with a deeper, more insistent register.

Sonia has heard it too. 'Is that the taxi plane coming in?'

Spratley shakes his head. 'Single engine. Mark Nine Spit, at a guess.'

They all fall silent, eyes and ears straining at the low cloud. Spratley's cigarette bounces up and down as he speaks. 'And they're on the same circuit. Which is not the brightest idea in the world…'

The first officer steps off the wall as a pair of wheels break through the grey vapour, and then a swoop of curved wings.

'Damn it, Spratley, you're right! A Mark Nine.'

But in a blink, the Tiger Moth is also there, dropping just below the Spitfire. Both planes are on the same trajectory to the landing strip. Vee feels herself inside a wave of other pilots as they lurch together off the wall. The planes pass each other, and for a second, time seems both to freeze and to lengthen.

Spratley points his cigarette into the air. 'Did they touch? My God, it looked that way.'

For some reason, Vee starts to run. By the time she reaches the edge of the mown strip, both planes have made a hasty landing and are travelling across the grass in opposite directions.

As soon as the Tiger comes to a stop, Freddie bounds out and strides towards the buildings. He flings off his helmet and goggles as he passes Vee.

'Did you see that damn fool? I'm going to report him to Ops and then give him a piece of my mind.'

Or her, Vee thinks. But the Perspex hood of the Spitfire has slid back and it is clear that the pilot is, indeed, a man. As he climbs out, ground staff are already swirling around him. He stands with his back to Vee, talking intently to Smithson the chief mechanic. His arms inside a sheepskin jacket sweep in fluid, descriptive arcs around the nose of the plane. The fitters are crowding around the pilot and she can't see his face, but there is something about the way he is moving…

Without quite thinking or knowing why, Vee sets off towards him. Her pace quickens. She is now walking as fast as she can without actually breaking into a jog. It is not far but Vee can't seem to get her breath. And then, when the airman turns, she sees why.

He catches sight of Vee as he is still talking and his ice-blue eyes latch on to her and do not leave. Then, as the ground staff start to clamber over the Spitfire, Stefan Bergel comes towards her.

'Vee.'

Vee's heart is beating so hard she has to cough before she can speak. And her face can't decide what expression to take on. There are so many to choose from – surprise, delight, cool reserve. She tries for wry amusement.

'What a coincidence.'

His smile becomes sheepish. 'Every cloud, as you English say, has something silver.'

'Is that why you're here then, because of the low cloud?' She cannot stop herself smiling too. 'Even with your radio?'

'No, no, I was not lost. A little mechanical trouble, that is all.'

'And this was the nearest aerodrome, was it?'

'Exactly, and I don't want to risk it in… these conditions.' Is he blushing? He turns to look at the fitters pushing his Spitfire towards the hangar. 'And I know ATA ground staff are good.'

He tilts his head in the start of a shrug. Then he grins and Vee's insides seem to liquefy. God, he looks good. In his sheepskin flying jacket he seems taller, broader. She can hardly breathe. She looks away. By the entrance to the administration block, heads are starting to turn.

Vee pushes back the loose hair from her forehead. 'I'd offer you tea but there is someone over there who is very keen to have a word with you and it might be best to avoid him.'

'Oh, that Tiger Moth…'

'Yes. That one you nearly crashed in to.'

'I think he was not expecting to meet any other plane.'

'That's an understatement.'

'Sorry?'

'Well, anyway, it might be best to keep out of his way and stay by your aeroplane.'

'With you?'

Her stomach somersaults. 'All right. If you like.'

Between patches of dirty snow, the grass is heavy with moisture. The toes of Vee's flying boots turn black as they walk to the hangar. Inside the cavernous entrance, Stefan leans his shoulder against the metal wall. Nearby, test bay mechanics in a scruffy mix of overalls, jackets and flat caps, crawl over the Spitfire; crouching on the wings and unscrewing panels on the fuselage.

Stefan's gaze turns to Vee and she cannot think of a single

thing to say. She laughs for no reason and looks away.

'What is funny?'

'Oh nothing. Would you have a cig, at all?'

It seems as good a remark as any.

Stefan unzips the sheepskin and takes a packet from his uniform jacket inside, tapping out two cigarettes. Vee does not really want it but she puts one to her mouth as he strikes a match. Stefan cups his hand around the flame, holding it to her face until the light catches. His head is close to hers now. Almost touching. There is one stray black bristle on his smooth cheek. She breathes in his breath. Then he moves away.

The smoke of the too-strong cigarette fills Vee's lungs and calms her blood. She throws Stefan an amused look.

'Funny that you don't seem surprised to see me.'

'Well, you told me, White Waltham is your home base.'

'Yes, I suppose I did.'

'And I want to find out if you have your Wings already.'

Vee blows a plume of nicotine smoke from the corner of her mouth then reaches into her trouser pocket. 'Funnily enough...'

The embroidered wings unfurl on her palm.

'Vee! Congratulations!'

His eyes light up and in what seems like a reflex, his hand is on her shoulder, squeezing. Slowly, he lets go and Vee wills him to touch her again. But, of course, he does not.

'Thank you.'

'You do not seem so happy about it.'

'They were given to me rather grudgingly, I think'

His brow furrows. She forgets, as she talks to him, that English is not his language.

'I mean... I was told, as I got them, that I am a rather reckless pilot.'

Stefan snorts and drops the stub of his cigarette. 'Then you should join 302 Squadron. That is exactly what we need.'

She laughs. 'If only that were possible...'

'In Poland you could.'

'Really? You have female fighter pilots?'

'A few, yes. When we had an Air Force.' He looks down at his smouldering cig-end and grinds it with his boot. His face is suddenly expressionless.

Vee shakes her head. 'I can't imagine having to fight as well as fly.'

'If you had to, you would do it. And you are a pilot now. That is the most important thing.'

He looks up at her smiling, but his eyes are troubled.

'And we must have a drink, yes, to celebrate?'

'Must we?'

'Of course. If you like.'

She folds her arms and points at him with the ashy tip of her cigarette. 'It's rather a long way to Bradwell Bay.'

'Oh, 302 is at Northolt now. And you go to London sometimes?'

'Sometimes, yes.'

A smile starts and Vee cannot stop it spreading. Does this mean he has asked her out? Or perhaps he was just being polite.

'Oi! 302.'

Vee jumps and looks round.

It is Smithson, the mechanic. 'There's nothing wrong with that Mark Nine.' He looks Vee up and down. 'And I can see now that you'd be surprised if there was.'

Stefan straightens, looking Smithson in the eye. 'On the contrary, old chap. Better safe than sorry, eh?'

Vee blinks. Stefan sounds almost English.

Smithson shakes his head. 'We'll put your machine outside and just as soon as you've finished with your... business here, I'll thank you to get it out of our way.'

Stefan gives a nod and a quick salute. Vee cannot decide if there is insolence in it. He takes a pair of soft leather gloves from his pocket, and with no great urgency, pulls them on. He does not seem embarrassed in the least. Did he really lie about a fault on his plane just because, as Smithson thinks, he wanted to see Vee again? The warmth of Stefan's smile makes her think that Smithson might be right.

Stefan leans towards her conspiratorially. 'So, would you like to meet Donald?'

'Who's he?'

Stefan points at the Spitfire being pushed out by three fitters. Painted on the fuselage are two garish cartoon birds.

'Donald Duck?'

'Correct!'

The duck, with his jaunty blue cap and half-quacking beak, holds up a feather like a warning finger.

'Why Donald Duck?'

''Cos I like the way he talks, lady.'

Stefan's squeaking, quacking American duck-voice is uncannily perfect. Vee laughs out loud.

'And the other bird, is it a crow?'

'A raven. A symbol of our squadron, the Poznański.'

'What's that?'

'From Poznań.'

It must be a place, but she has never heard of it. From the corner of her eye she sees Smithson scowling.

'Come on,' Stefan places a hand lightly on her back and they go outside. 'Have you been inside one before? Sit in, if you like.'

'In your Spitfire?'

'For sure.'

Close up, the plane's metallic curves are speckled with rivets. Stefan climbs on to the wing and lowers the door flap. His hand seems to hoist Vee directly into the tight cockpit. She sinks on to the bucket-seat, eyes flickering across the confusion of instruments and gauges. She can't imagine ever getting the hang of them all. The Tiger's few dials and pointers are hard enough.

Stefan's shadow looms. 'What do you think?'

'It's cramped, isn't it?'

'Sorry?

'You know, small.'

'Ah yes. But it has to be. When you are fighting, you must wear the aeroplane like a coat.'

The cockpit smells, as all cockpits do, of engine fuel and greasy metal, but in this one there is also a tang of just-exploded firework. Vee's hand rests on the Spitfire's control column, her thumb caressing the black button inside the circular handle.

'Is this the trigger?'

Stefan is silent. She looks up and his face is expressionless, his eyes locked open, as if on a target. He turns then, and jumps to the ground. The cockpit feels suddenly bigger without his shadow across it. Vee curses silently for having reminded him, as she must have just done, of some ghastly kill that he would rather forget.

Her pulse quickens as she climbs out. Painted on the fuselage, next to the raven and below the red and white chequerboard of Poland, are three small black crosses edged in white. Three kills, then, at least.

Stefan is standing on the grass with his hand outstretched. He has taken off his gloves. Vee resists her impulse to climb down unaided and takes his hand which is cool and surprisingly small around hers. He does not let go as she stands beside him on the ground. And then, before she has realised what he is doing, Stefan brings the back of her hand to his mouth, pressing her knuckles to his lips. Vee stands, unable to move. His pale eyes fix on hers as he turns her hand over and this time brings her palm to his mouth. Heat flickers from his lips to the flesh of her hand and into the pit of her stomach.

But then, without a word, Stefan drops Vee's hand and turns away. He leaps on to the Spitfire's wing and into the cockpit. His arm is raised in a stiff wave. And Vee can't quite tell whether he is bidding her farewell or simply signalling for ground staff to help him take off.

Posen, Greater German Reich
Monday 12 April

A big black car, an Opel, is parked in a square of sunlight across the street. Ewa rubs her eye to slide a look past the chrome headlight perched on its wheel arch to the bald head squashed against the driver's window. The man is not really asleep. There is a clear sight line from his rear-view mirror to the entrance of the stone-faced apartment block. Ewa squints up through the criss-cross of overhead tram wires to a fourth-floor window. The blind drops. She is expected.

Her heels clack on the pavement. After a few more steps over the grid of slabs she will need to decide whether to cross the road or keep on going. Perhaps she should forget the drop for today. She has probably been to this address on Hindenburg Strasse too many times already. The papers in her basket should probably return to her secret wardrobe cavity for a little longer. But then, with a yap, a black and white terrier runs into the path of a coal lorry that is lumbering up the hill. The driver honks his horn and Ewa takes a quick breath. Now.

Her ankle buckles on the cobbles but she hurries behind the truck and on to the pavement. Up two stone steps and she is at the wide front door. It eases open and she closes it behind her, clicks off the latch and breathes out.

Perhaps it was too obvious to use the dog as a distraction. And a door left on the latch is a sure giveaway. She holds her breath, listening for footsteps outside. But all is quiet. Perhaps the man in the Opel is waiting until she leaves before he stops her. There must be, please God, a back way out.

Electric bulbs buzz and flicker up the stairwell as Ewa turns on the ticking switch. The dial whirrs, trying to make her rush, but her footsteps echo evenly on the tiled stairs. On the fourth floor she stops, breathing in a smell of mildly blocked drain as she gives two short knocks on the nearest door, a pause, and then another knock.

'Do you have a newspaper for me?'

The words come through the door in heavily accented German.

'Yes, I have brought you this morning's *Ostdeutscher Beobachter*. The news from the front is excellent.'

The door springs open and Ewa steps inside. The woman's greying hair is pressed into flat waves against her head in a style that went out of fashion years ago. And she is wearing too much make-up. Gertruda might even be her real name.

'You have it?' Gertruda slips into Polish, holding out her hand.

The package in Ewa's basket is wrapped in the wide-winged eagle of the newspaper's masthead.

Ewa passes it over and whispers. 'Have you seen that Opel outside?'

Gertruda's eyes narrow. 'Is it still there?'

'Can I go out the back way?'

'No. There isn't one.'

'Holy Mary! I'm not coming here again. I have been too many times. Tell Haller there must be a different arrangement.'

Gertruda purses her lips. 'Just say you brought stout and soup for the old lady in apartment 3-B, Madame Ratajski. I will go down now and warn her, just in case. Don't worry. She speaks German and will say the right things. And she always has stout in the house. Paulaner stout, remember. Be sure to walk past the car when you leave. Not too fast. And think about where you will say you are heading.'

'Seriously, I'm not coming back here.'

Gertruda's voice becomes a hiss. 'Pull yourself together. It might be nothing.' She jerks open the door. 'Now, go.'

At the bottom of the staircase, with her hand on the front door handle, Ewa stops. If she turns right, towards home, it is not far to the apparent safety of the crowd shuffling around the tram stop. But if she is to pass the black car as Gertruda has advised, she must turn left up the empty street. She knows that Gertruda, annoyingly, is right.

Ewa turns left and walks without hesitation. The Opel and the man inside it have not moved. She keeps her pace steady and does not look at the car. Except for a peasant family pushing a handcart up the cobbles, the street is quiet. The peasant boy's dirty feet are bare.

Then, as she comes level with the car, Ewa makes herself throw a casual glance at the driver. His smooth head is still flattened against the glass: his eyes are closed. Perhaps he really is asleep. Ewa's step cannot help quickening on a surge of elation to get past him. For the last twenty minutes she has thought of nothing except the wide street, the car, Gertruda; things that she can see, touch and hear. There has been no room in her brain for the past or the future.

And this is exactly the mental effect she was hoping for when she joined the AK. In that first spring of the war, Ewa had sensed that the intense concentration accompanying each illicit task would be the best way, apart from insanity to blot Stefan out of her thoughts. Because as the days warmed through those fractured weeks and Ewa began to realise that Stefan's letters might have stopped for good, she would do anything to avoid waiting in the house for Jabłoński to come with the post. That waiting had almost sent her mad.

Then, as weeks without word from Stefan turned into months, Ewa started each day feeling that this would be the day when news of him would arrive. It might come on a scrap of paper from a neighbour, or from an unknown man in the dining room whispering as she served him cognac. But always, in her imaginings, it was Stefan's death that was revealed. She began to want it. At least then the waiting would end.

At last, almost a year after his first letter came from Russia, Ewa began to understand that she might never know what had happened to her lost love. And it was at that point, when hope had petered out, that she joined the AK. Miraculously, her tactic worked. The adrenaline that washed through her during undercover activities seemed to bring her back to life.

'Excuse me.'

Ewa's insides freeze. It is a man's voice, speaking good German. Her feet want to run but she stops and looks back keeping her face, she hopes, neutral. Her legs weaken with relief. It is just Obersturmführer Beck, his hand raised in a greeting. His eyes, beneath the peak of his cap, reflect the gleam of his smile.

'Fräulein Hartman.'

He is a little out of breath. Did he hurry up the street fast enough to see her come out of the apartment block? She must assume that he did.

'Obersturmführer. Good morning.'

'May I walk with you? And carry your basket?'

'Oh, it is empty now. But yes, of course, do walk with me. I'm surprised that you are not already in the library.'

'Well, a small errand brought me out, but I am on my way back there now. And you?'

'I took some leftovers to an old lady who lives here on Hindenburg Strasse.'

'And you are not going back to the guest house?'

She is indeed walking away from the Old Square and away from most of her usual shops. Reluctantly, she offers thanks to Gertruda for suggesting that she should have a story prepared.

'I am going to call at the coal merchant. The weather seems set fine, so I think we will change our order.'

Beck falls into step with her. His face glows and his tall boots are polished to a ripple of gloss. Ewa wishes now that she had been brave enough to wear her good jacket instead of this old winter coat. The coat is so dowdy that it helps her to feel invisible. But the warming spring air makes a coat that is loose enough to hide contraband look suspicious. With an inward wince, she realises yet again how cowardly impulses can put her in peril. From now on, she will dress to be noticed and then assume that there is always someone watching.

Near the top of the street, Beck puts out an arm to shield Ewa from any oncoming vehicles as they cross. But the traffic in all directions is light. Up on the boulevard, two empty trams pass each other and ring their bells. One of them has a misspelt sign in the window, *hier wurde nur Deutsch gesprochen*. This is amusing, almost. Whoever wrote the sign clearly isn't proficient in German, despite the words declaring that no other language must be spoken on board. Ewa used to make the same error herself but it is a long while since she got her German tenses mixed up.

'It is considerate of you, Fräulein Hartman, to help an old lady.'

'Oh please call me Eva.'

Perhaps she might like him less if he does.

'Thank you, Eva. I will.'

Beside the blackened portico of the museum, the pavement is wide but a man in a baggy suit steps off it and cowers out of their way as they pass. The man does not look at Ewa but she knows what he is thinking about her friendliness to an occupying soldier, and what the man might like to do to her in revenge. She wants suddenly to punch him, that Pole standing there in the gutter, clutching his trilby to his chest. *What do you know?* she wants to yell. *How much are you risking for your dead country?*

Instead, she swaps the empty basket to her other arm and moves ostentatiously closer to Beck, touching her hand to his grey-green sleeve.

'And perhaps, if we are alone Obersturmführer, I may call you Heinrich.'

Is it her irritation with the Pole that has freed her to be quite this forward with Beck? Or is her irritation a convenient excuse?

Beck's face flushes. 'Gladly.' He comes to a stop by the kerb. 'I am going across the Platz. Which way is your coal man?'

'On Friedrich Strasse. I will cross with you.'

Even though the nearest vehicle, a wagon pulled by a thin horse, is some distance away, Beck again puts his hand out to shield her across the wide boulevard. Ewa realises how much she likes walking beside him. Not just because of the imposing figure he cuts on the grand street but also, ridiculous though it is, because his presence makes her feel safe.

Around the edge of the square, the long red and black banners mounted on flagpoles stir in the faint breeze. Sunlight illuminates the library's pale columns. Perhaps the weather actually is turning fine. Ewa might make her cover story real by changing the coal order when she gets to the yard.

Beck comes to a stop by one of the benches on the square and takes out a cigarette packet.

He taps the open end against the black leather of his glove. 'I will take a five-minute smoke before I return to the reading room. Would you care to join me?'

'Yes, certainly.'

It is not a lie. In the past week or so that he has been a lodger, Ewa has come to savour time spent alone with Beck, admiring his handsome face and listening to his flow of melodious German.

She crosses her legs as they sit on the bench with the basket between their feet. Beck pulls off his gloves to offer his cigarette packet and Ewa leans in towards him as he strikes a match. Across the square, the bell tinkles at the tobacconist's door. The shop sign is so thinly painted that a *y* and a Polish *ń* ghost through the German word *Tabak*.

Beck blows out a plume of smoke then smiles. 'Are they natives of the city, those old people that you help?'

Ewa knows he does not mean Polish natives of the city, but she nods. 'We Germans have always helped each other. But I do not do much for them, really. Some leftover soup, a bottle of stout, that is all.'

'Would you like to do more?'

She feels a stab of warning. 'How do you mean?'

'To help other German people, those new to the city perhaps.'

'Settlers?'

He nods. 'It can be hard for them to adjust to life in the town. Most of those from the east have been farmers. And I think that there will be many more coming this year. The Ethnic German Resettlement Office is always in need of local women to be settlement advisers.'

'It's a good idea, Heinrich. I should have thought of this before.' His face brightens as she says his name. 'It is just that I must give first priority to the guest house.'

'Of course, I know how busy you are already.'

'But perhaps I could talk to the Office about what I might do for them in the future.'

Now her mind is whirring. She can well imagine the shitty mess that is left by soldiers after they do the evictions. Why on earth would she want to clean up after them and then have to be civil to some swaddled-up Moldavian peasants who hardly speak German and have no idea how to live in a modern apartment? On the other hand, there would, now she thinks of it, be an advantage in knowing which Polish households were about to be evicted next...

Beck does not seem to notice that she is distracted. 'You are so efficient with your housekeeping, Eva. I feel privileged to be your guest.'

Ewa laughs and shakes her head. 'I am used to it. I have been in charge of the bedrooms and the kitchen since I was thirteen.'

'When your mother died?'

'That's right.'

'I'm sorry.'

For no good reason, tears well into Ewa's eyes. Beck lifts the basket out of the way and moves closer to her, their legs almost touching, and covers her bare hand with his. Ewa nods as his fingers squeeze hers. Stefan's ring presses into her skin and she finds that she cannot quite speak.

Beck's voice becomes jaunty. 'So, come. It is time for your daily guess.'

'My guess?'

'About my home town.'

Ewa laughs and rubs her nose. 'All right.'

She studies his angular jaw line and light grey eyes, as if they might give a clue to his origins. For no good reasons she says, *Leipzig*, and his brows knit in theatrical surprise.

Ewa grins. 'Am I right?'

'It is not my home town but I studied at the university there, so you are getting close.'

'I will be right very soon. I know it!'

They smile at each other and then their mouths relax into silent awkwardness. Ewa starts to ask some empty question about Leipzig as Beck also begins to speak.

'Sorry, Eva. You first.'

'No, Heinrich, tell me what you were about to say.'

'I just wondered about the ring I see you wear.'

'Oh, this. It's not real, just a piece of costume jewellery.'

'Was it your mother's?'

In a flicker of indecision Ewa wonders whether to be truthful, to say no, it was given to me by a Polish officer I once loved. But even if she were to justify the relationship by explaining more about Stefan's background, she would still be opening a box of nasty and perhaps incriminating complications. It is so much better that they all think she is an innocent girl, and as German as one from Hamburg or Leipzig.

'Oh, no. It's just something I like. Why do you ask?'

'I thought it may have a special meaning. And I wouldn't like to feel that I was intruding into any existing understanding you might have by sitting here with you now.'

'Oh no, no.' Ewa laughs too loud. 'Look, it is on my right hand.'

'I know, but the tradition about these things is different…'

He is about to say '*in Poland*' but she saves him the embarrassment of having to mention the word.

'No, Heinrich, I assure you, there's nothing like that to worry about!'

She wonders if she is protesting too much but Beck nods and seems reassured. He points his cigarette in the air towards the wedding-cake white theatre at the head of the square.

'Do you like the theatre?'

Ewa's heart drops a beat as she feels the weight of a choice, which she knows is coming, press down from above. 'Not much, I'm afraid.'

'Or the cinema? I hear that the Apollo is showing *The Great Love* this weekend.'

'Really? That's a super movie.'

'You have seen it already?'

Here it is; the moment when she must decide. Ewa senses that all of the future paths in her life are about to compress into this one reply. Will she choose the ghost of Stefan Bergel over Heinrich Beck, who is here beside her and pulsing with life? Will she choose loyalty to the AK and loneliness, or love? Her decision hangs in the air.

Yet Beck's interest in her seems so genuine, as does his gentleness. And Ewa imagines, in that instant, the tip of his forefinger drawing a figure of eight on the inside of her thigh.

'I saw *The Great Love* when it first came out.' She smiles. 'But I would love to see it again.'

'Would you? Then please, let us go together. On Friday, yes?'

'That would be delightful. Thank you.'

Beck's smile reveals his flawless teeth. 'I shall look forward to it very much.'

'Good.'

Her decision can be justified, she immediately tells herself, as intelligence-gathering. She might glean some useful information from Beck whilst he is relaxed and enjoying himself. But as Ewa picks up her basket and stands, she feels sick. Swaying slightly, she turns her face to the sun, looking for strength. No, she will not let a ghost control her life. Stefan must be banished from her heart, and there is only one way to evict him cleanly and forever.

Warmth swills through the breeze and a green haze seems to coat the bare branches of the trees. Yes, the weather has definitely turned. She will certainly be able to wear her double-breasted jacket on Friday night and it will go well with her new hat with the blackcock feathers.

'Are you all right, Eva?'

'Oh yes. Just running a little late now. I must dash.'

She raises her hand as she says goodbye, then scans the square to check if anyone is watching. But if any of Haller's people have seen her they should be pleased. Haller, after all, is a fully paid-up member of the Nazi Party which, he argues, is the perfect cover for a komendant of the AK. And there must be all sorts of things that he might want Ewa to find out from Beck. How big a step is it anyway from hosting and feeding the occupiers, to going for an evening out with one of them?

A truck and some bicycles turn into the side street that leads down to Friedrich Strasse. The new street name seems so much more dignified than the old Polish name, *Pocztowa*, Mailbox Street. Just before she turns into it too, Ewa glances over her shoulder at Beck's impressive silhouette striding towards the library. She takes a short breath. Nothing is final, yet. If she thinks better of their night out, she can always change her mind before Friday. A headache might perhaps arrive, which everyone knows is a woman's code for *you're not really my type*. Except that Beck is so much Ewa's type that she finds herself smiling stupidly at the thought of sitting beside him on the cinema's plush red seats as the lights dim.

A cloud has crossed the sun and the air is suddenly biting. Winter might not be finished yet. Ewa rearranges her face and decides that the coal order should stay as it is. But when she gets to the merchant's yard, she will make a point of going inside and then simply pretend that she has forgotten the date of the next delivery.

She pulls up the collar of her coat. An approaching cloud looks so low and so yellow that there may even be sleet on the way. But whatever the weather on Friday, Ewa will wear her double-breasted jacket and her new hat to go to the pictures with Heinrich Beck. She will pin her hair in braids too, and be sure to top up her blonde rinse.

Gosport, England
Monday 12 April

No one else gets off the Anson taxi plane at Gosport and it hardly comes to a stop as Vee clambers out. She hurries to the edge of the concrete strip then turns to wave but the Anson is already rising into the squally sky. It hangs apparently motionless until one wing tips down and the plane banks landward. Soon the Anson is buffeting up into the ragged clouds, its outline indistinguishable from the seagulls.

Vee scans the wind-blasted aerodrome; factory hangars inside a barbed-wire perimeter fence; airborne barrage balloons shimmering above grounded fighters. At least one of the distant Spitfires has the four propeller blades of a Mark Nine. Vee squints at the planes, straining for a clearer view. Then with a start, she realises what she is doing. She is looking, pathetically, for any sign on a fuselage of a painted raven and a cartoon duck.

Head down, she sets off towards the dilapidated caravan that must be Watch office. Really, it is worse than pathetic to become so distracted on her first ferry job in an aircraft type she has never even seen before. The conditions are poor, too. She must keep herself focused entirely on flying the Swordfish as competently as she possibly can. And on staying alive.

Vee tries to recall the flying particulars printed on the card headed *Fairey Swordfish* that is in her overnight bag tied to the other *Ferry Pilots Notes* with a shoelace. She mutters into the wind the numbers that she has tried to commit to memory during the short flight in the Anson.

'Final approach speed – 65 knots, revs per minute – not to exceed 2200, stall speed – 53 knots.'

Or was it sixty-three knots? But now she is at the caravan and there is no time to double-check.

A fug of cigarette smoke hits her as she opens the door. Behind the crooked desk, the Watch sergeant looks up.

'Oh. I see.' He winces, which is as good as saying out loud that he was expecting Vee to be a man. 'Here for the Swordfish, are you?'

'Yes.'

She pulls the chit from her pocket and hands it out but the sergeant leans back and nods at a deck chair in the corner.

'Well, make yourself comfortable. You can wait in here till the wind drops.'

'Is that really necessary? The Anson got away all right.'

He stubs his cigarette butt into an overflowing ashtray. 'We'd have to lower the balloons again to let you out.'

'Yes…'

'And I'm not going to bother if you can't manage to take off.'

'I'll manage.'

'It's not up to you to decide.'

'Actually, it is.'

Vee fishes for the Flight Authorisation Card in her bag and lays it on the desk. The sergeant glances down at Vee's self-satisfied face in the photo and puts a sarcastic finger under the words as he reads.

'"Third Officer V Katchee... Katchee... something... Miss, is hereby empowered to authorise *his* own cross-country flights..."' He puts another cigarette between his teeth, '... and your own funeral.'

Anger flares in Vee's chest. 'I hardly think so. It's no more than force five.'

'Gusting to six.'

Vee shrugs. 'The sea looks flat.'

'It always does from the air.'

'I am, as it says, empowered to authorise...'

'Fiery one, aren't you? Where do you come from?'

'Teddington.'

He raises an eyebrow. 'I mean originally?'

'Originally? I was born there.'

'But, you know, before that.'

'Before that?' Vee is always wrong-footed by questions like this, although she usually finds some sort of reply that shuts people up. 'I think I was conceived on a family holiday in Eastbourne.'

The sergeant shakes his head and grabs the chit from under Vee's fingers. 'Like I say, it's your funeral.' His pen scratches an unreadable signature before he rips the typed sheets apart. Then he points his thumb backwards over his shoulder. 'The plane's over there.'

Turning his back to Vee, he starts to pull at the dial on the big black telephone. Vee is out of the caravan before he speaks.

She strides towards the grid of planes at the far end of the strip. Indignation has made her bolder, but when she sees the Swordfish her gut tightens. The wingspan is at least forty feet. The three open cockpits in the fuselage sit high above an empty torpedo cradle between the wheels. And the wind, if anything, is stiffening. A yellow windsock points, rigid, away from the sea.

As she does the walk-around checks, gusts tug her hair out of the leather helmet and into her eyes. Perhaps the Watch sergeant was right.

A mechanic holds the ladder to the cockpit but it is too windy to ask him much about the plane. He seems impatient and so there is no time, either, to double-check the card from her *Ferry Pilots Notes*. Vee glances at the seaward runway. The strip is edged by vertical black cables like the bars of a cage. Hovering at the top of each cable is a whale-like silver balloon. Some of these balloons are wobbling towards the ground. Along the perimeter fence, poplar trees lean and flicker in the wind.

Vee pulls the straps over her shoulders as tight as they will go. *Fuel Mix – RICH, Flaps – UP*. But even now she finds herself staring at the paintwork on a single-engine fighter that has just come in to land. It is a Defiant, though, not even a Spitfire. She must, damn it, get a grip.

From the front of the plane, the mechanic shouts through the wind. *Contact!* And the propeller-engine roars black smoke into the cockpit. Vee tries to breathe steadily as she waits for the engine to warm. But she finds herself panting as she signals for the chocks to be pulled from the wheels.

And then she is turning the bulk of the Swordfish into the wind. She edges the stick forward and almost as soon as she feels the bump on to concrete, the plane begins to run away from her, fighting for control. The thrust behind the throttle is as terrifying as it is thrilling.

'Whoa there!'

She is actually shouting, like an idiot, at the Swordfish. *Breathe*, she tells herself, *stay calm*. Again, she eases the throttle gently forward. But the Swordfish is already leaping into the air.

Wingtips flex and creak, and Vee's head swims with the howl of wind and engine, and then the floating sensation of flight. Lifted by the headwind, the ascent is achingly slow and almost vertical. She glances down at the barrage balloons twitching on the ground and a huddle of overalled figures standing between the balloons and the fighter planes. Her eyes stay on the men a moment longer than they should and she realises that she is looking, insanely, for one that might be Stefan.

The Swordfish rises higher and Vee's hands tighten on the control stick, fighting to keep the angle gradual. Tiny boats leave silver trails across the grey sea. Soon, very soon, she will need to start the inland turn. She has no feel for the Swordfish apart from its strength and no sense of how forgiving it will be on the turn. Ready for a fight, Vee holds her breath as she tilts the stick and works the pedals. But as the angle comes, it feels smooth and controlled. With the wind behind her, the nose dips but there seems no loss of height.

The long perimeter of the aerodrome comes into full view. Vee blinks through her goggles at the figures, now scattering beside the deflated balloons. And one of the men does, indeed, seem tall and dark-haired. And he seems to be staring at the Swordfish. Vee cannot quite take her eyes off him. Then, he starts to run. He is coming her way. And, when he comes directly below, he raises an oversized pistol and points it at her plane.

A red glare flashes across the double wings. The reflex from Vee's shoulder transmits itself to the plane and automatically the Swordfish banks away from the flare. Vee looks up. And there, bathed in pink light and so close she feels as if she could touch it, is the soft belly of a balloon. Directly beneath it, almost in the space where the Swordfish's wings have just been, is the balloon's metal anchor cable. Without that warning from the Very flare, the cable would have sliced through the Swordfish like a cheese-wire.

Coldness sweeps through Vee's core. How could that balloon have been invisible? And how could she have almost lost an aircraft, lost everything in fact, because she was distracted by a dark-haired chap who looked a bit like the one that yesterday kissed her hand? Vee looks at the balloon that is flopping belatedly downwards and her stomach heaves. This is the closest she has ever come to catastrophe.

Hot bile jabs into the back of Vee's throat but she cannot risk leaning over the side to be sick. If she is going to throw up it will have to be on to her lap. Swallowing hard she takes a long breath then glances at her map. Easily, she finds the right bearings. The vis below the cloud base is arctic sharp and the Swordfish, now comfortable in the air, feels calm and obedient.

China blue wedges open through the cloud and Vee takes at last a lungful of air. Is she really allowing herself to jeopardise her future as a pilot, indeed her future full stop, because of a school-girlish crush? Clearly, she is incapable of flying and having an admirer at the same time, so one of them will have to go. And there is no contest at all about which one it will be.

The tailwind whips the Swordfish along, and before Vee is expecting to see it, a shaft of light picks out the familiar gasometer at Reading. Then, it is only a short skip above the railway line towards London before the familiar aerodrome, billiard green and dotted with planes, comes into view.

Captain Mills is bound to be looking out for her. Perhaps that sergeant at Gosport has already telephoned him to report the near-catastrophe with the balloon. And Vee cannot blame the mistake on anything except her own carelessness. So, if she is going to prove Captain Mills wrong, now is the time. An ill-judged pancake landing might be enough to give her the shortest career on ATA record.

Vee scans the sky. Another plane is already circling above the mown X of landing strips. Four engines. A Lanc. Vee watches it spiral on to the ground as she circuits the field and gets the hang of the wind. But a firm breeze seems to suit the Swordfish. Nose slightly up. Tail-wheel ever so slightly down. The three-point touchdown is textbook smooth.

Vee steers towards the holding area, relief deflating the tension inside her. Nothing went horribly wrong. The Swordfish has been delivered on time and in one piece despite the wind. But that flare… someone here is bound to find out.

In the Ops room, though, Captain Mills has no comment as she hands him her copy of the chit for the Swordfish. He says nothing at all, in fact; nothing about the balloon, or about her near-perfect landing. Her pulse which has been racing begins to slow. Then, as she picks up her bag he raises one eyebrow in her direction.

'Ah yes, Katchatourian.'

His voice is flat and Vee's pulse again quickens. Is he about to give her another job? Or has the sergeant at Gosport already ratted on her? But Captain Mills' face, as always, is unreadable.

'Would you please take this greenery out of our way?'

Vee blinks. 'I beg your pardon?'

'This foliage, here. It's aggravating Miss Blunt's hay fever.'

He nods to a filing cabinet in the corner by the door. On the top of it, wrapped in pink cellophane and tied with a silk ribbon, are at least twenty white roses. Vee stares. Her brain cannot quite process the possibility that they are for her.

'Flowers?'

'That is what they look like from here.'

'For me?'

'So it says on the label.'

'There's some mistake…'

'I don't think we have any other *V Katchatourian* here do we, Miss Blunt. It's a singular sort of name.'

The tweed-suited woman clacking at a typewriter inclines her head and smirks.

Cellophane crackles in Vee's hands. The blooms are tightly furled and odourless. Each one must have cost several shillings. Blood starts pumping faster around her body. She has the sense of life blowing her forward like a tailwind behind the Swordfish.

There are winks and grins as she carries the lavish bouquet along the corridor and past the mess. The flowers are entirely out of keeping with Vee's everyday unlipsticked appearance. And indeed, until this moment, twenty white roses would have struck her as an embarrassing cliché of romance, yet she finds with surprise that she likes being seen with them. She feels a glow of, yes, pride. And there is nothing quite as satisfying as taking people aback.

As Vee pushes open the locker room door, Sonia looks up from the make-up compact in her hand.

'Oh my!'

'I know.'

'From Mr 302?'

Vee cannot quite say anything through the turbulence of her facial muscles. She is beaming, frowning, blushing, shrugging, all at once. Is her resolution which she made to herself less than an hour ago, to put flying ahead of love affairs, going to be blown away by a bunch of flowers? She hides her face in the bouquet as she puts it on a bench. The tightly furled petals do have a smell, but one that is vaguely antiseptic.

'I don't know.'

'What does the card say?'

But Sonia has already pulled a little pink envelope from the ribbon and is handing it to Vee. It is addressed to: *Third Officer Miss V Katchatourian*. She cannot quite bring herself to tear it open.

'Come on, Vee. I've got to go for my Master lesson in a sec.'

Vee tries to laugh but it turns into a cough. It would probably be for the best if the words inside the envelope make her cringe – some badly translated declaration that sounds flowery and ridiculous. Then it will be easy to send Stefan a cool response that ends his interest in her once and for all.

'Go on, Vee, open it!'

Vee fumbles at the miniature envelope and half exposes the card inside.'Well, what does it say?'

Vee skims the card bordered with daisy chains. *Please attend a tutorial in flying blind. 9pm, Saturday 17 April, The 400 Club, Leicester Square.*

Sonia folds her arms. 'Well, that's not very romantic. And he doesn't bother to put his name. Is it even Mr 302?'

'Yes. It's him.'

'Will you go?'

Vee shrugs.

'I thought you liked him?'

'I…' Vee opens her mouth to say that she thinks she likes him too much, that he has taken over her thoughts to the point where she is not safe in the air. And, anyway, if she wants him that badly, it all probably leads to dreadful upset. But Vee finds that her throat has tightened so firmly that she cannot speak. For a horrifying, ridiculous second she wonders if she is going to cry.

'Well, even if you don't like him, darling, you'd be a fool to pass up an invitation to The 400.'

Vee gives an exaggerated shrug of both shoulders. 'I must though, especially as all this, these flowers, The 400, it's all so extravagant…'

'What are you on about?'

'Doesn't it make him look, you know, too keen?'

'Like he wants sex, you mean?'

'Sonia!'

But as usual, Sonia is right. Vee sees that this is exactly what she has been thinking. And if a kiss on her hand can distract her so completely, what sort of ridiculous state would actual love leave her in?

'But you like him don't you?'

'I don't know him. At all. How can I say?'

'So you must go along to The 400 and find out. And don't feel at all intimidated by how much everything costs. Those foreign RAF chaps are rolling in cash. It's not as if they can send their wages home, is it?'

'No, but…'

'No buts. If you don't want sex with him at the end of the evening then just say cheerio and thanks for the blooms.'

'And if I do?'

'Then bloody well get on with it!' Sonia glances at her watch then bangs her locker door shut. 'Sorry, darling, must dash, McKay will be warming the engine. And I need all of my wits about me so that I don't actually scream when we land this time.' She blows a kiss. 'Get those in water, pronto.'

Perhaps it is Vee's imagination but the roses do seem less fresh than they were – the heads a little less upright, the white petals less tight. She pushes Stefan's card inside the tiny torn envelope and hides it amongst the flowers. Then she takes them to her locker. The roses buckle as she squashes them between her sheepskin flying boots and overalls inside the metal walls. She clanks the door shut and has to lean her weight against it to turn the lock.

 ## Posen, Greater German Reich
Friday 16 April

Ewa stares at her face in the wardrobe mirror and sighs. Her skin is pale and flaky. She has tried pinching at her cheekbones but this just leaves blotches that make her look as if she is coming down with something.

In her hand, a gold tube of crimson lipstick hovers and Ewa's mouth slackens, automatically, into a half-open pout. The reflex is well worn even though her lipstick has not been used for months. As soon as she read an article on 'natural complexion' in a German women's magazine, Ewa began to feel self-conscious about using her powder compact and lipstick. True Aryan women never wear make-up, the article had said, although quite why was not made clear.

Ewa rolls her eyes at her reflection and dabs three crimson

spots on to each lip. Even the most fervent party member could not object, surely, to a bit of lipstick for an outing to the pictures? She rubs her lips together and runs her tongue over the greasy-sweet staleness. If Beck kisses her tonight that is how she will taste. Perhaps that might put him off. She half hopes it will. But she can see that the lipstick has widened her mouth and whitened her good-enough teeth.

Her eyes flick, then, to the bottom of the wardrobe with her recollection of a lipstick mentioned in one of Stefan's letters. The Polish prisoners, he had written, were allowed to spend whatever roubles they could scrape together at a mobile canteen that circulated the camp. One winter day, amongst the writing paper and shoelaces and Turkish cigarettes that were for sale on the cart, Stefan had spotted a lipstick.

He wrote about this in a wry tone that was clearly intended to make Ewa smile. But as the letter went on, it had the opposite effect: '... *there is only one prisoner here who might make use of a lipstick, for we have in the camp, amongst the thousands of men, one solitary woman.*'

Even now, the thought of that one woman sends a hot wave of jealousy through Ewa. Why, damn him, did Stefan not realise what effect his mention of another woman would have? Ewa's resentment for this mythical female prisoner only grew with his subsequent letters. '*I had the good fortune last week to speak to our sole female compatriot in the camp. The guards allowed her out of the solitary confinement where she is usually kept to pass a jolly evening with her countrymen. This lady, First Lieutenant Janina Lewandowska, is a female pilot officer of the Polish Air Force. She is a well-known aviatrix and parachutist. I managed to fight through the throng around her in the dining area and introduce myself. She confided that she also did her flying training in Poznań and knows the city well. She has even eaten at your father's guest house! We reminisced about the Aero Club. I wondered, in fact, if I remembered her sitting at the bar there, but in those days I would not have had the courage to speak to such a glamorous and distinguished flyer.'*

Ewa, who had no memory of such a person at the Aero Club or the guest house, began to dread seeing this woman's name on the page. When a letter from Stefan arrived, she would let her eyes scan over it for a capital *J* or *L* and then leave the reading of this part until last. It began to seem to Ewa that Stefan was more intimate with this female than the other prisoners, perhaps because they were both pilots. He even relied on her to help him out: *'I have run out of roubles and soon may have to sell my Pelikan pen (you know, the one with the lizard-skin pattern that you used to like). Luckily, Janina, who also admires it, has offered me a good price...'*

As she stands there remembering, Ewa twists the paste engagement ring around the ring finger of her right hand. She continued to wear Stefan's ring after the occupiers came as a secret defiance. They all assumed that as a German, she would wear an engagement ring on her left hand. So it gave her secret satisfaction to hoodwink them about the ring's significance. But the paste jewels have been so long on her Polish ring finger, longer than any genuine engagement should be, that the gesture now feels hollow. Then she wiggles the ring off and flings it into her stocking drawer.

Going back to the wardrobe mirror, Ewa presses an arc of lipstick to her top lip, then completes the thick red O around her mouth. This will be a test for Beck. Has he enough party loyalty to tell her to wipe it off, or will he kiss her anyway?

Ewa buttons her jacket then clops down the stairs in her good shoes. Beck is waiting for her in the passageway, moulded into his grey-green uniform, freshly shaved and beaming, with his peaked cap under one arm. His heels tap together softly.

'All set?'

'Just my hat.'

She reaches for the one with the blackcock feathers and goes to the hallstand mirror to position it on to her blonde braids. An unfamiliar woman looks at her from the reflection; dark eyes shining, red mouth smiling. Smart and confident. German.

Once they are out on the square, Beck offers his arm and Ewa does not hesitate. Heat rises inside her as her elbow links with his. She knows that this is reckless but the closeness of a man after being so long on her own makes her feel like a girl again.

Beck's gait is purposeful and she has to skip to keep up as they stride across the cobbles. In the crisp twilight, the narrow painted houses seem to float above their dark colonnades. The old town hall's ornate layers shimmer.

He smiles down at her. 'A capital evening for a stroll.'

His German is more casual than she has heard it before and his whole demeanour more intimate. If he has planned this night out because he suspects Ewa of underground activities, he is a better actor than any she will see on screen tonight.

'It is a lovely evening.' Ewa's arm presses into the crook of his elbow. 'Have you visited Po… Posen before?'

For a split-second, she was about to say *Polen*. Did he notice her change the word from the country to the city when the first syllable was already in her mouth? But his smile does not waver.

'No, I had never been to the Warthegau until being posted here. It has proved an unexpected delight of my service.'

'We are quite a provincial place, though. Please don't expect the cinema to be like those in Berlin.'

'Oh, but the Apollo is so stylish. Beautiful, even. Everything here is beautiful.'

They are on the pavement beside the grey-walled hospital. Just ahead of them, a middle-aged woman scuttles off the kerb and across the road. She does not look their way but there is terror on her face. Winter curfew hours are still in place and it is only half an hour until all Poles must be off the streets. Beck does not seem to see the woman at all.

'And the plans to improve the city will make it one of the most modern in Europe.'

'Is that so?'

'Certainly. Along with the improvements to existing buildings like the Castle and the swimming pool, there's the new park and lakes which will be spectacular once the work on them is complete. Perhaps we could visit them together when the weather improves.'

'That would be super.'

'And of course, there are the new roads. The airport, I hear, is to be entirely upgraded from what it was before.'

He slides her a sideways look that implies she might have some special interest in this location. Her pulse quickens. Has someone told him how much time she used to spend at the Aero Club, and who with? Her face must not give her away.

'All German people in the city are so grateful for what is being done.'

Beck looks pained. 'I'm sure that every inhabitant will see the benefits of Germanisation in the end.'

Saints in heaven. Why did she even allude to this embarrassing fact about the city? Just mentioning that some residents are German implies that others, the great majority in fact, are not.

'Of course.'

But Ewa notices, with a detached part of her brain, what Beck's words also suggest; that the occupiers' plan to make the city entirely German is not expected to succeed. Perhaps they have already admitted, to themselves at least, that it will be impossible to replace every native Pole with a pidgin-speaking Balkan peasant.

Beck puts a restraining hand on Ewa's arm as an official car speeds past on the boulevard. Then he steers her across. In the budded branches of the tree-lined central walkway, birds trill.

The street lamps have come on, but dimly. From what she has overheard in the dining room, Ewa knows that this is because there are fears, despite the vast distance, of English bombers reaching here soon.

The narrow commercial streets are almost deserted but there is a spill of yellow light from the glass doors of the cinema.

'Do you already have the tickets?'

'Of course.'

Beck pats his breast pocket and opens the foyer door for Ewa to enter. Breath briefly deserts her at the sight of so many field grey uniforms clustered across the chess-board tiles. Chrome gleams against the red walls and German voices, loud, indignant, excited, crowd the air. There is a sense of occasion, as if something momentous is about to happen, and the few women there are tastelessly overdressed in pale fur and lace-covered hats as if for a wedding. It seems a ridiculous fuss for a film show, not even a new film, at that. But Ewa feels suddenly out of place in her sober jacket. At least she put on the lipstick.

Beck nods and smiles. Hands raise to him in casual half-heils, but he seems keen to move forward and does not introduce Ewa to any of his colleagues. Once cocooned by the plushness of the auditorium, Ewa begins to breathe more freely. The cinema always gives her a rush of childish anticipation. She remembers how she would hold her mother's hand throughout the show, gripping it at moments of high emotion, or whenever she wanted her mother to return the squeeze. She wonders what her mother would think, seeing her here with Beck, and for a sudden horrible second she is glad that her mother is dead.

The auditorium is stuffy and overheated. Beck indicates seats at the front of a shallow tier which are the best in the house.

'Is this all right?'

'Of course. Lovely.'

As he sits, Beck takes off his gloves and places his own bare hand over Ewa's as it rests on the arm of the seat. It is so long since anyone held her hand. She does not return his pressure, but neither does she pull her hand away.

The red velvet curtains swish, the lights dim and stale heat settles on to Ewa's limbs. Despite the heave of grey uniforms around her, she finds herself relaxing into her seat. Without exactly meaning for it to happen, her hand turns over so that it folds into Beck's.

His profile flickers in the white light from the screen. Then, he leans his head towards Ewa so that hairs from both their heads entwine. 'Can you see all right, and hear?'

Ewa nods and leans her own cheek towards his, although she has nothing actually to say. One of her forefingers presses against his with a pressure so slight she is not sure what she herself means by it. Heat flushes through her chest and she cannot stop herself unbuttoning her jacket.

Orchestral music, overloud and tinny, wraps the curving auditorium. Ewa glances vaguely at the newsreel procession of Russian fields and rivers before casting a look across the front of the stalls. The cheap seats are sparsely occupied and no one there is in uniform. In the swirl of cigarette smoke through the projector's beam, a woman's head is illuminated. Ewa stares. Is that Gertruda? The waved, flat hairdo is identical, but Gertruda is a Pole. She would not be allowed in here without a DVL badge, like the blue enamelled '*Wartheland*' pin on Ewa's own lapel.

It looks like Gertruda though. Why on earth would she come here? Her German is no better than a five-year-old child's. She'd be unlikely to understand all of the dialogue in the main film, let alone the more complicated explanations about the Eastern Front that are rolling through the newsreel.

Ewa feels, faintly, the weight of Beck's hand lifting away from hers. And then there is a word from the announcer that flips Ewa's eyes from Gertruda's crimped hair up to the screen. The word is *polnischen*. Polish. Not *der Pole*, as in '*the backward ways of the Pole*', or '*the filthy habitations of the Pole*'. No, *polnischen*. The respectful adjective – a word that implies a nationality, a real country. It is not a word that she can remember hearing in

German since the start of the war. A drip of perspiration runs down Ewa's neck and between her breasts.

But her attention is now fixed to the screen. A sunlit black and white river curves beneath an escarpment. The roof of a wooden mansion towers above waving larches. Then there are men milling about in cold sunshine, some in long leather coats and stiffly peaked caps, others in grubby side-buttoned tunics. Spades pitch. Sandy soil sprays into the air.

Ewa squints then as the camera passes over strangely shaped bulges in the ground. The announcer speaks quietly over the choir of male voices that sing a murmuring song. Ewa concentrates on the lumps of soil but there is no telling what they might be. *Polnische Offiziere,* says the voice through the sad singing. *Polish officers.* The air in the auditorium is growing thicker and hotter. Ewa realises that she can hardly breathe.

But Beck, she senses, is moving. Or not moving, in fact, but tensing into rigid stillness. The screen fills with more lumps in the soil. And then these lumps turn into arms, hands, heads. Not real limbs or heads, of course, they are too dusty and weightless. Hollow. Like deflated footballs, or rag-dolls left too long in an attic.

Live people now fill the screen. Women. Babies. Although as the camera moves away it is clear that they are not really alive; their smiles are too fixed, their clothes too old-fashioned. It is just a pile of photographs being sorted by a German soldier. The photographs must be from the soil. The loved ones of the empty men; their rosy babies having baths; their young women with hopeful eyes and just-trimmed bobs. Other things are brought out of the soil; a pair of spectacles, the glass unbroken; a pen, that even through the crusted soil, seems to display its lizard-skin whorls.

'Oh, Jesus!'

Ewa's hand leaves Beck's and flies to her mouth, pressing against it, stopping any other involuntary sound that might seep out. But the announcer's voice continues; his clipped German is doleful but indignant: *'what we have found here in the forest of Katyn reveals the work of the Bolshevik monster in all of his inhuman savagery...'*

Beneath larch trees, workmen in side-buttoned shirts begin to pull the empty men out of the earth. There is clearly no weight to these toy-like humans. They emerge easily, dust-covered and shredded, but still in one piece. The labourers poke at the empty men, rearranging limbs and rotted clothing. One persistent worker raises, again and again, the bare white globe of a head until it balances upright on a neck. Ewa's hand presses harder against her mouth. Heat seems to have robbed the air of oxygen.

And then, one of the peasants, a wizened old man in a brimless cap, takes up a hacksaw and sets about one of the empty men's arms. Sawing. Through the raggy sleeve and into the arm. The empty man shudders and gives off a small cloud of dust as if to protest, but he is unable to stop the peasant cutting into his bone.

It is too much. Ewa's hand leaves her mouth.

'What is he doing with that hacksaw? Why in God's name is he sawing off someone's arm?'

She has directed the question to the screen, but then she looks around and sees that every face on the balcony is turned towards her. In the white glimmer of the screen all of the faces are the same colour and each has the same look, both baffled and irritated. Only Beck's expression reflects her own, although his eyes, when they come to rest on her, are blank.

Ewa begins to rise. 'I'm sorry, Heinrich. It's so hot... I must leave.'

He stands and moves aside. But as she bursts up the stairs, out of the darkened auditorium and through the deserted lobby, he is close behind.

In the cold night air, she stops and clings to the wall beside the foyer doors. She does not feel faint. Not in the least. But she bends over anyway with her head pointing to the ground to look more convincing. The reassuring hand that she expects to feel on her back does not come. Instead there is the strike of a match. Slowly Ewa straightens and sees that Beck is beside her, his cap pulled low over his eyes, his cheeks hollowed by the drag on his cigarette. He tilts the packet towards her but she shakes her head.

'I'm so sorry, Heinrich. Those bodies… and the heat made me feel unwell.'

He does not say anything. His face is half-lit by the yellow glow from the foyer but his eyes are in shadow. Ewa feels that she must say something else to fill the silence, to explain.

'Usually, I don't mind what they show of the battlefields, but it was just those close-ups…'

'I think he was recovering the wristwatch.'

Beck's voice is thin and distant.

'What?'

'The man with the hacksaw who you were asking about.'

'Oh, I…'

'He was trying to take the wristwatch from the corpse. Items like this, as well as the photographs and personal effects that you saw, will be extremely useful for identifying the bodies.'

'I see. I'm sorry, Heinrich. I hope I did not embarrass you.'

He shrugs and a cold wave builds inside Ewa's chest. She has not seen him like this before, so locked into himself and distant.

She stands tall. 'I feel much better now. Shall we go back in?'

Beck taps his cigarette against the wall and leaves a grey smudge on the white paintwork.

'No, I don't think that would be a good idea. They all heard what you said.'

'I only said…'

And then, as Ewa remembers her exact words, she understands what he means. The subject of her question about the hacksaw, even her mention of God, did not really matter. But with a drench of horror, Ewa realises that she asked the question in the wrong language.

Beck flings his cigarette stub to the ground and sets off. Without speaking, Ewa walks alongside him down a passageway on to the dark street. And as Ewa glances up at Beck's face, she realises that he, and perhaps amongst all of the Germans there, only he had understood, without any need for translation, every Polish word that she had said.

White Waltham & London, England
Saturday 17 April

'Still here?'

Vee looks round. She has been standing by the locker room's high window, arms crossed, watching a condensation trail dissolve into sky.

Sonia pulls off a knitted red pixie hat as she comes in. 'I thought you'd be all dolled up and gone by now.'

'What?'

'For The 400.'

'Oh, that.'

'Yes, that!'

Vee shrugs. But she has thought of little else since reading Stefan's peculiar invitation. And that's the problem.

Sonia puts a hand on her hip. 'You are going, aren't you?'

'No, I don't think I am.'

'Why ever not?'

Vee sighs. 'It's too much of a distraction.'

'What is?'

'Men are.'

'Obviously. That's what they are designed for.'

'But things are complicated enough without… you know…'

'Sex?'

Sonia's eyebrows arch and Vee shrugs, not quite able to admit to herself the depth of her longing for Stefan to touch her.

Sonia leans forward so that the woman in the other corner cannot hear. 'Well, all I can say is I'm bloody glad that Tony and I have done it while we've had the chance. You never know…' Sonia's voice tails off as her eyes slide to the high window and the haze left by the contrail. A shadow seems to pass across her gaze. 'He's rather late back from Cosford now, as it happens.'

'I'm sure he'll be all right, Sonia. He's such an experienced pilot.'

'Oh, I know. Probably holed up in a pub somewhere waiting for the weather there to change.'

But Sonia bites her lip and Vee is glad to change the subject back.

'I haven't got the energy for a night out in London anyway, or the clothes.'

'Buck up, Vee.' Sonia goes to her locker. 'I'll lend you my uniform skirt if you don't want to dance in slacks.' She fishes around inside the metal walls. 'And I have something here to perk you up.'

Sonia pulls Vee down to sit beside her on the gym bench and unscrews a small brown bottle. Squeaking out a plug of cotton wool, she shakes two white pills on to her palm.

Vee blinks. 'Benzedrine?'

'Just the thing.'

Sonia goes to tip the pills on to Vee's hand. But her face turns again to the window at the drone of a distant engine. Vee knows, instantly, that this plane is twin-engined and high horsepower, a Wellington, probably. It is most definitely not the single-engine Fairchild in which Tony is expected, and has been expected for some hours. For a second, Sonia's dark eyes deaden and Vee knows that she must have realised that the plane is not Tony's.

The brown bottle hovers in Sonia's hand. Vee wonders if she should say something, some platitude, perhaps, about Tony staying on for another pint in that mythical pub. But words would only turn foreboding into something more plausible. And reassurances, Vee knows, have a nasty habit of being proved wrong.

Vee grasps at the grooved white tablets from Sonia's cupped palm. She sees suddenly that there's no point trying to stay away from Stefan. He will remain a dangerous distraction whether she sees him or she doesn't, because either way, she will not be able to stop thinking about him.

'Two?'

Sonia's eyes gleam. 'Why not? They'll perk you up no end. Get you to London and back fresh as a daisy. And here's something to wash them down.'

She pulls a silver hip flask from her greatcoat pocket and holds it out. The whisky stings and then coats Vee's throat with smokiness.

'Glen Elgin. Daddy's best.' Sonia takes a long swig then puts the flask back in her pocket. 'I think we deserve it.'

Vee closes her eyes for a second. The heat from the whisky is searing into her gut, fanning across her lungs, bringing warmth and energy to her arms and legs. She could almost start dancing right this minute.

'Will everyone else be in evening dress, do you think?'

'No, no, darling. Even at The 400 women are starting to wear their uniforms. It would be unpatriotic to stop them.'

'Will your skirt fit me?'

Sonia is already up, rattling at the metal door, pulling out her tailored navy skirt, and signalling Vee to stand up and have it held to her waist.

'It may come up a bit short, but respectable enough. You don't need to bother with stockings now the weather has cheered up. And look, you can borrow these too.'

The silky ball that Sonia slips into Vee's hand unfurls into a pair of French knickers. 'Go and change in the lavs while I find Marjorie. I think she is going up to town tonight and I'll ask her to make room for you.'

Vee's heartbeat is quickening. Tiredness evaporates into a little halo of light around her head. Yes, she will go. And even if Stefan isn't there, a trip to London will be better than mooching around in her digs at the farm with nothing much to do. She takes Sonia's skirt to the Ladies.

As soon as it is on, Vee feels a thrill of anticipation. Without quite admitting to herself why she is doing it, she wriggles off her flannel bloomers and feels the stroke of Sonia's silk underwear run up her bare thighs. The skirt lining is silk too, and the cut as close-fitting as an extra layer of skin. She is rather glad, in fact, that she has no stockings.

Sonia was wrong about the length, though. The skirt's hem is definitely shorter than regulations permit. But Vee is pretty sure, as she slips out of the Ops block, that she can make it into the back seat of Marjorie's Lagonda without Captain Mills seeing her knees.

As the car engine booms, Marjorie Hyde-Barker looks over her shoulder from the driver's seat and gives Vee a tight smile.

'I've left the hood down to give a bit more space. I do hope it's not too blowy, or too much of a squash. Sonia said you'd not mind.'

The back is not really meant for passengers. Vee's legs are wedged up against the front seat where Freddie Dunne is sitting.

'No, of course not. It's very kind of you, Marjorie.'

'Well, quite a coincidence us all wanting to go to The 400 tonight. And we must make the most of the petrol ration, mustn't we? All set?'

Marjorie lays a fuchsia scarf over her rolls of auburn hair and ties the points under her chin. Feathery pink chiffon leaks from the bottom of her greatcoat as she stamps on the accelerator and the Lagonda exits the aerodrome gates with a roar like a Hurricane. Vee's head is pushed back against leather upholstery and polished wood. Above the lane, evening sunshine filters through half-bare branches. Grassy verges flash past, and then pavements, lamp posts and a parade of shops.

As they join the by-pass, Marjorie crunches the gears and the Lagonda thrusts forward. Vehicles around them seem to ease back into slow motion. Marjorie drives as if she expects everyone else to get out of her way and mostly they do. The roar of engine and wind fills Vee with lightness. She never knew that driving along the Great West Road could feel so much like flying. Or perhaps it's just the Benzedrine.

Dusk gathers around crowding houses. Despite the dimness of tape-choked headlights, the Lagonda's speed does not let up in the blacked-out streets. When the engine is finally silenced and the headlights extinguished, Leicester Square's lollipop trees loom black in the darkness.

Vee spills out of the car onto the pavement, uncramping bent ankles and strained calves. Her head fizzes, and her eyes are alert to every shadow. Freddie is stuffing greatcoats into the car and pulling up the roof. Marjorie shimmers on the pavement in a haze of pink chiffon.

She unties her headscarf and strides off, beckoning. 'This way chaps.'

Vee follows her into a narrow doorway and down a dim staircase. The stairs widen. Curved chrome is cool under her hand. A blaring saxophone wail cuts through the buzz of voices and the fog of tobacco smoke. Cigarette sparks stud the shadows.

'Johnnie!'

Marjorie floats towards a tall figure in air force blue who kisses Marjorie on both cheeks. Vee stands alone by a fake marble pillar; her head, her heart, her whole body, thump in time with the double bass. She scans the darkened tables but all uniforms look the same colour in the dimness and the faces all look blurred. She probably would not even recognise Stefan Bergel if he were standing right in front of her.

If he is not here, she will have to turn around, go back up the stairs, find the nearest Underground and return to base. Perhaps that is what she should do anyway. But Marjorie is pulling Johnnie Vee's way.

'Johnnie, Vee here is looking for a chap from 302. Are there any in tonight?'

He nods at Vee, and gives her a look that is ever so slightly the once-over. His voice is made of sharper cut-glass even than Marjorie's.

'302? They're always in! Over there, in the corner.'

It seems rude not to follow the lift of his chin and Vee sets off, winding between candlelit tables around the dance floor. Sonia was wrong about the uniform. No other woman here is wearing one.

As she reaches a circle of dull jackets, Vee stumbles and all of the heads that had been bent together look up. At once, she recognises a face but it is not Stefan's. Piotr Double Whiskey's hair is slicked back, his face blank. Vee stands for a long moment staring at him. Clearly he does not remember her. Perhaps without her flying helmet...

'Vee.'

It is Stefan's voice. At first Vee cannot see him in the tight circle of men. And his voice sounds far off. Cool. Not pleased to see her. When she sees his face, it is deathly white.

He must have forgotten she was coming. And there is no doubt about it now, she should just go. In the second it takes to turn her head away, the whole thing plays out in her head; how she will leave with a flourish, bound up the staircase and march off into the cool air...

But his hand is on her arm. 'Vee.'

She realises that she has not actually moved and Stefan is still beside her, touching her. His face seems far away, and then very close.

'Vee, you came.'

'Yes, I'm afraid so. You asked me, if you remember.'

His hand leaves her arm but he stays close. 'Of course. I am sorry, I should be waiting for you by the door. But Piotr has brought news of something and I...'

Vee snorts and sounds angrier than she intends. 'Well, I won't keep you.'

This time, she does turn away.

'No, Vee.' Stefan's hand takes her elbow. 'Don't go. Please.'

She turns to him. His face still looks washed-out, but his eyes flash, intent on her, and full of pleading.

'I must let you finish your talk with your comrades.'

Perhaps she really has interrupted something serious; planning for a raid across the Channel, or working out why some op went badly wrong. Stefan is reaching for a plush-covered stool from another table and Vee sinks on to it without really making a decision to stay. Her heart is pounding. It is clear that none of the stony-faced men want her here. And none of them seem to feel like speaking English.

Piotr gives Vee a smile but it looks forced. Then his hand is in the air, fingers clicking. Almost instantly, a white-coated waiter brings a jug and glasses. Liquid, blue enough to go into an engine, is poured and a glass is put in front of Vee.

'What's this?'

Stefan's face has more colour and his features start to relax. 'A Messerschmitt.'

'Right. And that is...?'

At last, he is smiling. 'Drink it, and tell me.'

Vee sips and then coughs. The cocktail is syrupy but leaves her mouth on fire.

She coughs again. 'Vodka.'

'Of course.' He laughs drily. 'And?'

'Curacao, I suppose, to make it blue.'

'That is right. Blue like our jackets.'

'And something sweet…' There is a cough-mixture taste that she cannot place. 'Pears?'

'Cherry brandy. The best. From Wielkopolska.'

'What's that?'

'Greater Poland, it means. The region where our squadron is from. The old heart of Poland.'

His knee pushes up against hers. She gulps another mouthful of the blue drink before taking a breath. A lovely looseness flows into her shoulders and then down her spine. The thumping in her head lightens.

The men begin to speak. Quick syllables ricochet and the solemn mood lifts. One of the airmen raises his chin, first at Vee then at Stefan, and after his whoosh of words, laughter erupts.

Stefan bats away their jibes then jumps up and holds out his hand to Vee.

'Care to dance?'

She nods and takes his hand. It is cool and firm. He weaves her into the heave of bodies and the pulse of beats on the dance floor. Stepping backwards on the polished springy wood, Stefan passes his arm behind Vee's waist and pulls her body into his. He feels strong and supple and warm. Her hand, still inside his, is lifted and they start to sway. But their feet stay rooted. A trumpet blasts and couples kaleidoscope around them.

Vee leans into Stefan. 'Aren't you supposed to dance, on a dance floor?'

He looks at her then with an intensity that makes a tingle rise up her neck. He is squeezing her hand too, quite hard. But he says nothing.

She tries to smile. 'You did forget about me coming tonight, didn't you?'

He sighs and gives the slightest of shrugs. 'I… yes, for a

minute I did. The news that we had was very bad.'

'From the squadron?'

'No, no from Russia.'

'Russia?'

Vee frowns. Why would news from the Eastern Front be so important to them? And anyway, she knows that although the fighting is fierce, the news from there nowadays is pretty good. Britain's Russian allies have begun to push the Germans back.

Again, though, Stefan's face seems to blanch. 'It is now certain that a great many of our Polish comrades, who were prisoners in Russia, are dead.'

'Oh. I'm sorry. Did you know any of them?'

'I…' He shakes his head and briefly closes his eyes. 'Vee. This is something… I cannot talk about it.'

'Of course, no need.'

He does not seem to hear and has a dark, faraway look. 'I do not want to hide the truth, but I did something bad… something I… I'm sorry.'

Again he shakes his head and Vee wonders what he can be talking about, what on earth would make him feel so bad. But then she thinks of his near miss with Freddie Dunne and does not really want to know.

She eases her body away from his. 'This wasn't the best time for our night out, was it? Perhaps I should come back next week.'

'No! Vee, please stay with me.'

'Are you sure? Wouldn't you rather talk to your friends?'

Stefan shakes his head and his feet begin to move against the vibrating floor. Although it is not dancing, exactly. His grip around Vee's waist tightens and then, with a shake of his head, his face lowers on to her shoulder.

She does not quite know what to do. It must look odd, how they are standing here clinging, not really moving. Marjorie might be looking, too.

She speaks close to his ear. 'Is this part of my instruction?'

His head lifts. 'What?'

'In flying blind?'

He looks at her, his eyes watery through a strobe of flickering light, but he is smiling. Their bodies lock together. Music lilts and swells as the dancing couples spin, but Stefan and Vee stay fixed to the floor and to each other. Heat flows through Vee, sharp as cherry brandy. She does not care if Marjorie sees.

Vee thinks then of how she left Sonia, glancing from wristwatch to sky. If Tony has not returned by now, Sonia's world will already have fractured entirely and forever.

Vee pulls away from Stefan although their feet still shuffle together on the dance floor. 'Stefan… I like you, very much. But I don't want to make life complicated for either of us.'

He looks at her intently, his eyes searching hers. Are there tears in them? But his voice is steady.

'I am glad you are here, Vee. Very glad.'

His voice, with its musical accent, reminds her suddenly of her father.

'Are you? Why?'

'You make me believe that things can be good again. That I can make things right.'

'Do I?'

'Yes.'

'How?'

But as her face moves towards his, his mouth presses down on hers and she cannot tell which of them kissed the other first.

Hesitantly, Stefan pulls away and smiles, but his gaze has locked on to Vee's. She cannot stop her hand rising to stroke a forefinger across his lips.

'Let's go somewhere, Stefan.'

He nods. Their linked hands drop to their sides but the fingers stay locked.

Then he is pulling her away from the vibrating floor and

around the circular tables, the serge of their jackets catching at tablecloths and velvet drapes. As they mount the staircase, their arms circle each other's waists; hips press against thighs.

And then they are out in cool air. The square is quiet. A half-moon lights the entrance to a side street, and then an alleyway. Vee stumbles as her foot slips on slimy cardboard and against cobbles. But she does not care where it is they are going as long as she is still holding Stefan's hand.

They enter another alley and Stefan looks over his shoulder but there is no one around. At a dark doorway they stop. The disused door is padlocked and thick with dust but Vee steps back and lets her jacket rest against it. Stefan buries his face in her neck – kissing, licking, biting. Then he is unbuttoning her jacket and her shirt. His fingers are inside, on the skin that no one ever sees. He seems to know how best to touch, with a soft insistence that shocks Vee even as it delights her. She tries to ignore a tiny voice at the back of her brain: *see, you are not his first, you are not the only one.* But all she wants, all that every nerve in her body is telling her, becomes one word: *more.* She says it louder, over and over as he pushes her flat against the dust-covered door and then upwards into the corner. A ridge of clammy bricks is pushing a line of pain into her buttock and she is standing on something with a nasty squish to it. But nothing matters except her need for *more.*

Stefan's hand is under her skirt now, rucking up the fine woollen cloth, pulling at her underthings. There is a tug then a rip, and silk trickles down her legs. She leans into him as she feels the soft heap of Sonia's knickers around one of her shoes. *Stefan.* Is she saying it? *Stefan.* And then he is pushing against her, pushing into her. He says nothing, only breathes, although his breaths might be words she does not understand.

'Stefan… more… please.'

But then he stops, and his breath is a single word. '*Scheisse.*'

'Stefan…'

They are both panting. Both still wanting. But the urgency has gone. Above them, a stripe of bleached sky divides the black roofs. Stefan's eyes catch a gleam of half-moonlight but he does not look at Vee.

'Stefan? What is it? I'm sorry...'

He mumbles words that she cannot make out and something cold goes through her.

'Stefan, it doesn't matter. I don't mind about not doing it... it doesn't matter.'

But he has already pulled himself away from her, and buttoned up. She reaches down to save Sonia's silk from the filth. And when she straightens, Stefan has already turned his back to her and is moving away, head down, as he pulls on his airman's side-cap and breaks into a run towards the street.

 Posen, Greater German Reich
Sunday 18 April

Ewa sits on the bedroom rug chewing her nails. Letters from the hidden drawer are scattered around her and she has at last found a private half-hour to scan them, again and again, for some clue that will link Stefan to a grand wooden house rising from larch trees above a curving river.

Beneath the curious address on each letter – *Gorki Rest Home, Moscow, PO Box 12* – there is plenty of detail about Stefan's life as a prisoner of war; the dull routine of queuing inside the monastery citadel to wash, eat and be counted; the occasional, apparently cordial attempts at interrogation by the Soviets. Stefan describes the bitter winter and then the brief thaw early in the spring of 1940. But there is nothing on any of his densely written pages about a dacha in a forest like the one Ewa saw on the screen at the Apollo.

Stefan's words can still make her heart ache. *'It cannot be long now, my love, until we are together, for today I saw the first release of prisoners.'* His confidence is both irritating and desperately sad. Excitement thrills through his account of a sentry marching the muddy pathways between the shacks calling out names from a printed list. *'Those who heard their own names cheered and punched the air as they were told to gather their belongings and report to the cinema hut. There, each of those happy souls was given a portion of dry bread and herring wrapped in white paper before they bounded into the hut and to freedom. Start praying, my darling Ewa, as many times a day as you can, that my name will be on the next list.'*

After this hopeful message, Ewa remembers imagining that Stefan himself would arrive at her door before another of his letters. And so the postman's next delivery came as a disappointment. In this letter, Stefan's optimism seemed to falter: *'Another prisoner cohort gained their release today,'* he wrote, *'but alas, my name was not on the sentry's list.'* Ewa's own dismay had prickled into resentment as she read on: *'... but I can report that one who had the good fortune to be called was my dear comrade, Janina Lewandowska, the aviatrix. When she saw me in the throng outside the cinema hut, she waved and shouted. "Lt Bergel, I will get your vodka martini ordered and wait for you at the Aero Club bar!"'*

At least that got the irritating female out of Stefan's way, Ewa had thought. But reading further, her unease began to build. Stefan told of waiting with the remaining prisoners in sleety rain to see what would happen next. But the camp's main gate stayed shut. Murmurs started up about what might lie in store for the officers inside the cinema if they were not to leave the camp. And then, Stefan wrote, *'... the cinema doors suddenly re-opened and a line of men (with one woman elegantly bringing up the rear) marched down a narrow path past some outhouses to a wicket gate in the perimeter wall. This low gate, which I had never noticed before seemed to have appeared by magic. One by one, our fellow prisoners ducked through it and were gone. Keep praying, dear Ewa, that I will be next to pass that way!'*

Ewa shudders now at the eerie image of the gate in the wall. This wicket gate was always there, but the prisoners had gone about their daily lives oblivious to its sinister presence. Friday's newsreel surely showed what lay in store on the other side.

Yet even Stefan's final letter, dated 7 April 1940, is relentless in its optimism. *'Again today,'* he wrote, *'some lucky men have been shipped to freedom through the gate in the perimeter wall. I watched them with a chess companion of mine from Katowice and later, over the chess board, we speculated about our freed comrades' possible destination. My companion is a charming but wary individual. What good, he mused, was one small packet of bread and fish for a journey all the way to the Polish border? In the current season, such a trip might take nearly a week. Our comrades, he argued, must simply be on their way to another prison on Russian soil. But I would not give in to his pessimism. The fact that our most senior personnel (as well as our only female officer) have been moved first proves to me that there must be privilege or at least compassion attached to these prisoner movements. So stay full of faith, my darling, I am sure that our spring wedding is drawing near!'*

But that is all there is. And these last words that Stefan wrote to her are now three years old. Ewa's heart gives a hollow beat. She suddenly has no doubt that the officer from Katowice was right. The wicket gate in the citadel wall led only to a dacha built on sandy soil above a curving river.

Ewa goes to her stocking drawer and slips Stefan's ring back on to her right hand. It feels good to have her finger encircled again. And if Stefan, loved as he was, is dead perhaps her guilt about finding someone else will at last start to lighten.

Since the embarrassment of Friday night, Beck has been absent from the dining room but it cannot be long until Ewa runs into him. She heard him last night in the room beneath hers, the oak-bed creaking as he thrashed about. There will be some initial embarrassment over Friday night as they meet again, but Ewa will suppress it under a bright veneer of normality. And she will be wearing the ring on her right hand as she normally does.

Downstairs, there is a commotion of footsteps and doors closing. Ewa glances at the clock and realises how long she has been sitting here on the draughty floor. The breakfast things have been cleared away, but it will not be long until she must make a start with the lunch. They like a hot meal early on a Sunday. She sighs. Meatballs, godammit. When she planned the weekend menu, she was fizzing with nervous energy, able to think only of the coming cinema night with Beck. Now, the idea of cutting and grinding raw meat brings to mind a man with a hacksaw…

Ewa jerks up, collecting and folding the letters, silently slotting the drawer back beneath the wardrobe. She cannot let herself be overcome. All of her concentration must go into facing Beck without slipping into embarrassment. Or fear.

With a slam of the front door, downstairs quietens. Perhaps, that was him, Beck, leaving for the day. Ewa smoothes her skirt and locks her bedroom door behind her but as she reaches the lower landing, the door to the oak-bedroom opens and he is there.

'Eva.'

'Good morning, Obersturmführer.'

She cannot quite look him in the eye.

'Would you mind stepping into my room for a moment?'

Her stomach flips. He is freshly shaved and gives off a faint smell of leather and soap.

'Certainly.'

His room is neat, the bed made. Beside the chest of drawers, a kit bag stands bulging into its fastened straps. Beck closes the door and gestures for Ewa to sit on the bed. But she does not like the idea of him standing over her, nor of him sitting next to her on the soft eiderdown. So she goes to lean, a little awkwardly, on the oak bedstead while Beck stands by the window. As he speaks, he looks down on to the side street that leads to the deserted square.

'I am sorry not to give you any notice, Eva, but I must leave today.'

'I see.' Ewa presses both hands onto the bedstead. Unexpected dismay washes through her. 'I hope it's not because of... of Friday.'

He turns to look at her and his face is ashen. 'It is, in a way.'

'Because of what I said, in the cinema? Does that mean you have to move out?'

'No, no. It is to do with what we saw on the screen. I am to go to the east.'

'To Russia? To that place?'

He puts his head to one side in assent. 'There is an aeroplane leaving this afternoon and I must be on it.'

'Will you be back in Posen again?'

'I hope so. With all my heart.'

But his eyes are so forlorn that she realises with the sink of her stomach that he is not really expecting to come back. Stupid tears prick at the top of her nose. Was every man she ever liked destined to disappear into the cold vastness of Russia?

'I'm sorry that you are going, and I am sorry for Friday. I hope that you will remember me fondly.'

He steps towards her and takes her hand from the bedstead. 'Dear Eva. I will not stop thinking of you.'

'Oh, Heinrich...'

'Perhaps I may write?'

'Of course. Please...'

But already his mouth is over hers; his tongue hot and searching, his body stiffening. She wants to give in to the kiss but she cannot quite relax herself against him.

Then, abruptly, he steps back. 'Forgive me.'

'No, Heinrich, there is nothing to forgive. I just feel anxious and sad that you are leaving.'

He throws her a guarded look then sighs and hangs his head. 'I should tell you that posters will be going up around the city next week. Police posters. In Polish. About what we saw at the cinema.'

Her pulse quickens and she sinks back to the bedstead. 'Yes?'

'They will be asking for Poles who know of any of their countrymen who were imprisoned by the Soviets in 1939 to bring forward documents and photographs.'

Ewa's heart is hammering. 'Why?'

'These things might help us to identify the many bodies that have been found.'

She swallows and tries to give a polite smile. 'I don't think I know of anyone who can help with that.'

But Beck shakes his head and sighs. His eyes fix on her right hand that is smoothing back and forth over the carved lip of the bedstead.

'You still have on your ring.'

'Ah, yes. A silly thing but I do like it.'

'And still on your right hand, like a Polish engagement ring.'

'But I am German!' Her voice is too sharp. She starts swinging her arms about as she tries to laugh. 'You know a great deal about marriage traditions, Heinrich.'

'Perhaps.' He shrugs with one shoulder. 'I know, for instance, that English women, like Germans, wear their engagement ring on the left hand. But the English put the wedding ring there too.'

Ewa gives a tiny frown. 'Do they?'

She cannot begin to imagine why he has mentioned the English. The oddness of his remark unnerves her.

She stands up. 'You have a long journey, Heinrich. Let me pack you some food.'

'Oh no, don't go to any trouble.'

'It is no trouble. I have already prepared a selection of cured meats for this evening's supper and it's only right that you should have your share.'

He sighs and puts out his hand to her as if trying to make amends but Ewa is at the door giving a nod and a smile before leaving the room.

Her stomach somersaults as she hurries down the stairs. If he really does know, as he seems to, about her engagement to Stefan, then he also knows that she has been lying to him. She must find out for sure what he knows, so that she can make things right with him before he leaves. And if Beck does know about Stefan, there is only one way he can have found out.

A metal cask is rolling along the passageway and Ewa stops on the bottom stair to watch her father heave it into the dining room. Then she follows him.

'Papa.'

He grunts and bumps the beer cask upright on the linoleum. 'What is it?'

'I must speak with you. In the kitchen.'

'Why?'

But Ewa has already turned back into the passageway. She holds the kitchen door open until her father is inside. Then she snaps it shut.

'What have you said about me, Papa?'

'How do you mean, Maus?'

He is standing with thumbs latched into his braces, cheeks puffed red behind his moustache. Ewa steps forward so that their faces are level and almost touching. The amused twinkle in his eye is infuriating.

'About Stefan.'

Her father's brow wrinkles. 'Nothing. Why should I?'

'Have any of them been asking whether I was spoken for?'

'You're not though are you? All that was years ago.'

His words seem to relegate Stefan far into her past like a broken toy or a dead pet.

'But we were engaged.'

Oskar's shrug suggests that this is long forgotten and was all some girlish whim anyway. That Stefan means so little to her father makes Ewa suddenly want to cry.

'But you must have said something to someone, Papa. Did any of them ask about me?'

'Not in that way.'

'In what way, then?'

'You know. Nothing much.'

'Something though?'

Her father lowers his voice. 'Obersturmführer Beck was asking the other day about your childhood.'

'What about it?'

'Oh, the usual things – what you were good at in school, what you liked to do in your spare time.'

'And what did you tell him?'

'That you were good at cookery. But he knows that anyway. And you liked to go up to the aerodrome to watch the planes. I've said nothing at all about Stefan. Why would I?'

Ewa folds her arms and turns away. She knows he is telling the truth. He has never lied to her in her whole life, even when, during her mother's illness, she had wished that he would.

'Is that it? Can I go back to the beer now, Maus?'

She nods, irritated, then goes to the cold cupboard. Three types of unopened sausage and two hams are piled on to the platter. At the table she selects the sharpest knife from the block to shear off a selection of thin slices then lays them on a sheet of waxed paper. It was dry bread and herring that went into the packets given to Stefan's comrades as they left prison. Stefan had believed, naively, that this would be enough for a journey back to Poland. But Stefan's sceptical friend from Katowice was right, Ewa can see that now. Those prisoners who left the monastery citadel did not travel far. And all of them, even that female pilot and Stefan himself, now lie in shallow graves under Russian larch trees.

Ewa folds waxed paper over the slivers of meat and tucks in the ends. A clear chapter of her life has ended. She no longer needs to imagine that Stefan is somewhere else. He is gone. And the sense of him being wiped from the world comes as a strange relief. She is suddenly glad that Beck is going too. She will not need to pretend to him any longer about Stefan.

Life will become simple again; cooking and cleaning for the occupiers, silent typing and information drops for the AK. Ewa will throw her whole self into this last part. There is nothing now to stop her taking more risks, like cultivating a relationship with the Resettlement Office and becoming a proper spy.

Beck is already in the passageway.

She holds out the packet of meats to him. 'It is all freshly sliced and will keep as long as you like.'

'Thank you, Eva.' He unbuttons the top of his jacket and pushes the packet inside. His voice softens. 'Take good care, dear. I will write.'

Ewa nods and quickly touches his hand, patting it as a mother might when sending off a child to his first day at school.

Beck's face brightens, suddenly. 'And so, now, this is your last chance.'

'For...?'

'For a guess – about my home town.'

Ewa sighs and shakes her head. 'You have outwitted me, Obersturmführer Beck. I have no idea.'

'The answer will make you smile.'

'Why?'

'Do you still have no idea?'

'No, I don't.'

'I am from Kattowitz.'

In a thump of shock, her face, she fears, becomes molten.

Beck picks up his bags but says nothing more, giving a final click of heels and a quick nod before pulling the back door behind him.

Ewa stands in the passageway hardly breathing. Had Beck deliberately saved that bombshell until he was leaving? For he must have known what her reaction to it would be. How could she be anything other than alarmed to find out that he, like her, had grown up in the Republic of Poland in a town with two names?

Ewa fears though that the agitation on her face has given even more than that away. And, impossible as it is, she wonders if Beck realised that she had been thinking only a few moments earlier about a man from the town that her dead lover had called Katowice.

 # White Waltham, England
Friday 23 April

Vee lifts the chit from the counter and her eyes do not leave the indents of black typeface on the flimsy top-sheet. The paper quivers in her hand.

Captain Mills raises an eyebrow above his round spectacles. 'Something amiss?'

Vee gathers the breath to reply. 'A Spitfire.'

'And?'

'Are you sure?'

'Am I sure that MK355 is a Spitfire?'

'No, sir. I mean are you sure that I'm ready to fly one?'

'You've got ten hours solo on a Master haven't you?'

'Yes.'

'Well. What more do you want?'

'A couple of circuits in a Spit, perhaps?'

'Oh we don't bother with that any more. Can't keep a fighter plane tied up as a trainer. And you're better prepared with your hours on the Master than most RAF men. If you're nervous, I suggest you fly round Castle Bromwich in the Spit a couple of times before you head south. Just watch for the balloons.'

Did he wink? Vee can't quite tell. But the thought that he might have produces in her a surge of irritation which is enough to steady the trembling paper in her hand.

'Very good, sir.'

She knows that Captain Mills is right about her hours in the Master being good enough preparation; the controls, the cockpit, the horsepower are all about as close to a Spit as you can get. It is just that the Master has two seats and the Spitfire only ever has one. At some point, every Spitfire pilot has to get into the fastest machine on earth and fly it, for the first time, alone.

In the corridor, though, she has to stop and lean a shoulder against the wall to look at the chit again. A brand-new Spitfire. A Mark Nine, just like the one that Stefan flies... Oh God. Vee presses her hand into a tight fist. For at least an hour she has not thought of Stefan but here he is again at the front of her mind.

Since the disastrous night out in London, Vee has heard nothing from him. At first, the shock of Tony's death overtook everything else. And Sonia's grief made her own disappointment in love seem more just. It would have been intolerable to have been blissfully in love whilst Sonia was in such despair. And anyway, Vee told herself, it was up to Stefan to make the first move.

But as the days wore on, a panicky voice inside her began to whisper that maybe the same thing had happened to Stefan. The Fairchild, with Tony at the controls, had smashed into a ploughed field for no apparent reason. Everyone is saying that it will be put down by the Accidents Committee as *pilot to blame*. But Vee is beginning to wonder whether all pilots end up being killed by an aeroplane, if they keep on flying long enough.

As the days have gone by and Vee has gone over again and again what happened in the alleyway, her doubts about what to do next have become more insistent. Perhaps she should make allowances for Stefan's sudden reluctance to go further with her. The stress of combat may have made things difficult for him in… in that department. Or the shock of that news about the massacre, as she now knows it to be, of Polish prisoners. It seemed as if Stefan had a very personal connection to that event, perhaps even guilt, in his own mind at least.

On the other hand, his apparent distress about events in Russia might have simply been a cover for ungentlemanly behaviour. Perhaps he became incapable only when he realised that it was Vee he was pushing up against the dirty doorway, and not his beautiful Polish girlfriend. Or even his wife. Because yesterday, with a start, Vee suddenly saw how easy it would be for Stefan to be a married man and to keep this fact hidden from her. If this is really how it is, Stefan's comrades must have all been secretly laughing at Vee, or feeling sorry for her. But this thought has become so distasteful that she commands herself not to think of it again.

Perhaps the only way to put these crowding, distracting doubts out of her mind is to make a telephone call and ask Stefan some straight questions. She would surely get a sense of whether he is lying in his replies. And perhaps, in order to rid herself, once and for all, of the agitation he has caused her, she must make this call before flying her first Spit.

She starts to walk down the corridor towards the parachute store. Speaking to Stefan may not make her braver but it should at least reduce the confusion she feels. That would be better than nothing.

One of the telephone cubicles is occupied. A woman's lace-up shoe, visible beneath the door, is tapping furiously. The other cubicle door is ajar. Inside, Vee can see the heavy black receiver on its plaited loop of brown cable. Vee goes in and lifts the receiver. Then she presses a shilling into the slot.

The operator's voice crackles with impatience. 'Exchange and number.'

'Northolt Aerodrome, please. I don't have the number.'

There is a long pause.

'Station Operations or Mess Office?'

'Er…'

'Pardon?'

'Mess.'

Another pause.

Vee stares at the sign on the back of the door: *Is your call really necessary?* Is it? Probably not. It's probably the opposite of necessary.

'Hello. Mess Office.'

Vee jumps and automatically presses the silver button. Her shilling clunks into the box.

'I'd like to speak to Flight Sergeant Bergel, 302 Squadron.'

'Sorry. Not here.'

'Oh. Right. Could I pass on a message?'

'Sorry, no.'

'Or find out 302's new location?'

'No, miss. You misunderstand. There's been no squadron movements.'

'But Flight Sergeant Bergel…'

Silence.

'… is he all right?'

'May I ask what this would be in connection with?'

'I'm just a friend.'

'Oh.'

Is there a sneer in his voice? She may be imagining it.

'Well, miss, I can tell you that he has moved on for operational reasons but that is all. Is there anyone else you'd like to speak to?'

'Erm… Piotr. Piotr Dev…'

'Drzewiecki.'

'Yes.'

The line seems to go dead. Then there are voices in the background. The pips will start going before long and she doesn't have another shilling, only pennies and ha'pennies and she's not sure how many of those…

'Please? Who is this?'

Vee recognises the strong accent with its impetuous edge.

'Oh. Hello. It's Vee Katchatourian, Stefan's friend.' Piotr does not answer. For all she knows, Stefan has lots of 'friends'. 'I'm from ATA. Do you remember? At The 400 Club...'

'The lady pilot.'

'Yes.'

'How I can help you?'

'I just want to make sure that Stefan is all right.'

'Yes. He is.'

'Oh. Good. Could you give me his telephone number?'

'No. I do not have.'

'Or an address?'

'No.'

'Could you pass him a message from me?'

The line goes quiet. Perhaps there is a sigh.

'Miss Vee, I think best you forget Stefan.'

'Should I?'

'Yes. Goodbye, Miss Vee.'

The pips start then.

'Oh. All right. Goodbye.'

There is a click and then the burr of an empty line.

Vee replaces the receiver on to the cradle but her hands stay cupped around the warm weight of Bakelite. What on earth did any of that mean? She can think of no good reason why they should be so evasive. Perhaps Piotr's English is at fault and he did not understand what she was asking. Or perhaps he was simply covering for Stefan who has no intention of ever seeing Vee again.

A bang from the adjoining cubicle makes Vee let go of the receiver. Beneath the cubicle partition, she sees again the shoe that was tapping but is now still. It is Sonia's shoe, she realises. And when Vee goes out into the corridor, Sonia is there, with a face that is, as it has been since last Saturday, the colour of morning ash.

'Sonia.'

Vee's hand folds over her friend's. She cannot think of a single thing to say. Sonia's mouth smiles although her eyes are dull as death.

'That was Tony's father. Just confirming the arrangements. I'll motor over there on Sunday.'

'Shall I come with you, Sonia? At least as a passenger. It's a damned nuisance not being able to drive or I'd offer...'

'No, no. I'll be all right.'

'Are you sure? What about today? What are you going to do with yourself?'

'Get my chit, of course.'

Vee frowns. 'You're flying? Today?'

'I have to. I'd feel even more ghastly if I couldn't fly.'

Vee shakes her head but cannot bring herself to say anything else.

From the corner of the corridor ceiling, the Ops tannoy blares: *'Hello, hello, attention please. Taxi Anson 9972 waiting outside for pilots: Thompson, Estes, Hurworth, Katchatourian and Cheng.'*

'That's you, Vee.'

'Yes.'

'Go on. Don't keep them waiting.'

Outside, the wind is brisk but the vis is telescope sharp. Cotton-wool clouds dot the porcelain sky. As she heads towards the Anson, Vee feels alert to every detail; the mechanic wiping oily hands on his overalls, the yellow Tiger Moths lined up like ducklings at a fair, the red cross on the ambulance that sits at the ready by the landing strip.

Suddenly, Vee is glad, no, she is overjoyed that Stefan has gone out of her life. Because it would be completely ridiculous to end up like Sonia and be madly in love with a dead man. Now Vee is free. And if she ends up ripping the brand new Spitfire into the ground, the loss of the aircraft will be the only thing that really matters. No one will mind too much about losing a third-rate Third Officer.

She waits on the grass behind Mike Thompson, drumming her fingers against her bag as he hauls his tall frame on to the wing and through the Anson's low door. Vee follows, stooping into the cabin as her eyes adjust to the light.

'Budge up!'

Jimmy Cheng, a burly New Zealander, is right behind her. Vee shuffles away from the door so that he can get by. Then he sees her face and looks aghast.

'Hey, miss, you feeling all right?'

'Yes.'

'You look a bit...'

'I'm all right.'

Vee sits on the narrow metal bench and pulls the straps tight. She will not admit, even to herself, that everything in her life recently has gone too far, too fast. Only three months ago, she couldn't fly at all; only a month ago, she had never been in love.

The fuselage wall thrums against Vee's head as the Anson accelerates across the grass. She grabs the edge of the bench and closes her eyes. Wheels shake before they give up the ground with a thump. Despite the straps, Vee imagines herself floating, weightless up into the sparse cabin.

She opens an eye and Jimmy Cheng's head is bent towards his neighbour in an earnest exchange but he is looking straight at Vee. They must think her ridiculous, clinging on to the bench like this during a perfectly comfortable take-off. If she is to fly a Spit, she must at least pretend to be all right. And if she does not fly the Spitfire today, she might as well give up on being a pilot for good.

Vee takes a breath as deep as she can manage and reaches into her overnight bag. The covers of her *Ferry Pilots Notes* are dog-eared and grubby. But the *Spitfire Mark IX* page is clean. Vee does her best to commit the instructions to memory:

'... *oil pressure gauge – 30LBS; air screw control lever – FORWARD; fuelcock levers – UP...*'

109

She knows all this off by heart but the words seem to have no meaning.

Beyond the Anson's cockpit windows, the pale sky is islanded with white clouds. On the horizon, above Birmingham's forest of tiny chimneys, the brown smog is studded by a glitter of defensive balloons.

Vee knows there is something missing from the *Notes*, something that Sonia had said about take-off in a Spit. An important piece of advice. Was it something about swapping hands from throttle to undercarriage lever? She could ask Jimmy but he now seems engrossed in a comic. And asking anything would make her look even more pathetic than she probably already does. They would not be surprised. They probably think that she has never been quite up to scratch as a pilot, even for a woman.

The Anson tilts away from the sun and Vee twists her neck with a crack of tense muscles. There, below, is the Vickers-Armstrong factory with its vast furrowed roofs and concrete roadways; a small rectangular city surrounded by fields. Between a giant hangar and the bleached X of landing strips, miniature Spitfires are tied down in earthbound battle formation. And one of them must be MK355.

Jimmy hardly looks up from *The Wizard* as Vee leaves the plane, and on the ground everything feels a little firmer. In the factory aerodrome office, the sergeant on the movements desk is pleasant and brisk. He seems unsurprised that Third Officer Katchatourian is not a man and as he signs her chit, he explains in detail where she will find the aircraft and he even kindly points the way to a ladies' room. This is not a thing Vee has ever found before in an RAF station or maintenance unit. She usually has to go to the gents double quick.

This factory lav even has a dish with real soap in it and Vee takes a long sniff of her hands as she washes them. Then she looks at herself in the mirror. Her skin is dull and spotty; her hair has not been washed for more than a week. She looks like a disappointment to herself as her mother would say. Neither of her parents is as proud of her as they should be. Being a ferry pilot is too out of the ordinary for them to comprehend fully what a remarkable thing it is that Vee has achieved. If this flight goes wrong, they will mourn her bitterly, but they might also feel vindicated. Flying certainly did turn out to be much too dangerous a job for a girl.

MK355 glints with fresh paint and unscratched Perspex. The ground staff are polite, telling Vee not to worry about a puff or two of smoke from cowlings on account of all the new grease in the engine. And *it's not called a 'Spitfire' for nothing!* they say.

Despite her foreboding, excitement sparks through Vee's stomach as she presses her parachute into the seat and herself on top of it. Instrument dials glisten. With the initial checks done, Vee shouts *Clear!* and presses the starter button. A blast from the propeller-engine punches her face and as she breathes in the smoke and noise, she is filled with a sudden lightness. She knows exactly what to do to fly this plane, and must now prove to everyone, including herself, that she can.

Hydraulics, down; booster pump, on; pressures and temperatures rising. Vee pulls the lever by her feet to release the brakes and the Spit jumps forward. She looks over her shoulder. Both of the mechanics are pressing their weight on to the tail. Vee edges the Spit forward, her feet on the rudder pedals, coaxing a zig-zagging path that allows her to see to each side of the plane's high nose. As wheels bump on to the glaring expanse of concrete, the nose lists down as the men riding on the tail leap off.

Throttle forward. A heavy hand of air pushes Vee against the seat as the Spit accelerates. Concrete, grass, factory buildings are all passing in a blur. And then, the nose begins to sink. Even though she knows that this is what always happens when the tail wheel rises from the ground, Vee's stomach lurches. The sense of

111

an impending somersault runs a drip of sweat into her eye. She looks for a second across the wing and a distant yellow windsock is underneath it. So the Spitfire must be in the air.

Vee holds tighter to the steel ring that tops the control column and eases it back. Up, up; easily, joyfully. Never has an aeroplane felt more at home in its element. Higher, higher. The Spitfire is cushioned by the air. Falling is inconceivable.

Vee suddenly remembers Sonia's advice to wait before switching hands from throttle to control column to undercarriage lever. And once the wheels have flipped into the body of the plane, it glides ever faster in a glorious, roaring symphony.

The altimeter needle teeters in the dial. Two thousand feet. Woolly clouds are not far above. Their curving undersides seem even more solid close up. It is hard to believe, this near, that she could fly through them, almost as easily as through air.

Vee sees then, in a moment of cold-front clarity, that she was stupid to pin any hopes on to Stefan. He is in love with someone else; someone who may be out of reach, but he cannot let her go. Vee will not let herself fall into the same trap. She will forgive Stefan for abandoning her if that is what he has done. And if she lives long enough, she will forget him.

Up ahead, a low cloud, bulbous as a cauliflower, sits directly in the Spitfire's path. Vee glances at the panel. Two hundred miles an hour. The correct cruising speed but faster than she has ever travelled, or might ever travel again. The cauliflower cloud is advancing headlong and Vee knows that she should avoid the uncertain turbulence of its interior. The dense white vapour looms. And before there is time to change course, Vee is swallowed by whiteness.

Autumn 1943

Cumulus

Rounded white clouds scattered across the sky and in constant movement. Associated with fine weather but may develop into cumulonimbus, the towering black clouds that produce lightning and violent storms.

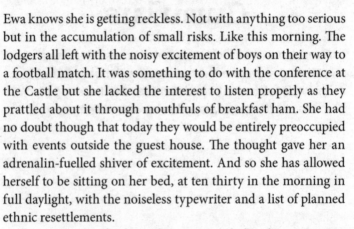

Posen, Greater German Reich
Monday 4 October

Ewa knows she is getting reckless. Not with anything too serious but in the accumulation of small risks. Like this morning. The lodgers all left with the noisy excitement of boys on their way to a football match. It was something to do with the conference at the Castle but she lacked the interest to listen properly as they prattled about it through mouthfuls of breakfast ham. She had no doubt though that today they would be entirely preoccupied with events outside the guest house. The thought gave her an adrenalin-fuelled shiver of excitement. And so she has allowed herself to be sitting on her bed, at ten thirty in the morning in full daylight, with the noiseless typewriter and a list of planned ethnic resettlements.

The work absorbs her. She turns each handwritten page, stomach skipping with apprehension in case she recognises the address of someone she knows too well; a school friend or a distant relative of her mother's, someone she would have to warn about what was coming. And such a warning would be very much more than a small risk.

Suspicion could so easily be roused. Even on the day of an expulsion, if the household lacks its radio and blankets or the kitchen is without any pans or knives, the question *'Who told you?'* will arise. It would be screamed, in fact, by policemen speaking bad Polish. And Ewa could not really blame any evicted family for saying the name of the woman who had tipped them off. Thankfully though, there has so far been no one on the lists worth that risk.

It has not taken Ewa long to become a trusted member of

114

the Resettlement Office team. In the summer, endless swaddled peasants, speaking a language that only their dogs and Bulgarian neighbours would recognise as German, had flowed westward. These borderland *Volk* are coming partly because they have heeded, patriotically, the Führer's call to populate the Reichsgau Wartheland with Germans. At least that is what the newsreels say. But mainly they are coming, in ever-increasing numbers, because they are not stupid. The Soviets are on the advance. And anything remotely German that gets in their way, even schnauzers and dachshunds Ewa has heard, will not live to meet more than one Red Army soldier.

When Ewa turned up to volunteer, Frida, who runs the Resettlement Office, was beginning to despair. Where were all of these new settlers to go? The Bessarabians all wanted farms, but they had already been snapped up. Only city apartments were left, and these, especially in their nasty post-expulsion condition, were not popular. We must make them nicer, Ewa suggested. Provide the new occupants with a hot meal, and flowers perhaps. Frida had smiled. Most of the other Resettlement girls were hearty Party types from the Alt Reich but Frida seemed delighted with Ewa's quiet domestic efficiency. And Ewa is now trusted with administration too. It will not be long until she is drawing up the eviction schedule herself and deciding which apartments, currently lived in by Poles, are required for 'German' settlers.

Downstairs, the back door bangs over a hail of men's voices. Ewa's fingers hover over the hollow keyboard. The carriage return is embossed with letters: *REMINGTON NOISELESS PORTABLE*. She has no idea what the words mean. The machine must be English or American and she can only guess where Haller got it. Her fingers again trip silently over the keys. There are a few more dates and addresses to add before this copy will be done. The liaison girl who will take it is only working on the flower stall until noon.

Did one of the voices below shout for her? Perhaps an officer has come back for something and needs to speak to Ewa about dinner arrangements. Her meal plan for the week is already messed up; it was only yesterday when most of them said that they were likely to be out each evening. And then, of course, there is the Gauleiter's dinner on Saturday. Her stomach gives a little flip at the thought of all the work she must do for it, and at the thought of the event itself.

Ewa types the final address and pulls the paper from the roll. Hurriedly, she starts to pack the typewriter and replace Frida's lists in the folder on the dressing table. But as she is fixing the hidden drawer back under the wardrobe, the words drifting up the staircase tell her that the voices below cannot belong to any of the officers. They are men's voices certainly, but they are speaking Polish. It must be her father with the postman. Because, much as the occupiers wanted to find a German for the job, they have found it impossible to replace old Jabłoński. No one else knows the city's warren of alleyways and ancient apartment blocks so well. And now that most of the streets have German names again, as well as new-fangled postal codes, the mix of languages would have flummoxed anyone who had not started out, like him, as a city postboy in the Kaiser's Reichspost.

It is time to get going anyhow. Today's apartment is likely to be in the same nasty state that they usually are. She already has enough to do this week, but the more Frida relies on her, the more Ewa is taken into Frida's confidence, especially since Helga, one of the most efficient girl-scout types at the Resettlement Office, has returned to Essen. Frida whispered to Ewa that this was because Helga's parents were frightened about the creep of the Eastern Front ever closer to Posen. The snooty Rhinelanders, Frida said, regarded Posen as a frontier town and so they imagined that some Cossacks, thousands of kilometres away, were more dangerous to their darling Helga than the nightly Allied bombardment they were getting in Essen.

The idea that the Allies could one day win the war had always given Ewa a glow of secret smugness. With Germany defeated, the Republic of Poland would return and all of her wartime sacrifices would be recognised. But, as Frida prattled on, Ewa began to imagine what the military conquest of German-held lands might look like to the people who lived there, and foreboding tremored through her.

The typed sheets remain face-up on the silky bedspread as Ewa locks the bedroom door behind her. The chance of anyone wanting to enter her room is so slim that it is not worth the time to clear them away. Below, her father and Jabłoński are shouting about traffic congestion, and the best way, whilst there are so many vehicles heading for the Castle, to avoid St Martin Strasse, or Święty Marcin as her father carelessly calls it. But nevertheless, it is *Eva* that he calls up the stairs and Ewa winces with irritation at her German name.

Jabłoński is smiling up at her from beneath the silver spread-eagle on his oversized cap and holding out an envelope. Ewa sees her father exchange a look with him then a wink and she whisks the envelope from Jabłoński's hand with a curt *Danke*. The word *Feldpost* is embossed above the address and instantly, she knows who the letter is from.

In the dining room, Ewa leans against the sideboard and studies the envelope. Her name and address are written in an elegant flowing hand: *Frl Hartman, Gasthaus Hartman, Alter Markt, Posen*. She wonders why he has not written before now. It is almost six months since he left. She has almost forgotten about him. The flimsy envelope crackles open.

Feldpost 00608 30. IX. 1943
Liebes Frl Hartman,

Please accept my sincere apologies for failing to write to you as I promised that I would. My only excuse is that I was never sure of what I could say to you apart from reminiscing about the joy of my stay at Gasthaus Hartman. But the very sweetness of these memories was painful amidst the distastefulness around me. So please try, if you can, to forgive me for my silence.

I write now in haste, but with some good news. I shall be returning soon to Posen. I have been tasked to deliver a lecture on 6 Oct so I shall be back in the city by that date. I have scant hope of a vacancy in your delightful establishment, but should there be one, could you and your father bear me in mind?

Even should a bed not be available, I intend dear Frl Hartman, to take a meal at the Gasthaus, and I hope sincerely to thereby resume our acquaintance.

Mit besten Grüssen,
SS-Obersturmführer Heinrich Beck

Ewa frowns. This sounds nothing like the man she remembers. She knows all of the troops' post goes through a censor, but that is no reason to keep up such a strange formality. '... *thereby resume our acquaintance*' sounds more like something he might write to one of his old professors rather than to a woman with whom he has shared a passionate embrace. But there has been no one else who has taken her fancy since he left, although a few have tried their best to entice her.

She folds the letter back into the envelope as her father puts his head around the door.

'News from the front?'

He has switched languages and seems even more jovial in German. Perhaps it is an impression of his long-dead grandfather.

'A booking enquiry actually. From Obersturmführer Beck. Remember him?'

Her father screws up his face then smirks. 'The one who tried to take you to the pictures?'

Ewa ignores his teasing. 'I thought we could put him into the balcony room.'

'When is he coming?'

'I don't know exactly. But soon. Before Wednesday.'

'I meant to tell you that they want us to keep our best room free this week for some Berlin big-wig who might or might not appear.'

'Oh.'

'Beck could go in the gable room.'

Ewa blinks. The room next to hers. Only a thin wall and a tiny landing between them. 'He could, I suppose…'

'Good. Then that would be a full house, on paper at least. Which is becoming something of a rarity. Will you get the beds ready?'

Ewa nods. She does not quite know what she feels about Beck's return but the knot of tension in her chest that started with her thought about the Gauleiter's dinner, feels suddenly heavier. She stuffs the envelope in her skirt pocket.

'But I must do the Resettlement Office's work first. There's no telling how long that will take.'

She follows her father into the kitchen to collect her basket from the top of the dresser and wonders if his eyes narrow as she carries it upstairs. Should he ask why she needs to take the basket to her room, she will say that the Führer's framed photograph is up there as well as a few knick-knacks for the settlers. But when she comes back down, and the basket is packed not just with the photograph of Hitler but also with a hidden scroll of typed addresses, her father says nothing.

Ewa stands at the kitchen table to cover the photo frame with cloths then pile the basket with brushes and a tube of scouring powder as well as potatoes, onions and a joint of mutton neck for the settlers' stew.

Her father drains his coffee cup and wipes his moustache. 'Have you decided on a menu for Saturday?'

'Mushroom soup. Veal Schnitzel. Apple strudel.'

He nods. 'There will be thirty of them you know.'

'I know. Will you speak to the butcher, Papa? If I do it, he will feel at liberty to throw saucy remarks at me in exchange for that much meat.'

'Yes, Maus, I will. And you must tell me if he ever does that to you. I know a good way to get our own back.'

Ewa looks sideways at her father and hopes that getting their own back does not involve calling in favours from the lodgers, although she knows that it probably does.

'See you later, Papa.'

'Take good care of yourself.'

As Ewa closes the back door behind her, she wonders if he meant something by that last, odd turn of phrase. He could not, surely, know about the roll of underground intelligence hidden in her basket. Maybe the fizz of energy that she always gets before making a drop has made her alert to danger signals that are not really there.

Outside, the clutter of cobbled streets and painted houses are washed in yellow light. Ewa wears her headscarf knotted on top of her head in readiness to clean the apartment. They are always left in a disgusting state after evictions. She braces her arm through the handle of the heavy basket and lets the sagging sleeve of her old cardigan cover the place where the roll of typed paper is stashed.

The streets are busier than normal, even for a Monday. A vast black Maybach with a Berlin number plate is edging down the street, clearly lost. Ewa has to move away from the kerb as it goes by. The fat man driving it glances up at her expectantly as if he is considering winding down the window to ask directions. Ewa catches his eye but the man turns away and the car purrs onwards. He must think from the way she is dressed that she is a Pole.

Sunlight stabs as Ewa turns the corner on to Sapieha Square and she puts up her free hand against the glare. For a moment, she is disorientated. All of the covered stalls on the market place look identical in the bleached light, and none that she can see are selling flowers. But once she walks into the maze of stalls and finds shade, she remembers the location of Wanda's kiosk and weaves her way towards it.

Wanda is not her real name, of course, and the girl does not spend much time working on the flower stall. But she has been there the last few times that Ewa visited and she makes a perfect costermonger with her ruddy cheeks and neckerchief.

'Asters! Dahlias! Phlox!'

Wanda has a lusty voice but her German is badly accented. She throws a side-glance Ewa's way as she shouts. Ewa stops and pushes at the wet stems of some garish, ball-headed dahlias in a metal bucket.

'How much are these?'

There is a note of condescension that inflects her voice whenever she speaks Polish nowadays. Wanda comes over pulling her hands in their fingerless gloves out of her apron pocket.

'I can do you six, assorted colours, for one Reichsmark fifty.'

'That's more than they cost last time!'

Wanda shrugs. 'All the hotels are full this week. And they all want flowers on the tables.'

'One twenty-five.'

'Sorry.'

Ewa sniffs and throws up a narrowed glance but Wanda's face is blank.

'All right then.'

Wanda picks out the dripping flowers, pink, red, orange, yellow and rolls them in a triangle of newspaper. She rolls her eyes at the two coins on Ewa's palm and makes a show of raking through the change in her pouch.

Ewa sniffs. 'I don't want all your little Reichspfennige clogging up my purse.'

'All right. If you come this way, there's a fifty in my bag.'

Ewa follows her behind the flower buckets and under the

awning, placing the heavy basket on the ground as Wanda opens a knapsack. And then, so swiftly that Ewa hardly sees how it is done, the dahlias are slid into the basket as Wanda removes the typed paper scrolls and transfers them to her knapsack.

Coins are exchanged as well as glances. Ewa is doing her best to keep her face neutral. But euphoria rushes through her as she turns away from the stall and strides off with nothing more incriminating in her basket than a bunch of ugly dahlias.

She cannot help smiling. Really, it doesn't seem risky at all. There are only women in the market today, and most of them seem Polish anyway. All of the Gestapo are preening themselves for the goings-on at the Castle. This morning turns out to have been an excellent opportunity to make the drop.

Ewa winds through the stalls and then back on to the street, heading up the hill. It looks as though a brand-new red and black banner has been put up on the post office. As she walks towards it, she cannot help but admire the striking effect of the colours against the pale stone façade.

And then, she feels a hand on her elbow.

'Fräulein.'

Her insides freeze. One word is enough to know that the man is German.

She should turn now, wrench her arm from his grip and say *How dare you?* in her best Berliner accent. But she can't speak, can hardly stand. The only sensation in her whole body is the pressure of that hand on her elbow steering her up towards the post office. From the corner of her eye, Ewa sees the man's shoes and trousers; mud on his toecaps, dark grey flannel rippling as he walks. A wide-brimmed hat is pulled down over his face.

'Keep walking. Don't speak.'

For some reason the man is speaking Polish now. And the voice sounds familiar. It sounds like his voice. *His* voice. Mother of God, she has gone mad. That is the only explanation. Living a double life so long has made her insane.

The man is walking next to her now, the grip on her elbow still firm, gliding her across the flagstones. And then she looks, just for a second, at his face and straight into his pale blue eyes.

Only his hold on her elbow stops her from buckling and falling over right there on the street. It is his face. His. And then she says his name but her throat makes almost no sound.

'Stefan.'

Posen, Greater German Reich
Monday 4 October

'Stefan…'

He pulls at the brim of his hat and steers Ewa away from the well-dressed couple about to enter the revolving door of the post office.

'Stefan… I can't breathe.'

She closes her eyes and the swastika from the red and black banner is imprinted inside her eyelids. The clanking of a tram is muffled as if underwater.

He grips her elbow harder. 'Come, let's cross over.'

His voice. It is still *his* voice. She tries to reply but cannot speak. He guides her across the cobbles and the grooved tramlines on to the landscaped centre of the boulevard. A man smoking a pipe is sitting on one of the park benches but the others, each with a neatly painted *Nur für Deutsche* sign, are empty.

Ewa sinks on to the seat beside a red-leafed maple bush. Blood drains from her brain. Jesus. Stefan is back. Blackness rims her vision and she leans her head forward on to her knees. There is a light hand on her back. Stefan's hand. This cannot be and yet it is. She turns her head and Stefan is still there, smiling.

'Ewa.'

Warily, she sits up. 'You are not dead?'

He shrugs as if the fact baffles him too.

123

Her hand goes to her mouth. 'But I saw your lizard-skin pen...'

'What?'

'... in the soil. Beside the hollow bodies.'

And she can still see those heads from the cinema screen, round and blank like airless footballs except for the gaping black shadows of the faces they used to wear. She starts to shake and Stefan rubs her back a little harder,

'There now, Ewa.'

Saliva slimes her fingers. 'You were there, in Russia... how... how...?'

'Here, have this.' Stefan puts a cigarette between her lips. His voice is quiet and he is still speaking Polish. 'Just smoke until you feel all right.'

On the other side of the ornamental shrubs, the man with the pipe has folded his newspaper and is walking towards them. Stefan brings his face close to Ewa's and flicks the lighter until it catches. His face is fuller than it used to be, the skin smooth and tanned – a grown man's face.

The pipe-smoker passes them, and walks away without looking back. The cigarette shakes in Ewa's hand but her breathing is slowing. Stefan smiles again and looks more relaxed, but more uncertain.

'So, aren't you pleased to see me?'

She sucks hard on the cheap cigarette, a wave of warmth loosening her limbs. 'Stefan... I...'

Suddenly his face drops. 'If there is someone else, I wouldn't presume...'

Furiously she shakes her head and, for the first time, looks at him properly. The gaze locks them together.

'No. There is no one.'

On the bench, Stefan's little finger edges on to hers and a spark quickens in Ewa's stomach like the first strike of a lighter.

'Is there somewhere, Ewa, somewhere we can go?'

She knows what he means. She feels the meaning in her fingertips, in her gut, in the roots of her hair.

She nods. 'It's not far, near Wall Strasse.'

He frowns. 'You mean Wały...'

'Yes.'

The name of the street has the same meaning in both languages. She realises that he cannot have been in the city long if the new name puzzles him.

'Will you go first? Can you stand up all right, Ewa?'

She runs a knuckle along her lower eyelash and whispers. 'Even if no one can hear you should call me Eva.'

His eyes narrow but he nods.

She takes a final drag on the cigarette before standing and stamping it under her shoe. 'Don't follow too closely.'

It would not do to be seen with him, whatever his story might be. It would not do at all. And she is glad to have a few minutes to gather herself from the shock, and to think. As she stops to cross Friedrich Strasse, she throws a look behind. Stefan is still there on the park bench. Stefan. Not a prison letter re-read a thousand times, nor a cheap ring, nor a ghost, but the man himself. And, saints in heaven, he looks good. His body is less boyish than it was – broader and more muscular. He looks well fed. He looks German.

She tries not to rush. Her breathing is still not right. And this is a moment to savour, one that she has tried to conjure into reality for the past four years. At first she never stopped imagining his return, hoping that if she thought of it often enough whilst awake, it would at least seep into her dreams. But it never did. Instead, nightmares infected her waking hours. As she was scrubbing the sink or brushing the yard, she would see Stefan collapsing on to a frozen railway track. Once, so lost was she in this imagining, that she thought a pile of rubbish sacks against the toilet block was his corpse. Day and night, her mind told her that he was dead. And yet today her eyes and her fingers and her gut are telling her that he is alive.

Walking up Garnison Strasse she senses his footsteps behind her but dare not look. The basket weighs on her arm, gaudy flowers wobbling. Each step clicks through her brain and triggers a question. Where has he been? How did he get back? What has he been doing? Any young man anywhere in what used to be Poland has already been drafted for labour duties. Stefan, in his smart suit and fedora, does not look as if he has been slaving in a munitions factory or a coal mine. But if he has not been in Poland, where has he been? And more pressingly, what will he, and what will she do now?

Her legs almost float her past the ochre and cream plasterwork of number thirty-two. She crosses the street, feels for the keys in her pocket and slips the larger one into the metal grille. Iron foliage quivers as the gate clanks open. A sideways look down the street brings a thump of her heart. Stefan is coming. Another key lets her through the main door to the apartment block. She leaves both gate and door ajar.

Inside, arched windows flood the entrance hall with light. On one of the landings above, a door closes and there are footsteps. Ewa's heart skips as the front door pushes open and Stefan appears. She puts a finger to her lips then points upwards where there is a man's gloved hand on the banister.

But Stefan's voice is loud and jovial, echoing up the stairwell. 'Oh, don't trouble yourself about that, Fräulein.'

He has put on a slight Bavarian accent. She goes to him and stands on her toes, whispering. There is a small white crust of shaving soap on his ear lobe.

'Someone from the eviction party might still be here.'

He shrugs and leans against the wall with one hand in his trouser pocket. The footsteps become louder on the stairs and then an elderly man in a Homburg hat appears alongside a woman with a fur stole. There is a tear stain across her cheek. Terror fills their eyes.

Ewa smiles and thrusts her right arm into the air. 'Heil Hitler.'

The man on the stairs hurriedly raises his arm too but seems unable to speak. Stefan pulls at the brim of his hat and lightly raps his heels as the couple pass. They cannot bear to look at him.

As the door slams behind them, Ewa whispers. 'They think you're Gestapo.'

'How do you know I'm not?'

Lightly, Ewa punches his waist and he seems to cave in, laughing. Her pulse quickens. She knows almost nothing about him any more and the thought charges her with excitement.

They start up the stairs. Stefan comes closer as they climb. By the third-floor landing, his breath is in her hair. He presses against her as she tries to turn the key in the apartment door. The lock is stiff. Rattling echoes down the stairwell.

'Let me.'

He reaches out, wrapping arms around her then yanks at the handle and twists as he turns the key. The door springs open.

Inside, Ewa goes to put the basket down but Stefan is already pulling her to him. The basket falls on its side as he pushes Ewa back and up against the closed apartment door, covering her mouth with his. Cardigan and headscarf fall on to the dirty linoleum. Then Stefan's hand is inside her blouse. With a gasp, Ewa remembers how this all used to go. Her hands reach under his jacket, loosening belt and buttons, feeling how ready he is.

Then his hand is under her skirt, lifting up her leg, keeping his arm under her thigh. She opens her mouth and throws back her head. She is trying to be quiet but a groan slips from her throat as she lowers herself on to him. He pushes into her. Slow hard thrusts, with his head buried in her neck. She moves her hands across the bare skin of his back. Then she finds his head, lifting it until his face is level with hers. His eyes seem far away.

'Look at me.' She tightens her fingers into his hair. 'Look at me, Stefan.'

And he does.

His shudder crumples on to her and his head falls back on to her shoulder.

Ewa stares into the dark hallway, breathing hard on a reek of pipe tobacco and damp. Awkwardly, she lifts herself off Stefan. The elastic in her knickers has snapped and they hang limp around her ankle. She slips them off and wipes herself, marvelling at the unlikeliness of what has just happened, and how different the world seems to how it was when she dressed herself this morning.

Stefan buttons himself as he follows her into the sunlit salon and picks up a chair from the floor. He sits down, breathing hard and looks around the wrecked room. For a moment he meets Ewa's gaze and they stare, each trying to comprehend the change in the other. Stefan is first to look away.

'Who lives here?'

The sound of his Polish makes her wince and she answers in German. 'No one, for now. The expulsion was this morning.' She goes to the window and tucks up the torn net curtain. 'But it won't be long until the new people come.'

'It's a pigsty.'

He has switched to German as if he hardly notices the difference.

'You think this is bad?' She collects the tipped basket and brings it to the table. 'We don't have long, Stefan.' Her eyes stay on him as she unpacks flowers, cleaning cloths and potatoes. 'I have to clean the whole apartment, spruce it up, make a meal for the settlers. They probably won't arrive till late this afternoon but it may be earlier and you must be long gone by then.'

His smile widens. 'Your German is good these days. Perfect, almost.'

'Why you cheeky...' Ewa picks up an onion as if to throw it at him.

He grins and puts up both hands with fingers crossed in surrender. He is right, though. When he knew her before, she spoke German in short impolite sentences like a child. The language comes out naturally now. She even dreams in it.

He reaches out a hand. 'Ewa... Ewa.'

Ewa entwines her fingers in his and he pulls her towards him. She sinks on to his lap and wraps her arms around his neck. His face is so close that she cannot see it clearly. She runs a finger down his profile – the tip of his nose, his lips, his chin.

'You've changed, Stefan.'

He sighs. 'Yes.'

'Have I?'

He turns to look at her but says nothing.

'Well, have I?'

'No. Maybe. I don't know.'

'Don't you?'

He sighs again and shakes his head.

'Why not? What are you thinking?'

'I'm trying to remember your face the last time I saw you.'

'From the train?'

'Yes. I was waving, desperately, from the window, but you didn't wave back.'

'I couldn't. I was shaking so hard I couldn't move.'

She shivers at the memory and he strokes the back of his fingers over her cheek. 'Hey, don't cry. I'm back now.'

'But for how long?'

'Let's just think about now, Ewa. This hour we have now, in this room.'

Ewa sniffs and lifts herself away from him. She goes to the basket and takes out an apron, looping it over her head. 'An hour at the most. And I will have to get on with the cleaning. But you can talk to me as I do it and tell me everything, and I mean absolutely everything, that has happened to you in the last four years.'

'Three and a half.'

'More than four since I last saw you.' Ewa pulls a scrubbing brush and a cardboard tube of scouring powder out of the basket and goes into the kitchenette. 'Where have you been all that time?'

'Well, first Russia, but you know about that.'

'Why did your letters stop?'

He rubs his chin and smiles. 'It's not very easy to send a letter here from England.'

'England? How in hell did you get to England from Moscow?'

'I was never in Moscow.'

He comes and stands in the doorway, leaning against the frame.

Ewa squeezes a puff of scouring powder into the deep sink then attacks it with a stiff brush. 'But that was the address, the *Gorki Rest Home, Moscow.* I sent letter after letter there for months after you stopped replying.'

'They made us put that address on our letters for some reason. But it wasn't real.'

'Oh.' Ewa feels oddly crestfallen that there had never really been any masseurs in white coats. 'So where were you?'

'Kozielsk. A long way from Moscow. I told you, didn't I? It was an old monastery they made into a prison camp. And thank you for the goose fat and sausage by the way. They saved my life that winter.'

Cold water gushes into the grimy sink, mushrooming the scouring powder into bubbles. Perhaps the porridge never stayed as hot as he said it did either. How stupid she had been to take everything in his letters at face value.

'And was that place near Katyn?'

His voice drops. 'Where?'

'The place where the ground was full of bodies. All the Polish prisoners of war, they say.'

He goes up to her and takes hold of both her forearms. His face is very close.

'What do you know about this?'

'It's hardly a secret. I saw it on a newsreel. In the spring.' Her voice trembles. 'I thought I saw your ink pen...'

'Did you tell anyone about me?'

'No.'

'Even when the police were asking for information to help identify the bodies?'

'You know about that?'

'There are still posters...'

'No. I said nothing.'

He tries to raise his mouth into a teasing smile but it does not quite come off; the effect is a little disturbing. 'Did you not want to find me?'

'I couldn't risk our lodgers knowing too much about me.'

As she whispers the words, Ewa feels a stab of guilt about Beck, and then irritation that Stefan has made her feel this way.

She pushes Stefan back and shakes a soft cloth from her apron pocket. 'So, come on then. How did you get to England?'

She cannot imagine him amongst the English with their cosy parlours and cold manners.

'Long story.'

'Tell me.'

'When we have more time.'

'No, now. What did you do in England?'

He raises one shoulder. 'I spent most of the time chain-smoking in a bollock-freezing hut on the side of a field.'

Ewa considers what he is saying as she wipes at the sink. Ceramic whiteness begins to gleam through the grime.

'You mean you've been a pilot in their Air Force?'

'Clever girl.'

He smiles again and reaches out for her but she bends to the floor where a broken bottle is lying on its side in a white puddle. Her cloth soaks through the milk then Ewa goes to the sink to rinse it. Perhaps he has been in England for years. Her stomach

131

lurches at the thought of all of the things he must have done there that she will never know anything about.

'Sometimes I used to wonder if you had stopped writing to me because you were in love with that lady pilot.'

His face darkens. 'What lady pilot?'

'The one in your letters, from the Aero Club.'

Stefan turns his back to her and goes to the table, pulling a cigarette and a lighter from his pocket.

Ewa's stomach lurches as she wonders if she has gone too far. She picks up the milk bottle from the floor. A rinse under the tap shows that only the neck is broken and she carries it, half-filled with water, to the table. As she starts to strip slimy leaves from the dahlia stems, she throws an uncertain glance at Stefan who is sitting on the dining chair with his legs stretched out.

'It might not be long until they arrive, you know.'

'Is anyone official coming?'

'With the settlers? I don't know. Someone from the SS probably, to make sure there are no problems.'

'Who will it be?'

'Does it matter?'

She squashes red and yellow blooms into the milk bottle. As she pulls the foliage down, Ewa feels the jagged edge of glass and looks at her finger. It hurts but does not quite bleed. She thinks then of all the pointless anguish, when she mourned Stefan as dead even though he was, the whole time, as healthy and handsome as he is now. She does not know whether she would rather weep or scream.

To hide the look on her face she turns to the wall and lifts an enamel plaque off its hook. The black-faced Madonna with an unfeasibly small Christ perched on her arm is crusted with grime. Ewa blows on to the surface and rubs a sticky corner until a flash of gold shines through. She puts the plaque into her basket and pulls out the framed colour photograph to go in its place. The Führer stares at her blankly, one hand on the waist of his brown shirt, as she fixes the frame to the hook and straightens it.

'There.'

She turns. Stefan's pale eyes are latched on to her.

'What?'

'I like your hair that colour.'

She pulls a sceptical face but then softens. God, he looks so good sitting there with his ankles crossed and his cigarette-hand hovering.

He rakes a hand through his hair. 'The braids look good too. And I'm glad you are still wearing my ring.'

She purses her lips. 'You might need to get another one for me soon, seeing as you didn't use any precautions just now.'

'No problem. Just say the word and I will book a priest.'

Her head shakes but her heart is galloping.

Stefan's face breaks into a smile, that broad teasing smile that lets her know he wants her. Whatever fear she used to have about getting pregnant, or the priest finding out, or even about eternal damnation, that smile always made her give in to him. As it does now.

Ewa pulls a half-wilted yellow dahlia from the milk bottle before crushing it in her hand. The arrangement looks better without it. Then she goes towards Stefan, trying to scowl.

'And will I see you again anytime soon? Or do you want to leave it another four years?'

But he has already stood up and is pulling her to him, kissing her like he did in those days before there was any war or any need to pretend to be someone else.

She pulls away from his mouth, breathless. 'All right then, Stefan, precautions or not. We'll have to be quick, but let's do it properly this time.'

Posen, Greater German Reich
Tuesday 5 October

Ewa leans against the stove, sipping barley coffee and telling herself that she is not going mad. Stefan was here. In the city, whole and healthy. Yesterday. She has her ruined under-things and an ache between her legs to prove it. But the reality of him, when he is not actually beside her, is still too far-fetched to believe.

Apart from the purr of Untersturmführer Lange snoring somewhere above, the guest house is quiet. Outside, the half-hour chimes jangle from the old town hall. Four thirty. Ewa tweaks the blind and peers up at a half-moon dazzling the gabled rooftops. If it were not for the curfew she would go now. It is light enough to cycle and every cell of her body is yearning to go. As soon after dawn as you can, Stefan had said. But inviting a sentry check by leaving before five would not, on this particular journey, be very clever.

Timings, preparations, ingredients run through her mind. The cycle to the farm should take no more than forty-five minutes but she must be back in good time to prepare lunch for midday sharp. What a good job she has already prepared split-pea broth and... Ewa freezes. Above, on the stairs, boards are creaking. Is one of them getting up? They rarely stir before six.

The kitchen door opens slowly, and in the double beat of her heart, Ewa cannot quite make sense of who is there. For a terrifying, euphoric second she thinks it is Stefan, and then the figure, in stocking-feet and an unbuttoned shirt, comes into the kitchen.

'Heinrich!'

His look is sheepish as he comes up to her. 'I am sorry, did I startle you?'

'A little. When did you arrive?'

134

'It was almost midnight. Thankfully your father was still up.'

'Oh, I see.'

She cannot believe that she slept through Beck's arrival. She cannot quite believe that she slept at all. Thoughts of Stefan and all that she had done with him yesterday should surely have kept her awake. But once between the cold sheets, she fell instantly into dreamless oblivion.

Beck stands awkwardly in front of her. Perhaps he is wondering whether to take her hand and kiss it. Perhaps a little too deliberately, she folds both hands over her apron.

'Would you like some coffee? I can make you a real one, or I have a pot of barley coffee already on the stove.'

'Thank you. Barley coffee would be most welcome.' He leans against the dresser as she pours milk from a striped jug into a bowl. 'You are up so early.'

'I have a lot to do this week. Are you sure barley is all right?'

'Perfect. I'm hoping to get a little more sleep.'

'You had a long journey yesterday?'

'At the weekend, actually. I have been detained with business at the Castle, and at the university, since then.'

Ewa expects him to say more but he is sipping from the bowl and staring fixedly at nothing.

'Thank you for your letter.'

He nods.

'So, how was it, in the east?'

He shakes his head and blinks heavily as he turns to her. 'Full of things that I wish I had not seen.'

His face is so drawn and empty that she cannot help laying a hand on his forearm and squeezing it. 'Poor you.'

Colour floods back into his face. Does she still find him attractive? He is undeniably good-looking – tall and taut, with close-cropped hair and soft grey eyes. And that haunted look he now has is magnetic. But Ewa no longer has any need to consider this question, because Stefan is back.

'And you, Eva, how have you been?'

'Oh you know, the same. Busy.'

'With the guest house?'

'And Resettlement Office work. I took your advice to volunteer.'

His eyes sparkle. 'I'm glad.'

She feels him begin to lean towards her and so she goes to the sink with her empty bowl. She must not let him get close enough for things to become awkward. Although, of course, they already are.

Ewa smiles. 'I helped with a resettlement yesterday as it happens. It quite wore me out, which is why I'm afraid that I was already asleep when you arrived.'

'Please don't apologise. I don't mind in the least. I just hope that the settlers appreciated your efforts.'

'Not exactly. Their German was quite poor but I think they were complaining that the accommodation wasn't as large as their house in Sarata.'

Beck shakes his head. 'If you could see what it is like in the east, Eva…' He sighs. 'When one thinks of what we have done for them; evacuating them to safety here in the Reich and providing them with excellent accommodation in a modern city, the cheek of these Bessarabians is breathtaking.'

His own German is still accentless, the hard syllables precise yet supple. Ewa wonders if all the Germans in Katowice talk like that.

'Well, I did my best with the apartment even though it was quite a mess when I got there.'

'I'm sure that you made it beautiful.'

She smiles and looks at her hands. He will think that the flush in her cheeks is the result of his compliment rather than the thought of the apartment near Wall Strasse and, in particular, of the worn oriental rug where she and Stefan lay together for a second time.

'And you will be busy this week, I suppose, Heinrich, with your lecture? That sounds exciting.'

He brightens and seems to stand to attention. 'Yes it is. I am hopeful that Reichsführer Himmler himself may even attend.'

'Oh my! What is to be the subject of your talk?'

'Did I not say in my letter? It is a summation of the work done this summer on the excavations.'

'The excavations?'

'At Katyn.'

Ewa feels all the blood in her body sink to her feet. 'Is that where you were?'

'Yes.'

She wonders why the name still chills her even though she now knows that Stefan's is not amongst the corpses in its sandy soil. Perhaps the memory of her embarrassing Polish outburst in the cinema still makes the name, *Katyn*, feel dangerous. Or perhaps it is the coincidence of having heard the name so recently in her own mouth, as if Beck had been eavesdropping yesterday at the apartment.

She tries to appear ever so slightly bored. 'And will you have lots of interesting things to mention in your lecture?'

Beck frowns. 'Yes.'

'Excellent. I wish you luck with it.' She arranges her face into a look of concern. 'I am sorry that your room is so small this time, Heinrich.'

'But it is next to yours.'

Ewa forces herself to smile as heat rises, unstoppably, into her neck. His attentions are embarrassing yet also a little exhilarating. She will have to work out how to keep Beck at arm's length without it seeming like an insult. All she can think to do at this moment is simply to ignore his remark.

'If the reservation from Berlin does not arrive we can move you into the balcony room. That will give you more space for your papers and what have you.'

Five chimes tinkle across the night air and into the kitchen. Curfew is ended.

Ewa rubs her hands on her apron. 'The city will be busy today because of the conference.'

'Indeed. The Gauleiters of every province in the Reich, along with many of their staff and other officials, have come to Posen to hear the speeches. I am honoured to be a part of it.'

Ewa smiles and wonders how to get away from Beck and out of the house without seeming impatient. 'Did you know that we will be entertaining our very own Gauleiter here in the guest house on Saturday night?'

'Gauleiter Greiser? Oh, I am very pleased for you, Eva. He cannot fail to be charmed by your hospitality.'

'You know him, don't you?'

'I have worked with him, when I was last here in Warthegau.'

'Ah, so perhaps you can help me. Do you by any chance know if he likes mushrooms? People can be very particular about them.'

Beck laughs warmly. 'Oh, I have no doubt about that. He is a native of this region and everyone here loves mushrooms!'

'Yes. I suppose that is true. Thank you.' Ewa laughs. 'So perhaps I shall get on my way to collect some this morning.'

'Really? In the city?'

'Not far outside it. There is a wood I have visited since my mother took me there as a child. The crop is always large and varied at this time of year.'

He looks at his wristwatch. 'If you wish, I can make a telephone call and ask a driver to take you there. It is for the enjoyment of the Gauleiter, after all.'

She forces her smile to widen. 'That is very kind. Could the car come straightaway?'

'Soon, I think.'

She scratches her head. 'Actually, no. Please don't trouble anyone. I'm sure that the drivers are very busy and I can be in the wood within the hour on my bicycle. I find that the flavour of mushrooms picked at dawn is so superior. Besides, I enjoy cycling and I don't do it often enough.'

Her heartbeat is echoing against her ribcage, but he nods. 'That sounds so pleasant.'

'It's a shame you cannot join me, Heinrich, on my father's bicycle.'

He looks at her steadily without blinking then licks a fleck of milky froth from his lips. Has she been too reckless in her attempt to seem convincing? Is he, sweet Jesus, going to say that on the contrary, he will come with her?

But he sighs. 'It sounds so tempting. But I must be at the Castle in a few hours and a short sleep is essential.' He steps towards her and takes her hand before she can move away. 'If you would allow me to accompany you on another excursion before the end of the mushroom season, the joy of such a prospect will help get me through anything.'

'Of course, Heinrich.'

Without her quite realising what he is doing, Beck has bent his head to kiss her hand. The hair on the top of his head seems to have thinned since she last saw him and his eyes as he straightens are melancholy. He seems to have changed more in six months than Stefan has in four years.

Gently, Ewa pulls her hand away from his and points up to the top of the dresser.

'The baskets. Would you mind?'

He reaches up. He is taller than Stefan as well as better looking, perhaps. He bows his head to present the baskets' wicker handles.

Ewa gives a wry smile. 'A million thanks, Obersturmführer.'

'My pleasure, dear Fräulein Hartman.'

Ewa watches him pad up the stairs as she puts on her coat and cannot help feeling a little sorry for him. How desolate he would be if he knew her real destination this morning. He would be angry too. She shivers and hurries out into the yard.

Baskets creak and slide on the handlebars as the bike bumps over the cobbles. The air is crisp and the narrow streets are spectral with early light. Once out of the old town and on to the tarred surface by the brewery, Ewa presses hard on the pedals to pick up speed. Dull lights glow in the Gestapo headquarters. She glances at the block's regimented rows of windows but most of the panes are greyed out with cement. She will not let herself think about what goes on behind the lifeless glass.

Soon, she is over the tram intersection and on to the straight streets that lead towards the airfield. Even this back road has been improved by the occupiers and once away from the houses, smooth concrete kilometres slip by.

Near the aircraft factory, Ewa watches an aeroplane descending between puffs of clouds. A lattice of rods, like something you could hang washing on, covers the aircraft's nose, and Ewa wonders what it might be. She cannot even name the aeroplane. Before the war, she could identify every plane in the sky, but there are so many new ones now that she has lost track. And plane-spotting is no longer a vaguely glamorous hobby helpful for getting acquainted with the opposite sex. She cannot imagine that the sky will ever seem innocent again.

Turning off the new road, Ewa passes a cart pulled by a mule. Startled by the bicycle, the beast stumbles and the old man holding the reins shakes his fist. But then his hand drops. Ewa must look like what she is – one of them. She scowls and imagines the shock there would be on his stupid face if he knew the real purpose of her dawn cycle ride. She stands up on the pedals to overtake the mule driver and does not look back.

Early sunlight flickers through young poplar trees that line the track between flat, empty fields. At the turn to the farm, Ewa takes a gulp of manure-laced air. She was not surprised when Stefan told her to meet him at Haller's farmhouse. As soon as Stefan said *England*, in fact, she had realised that the AK must be involved in his return to the city. Although quite why it is suddenly all right for her to visit the komendant in person at his home, Stefan did not say.

She has been here only once before, last year, when there was a scare about one of the liaison girls and Ewa was told to deliver her typing direct to the farm. She had been stiff with fear on the journey and her teeth had chattered as she held out the package to Haller. But he had laughed and put a cup of steaming coffee into her hands. Today, for no good reason, she is not nervous at all. Desire to see Stefan again has cancelled out every other sensation.

As the village rises into view, the track turns to mud. To save her skirt, Ewa gets off the bike and pushes it around a wide oozing puddle. Haller's pink-washed single-storey farmhouse is the only building, apart from the church, with a proper tiled roof. Other buildings are topped with corrugated iron or thatched with grass. Rough plank fences line the village street. No one is around.

Ewa picks a path through a churn of cart-ruts and hoof-prints. A twist of smoke rises from the farmhouse chimney. Yellow light illuminates a net curtain. She pushes the bike into the sloping yard and pulls the baskets from the handlebars. If anyone except Haller answers the door she will simply ask permission to gather wild mushrooms from the wood beside the lake. But before she can even knock, the door swings open.

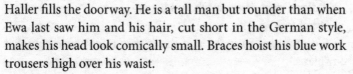

Lüssow, Greater German Reich
Tuesday 5 October

Haller fills the doorway. He is a tall man but rounder than when Ewa last saw him and his hair, cut short in the German style, makes his head look comically small. Braces hoist his blue work trousers high over his waist.

He beckons Ewa in and stands aside. '*Prosze.*'

She blinks, never quite sure which language it will be.

Warmth draws her into a kitchen that smells of wood-smoke and day-old soup. Her eyes dart around the room to the figure leaning against an in-built stove in the corner. Stefan stares back at her unblinking and not quite smiling. He looks lithe and stylish beside the bulky komendant and another younger man in working clothes who sits at the wide table.

Haller pulls out a chair. 'Coffee?'

He opens a glass door in the dresser and takes out a cup, filling it with milk and coffee, and putting it on the tablecloth. Ewa sits down. As she takes a sip over the rim, she glances at Stefan. His face is still unreadable. The young man at the table, with reddish hair and an uneven smile, is staring at her too.

'So.' Haller's chair scrapes on the polished tiles. 'We have a job for you, Ewa.' Haller nods at Stefan. 'Tell her.'

Stefan's arms are folded across his white shirt and a dark tie. Ewa is not interested in the job, only in him. She cannot let her eyes leave him for a second.

Stefan raises one shoulder. 'It's not really a job. Just do as you are going to do anyway and wait table for the Gauleiter and his pals on Saturday night.'

Unease slides through her. She looks from Stefan back to Haller. 'You know about the dinner?'

Haller smiles. 'Of course. One of our people suggested to the Gauleiter's office that the Guest House Hartman would be a perfect place for Greiser to celebrate the end of his triumphant week hosting the conferences.'

'Oh.' So the whole dinner is some sort of AK ruse. A wave of dread ripples through her. 'And what am I to do there?'

Haller shrugs. 'Just watch and listen.'

'What for?'

'For anything to make you think they might have rumbled our plans.'

'Which plans?'

'A special job. Operation Eagle.'

'Another warehouse fire?'

Destroying the warehouse full of Wehrmacht winter supplies destined for the Eastern Front has been the local AK's biggest success to date.

'No, no.' Stefan waves his hand dismissively. 'A new type of operation. A transport from Britain.'

'We've had those before, for what they're worth.'

The Allies' air-drops of weapons, transmitters and cash usually land in the wrong place and end up in exactly the wrong hands.

But Stefan's eyes gleam. 'Not a parachute drop. A Dakota.'

'What's that?'

'A twin-engine heavy transport plane. American.'

Ewa frowns. 'But not with parachutes?'

Smiling, Stefan runs a hand through his hair. 'No. The aeroplane will land. Here.'

The man at the table looks from Stefan to Haller. 'An aeroplane landing? How the hell…?'

Stefan seems not to have heard him. 'Next Saturday, whilst the Gauleiter is enjoying his Schnitzel at Guest House Hartman, a C47 Douglas Dakota will take off in England and land here in the komendant's clover field.'

The red-haired man pushes back on his chair and laughs. 'You're serious, aren't you?'

Irritation flashes across Stefan's face. 'It has been done before.'

'Where?'

'I can't tell you.'

'Not round here, though.'

'No. But it went without a hitch, I can assure you.'

Ewa picks up the coffee cup with a pattern of angular pink tulips circling the rim, and brings it to her lips. She wonders if Haller has a wife, and if he does, what she thinks about the AK meeting in her kitchen.

The red-haired man shifts on his seat. He clearly does not like Stefan. 'You really think no one is going to notice a massive American bomber coming down to land just a few kilometres from the city?'

Stefan seems unperturbed. 'It's not a massive bomber, it is a Dakota. Only two engines. That is the beauty of it. We are close to the airfield so the observers will think it is just a Junckers or a Heinkel coming in to land. And the plane will be on the ground for no more than eight minutes before turning around and taking off again.'

Haller leans forward and puts his elbows on the table. 'We are confident that this will be the first of many landings in this region, the start, we hope, of a powerful "air bridge" from and to England.' He looks at the red-haired man. 'The Allies can send us the usual supplies that come by air drops but in much greater quantities and with fewer losses. We might get heavy artillery, perhaps even vehicles. And maybe more importantly, we can send things back to England; intelligence information to the Polish government in London, samples of German weapons and equipment to the British.'

Stefan keeps his eyes on Ewa. 'And we can send people.'

Ewa shrugs and turns to Haller. 'I'm not sure I'll be much help. The officers never give anything away whilst I am around. You know that I've heard almost nothing in the guest house that has ever helped us.'

Haller leans forward. 'This will be different, we think. Gauleiter Greiser and his staff are hosting a get-together for the highest leaders of the Reich. So, once it is over, he will be inclined to relax and celebrate. And if, that night, the Gauleiter has already received intelligence that will allow his forces to intercept the AK's biggest operation in his province, he will not be able to resist giving away something about it.'

Ewa stiffens. 'And what should I do if he does?'

'We will give you a runner for the evening who will report

instantly to our comrade, Robak,' Haller nods at the red-haired man, 'who always drives to the station with milk churns for the midnight train to Berlin. A warning from your runner to him will allow our people waiting by the landing ground to dissolve into the dark and the Dakota will not come near. You will keep us safe.'

'Who is the runner?'

'A girl. To help you with the Gauleiter's feast.'

Fear spikes into Ewa's gut and she tightens her grip on the coffee cup. 'I can't risk having a runner in the guest house. It would implicate my father too closely.'

Haller's fingers drum on the table. 'But you already keep a silent typewriter there, and store documents.'

'That's different. My activities are entirely separate from the work of the guest house.'

Stefan stands upright. 'Believe me, your role in this is vital.'

She glances up at him. 'Vital or fatal?'

He takes a step forward. 'And the cargo we will send to London could completely change the course of the war.'

She senses that he wants to reach out and touch her but his hands stay in his pockets.

'And what is that cargo?'

Haller's drumming fingers become louder. 'Do you agree to your assignment?'

Ewa sighs. A row of dancing pink tulips, exactly like those on the cup, is stencilled in a precise line around the top of the kitchen walls. Haller is risking everything, as they all are, if the landing goes ahead. But how can she refuse the mission when her role is to help keep Stefan safe?

'All right.'

'Good. Then we are all on board.' Haller inclines his head towards the red-headed man. 'Robak here is our contact at the Focke-Wulf factory. He has already arranged to provide us with a complete Neptun airborne intercept system, which is built here at the factory. This is a large piece of equipment which, instead of being dismantled and sent slowly by many couriers to England, can now be loaded in one piece on to the aircraft and delivered to British scientists the following morning.'

Robak raises his eyebrows and whistles.

Haller puts up a hand. 'The Neptun will be collected by you from the factory on Saturday night on your return from the milk-churn run. The device will then be brought to the field to await the Dakota.' Haller folds his arms and nods at Ewa. 'So, you see, *Dakota* and *Neptun* are words that you should be listening out for during the Gauleiter's dinner.'

'And others?'

'I will be in contact. All you need for now are the code names. I will be Jan. You now know Robak, and the mission will be co-ordinated by Anatol over there.' Stefan puts his head to one side and smiles. 'And you, young lady, will be Julia.' Haller stands up. 'Good. Now we are all acquainted and the mission agreed.' He nods at Ewa's collecting baskets. 'And if you are to get the day's best mushrooms, you had better be on your way.'

Stefan reaches for his jacket. 'I will show her where they are.'

Haller nods and moves out of his way. If he winks, Ewa does not see.

She follows Stefan into the farmyard and towards a beech copse. Ewa stays a pace or two behind him, mesmerised by the tilt of his shoulders despite the needle of doubt inside her. How much does he really care for her? If it is as much as she feels for him, he would surely have shown more caution about the placing of an AK action right inside her home. And he could certainly have stuck up for her a bit more. As it is, she feels bullied. The komendant assumed that the 'young lady' would do whatever was asked of her and Stefan merely egged him on. Ewa wants to feel the same surge of yearning for Stefan that she did yesterday, but now anxiety and indeed irritation have got in the way.

Once in the trees, Ewa falls back and starts kicking at the papery leaves on the ground. Stefan turns to her and reaches out a hand but she does not take it.

'I don't have much time. I must collect some mushrooms to take back or it will look suspicious.'

He nods. 'I will help.'

He begins moving the desiccated leaf litter aside with his foot. When his shoe touches against hers, Ewa feels not desire but a sudden wave of vexation. She strides off towards a nearby oak tree and kneels down by the spongy yellow growth at its base, tearing off the feathery stalks of fungus and laying them in a basket.

Stefan follows her and leans his shoulder against the gnarled trunk. 'Those chicken mushrooms are no good for soup.'

She looks up. 'How do you know I'm making soup?'

He shrugs. 'Well you are, aren't you?'

'And the Schnitzel. How did you know about that?'

He taps the corner of the other basket against the tree. 'A good guess.'

Ewa's eyes narrow as she stands up. 'How long have you been here, Stefan?'

'At Haller's?'

'Yes.'

'Three weeks.'

'Please tell me you're joking.'

'Ewa... I wanted to contact you sooner but it was safer for you if I didn't.'

'Thank you for your concern.'

'Come on, Ewa. My cover story is tied up with the farm here. I can't go into town too often.'

'So yesterday was the first time?'

'Not exactly.'

She closes her eyes.

'Ewa...'

Pulling her arm away from his hand, Ewa flicks at a crumble of leaf litter on her coat sleeve. 'We have you to thank, do we, for this new action, the "air bridge"?'

'Not just me.'

'Well, clearly not that Robak guy, he seemed as sceptical as I am.'

'Don't take any notice. He works at the Focke-Wulf factory but lives here on the farm and will do whatever Haller tells him. He can be trusted one hundred per cent.'

'No one can be trusted one hundred per cent. I can't trust myself that far.' Ewa shakes her head. 'This Operation Eagle is madness.'

'It has been done before, safely, near Lublin...'

Ewa kicks again at the leaf litter where the sunlight falls across it. Then she crouches down. 'Bringing a runner into the guest house could destroy my cover.' Her fingernails push into the crumbling earth. 'It could destroy everything.'

'But it will be worth the risk, believe me.'

'That's easy for you to say. You are only risking your own life.'

'I will keep you safe, Ewa.'

'And my father?'

Stefan's face does not change.

A cluster of brown bumps pushes from the spot that Ewa has cleared of leaf litter. She takes her penknife from her basket and opens the blade. But before pushing it into the soil, she points it at Stefan.

'I didn't feel very safe yesterday when you accosted me in public.'

'I knew it would be my best chance to catch you.'

Ewa does not reply but bends to lift the mushroom caps and check the colour of the gills, then she digs the blade into the earth.

Stefan squats down and puts his head beside hers. 'You must get rid of that noiseless typewriter, you know. Before Saturday.

As soon as you can really. And also anything you have that might link you to me.'

She levers out the mushroom's bulbous root and tries to imagine orange flames turning Stefan's prison letters to ash. But she knows that she will not burn them. Not even for him.

'I'll do what I think best. You don't have to tell me, Stefan. I have been doing what I think best for the past four years.'

'Where will you hide the typewriter?'

'I'll find somewhere.'

'In the old town?'

'Why are you so interested?'

He puts a hand in his trouser pocket. 'I might need a hiding place for something else. Just until Saturday. But it could be something quite large.'

'There are plenty of hiding places out here on the farm.'

'No. It needs to be in the city.'

'Why? What is it?'

'Something I'm going to pick up in town. I'll tell you more when I know for sure.'

'Thanks.'

'I'm sorry, it's just that nothing is certain yet.'

'Perhaps I should report you to the komendant. How do I know that this isn't part of some secret instructions you have from the English which will betray the AK? Or that you weren't joking yesterday about being from the Gestapo?'

'Be kind to me, Ewa. We don't have much time together.'

She stands up and looks down at his face. It is still so hard to remember that he is really here, that it is less than a day since everything she could foresee in her life was reshaped like the twist of a kaleidoscope.

He must be right that whatever happens, they will not have long together. And when he is gone, her life will go back to what it was before; so empty and numb that only the terror and exhilaration of insurgency will make her feel alive.

She puts a hand to his cheek. 'When will I see you next, Stefan?'

He does not answer but pulls her to him, kissing her neck, her face, her hair. They fall together. Baskets drop into the brown blanket of crumbled leaves and Ewa is lost in the feel and smell and heat of him. But when she senses that he is trying to go further with her right there in the open, the needle of irritation returns.

'No, Stefan. Not here.'

He scans the sparse woodland of grey trunks and fallen leaves, his arms still cradling her. 'There's a grove of holly bushes over there...'

'No!' Ewa wriggles away. 'We can't keep doing it anyway, Stefan. What if I am already pregnant?'

'We'll get married.'

'Don't joke.'

'I'm not. Look...'

He fumbles inside his jacket pocket, pulling out a tightly folded slip of paper then opening it between his hands. A crowned eagle unfurls above serial numbers stamped in ink. The words are in Polish and in French: *Rzeczpospolita Polska, Certificat de Mariage*.

Ewa's hand goes to her mouth. It is not a joke. Everything inside her, apart from the firm knock of her heart, seems to freeze.

But Stefan is covering her face with light frantic kisses. 'Darling, darling Ewa, marry me.'

'How can I?'

He doesn't seem to hear. 'We just need a priest and a few signatures; the komendant and Robak will do.'

'Stefan, Stefan...' Tears well up and she tries to cover them with a frown. 'What sort of husband can I expect? One who goes to work in the morning and doesn't come back for four years?'

'No, no, it won't be that long this time.'

'What do you mean, *this time*?'

But as she says the words, instantly she knows. As Stefan himself said, the transport plane can ferry not just documents and equipment, but also people. A pang of grief waves through her. What an idiot she is not to have realised sooner.

'You're going back to England, aren't you? On the Dakota?'

He looks at her but says nothing.

Ewa shakes her head and takes a gulp of air. 'But we can have a nice little wedding party before your flight. And then you can leave me more desolate than I was before you came.'

'Just marry me, Ewa.' He pulls her tighter. 'The certificate will be lodged with the Polish government in London. Records will be changed. You will be my wife, forever, no matter what happens. I want you to be mine, Ewa. And I want you, and everyone else, to have no doubt about that.'

Her eyes search his. The pupils have shrunk to black dots on blue ice.

'And then everything in my life would be even more complicated than it is now.'

She pushes him away and picks up the larger wicker basket. There are hardly any mushrooms inside it. Stefan is chewing his bottom lip and staring at the ground as he folds the marriage certificate into a tiny rectangle.

'Is there something else in the way of us marrying, Ewa? Someone...?'

'No.'

'You are sure?'

'There is no one.' She studies his face. 'And you, Stefan? In England...'

'No.'

He pushes the folded certificate into his inside pocket and steps up to her, taking her face in his hands. 'Once we are married we can forget that the last four years ever happened.'

A pair of wood pigeons thrash up from a treetop, wings flapping like a round of applause. Ewa remembers suddenly how the world used to feel before Stefan had grasped her elbow by the flower market, and how close she had been to taking up again with Beck. It is not fair for Stefan to ask so much of her. He has not even tried to understand what she has been through.

'So, once you're sipping your English tea again, that piece of paper is supposed to keep me faithful, is it? Even if I've no idea, as I hadn't until yesterday, whether you are alive or dead?' Stefan says nothing and Ewa shakes her head. 'Well, if that's what you think, think again. Because when you've gone and I need to cheer myself up by fucking a good-looking officer in a black uniform that is exactly what I will do.'

Stefan looks down into the smaller basket, shaking white and brown mushrooms across the base. Shafts of sunlight pierce the woodland canopy as he turns away and begins walking back towards the farm.

Ewa immediately regrets what she has said. There are only three more days before Saturday and then he will be gone. Without warning, a hot sob rises in her throat.

'Stefan. Wait. Wait.'

He turns. His face is blank.

'Stefan, I'm sorry.' Her voice cracks. 'Can I see you tomorrow?'

'Not tomorrow.'

'When, then?'

'Thursday. That's when I might need the hiding place.'

She wipes her wet cheek. 'This thing you want to hide, how big is it?'

He frowns. 'A suitcase, perhaps...'

She comes alongside him and takes his hand, folding it between hers. 'How big is the suitcase?'

'Not over-large but quite heavy.' His voice is flat. 'And it may have a very strong smell.'

Posen, Greater German Reich
Wednesday 6 October

'Did I tell you, Eva? Eight more for dinner on Saturday.'

Her father kneels on newspaper as he uses a wire brush to knock soot from the stove's baffle plate.

Ewa winces. She is trying not to think about Saturday. 'How are we supposed to find extra veal for that many?'

'We'll just have to beat the Schnitzels a bit harder.'

She clatters breakfast plates into the sink. 'And why are they having their celebration here anyway? We haven't got the space.'

'Just be glad of the business. Have you seen the dining room bookings for next month?'

'No.'

'There aren't any.'

Ewa turns the tap on hard. 'What else can we expect when most of the population aren't allowed to eat here?'

'Keep your voice down, Maus.'

'It is down.'

'Maus…'

His voice has a careworn edge. Instantly, Ewa wants to say sorry, and that it is only the stress of planning for the Gauleiter's dinner that is making her bad-tempered. But she knows that if she starts to apologise, her voice will crumble into tears and it will be hard for her not to tell him what is really tying her heart in knots.

Because she won't see Stefan today. And that means one whole day of the four they have left will be wasted. Ewa will be scrubbing crockery and peeling carrots when he is less than an hour's bicycle ride away. This thought, if she lets it, is enough to make her punch the wall.

But she must keep herself calm in order to dispose safely of the noiseless typewriter; a task which is now a welcome distraction. They have told her the address and the timings so she just needs to package the machine discreetly and get it there. Already, Ewa is thinking of the route. The direct tram will take her straight past the Castle so she will need to hold her nerve, but she knows that plain sight is always safest. AK work is still the best way to push Stefan out of her mind.

Ewa glances at her father. 'All right. I'll make the food already ordered go further by doing two types of potatoes. Roasted as well as mashed.'

He smiles from under his eyebrows. 'Good, Maus. I'll go to the wholesaler later. He owes me a favour.'

'Can you get some cream too? And cottage cheese?'

'I'll try.'

She rolls her shoulders as she wipes a greasy plate. 'What time will you go?'

Her father glances at the clock on the dresser. 'As soon as I've done this.'

She nods. The officers will be gone soon too. She heard Beck get up and leave the house before she was dressed. She has hardly spoken to him since he got back. He ate at the Castle last night and was clearly too busy today for breakfast. Within the hour, the guest house will be empty and that will be her chance to pack the typewriter.

Oskar Hartman's army knapsack has faded from khaki to beige on the top of his wardrobe. Once the guest house is quiet, Ewa stands on a chair to lift it down. The old knapsack is rather stained on one side, but all of the buckles are intact and the straps are still so supple that she wonders whether her father has been greasing the leather. She wonders why he does not use the bag any more. Perhaps, when it comes to anything to do with the World War, he is proud of his service but does not want to be reminded of it too often.

Ewa takes the knapsack to her room and packs it methodically.

There is just enough space to bury the noiseless typewriter within a thick wrapping of threadbare summer frocks and grey underwear. She carries it downstairs to the dining room on her shoulder. The knapsack is heavy but she concentrates on holding it in a way that will make it appear light.

Leaving the bag by the sideboard, she goes to the window and stands on her toes to peer over the half-nets. Across the square, a few men in suits loiter under the turrets and arches of the new town hall. One of the men, in houndstooth check, catches her eye and raises his hat. Ewa makes herself smile back at him.

Then the back door bangs and her heart drops. For a nasty second she imagines the men in suits filing through the passageway and making straight for the typewriter. But that is plain silliness. She has only just packed it up and has told no one of her plan to transport it.

Ewa holds her breath and listens. Is it her father? Surely not yet. And none of the officers are likely to come back so soon. She must not worry. Her cover story is good and unless someone actually unpacks the knapsack, she has nothing to fear. It will not do to let herself be so nervy. On Saturday she must keep her hands steady enough to serve Gauleiter Greiser's Schnitzel without spilling gravy on his brown uniform.

Footsteps pad from the passageway on to the stairs and Ewa waits for a bedroom door to click before she leaves the dining room. Looking into the hatstand mirror, dark roots show through her blonde hair like a crack in her skull. She pulls the hat with blackcock feathers over the dark growth and tilts it to one side. The weather is still fine enough for her double-breasted jacket too. Upstairs, something heavy like a man's shoe drops on to the floor. But she cannot let a lodger delay her. It is gone ten and she must be at the safe house by eleven or nobody will be there. The over-bright lipstick smears but that will have to do. She looks German at least.

Ewa goes back to the dining room and grabs the knapsack,

but feet are cantering down the stairs. And before she has a chance to slide the bag behind the sideboard, a man in a black uniform comes into the room.

'Do excuse me. Did I startle you?'

It is Beck. Ewa gasps, not so much in alarm, as at the magnificence of his appearance.

'No, not at all. It's just… I haven't seen you in that uniform before.'

Beck frowns. His hair is slicked back and there is a whiff of chlorine as he looks down at himself.

'Is it all right?'

'Oh yes, marvellous. You look extremely smart.'

The jacket has a close, elegant cut that accentuates Beck's broad shoulders and the fabric is raven black. The stiff peaked cap, with silver rope-braids and a grinning silver skull, is clutched under his arm.

'Good. Thank you, Eva. It's a big day for me, you see. My lecture…'

'I know. I thought you had left for the Castle before breakfast.'

'Forgive me.'

The look he gives her is long and unblinking. It makes her uneasy.

'Have you eaten?'

He shakes his head. 'I went for a swim. It usually helps to get my thoughts straight.'

'And did it today?'

'Not as I would have liked.'

Ewa almost asks why, but realises that she would rather not know.

'I am happy to give you something to eat now, Heinrich, although breakfast is finished. Would you like bread and ham?'

'No, please, Eva, don't put yourself to any trouble, I can see that you are about to go out.' His eyes drop pointedly to the knapsack. 'An old army pack?'

'My father's.'

'He fought for the Kaiser?'

'Of course.'

'I didn't know. Was he in France?'

'I think so, yes. Although he rarely talks about it.'

'My father too.' Beck smiles. 'It is good to see that you are still using it.'

Ewa finds with a jolt that she has for a moment entirely forgotten about what is inside the knapsack.

'I just use it for my work with the settlers.' She laughs, perhaps too brightly and drops to her knees unbuckling the flap and the other straps beneath. 'See how useful and roomy it is!' She peels a corner of the top layer to show a printed skirt and a cotton slip. Only an edge of the towel, which is wrapped around the noiseless typewriter, pokes out of the clothes.

'They were my mother's things. But I have no use for them. It's too selfish to keep them when there are so many citizens in need. So I am taking them to a family of settlers from Volhynia. They are country people and the woman does not go out because she is ashamed of her peasant clothes.'

Beck's eyes shine. 'You are very thoughtful.'

'I should have done it before now.'

He sighs. 'Too many farmers have ended up in the city.'

As Ewa re-buckles the inner flaps, something shiny catches her eye; a small silver knob, one of the screws that holds the typewriter ribbon in place, is protruding out. Mother of God. Has Beck seen it? She pulls over the outer flap and fastens the buckles.

'Please,' Beck steps towards her and bends to pick the knapsack up. 'Let me help you.'

'No, no.'

Her hand gets there first and she puts all of her strength into making the pack seem lighter than it is.

'Are you sure I cannot get you some breakfast?'

157

'I will eat something at the Castle. I must not detain you. Which way are you going?'

'Near the zoo.'

'By tram, up St Martin Strasse?'

She can think of no way out and smiles. 'Yes.'

'Let me walk you to the tram stop.'

'That would be lovely, Heinrich.'

'And please, Eva, allow me to carry the knapsack.'

Shit, shit, shit.

'Thank you, Heinrich. You are so kind.'

But if Beck thinks that the knapsack is absurdly heavy for its cargo of ladies' lingerie, he does not say. In fact, he says nothing. In the street outside, only the marching of his top-boots echoes off the painted house-fronts. Perhaps he is nervous about his lecture, or perhaps the memory of their last walk this way, on a mild April evening, is shadowing each step.

Their silence, as well as the grandeur of Beck's black uniform, begins to weigh down on Ewa. She winces up at the blue strip between the overhanging gables looking for something, anything, to say.

'How nice that the conference visitors will see Posen in fine weather.'

'Yes.'

He marches on. Pedestrians ahead of them on the street melt out of their way.

'We had a very pleasant summer here. Was it hot, where you were?'

Beck sniffs. 'Damnably.'

'Oh.'

His pace slows. 'I'm sorry, Eva. Please excuse my grumpiness this morning.'

With one finger, Ewa touches his black sleeve. 'Don't apologise. I understand perfectly.'

He frowns but then smiles. 'Perhaps you do.'

As they approach the tram stop, a woman in a tight headscarf flashes Ewa a scowl before darting away. Ewa knows how she must look, in her smart jacket and jaunty hat, beside a man resplendent in SS black. But if that woman could see inside the old army knapsack that the officer is carrying, the sneer would be wiped off her face.

The old street opens out into the Platz where the tram intersection is crowded with people. But they must all be Poles because none of them are actually waiting for a tram.

Beck puts the knapsack on the ground and brushes his black gloves together. Ewa's heart skips. If he is going to say something about the weight of the pack, it will be now.

She gives him the widest smile she can muster. 'Thank you. I hope you find some breakfast before lunchtime.'

'I will survive.'

She smiles on, waiting for him to say goodbye but he does not move.

The muscles in her cheeks twitch. 'Are you… also taking the tram?'

'Yes, why not?'

'It's only one stop to the Castle.'

'But still a little quicker than walking, I think.'

It must be because of the knapsack. He wants to open it on the tram where she cannot run off.

She smiles. 'Excellent, Heinrich. You can keep me company.'

A bell trills as the green and white tram clatters down Hindenburg Strasse and comes to a stop. A mis-spelled *Nur für deutsche Farhrgäste* sign is taped to the glass. Beck motions for Ewa to get on first and picks up the knapsack. Perhaps he will place it on the wooden seat and, right there, unpack the noiseless typewriter from its nest of laddered stockings and creased frocks.

But Beck sits beside Ewa on the tramcar bench and puts the pack in the aisle. The only other passenger, an elderly bearded man carrying a dachshund, does not look their way.

The driver waits. Workers in flat caps stream past but no one else gets on board. Beck crosses his legs and balances the silver and black cap on his knee. Again, he does not seem inclined to talk and Ewa cannot abide the silence.

'So, will you be stationed here in Posen now?'

'For the moment, yes, I am very glad to say.'

'And billeted permanently at our guest house?'

'It is not yet confirmed, but I do hope so yes. As long as you are still happy to have me there, Eva.'

'Of course.'

Ewa feels herself start to flush. Is he going to mention, out loud, their disastrous night out at the Apollo? She is still not quite sure what she could say to excuse her mortifying lapse into Polish. The incident has become all the more humiliating and menacing in her memory since learning that Beck also grew up as a citizen of the Republic of Poland. He is more likely than any of the other occupiers to realise that involuntarily speaking the wrong language could be a symptom of questionable national loyalty.

Ewa brushes her skirt with a gloved hand to steady her nerves. 'Are you going to work again on the re-naming project?'

'No. Not that.'

'So, no longer in the library?'

'No. But nearby. At the university.'

Silence returns. But then the bell rings as the tram rattles off. The man on the opposite bench starts to stroke his quivering dog and Ewa puts her foot against the knapsack to steady it. She sees Beck glance down at it and cannot quite read his face.

Again she tries to fill the silence. 'The knapsack makes it look as if you are about to take a few days leave. Where would you go if you could?'

'If the war were over?'

The skin on Ewa's back prickles but she smiles brightly and nods.

'Home, I suppose.'

She presumes he means Kattowitz but it feels too awkward to say the name aloud.

'Can you not go there now?'

'Returning would be... complicated.' His fingers tap on the brim of his hat. 'But once the war is over, we must hope that life will become more straightforward.'

'Indeed.'

His home town, from what she has heard, is even more riven between people who grew up speaking different languages. Beck must have left there before the war to pursue his studies in Leipzig. Perhaps that way he was able to avoid being called up to fight for Poland.

Rows of architraved windows and stone-fronted office buildings judder by. Ewa tells herself not to look at the knapsack, even though she is itching to pull it closer. She will have to warn Stefan that if he wants her to hide a large, heavy suitcase, it will not be straightforward. Even a modest knapsack that is not at all smelly is far from inconspicuous.

The thought tightens her throat and she coughs, making Beck turn to her with a look of concern. 'Are you all right?'

She struggles to get the cough under control. 'Oh... yes...'

'Are you sure?'

'Certainly.' And then, she has the idea. 'I was just about to say, to ask that is... I am intending to go swimming later.'

Beck beams. 'Do you go often now?'

'No. I must confess that I have not yet used the pool.'

'Well then, you certainly should go today. Perhaps we could go together this afternoon.'

Ewa smiles playfully. 'That would be two swims in one day for you.'

'I would not mind. It is so calming.'

'Unfortunately, I am busy in the kitchen this afternoon. Is the pool open late?'

'Until 8.30pm on Wednesdays but I'm afraid that I will not be finished with my duties until after 9pm today.'

'Oh, that's a shame.'

'Never mind. Go alone tonight and perhaps we will swim together another time. Remember to take your Deutsche Volksliste papers for entry.'

'Thank you, I will.'

Beside the Imperial Castle, the road widens. Red and black banners blaze across the bulky stone arches and pennants droop from the wheel arches of sleek black cars lined up outside. On the Platz, a crowd of elaborate uniforms, black, grey-green, and brown are gathering. Beck scans the throng, eyes oddly wary then glances at his wristwatch. Surely to God, he will get off now.

Ewa's hand goes to the bell-button above the bench. 'Shall I ring for you?'

'What?'

Blood begins to ebb from Ewa's head. Perhaps he is not going to get off. Perhaps instead, he is going to insist on carrying her absurdly heavy knapsack all the way to the apartment of the non-existent Volhynian peasants.

Ewa's hand hovers by the button. 'Shall I…?'

Then Beck smiles. 'Oh, yes. Please.'

The buzzer whines.

'Thank you, Eva.'

Wheels rattle to a halt and Beck stands, pulling the silver-braided peak of his cap low over his eyes.

'I wish I could be of more assistance with your luggage.' He nods at the knapsack. 'It's quite heavy.'

She feels herself flinch. 'Oh, it's no bother at all. I hope that all goes well with your lecture.'

Beck glances outside then half raises his arm as if to give a full *Heil Hitler* but then lets it fall to his side. Instead, he nods, clicking his heels before turning to the exit. He waits behind the other passenger who is lowering his dachshund on to the pavement then marches off into the uniformed crowd.

The tram driver has shut off the engine and taken out a newspaper, spreading it over the control levers. The tram must be early. Or perhaps it isn't worth being on time when you only have one passenger. Ewa leans her face closer to the window to keep her eyes on Beck and make sure that he keeps walking away.

All of the faces beneath the variously decorated hats seem extremely pleased with themselves. Overloud laughter seeps into the tramcar along with an atmosphere of anticipation and smugness, not unlike some society race meeting or opera, except that amongst the hundreds of people milling around the Kaiser's fake Castle, there is not a single woman.

Ewa's gaze drifts around the crowd but she has lost sight of Beck. At the side of the Castle the scaffolding is still up where the builders have not quite managed to finish all of the renovation works. They will be in for it over that.

With a shudder, the tram starts up again and begins to trundle away from the square. The boulevard is at its widest here and there is a clear view of the university's gables and turrets. The tram hiccups as a group of hatless youths in cheap suits and pullovers run in front of it across the tracks in the road. They leap on to the pavement ahead of a man who is also heading for the university – a man in a perfectly black uniform. Ewa shifts in her seat. It looks like Beck from behind, but it is hard to tell, and he should be going to the Castle to deliver his lecture soon, not the university.

The hatless youths crowd around a revolving doorway. The brass plaque beside it says: *Institut für Gerichtsmedizin*. Ewa knows both parts of the long word, of course; *legal* and *medicine*, but she has never seen them put together like that before. Her mind becomes briefly distracted by imagining what exactly is being studied behind the revolving door. At that same moment,

Ewa's eye catches something familiar about a man who is leaning against the wall not far from the plaque. It is the way he is standing; one foot crossed over the other, shoulder buttressing the wall, wide-brimmed hat pulled down.

The tram is almost level with the doorway and with the striking black uniform that has come to a halt behind the students. Ewa twists on the bench, putting her hand between her cheek and the glass. It may not be Beck, of course, but if it is, she would not like him to see her staring. The tram jerks then speeds up as the officer puts out his arm to the revolving door. It is Beck. And at the same moment, the man in the wide-brimmed hat looks up at him and nods. Ewa sees the side of this man's face only for a second, but it makes her heart stop.

Nausea floods through her. She stands up and spins around, grasping at the benches as she clambers to the rear of the tramcar. The knapsack slaps over on to the floor. But Ewa does not take her eyes from the two men beside the revolving door. Her face is pressed up now against the back window, breath blurring the view, her gloved hand flattened against the glass.

The tram lurches as it accelerates, pushing Ewa off balance. But as she sees the revolving door rotate over the back of Stefan's dark suit, she suddenly realises the correct translation for *Institute of Forensic Medicine*.

Posen, Greater German Reich
Wednesday 6 October

From the outside, the swimming pool is smaller than the synagogue used to be but its newly brutal profile seems to occupy more space. Gone are the curving walls and decorated arches; unbending rooflines and rectangular windows now take their place. The building has been stripped of cupolas and pinnacles like a head shaved.

When it was used for worship, Ewa would pass the synagogue on her way to St Adalbert's and take little notice of the place. Only when it was mutilated beyond recognition did Ewa realise that the synagogue had been one of the city's finest landmarks. So now, normally she does her best to avoid the indoor swimming pool and the stomach-flip it gives her to realise what the occupiers have done already to her city, and what else they might be capable of doing. But today she is going for a swim.

The entrance door is heavy and there is no one in the reception area. Ewa parks the string bag with her towel and swimming costume on to the desk and wonders if the pool is really open. Then, in a warm waft of chlorine, a man in a brown coat swings open the door. He hardly looks at her face as he checks her papers and takes her Reichspfennige.

'Ladies' changing is under the spectator gallery, on the left.'

She nods and enters. The warm bleachy smell is pleasant and the pool outlandishly blue. Untroubled by swimmers, a glass-still surface mirrors the roof's soaring arches. Ewa feels a sudden urge to smash the calmness by falling in, jacket, hat and all. She shudders at how easy that would be. And although it is not the reason that she is here, Beck may be right that a swim could be the best remedy for her fizzing nerves.

As she pushes on the door marked *DAMEN,* the squeak from it echoes around the high dome.

'Oh!' Ewa jumps and looks away. There is a woman inside and she is entirely naked. 'I'm sorry. I didn't think anyone…'

'Well, don't worry. I'm delighted to see you here, Eva.'

'Frida! Hello. I'm sorry, I didn't recognise you…'

'In the nude?'

'Well, yes!'

They both laugh and Frida, who is always tidy and businesslike at the Resettlement Office, seems entirely untroubled by her nakedness. She goes to her belongings and fishes out a cigarette packet. Ewa waves a refusal but Frida lights up anyway and goes to sit on the bench, crossing her legs. Ewa struggles to keep her eyes off Frida's pendulous breasts. They seem to hang below her waist and are darkened by unfeasibly large nipples. Frida looks like an entirely different woman with wet hair pasted to her skull and her clothes off.

She leans back as she smokes, allowing Ewa an even better view of the unusual breasts. She must be proud of them.

'So, you are a swimmer too, Eva?'

'No, not really. But I have been so busy this week, I must somehow make myself relax or I will go crazy.'

'I hope it wasn't those Bessarabians who troubled you. You mustn't mind what they say. And we have every right to throw them out on to the street if they cause a nuisance.'

'Oh no, they didn't trouble me. It is the guest house work that is the worry. I have a big party to cater for on Saturday. We don't really have the space…'

'It will be fine, darling. I have seen what you can do with a few onions and a carrot. You are a gastronomic miracle-worker! The Poles could venerate you like one of their ridiculous saints.'

Her laugh is loud and braying. She uncrosses her legs and leans forward, resting an elbow on her knee. Ewa tries not to stare at the black thatch between her legs.

Frida points the smoking cigarette at Ewa. 'They have let you out, have they, even though it's almost dinner time?'

'They are all out tonight, a grand dinner at the Castle, I believe.'

'Ah yes, the conferences. It's all hush-hush what they're talking about up there.' Frida raises her eyebrows and hunches her shoulders as she puts a finger to her lips. The breasts jostle and Ewa averts her eyes.

'Really? One of the officers has told me about his speech.'

'What is that about, then?'

'Those graves they found in Russia, full of Polish officers.'

'Oh, that.'

'You have heard of some other things being discussed?'

'Well, between us, I think that the main point of the whole jamboree is not entirely unconnected with the original filthy usage of this lovely swimming pool.'

Frida giggles and Ewa cannot face hearing more of what she has to say on this subject. But more than anything, she wishes that Frida would muzzle her horrible breasts inside their brassiere.

Ewa turns away to undress but she leaves her skirt on as she removes her underwear. Frida's eyes follow each of her garments as they are removed. Ewa wonders if she hears a tut of disapproval at her prudishness but she is damned if she is going to put her parts on display under Frida's calculating eyes.

'What about you, Frida, do you use the pool very much?'

'Now and then. I like to swim, but prefer to do it with my girlfriends. This pool is so boring. You are the only other lady I have ever seen here. Look at this changing room.' Frida stretches her legs apart as she reaches out to wipe the corner of the bench. She holds up her fingers. 'See the dust? Hardly ever used. I would not be surprised if we are the only ladies who have ever used it.'

'And do you usually come at this time of day?'

'Why, yes. Let's make a habit of it, shall we? I would come every week if I had you to chat to as we swim!'

'Good idea! Once this busy week is out of the way we should make a regular date of it.' Ewa wiggles her woollen swimsuit under the waistband of her skirt and pulls the straps over her arms before removing her brassiere. Frida's greedy eyes follow the escapologist's jig.

Ewa folds her slip on to the neat pile of clothes. 'What about the men? Are there many swimmers?'

'Want a good look, do you?'

Ewa laughs although her hand clenches on her rubber hat. Frida really is asking for a slap.

'There must be some hunky torsos to admire.'

'One or two, maybe. But they hardly ever go up on the diving board where you'd get the best chance of seeing something juicy a bit further down!'

Frida's laugh becomes a snort and Ewa tightens the strap on her swimming hat with a thwack. 'Well. I had better start on my lengths.'

'Yes. Off you go, Eva.'

Ewa feels Frida's eyes on her back as she leaves through the louvered door.

The pool is still empty of swimmers and Ewa lowers herself gingerly into the cool water at the shallow end. She hunches her shoulders, splashing herself and patting wet hands on her arms. But in the end, it is better just to plunge.

Gasping, she tries to find her rhythm. She cannot remember the last time she swam. Not during the war, that is for sure. Maybe not since the summer before it started when she cycled with Stefan to the lake. It had been hellish hot. They found a rush-shielded spot away from the beaches, where they could swim naked. But they could not keep their bodies apart for long enough to swim very far.

Her arms settle into their crawl and her limbs start to warm. Her head relaxes below the surface as she turns to breathe. But her flat hand tightens into a fist each time she thinks of Stefan.

Was that him, was that really him, who followed SS-Obersturmführer Beck into the *Institute of Forensic Medicine*? At the time, she had no doubt about either of them. But now she is not sure if it really was Beck, let alone Stefan, that she saw. Stefan seems now so different to the young lover who swam naked with her between the bullrushes. And if that was him with Beck, the new Stefan would be as different to the old as a synagogue is to a swimming pool.

Ewa punches the water as she swims, searching for an explanation about why Stefan, if that was him, might be meeting on a busy street with an officer of the SS. Is this part of a more elaborate AK plot around the Neptun transmitter? One which requires Stefan to become a double agent? But airborne radio location surely has little to do with forensic medicine. Could Beck himself, difficult though it is to imagine, be some kind of double agent, passing secrets to the Allies through Stefan? But surely he would not then meet a partisan in full view of the most senior officers of the Reich. Unless, of course, he knows, like Ewa herself, about the power of hiding in plain sight.

There is another explanation, however; one that seems to be hovering just out of reach above the shimmering surface of the pool. Stefan might be working in reality for the occupiers. But the word *traitor* will not fully form in Ewa's mind. Stefan, like her, like Haller and like many people in this part of the country, has German forefathers and relatives. But Poland is their homeland, the country where they were born and grew up. The country they love. Although, of course, Stefan is more German than her. His own father was born in Bavaria...

'Goodbye then!'

Ewa splutters and looks up, treading water. Frida's clacking heels make a watery echo along the poolside. She is neat and ladylike again, apart from the wet hair still clinging mannishly to her scalp.

'Till next week!'

Ewa gives a wave in reply and paddles to the edge of the deep end, entirely put off her stroke. She holds on to the bar, stretching her leg muscles downwards, pointing her toes as straight and deep as they will go.

Above, a soaring barrel arch mirrors the pool's blue eddies. Ewa plunges her face into cool bleachiness then flattens her back and kicks off into the swirl of her own current. She cannot blame Stefan for keeping secrets. It would not be surprising if he has been given a special assignment, separate to the work of the AK. The British may want something in return for sending him here, something more than a prototype night-transmitter. The landing of a transport aeroplane so deep into enemy territory is a perilous, expensive operation. Perhaps this is what the suitcase is all about. The one with the smell, and the real reason that she is here, swimming in a former synagogue.

At the far end of the pool, behind the diving board, the light from a row of tall thin windows turns suddenly pink and a water-born sunset ripples across the pool. Ewa pushes off then flips on to her back, arms windmilling in reverse. It could be perhaps that forensic medicine is the key to the likely contents of Stefan's suitcase. That would account for its possible smell...

A shudder forces Ewa's chin below the surface and she swallows a chlorine-filled mouthful. She splutters then lies motionless in the water. Above the spectator gallery, the barrel arch merges into a dome. Translucent blue darkens towards the apex like the sky on a summer evening.

If she loses her faith in Stefan, she may as well not believe in anything. And marrying him before it is too late might be the only way to prove that she still has faith in herself.

Ewa's hands start to make figures of eight to keep herself afloat. Water seeps under the rubber bathing cap and rumbles inside her ears. If she does marry Stefan, he might at least think twice before rushing back into the arms of some English girl. Because she is beginning to realise that there must be an English girl. It is impossible that Stefan would have been without a woman for so long. Ewa can smell this girl in his jokes and evasions. And she can picture her too; one of those willowy English types who is careful not to scratch her perfect nails as she telephones from a government office inside Buckingham Palace, perhaps to organise this very mission.

Ewa closes her eyes and attempts to empty her head of everything but the echo of water. Her legs sink from the surface so gently that the tile against her foot comes as a shock. She stands up and puts her hands on her hips. At the far end of the pool, the high diving board looms against the darkening windows.

Water trickles out of the bathing cap as Ewa wades to the steps. Her woollen swimsuit gushes as she climbs out. She seems to have the whole pool to herself. The door to the reception area is closed and that attendant must be snoozing on the front desk. She goes to the ladder and starts to climb, bypassing the springy diving board and stepping up on to the high platform.

It is much higher than it looks from below. She has not dived off anything this high for at least ten years. Not since her mother died in fact. She can remember leaning over the outdoor pool, head first and fearless. But she cannot remember how that fearlessness really felt. At the edge, she takes a breath. Far, far below, a locker key has been dropped on to the blue floor of the deep end. Through the water's glassy surface, the lost key, with its red band, looks close enough to scoop up. As if there is no water in the pool at all.

Ewa swallows and glances at the door to reception. But there is still no sign of the attendant. No one has seen her come up here, so there is no need for embarrassment. She turns and scurries back down the ladders and into the door marked *DAMEN*.

Only Frida's wet footprints pattern dusty tiles. There are not enough Germans in the city to make use of all of the sports facilities, rush-hour trams and guest house dining rooms that are reserved for their sole use. In the shower, Ewa turns the dial and pipes groan and splurt into a thin hot stream. She scans the shower area and changing room, but there is no sign of what she was hoping to find. Perhaps she will need to look elsewhere in the city for a hiding place.

She slips off the fuzzy, sagging swimsuit to wring it out and water cascades into the drain at the end of the line of showers. As she throws the swimsuit over the side partition of a changing cubicle, her wet skin recoils from a draught of cool air. With her face to the gap between the back of the cubicles and the wall,

Ewa feels the air pouring from a wide metal grille by her feet. She reaches in to feel for the screw heads. One at each corner of the grille – flat slots. There is a metal nail file at the bottom of her handbag and if the attendant comes in she will say that her earring has rolled behind the cubicles. Except, of course, that she would not have to say anything. Her nakedness alone would scare him off.

The top screws come out easily and the grille tilts forward. Ewa crouches to look into the hole. It is dark, but seems dry and empty. Just an air vent in the wall that should have a corresponding metal grille somewhere outside. If that can be removed, there would be access to this vent from the street, even if the pool is closed. And so, if she is not mistaken, this ventilation shaft might be somewhere that a suitcase, even a very smelly one, could remain unnoticed for as long as Stefan wants.

Posen, Greater German Reich
Thursday 7 October

'Eva.'

Ewa stops, heart pounding, at the bottom of the stairs. She has had word, via the butcher's lad, to meet Stefan at three and it is almost half two. But now Beck wants her.

'Is that you, Eva? Do you have a moment?'

He is in the dining room. When he did not come down for luncheon she assumed that he was tired or too busy. But if he wants feeding now she will not make it to the cemetery in time. She eyes her hat still on its peg then sighs and goes through the half-open door.

'Obersturmführer.' She smiles. 'Can I get you something?'

There is no need for this formality, they are alone in the house. But perhaps it will signal to him that she has other things to do.

'No, Eva, thank you.'

His chair is pulled at an angle from the table and his feet stretch out, one ankle crossed over the other. He rests an elbow on the table, smoke rising from the cigarette in his hand. He looks terrible.

'Heinrich? Is everything all right, are you unwell?'

'Possibly.'

'Some camomile tea, perhaps?'

'No, no. Can you just sit with me for a moment?'

'Of course.'

She perches on a chair at the same table. 'Is it something you ate at the Castle perhaps?'

'No, I don't think it's that.'

He is grey-pale.

'Or stress. Do you have another lecture to deliver?'

'Eva?'

'Yes?'

'You know, don't you, that if you ever need me to help you, I will do it.'

Her heart gives a hollow beat. 'What do you mean, Heinrich?'

'I mean that you can rely on me, as a person. You may not want to know me more… intimately than you already do, but my regard for you is profound and sincere. And, whatever happens, I would always put your welfare before any other consideration.'

She tries to laugh. 'Oh, you sound so serious, Heinrich. You are really under the weather.'

He looks away, taking a long drag on the cigarette and does not answer. Then he sighs.

'Did you have your swim yesterday?'

'Oh, yes. The pool is a truly marvellous facility. Such an improvement.'

He holds out the yellow packet of Mokri Extra Strength to her. She smiles and puts up a hand.

'I can't, I'm sorry.'

'I know you are busy. Always out and about on your errands.'

'Only to see the coal merchant today. I am going to start negotiating for a good rate. Winter is coming.' She straightens her skirt as if to stand up. 'Are you not busy with the conference this afternoon?'

He shrugs and leans forward to stub the cigarette in the ashtray. Scarlet flashes from the silk lining of the black jacket hanging on his chair.

Ewa takes a breath. 'Or at the Institute of Forensic Medicine?'

'The Institute? Why do you ask?'

She keeps her face as blank and open as she can. 'Is that not where you are doing your new work? I thought I saw you going in there.'

'You were mistaken.'

Coldness washes down her spine. She has gone too far.

Beck stands suddenly and throws on his jacket in a swirl of scarlet and black. 'I will not keep you any longer from your coal merchant. I must be off too.'

Ewa's heart pumps against her ribcage as he lifts the gunbelt that has been hanging on the chair and straps it across his body. The silver skull embossed into the holster grins; a metallic whiff of revolver crosses the table. He definitely has something to hide.

Ewa tries to rein in her features and smile pleasantly. 'I hope you have your appetite back by this evening.'

He nods slowly as he tightens his waist buckle and adjusts the weight of the gun on his hip. Then with stiff elegance, he raps his heels together and thrusts his arm into a precise salute.

'Heil Hitler.'

'Heil Hitler, Obersturmführer.'

Ewa runs over this conversation again in her mind as she buttons her jacket and hurries over damp cobblestones. Beck clearly does not want her to think that she saw him at the Institute of Forensic Medicine. Which means that she very likely did. Can he really be in league with Stefan? And why? But if they really are working together, it is as good as pointless to try and hide her own connection with Stefan.

Ewa's legs weaken at this thought. Even though there is no traffic on St Adalbert Strasse, she stops and waits on the kerb to gather her strength. She must stay strong, and not let her mind spiral into anxiety with every possible risk. Bravery is no longer optional.

Three clangs reverberate from the squat wooden belfry beside the church as Ewa hitches up the handbag on her shoulder and crosses the street. Her towel and still-damp swimsuit make the bag bulge but she doubts that Stefan will notice.

Inside the cemetery walls, her pace quickens. Her heels skip on flagstones and then gravel. *Beside the obelisk to the drowned children*, the butcher's lad had said. Ewa shivers as she hurries towards the wooded hollow.

In the new cemetery where Ewa's mother lies, everything is clean and orderly, especially since the enforcement of German rules; no photographs on the graves, no coloured lamps or artificial posies. But here in the old cemetery, red and green lanterns flicker around some of the headstones in the afternoon gloom. But most of the graves' inhabitants have been dead too long for any living relatives to trouble the German occupiers with the vulgarity of their traditions.

Ewa's feet slow. Someone in a swinging grey mackintosh is half-hidden behind a sandstone obelisk. She cannot see enough to know that it is Stefan, but neither can she stop herself lunging forward. The figure turns.

'Ewa!'

They fall together. Stefan wraps his mac around her, pinning her inside its stiff folds. Ewa clings to him, desperate not to loosen the embrace. But already Stefan is pulling his mouth away from hers and sliding his gaze over her shoulder. She turns to see an old woman swathed in a shawl who is hobbling towards them down the path.

'Ignore her, Stefan.' Ewa takes his face between her hands,

forcing him to look into her eyes. Her voice catches. 'By Sunday you'll be gone.'

He lifts her hands from his cheeks. 'You must put that out of your mind, Ewa.'

'How can I?'

He sighs and steps back, buttoning his coat and fastening the belt. The coat is too big and makes him look overweight, as he might look, Ewa imagines, ten years from now. She bats away the unimaginable thought – *ten years*. Time seems elastic now. Making it past Saturday is hard enough to imagine.

Stefan bends to pick up something from behind a granite tomb. A dead smell, like a pot of bone broth left too long on the stove, seeps up. Ewa gives a start. The smell is coming from a suitcase, medium-sized but pale turquoise and shockingly obvious. Has Stefan carried it all the way from the farm? Or maybe, she thinks with a jolt of understanding, just from the Institute of Forensic Medicine.

Stefan nods towards a tree-arched path that undulates into the heart of the cemetery and they set off. As they pass the obelisk, Ewa blinks at the carved words on the other side.

Friedhelm Carl Schmitt 1888–1895
Drowned alongside his dearest friend Zygmunt Solski 1885–1895
Always together

In the faint breeze, leaves creep around the gravel paths. Moss-grown gravestones slump into uncut grass.

Ewa skips to catch up with Stefan and fumbles for his free hand. She glances at his face under the brim of his hat. 'Is it heavy, that suitcase?'

'Not really. You'll manage it all right.'

'I haven't said I'll take it yet.'

'Then why did you come?'

'To see you, you fool.'

Stefan slides her a half-smile and squeezes her hand. 'I like you in that hat.'

'I look like a Tyrolean housewife.'

'You look like a film star.'

'Shut up.'

'It's true.'

She sees that look in his eyes again.

'Where are we going, Stefan?'

His pace slows. They have come to an overgrown dip between low bushes. 'Over there?'

She guesses what he is thinking 'Mother of God, Stefan. Are you serious? We can't do it here.'

Yet even as she says it, Ewa finds herself scanning the vegetation for some other place where they might not be seen from the paths.

Then she bites her lip and comes to a stop. Is this as much as their lives together will ever be? A hasty, furtive coupling in an overgrown graveyard? She closes her eyes.

'Are you all right, Ewa?'

'No.'

'What's wrong?'

'Can't you see? If you leave me again I think I will die.'

'Ewa...'

His warm hand is on her cheek, his eyes trying to search hers but she turns away. Everything is so much easier for him. He will slip back into his life as a spy or a pilot or whatever that English girl tells him to be next. But Ewa's carefully assembled world will be ravaged by his absence. How will she bear it?

She ignores the yellow cigarette packet that Stefan is holding out. 'How long have we got?'

He shrugs and lights a cigarette. 'I have to be back at the farm before curfew. But we could hang around here a bit longer.'

Ewa's head throbs with fatigue. This is not how they should be spending their precious minutes together. Her fingers press against her forehead. She cannot look at Stefan.

'When we are apart I can't think of anything except seeing you again. But now that you're here, all I can think of is the moment when you will go.'

He does not reply but is staring at the top of the path where overhanging trees create a doorway of light.

'Stefan...'

'Is St Adalbert's church kept open?'

His voice has thickened.

'It should be. Why?'

'We can go in there.'

'Not to...'

'Just to see what's what. Come, take my arm. Talk to me about something, anything, whilst we walk. This place would make anyone gloomy.'

As he moves the suitcase, the peculiar odour makes Ewa catch her breath. Then she steps forward and links her elbow with Stefan's.

'What is your cover story?'

'I'm Haller's Polish cousin from Warsaw. Come to do the book-keeping. A special favour to Haller from his Party pals.'

Ewa gives a snort. Haller's membership of the Nazi Party is like this turquoise suitcase. Who would believe anything so conspicuous could conceal enemy secrets? If that, of course, is what the suitcase contains.

They are out of the trees now. The steeply gabled roof of St Adalbert's rises from the brow of the hill. He can't really be intending, can he, that they fornicate inside the church? She wants him, more than anything, but the idea of having those sorts of relations on hallowed ground, where the priests might see or hear... Holy Mary, the very thought is impossible.

'There's bound to be people in there, Stefan. St Adalbert's is the only church near the old town that Poles are allowed to use. All we can do in there is pray.'

But his pace does not slacken and when the ancient church door opens, the clunk of the latch echoes into stony silence.

Ewa stands with Stefan at the rear of the pews. The colonnaded nave, intricately painted in dark reds and pinks, seems deserted. Through odours of polish and incense, a thread of burning weaves up from the little flames that dot the darkness below a statue of Our Lady. Whoever lit the candles is no longer here.

Stefan takes Ewa's hand and brings it to his lips, but his eyes are darting around the church.

He whispers and nods towards the shadows at the side of the aisle. 'What's behind that door there?'

Ewa has been through the door once, with her mother, to arrange a basket of flowers.

'No, Stefan. It's the sacristy. One of the priests might be in there.'

'They are probably all sleeping after their lunch.'

'Stefan...'

But he is still holding on to her hand and pulling her towards the door. Ewa tells her feet not to follow him but they will not listen. Stefan puts down the suitcase to press on the door handle. It is not locked.

Inside, the room is as she remembers it – a cramped sacristy with lace-edged vestments crowding the hooks around the walls. The key is still in the lock on the inside of the door. She hears Stefan turn it before he comes up to her and puts a hand on her cheek.

Ewa whispers. 'No, Stefan. This is not right.'

'Please, Ewa. We may not get another chance. Perhaps God is giving us this opportunity.'

'Stefan...'

But there is uncertainty in her voice. The scent of candle-wax fills her lungs as Stefan's mouth covers hers. She knows then that it is too late for pious objection. All she cares about is him.

They make almost no noise on the stone floor. Ewa tries to

clamp her moans behind a grinding of teeth, but the effort of stifling her final feverish cry leaves her heaving gulps of air. Icy flagstones bite at each of her vertebrae as she sinks back. The cold track of a tear trickles into her hair.

Stefan is looking away from her as they lie twisted and sticky. This should be a time for tenderness, for words of love, but the turquoise suitcase is filling Ewa's vision and the shadow of it is seeping across her thoughts.

She puts her lips to Stefan's ear. 'Did you get that suitcase from Heinrich Beck?'

The twitch in Stefan's eye is so slight that Ewa is not quite sure if she has imagined it.

'Who?'

'I saw you with him. Going into the Institute of Forensic Medicine.'

'The what?'

'Forget it.'

If he hasn't told her straight, badgering is not going to make him change his mind.

Stefan frowns. 'Is this Beck one of your lodgers?'

'Yes. You know him, don't you?'

'No.'

And as she looks at him, she is no longer sure what she believes. The figure by the *Forensic Medicine* plaque was wearing a hat with a wide brim, much wider than the trilby that Stefan has on, but darker in colour than the fedora he wore on Monday. Perhaps…

'How well do you know him, Ewa?'

'What do you mean?'

'It can't have been easy living with so many attractive young men under the same roof.'

'Shut up, Stefan. You have no idea what my life has been like.'

Stefan sighs. 'I could not blame you, you know…'

Ewa's voice, fighting the need to stay quiet, becomes a hiss.

'Could you not? Is that because of what you got up to in England? It would be convenient for you perhaps, if two wrongs could make everything all right.'

Outside the door, footsteps echo through the darkly cavernous church. Hurriedly, Ewa sits up and straightens her stockings, clicking them securely on to their straps. Stefan is staring at her. Perhaps it is just the dim light that makes it look as if there are tears in his eyes.

The footsteps on stone are suddenly very close. Swiftly, Stefan buckles his belt. He signals Ewa to keep still and tip-toes to the door with the suitcase in his hand. Then he is beckoning her forward and unlocking the door. As they leave the sacristy, the priest turns and asks, loudly, what they are doing, but Stefan and Ewa are already on their way out of the main door.

They hurry past the wooden belfry and the scrubby lawn beyond. When they reach the road and Stefan is sure that no one is following, he puts the suitcase on the ground and lights a cigarette.

He waves the match to extinguish the flame. 'When we go, you pick up the suitcase.'

'Perhaps I don't want to take it.'

'Ewa, listen to me. If you knew the importance of what is inside it, what this evidence might mean for the Polish nation, for the whole way that the war is being fought…'

'Perhaps I don't care about any of that…'

'Ewa!'

'…compared to the hurt I feel hearing you lie to me.'

'Lie? What about?' Stefan takes hold of her hand. 'I swear to tell you the truth. Ask me anything you like.'

'All right then. But if I detect any hint of a lie, you will be taking that suitcase away with you again.'

'Yes. I understand.'

He is trying to smile but his eyes are wary. Ewa pulls her hand away.

'All right then. The girl. In England. I know there was one. Tell me.'

He looks faintly relieved, then serious again. He nods. 'You are right. I kissed her, but that was all, I swear.'

There. He has said it. But Ewa feels winded as if punched. She covers her stomach with her arms as questions foam into her mouth: *so, what does this English girl look like? Is she taller than me, prettier, funnier? Did you go dancing, drinking, swimming together? Did you try to fuck her, and it was just that she wouldn't let you?*

Only one question seeps through.

'Did you take her up with you in your aeroplane, like you used to take me?'

He shrugs. 'No point. She flies them too.'

'Herself?'

'She's a pilot.'

Oh, Judas. A lady pilot. Another one. Ewa imagines the English aviatrix, tall and rangy with a silk scarf around her neck, laughing as she jerks back the stick to loop the loop. Damn her. And damn him. But Stefan says he has not slept with her. Ewa has to believe that.

She flattens her hand against her brow. 'Shit, Stefan.'

'What?'

'What do you think?'

'You asked me to tell you the truth and I did.'

'I wish now that you hadn't.'

'Ewa...'

She picks up the suitcase. 'I'm going now.'

'Don't you want to know what is inside the case?'

'Does it matter?'

He shrugs. 'Just make sure that the authorities can't find it.'

'Obviously.'

'Where will you hide it?'

'Don't worry. I have somewhere.'

'Where?'

'Somewhere.'

The suitcase is heavier than the old army knapsack with a noiseless typewriter inside it, but not much.

'Where?'

She turns to go and Stefan puts a hand on her arm. 'All right, Ewa. But come to the farm tomorrow, to Haller's wood shed at eleven. There will be a priest.'

Her heart drops a beat. 'You're serious, aren't you?'

'I am.'

'Why bother? We're as good as married now we've fucked in a church.'

But just saying the words is enough to send a wave of cold dread through Ewa's insides. If she has not invited the wrath of heaven to descend on her head by this act of sacrilege, then heaven cannot exist.

She walks away, tears clouding her eyes. It would be crazy to go to the farm tomorrow. The last thing she needs is the drama and complication of a clandestine wedding. But if she does not go, she will not see Stefan again before he leaves on the Dakota. And so she might never see him again.

Posen, Greater German Reich
Thursday 7 October

As Ewa wipes her eye, she sees Jabłoński coming towards her up St Adalbert Strasse and her stomach does a quick somersault. He must have seen her with Stefan. But how much did he see, and what did he make of it? There is no way to avoid him though. Ewa must pull herself together, and she is already close enough to see the knowing grin on the postman's round face.

He pulls at his cap. 'Good afternoon, Fräulein Hartman.'

His German has the characteristic lilt of the region.

183

'Good afternoon.'

She pulls her handkerchief from her pocket and blows her nose. Hopefully he will think she has a cold.

Jabłoński winks. 'Don't worry, I won't tell Papa.'

'What about?'

'Your secret assignation.'

'What?'

His smile widens. 'With that mystery man outside the church.'

Ewa is torn by sudden indecision. Should she laugh dismissively and pooh-pooh his insinuations, or admit everything and beg Jabłoński to keep her secret?

But she does not blink. 'Oh, him.'

'Do I recognise him from somewhere?'

'I doubt it. He said he is a newly ordained priest from an underground seminary in Krakow, and is hoping to join the holy fathers here.'

'He told you all that just then, did he?'

She nods. 'He seemed to think I would be able to put in a good word for him with the priests even though I told him that I hardly ever go to Mass nowadays.'

'And that's why he took hold of your hand?'

She shakes her head. 'No, no. You are mistaken. It must have been the way we were standing.'

'He didn't look much like a priest.'

'They often go in disguise these days, don't they?'

Jabłoński is smiling but she can see that he is sceptical. He adjusts the postbag over his shoulder and they both look, automatically, back up the street towards the church. The pavements on both sides of the cobbles are deserted. Most of the apartments have been empty since the evacuation of this neighbourhood at the very start of the war. The settlers seem particularly reluctant to live in the former Jewish quarter.

Jabłoński glances at the turquoise suitcase. 'And I thought that was his too.'

'No, no, just some old clothes I have collected for the settlers.'

'Very old by the smell of them.'

'Yes!'

Ewa laughs, perhaps a little too energetically. Stefan must have gone back into the city down Kanonen Strasse. At least he is not following her. His insistence about wanting to know where the suitcase is to be hidden has made her wonder if he might. If she talks to Jabłoński a little longer, she will ensure that Stefan is not on her tail.

'Have you not finished your rounds yet?'

Jabłoński blows out his cheeks. 'Almost. So many sweethearts' letters coming to and from the Front these days,' he winks again, 'it keeps me on my feet all afternoon.'

But Ewa cannot stand his saucy innuendo any longer. 'Well, do not let me detain you further. Heil Hitler.'

Jabłoński seems momentarily flummoxed by Ewa's salute before she sets off down the street. At the edge of the as-yet-unnamed Platz, she looks back at the postman. He is still strolling up St Adalbert Strasse and there is no sign of Stefan. At least she did not tell Stefan where she is going with the suitcase. Whatever is inside it means a lot to him, that much is clear. And so, if he wants the suitcase back, whenever that might be, Stefan will have to find Ewa first.

She waits for the tram to roll by before crossing the wide roadway between apartment blocks and heading to the main entrance of the swimming pool. The glass door allows her a clear view of the unattended reception desk. She pushes in and there is still no one around. Ewa goes straight through the swinging door and into the chlorine steaminess of the poolside.

The blue water is ruffled by a fat man floating on his back with a fondant dome of belly exposed to the air. He does not look Ewa's way, and even though her heels echo on the tiles, the attendant does not appear.

The louvered door of the ladies' changing room closes softly behind her. She does not take a proper breath until she is inside the lavatory cubicle, the turquoise suitcase balanced on the toilet seat and the door bolted.

The suitcase is locked but the fastenings are old and loose. Luckily, Ewa has brought several screwdrivers in her handbag. It does not take much fiddling and poking before the clasps jump open.

A sweetish sickly smell blooms up. Ewa puts a hand over her mouth and nose and half closes her eyes, cowering from what she may see inside. But there is nothing repulsive, just a pile of brown envelopes each with a number inked on the top right hand corner. Some of the bulging buff packages are spotted with grease.

Gingerly, one hand still over her mouth, Ewa picks up envelope *2539*. The seal is gummed but she uses the screwdriver to tear the paper. Crouching to the floor, she eases out the contents: a small clothbound notebook, now grey; a medical card, too faded to read; a silver St Christopher medal that has clearly failed to protect its wearer.

Ewa puts a fingernail to the crinkled pages of the notebook and a vinegary odour wafts out. It looks like a diary with dated entries in spidery indelible pencil. Many of the words have been erased in a blur of watermarks and dirt. But the Polish ź's and ł's are unmistakable. At the front there is a date; *November 30, 1939*, and at the back before the blank pages begin, a rushed final entry:

April 9, 1940
…. we were brought to a place in the forest – something of a summer vacation spot. Here, a thorough search. They took my watch, which showed 6.30am. They asked about my wedding band which… they took my roubles, my penknife, my belt…

Ewa's heart quickens. She replaces the contents and folds the top of the envelope. Then she takes another from the suitcase. *3765*. Greasy litter spews from the envelope along with a stink of week-old broth. Wire spectacles, one lens cracked; a tortoiseshell comb with brown hairs still caught in the teeth. Ewa stirs the contents with the screwdriver and the bad-meat smell thickens over a dark-haired woman with big sad eyes who stares up from a studio photograph. On her lap, a small girl half covers her face with a toy cat. Underneath the photograph is a sheet of stained writing paper:

My darling, I cannot eat or sleep or think of anything but you...

Ewa feels a cleave of sympathy for the dark-haired woman who, if she is alive, may still be living in the same deadened twilight of not-knowing that Ewa inhabited until last week. This envelope on the lavatory floor may be the only proof that the dark-haired woman's man is dead, and unless she sees it, the woman will never know what became of him. Because Ewa can see what all of this is – the same sort of unearthed personal effects that she saw on the cinema newsreel six months ago. These items have become evidence of a war crime; evidence that has now been stolen.

Ewa wants to believe that this is why Stefan has taken such a risk with this stuff. His motive for placing himself, and her, in such danger could be compassion for the families of his murdered Polish comrades. Perhaps the AK can somehow contact the families of the dead to let them know the true fate of their loved ones.

But the unlikeliness of this task makes Ewa uneasy. Tears needle her sinuses as she refills the envelopes and folds them back into the suitcase. She knows now what the contents of all of the envelopes will be like, and she cannot bear to see any more.

With the screwdriver, the grille comes away easily. Placed sideways, and angled up from the gap beneath the changing cubicle, the suitcase slides neatly into the vent. Ewa undresses to her slip, then gets down on her knees to wriggle her shoulder into the gap between wall and changing cubicles. She reaches in and gives the suitcase a shove. The inside of her forearm scrapes on the metal edge of the grille, but the case shunts forward and is well into the air vent before it seems to hit the outside wall. If the swimming pool is closed when Stefan decides he wants the suitcase back, he can pull it out from the street.

Ewa takes off her underwear and stands naked, sniffing the lardy air that seems to waft back and forth through the vent. But the overarching reek of chlorine from the pool is doing its work. Ewa turns on the shower and rinses her hands again and again in the flow before putting them to her nose to make sure that the suitcase smell has left no trace. Then she cups both hands and sloshes warm water up between her legs. She is suddenly glad that Stefan took no precautions and so she can still feel the stream of leaking hotness that he left inside her.

Ewa's swimming costume, still damp from yesterday, seems to have grown to twice its normal size. She arranges the armholes around her breasts and pulls the tape belt tight. The smell of the suitcase is not particularly noticeable in the changing room now. Perhaps Ewa has got used to it. But as long as the air vent does its job, she doubts that anyone will be troubled by the undertone of bad meat. And if there are complaints, she is sure that the lazy attendant will not bother to investigate.

That same attendant is still nowhere to be seen on the deserted poolside. The fat man is ratcheting down a roped-off swimming lane with arm strokes that are infrequent but surprisingly efficient. Ewa takes a long breath and looks up at the diving board. Then she begins to climb.

The high platform does not seem so terrifying today. Perhaps it is because the fat man's strokes have churned up the surface of the water and so obscured the true depth of the pool. Or perhaps she has got used to the fear.

Yesterday, Ewa did not notice the striking view of the roof from the high board. She stands at the end of the fixed platform, her eyes following the angles at the intersection of dome and barrel arch. How elegantly the disparate shapes fit together. How naturally the architectural lines flow into each other. Despite everything weighing down on her, Ewa feels light-headed and slightly euphoric. If hiding the suitcase of evidence is, as Stefan says, a momentous act of resistance, then this is something that they have achieved together. Ewa realises then that she cannot bear for this triumph to be their last shared act.

'Hey, you!'

It is the attendant, standing beside the *1.8M* depth marker with his hands on his hips.

From the top board Ewa smiles and waves. 'Hello there!'

'You must not swim until you have shown your papers and paid for your session.'

'Don't you remember me, from yesterday?'

'You must pay.'

'Of course, I know that. But I stood by the desk, waiting and waiting and no one came. Is it a problem to pay on my way out?'

'No, the rules say that you must pay before you swim.'

'All right. Do you want me to come now?'

'Yes.'

'As quick as I can?'

'Yes.'

'Very well.'

Ewa puts her toes over the edge of the platform. Through the water's choppiness, she sees something red wobbling on the floor of the deep end. The bottom of the pool is a very long way down. But without pausing to think, she puts her hands together, prayer-like and points them at the lost locker key. Then she leans forward and lets herself fall.

Posen, Greater German Reich
Friday 8 October

Broom handles are crossed over the toilet-block doorway but Lange is still trying to get in.

Ewa's father puts up both hands. 'I'm sorry, Untersturmführer. Our hygiene service is in progress.'

The straps of Lange's braces already hang around his haunches. His face drops. 'But where can I...?'

'Use the old outhouse if you like. The water's turned off but there's a cinder pail...'

Lange has already set off across the yard and is scraping open the outhouse door.

Oskar Hartman goes back to mopping the linoleum and mutters under his breath. 'We wouldn't have to clean up in here so often if they were a bit more particular in their ways.'

'Quite so.'

Ewa squirts a puff of scouring powder at the tiles. The dried orange dribble beneath the powder is some distance from the urinal. When the occupiers came, her father took out a considerable loan in order to build this wooden sanitary block in the yard. The occupying authorities made it very plain that no officers would be billeted in the guest house unless modern, plumbed-in conveniences and a shower were installed. But the toilet chalet is already riddled with black mould. It has to be cleaned at least twice a day to keep the damp and the smells at bay.

Ewa snaps off her rubber gloves and tosses the scrubbing brushes into the bucket. 'There. I've done. And I will get out of the way so that you can let the desperate dears back in.'

Ewa's father chuckles and leans on his mop handle. 'Going somewhere?'

'Nowhere special.'

'Or meeting someone?'

'No. Why?'

'You've got your mother's blouse on.'

Ewa pushes a loop of the lilac bow back inside the collar of her sweater. 'I couldn't find anything else clean to put on.'

There is more to it than that, of course. But her father will not remember that it was the silk blouse that Ewa had on when she first saw Stefan in the Aero Club bar. As she'd walked in, he had looked straight at her and his pale eyes would not then look away. Once he came over and started speaking to her, Ewa knew that, before long, his fingers would be undoing the silk-covered buttons.

Oskar shakes his head. 'That blouse cost me a fortune. Your mother had fallen in love with it and was determined. Said it would last her a lifetime. It did, I suppose.'

'Papa…'

'I'm sorry. Where are you going, Maus?'

'Back to the woods, for more mushrooms.'

'This late in the day?'

'I'll get what I can. They'll be fresh at least, for the Gauleiter's soup tomorrow. And they're free.'

'Good, Maus. What would I do without you?'

'You'd manage, Papa.'

Her voice sounds thin and peevish. She does not mean it to but a tight band of muscle, like a surgical brace, has suddenly constricted her breath. How can she lie to her father about this of all things? She can well imagine the look of hollow sadness there would be in his eyes if she told him where she is really going this morning. She is going to her wedding, and he is not invited. He is not even to be told. The thought makes her want to retch. As she puts her face up to kiss her father's whiskery cheek, Ewa hopes he will imagine that the tears in her eyes are for her mother.

But even as she pedals past the Gestapo building on her way to the farm, Ewa still cannot believe that she is going to be Stefan Bergel's wife. The idea is both magical and absurd. And it will complicate her life entirely. After tomorrow night, when Stefan has returned to the other side of Europe, she will, very likely, never see him again, and so she will return to the grey half-world of not knowing whether he is alive or dead. And yet she will never be able to marry anyone else.

Ewa stands up on the pedals and speeds along smooth German concrete as she tries to make herself care about this fact. But she cannot. She wants Stefan to be hers, so that even if the Dakota he is travelling on disappears into the clouds forever, she will always be able to say: *I am Stefan Bergel's wife.*

Turning off the highway, Ewa raises her face to the weak sun. It is not far now. She pulls off the track by the beech copse and dismounts, leaning the handlebars against a smooth grey trunk. Then she makes for a clump of holly bushes and crouches behind them, shivering, to piss on the dead leaves.

When she stands, Ewa peels off her sweater and the lilac blouse shimmers in the dull woodland. But as she looks down, she notices that one of the silk-covered cuff buttons has popped from its eyelet and fallen into the crumbled ground. She drops to her knees and scrabbles through crackling leaves as she looks for the button. There is no spare and without this one, the blouse will be ruined. A dank earth smell rises from beneath the leaf cover, but the button has gone.

Ewa shakes her head, hot tears prickling. This is her wedding outfit, for God's sake, because today, ridiculously, is her wedding day. When she was twelve, she would imagine the proceedings of this day over and over with her mother always asking the same questions:

And your dress?

White satin with a four-metre train.

And the church?

St Mary Magdalene, of course.

And the flowers?

Orange blossom around the door, lilies by the altar.

Her mother never seemed to tire of this conversation until her last months when she tired of everything and no longer spoke. Ewa presses her hand to her mouth. She will not let herself cry. A new life is coming, she tells herself, a better life. She has had enough of being Eva, the blank-eyed blonde on her identity card. Neither does she want to go back to being a naïve, passionate girl called Ewa Hartman. It is time to become a grown woman – someone self-assured, clever, brave. And for that she needs a new name.

Folding the sweater into the bicycle basket, she remounts and bumps the short way down the track towards the wood shed. Through the pale trees, she sees that someone has hung berry-covered rowan twigs and trailing woodbine around the shed's plank door. Icy silk strokes Ewa's arm as she pushes the door open.

Inside, dirty light filters from a high window on to log-stacks and paint-peeled walls. A low table is covered with a white cloth and draped with dark leaves and red berries. Faces turn to her, smiling; Haller with his hair slicked flat, Robak's neck pinched into a celluloid collar. Behind the low table, a man in working clothes picks up a length of cream fabric that is stiff with gold embroidery, and hangs it around his neck.

Stefan steps from the shadows into the light. And as Ewa goes towards him, she sees only the searchlight blue of his eyes. He reaches for her hands, lifts them to his mouth, presses her cold knuckles to his warm lips. She cannot speak.

The man with the embroidered stole has dark stubble and nervous eyes. He mutters words, familiar and meaningless: *In nomine Patris et Filii et Spiritus Sancti...* then he says her name: *Ewa* and makes the sign of the cross. He asks her a question she does not quite hear. But she says *yes*. Yes to anything, in any language.

193

Stefan opens his hand. Inside are two plain copper bands, bent and soldered like something from a plumber's tool bag. He takes Ewa's right hand and slips on the ring. Their heads are touching and she feels the pull of his hair entwined with hers.

The priest wraps the embroidered stole around their joined hands, gold thread crackling softly as it bends. Hidden in the folds, Stefan's fingertips flutter inside Ewa's palm. The priest again makes the sign of the cross. Ewa is now, miraculously, Mrs Bergel.

Stefan's kiss is hard and quick. Then he fishes in his jacket pocket and pulls out a folded rectangle of paper and an indelible pencil sharpened with a knife. Clearing a space amongst the trailing woodbine he opens the marriage certificate, flattening it with his hand. His signature loops along the dotted line. He holds out the pencil to Ewa.

'Here.'

'What shall I write?'

'Your name, of course.'

'Which one?'

He smiles as if she is joking. But is it *Ewa*, or *Eva*; *Hartman* or *Bergel*? Each one speaks and acts like a different person.

'The one you were born with.'

She takes the pencil and writes *Ewa Hartman*. Stefan passes the pencil to the priest who signs illegibly. The embroidered stole is already hidden behind the bib of his dungarees. He seems to have said nothing to Ewa except in Latin.

The pencil goes from Haller to Robak. She sees what they write: *ZJ Haller* and *Tomasz Puźniak*. Haller produces a bottle of pre-war vodka and thimble glasses.

'Cheers!'

Incredibly, Haller is also handing round tiny triangles of white bread topped with black pearls of caviar. Perhaps his unseen wife has prepared this as a wedding breakfast. Salt is then sprinkled on a few cuts of dry bread, tasted by them all then thrown on the ground. Ewa looks over her shoulder but the priest has already gone.

A plump damp hand takes hold of hers and Ewa finds Robak, or Tomasz as she now thinks of him, squeezing her fingers to his lips. Robak, the worm, may have been his code name but it suited him.

'I wish you happiness.'

She laughs. Happiness seems as unlikely a prospect for her marriage as caviar at a wood-shed wedding. But she wants to believe him.

'Thank you.'

Tomasz's dark eyes are still fixed on her and she has to pull her hand free.

He gives a half-smile. 'You should cry now, Mrs Bergel, should you not?'

'Why?'

'You know what they say: a bride must cry at her wedding or she will spend the rest of the marriage in tears.'

'I don't take any notice of those old Polish sayings.'

'Don't you? Let's hope they are not right.'

'How can they be?'

Ewa is not as sure as she sounds and her heart is thudding. But she is glad that her voice seems steady. Because if she starts to cry now, she knows that she will not be able to stop.

Lüssow, Greater German Reich
Friday 8 October

'And now for our honeymoon.'

'Very funny.'

'Have faith in me, Mrs Bergel.'

'Don't, Stefan.'

His fizz of good humour makes Ewa feel even more bereft.

'Why not?' He is wheeling her bike from the shade of the trees on to the open field beyond. 'You see? A walk in the beautiful Polish countryside. Who could wish for a nicer honeymoon?'

She tries to smile. White flowers unfurl in the short yellow grass and autumn sunshine makes a circle of silken heat on Ewa's back, but it will not lift the heaviness inside her. Since leaving the wood-shed chapel, the seriousness of this step she has taken and the likelihood of it ending in grief have tightened into a hard lump at the top of her chest. Stefan's lightness is becoming infuriating. But she knows how to put a stop to it.

'I looked inside the suitcase.'

'Did you?' Stefan comes instantly to a stop. 'Where is it now?'

'Somewhere safe.'

'Where?'

'Can we sit down?' Ewa throws her sweater on new-mown grass at the edge of a ditch. 'All that stuff… it's from Katyn, isn't it?'

Stefan lays the bike on the ground and sits next to her. 'You can see, then, why it is important.'

'To the families?'

'That as well.'

'As well? What do you mean?'

'The evidence is too important to be returned to the families yet.'

'What?'

She turns to him aghast and his face darkens.

'Each package holds the possessions of an identifiable Polish officer.'

'So all the more reason to find the families…'

'No.' He looks at the sky. 'A thorough examination of this evidence has already been carried out. There are many dated objects amongst the dead officers' possessions. And no date is later than April 1940.'

'What does that prove?'

Stefan sits straighter. 'It proves, conclusively, who are the murderers. You see, the Wehrmacht did not advance into that part of Russia until the summer of 1941. So even though the British are saying that this is Hitler's crime, Germany could not have committed the massacre at Katyn. When the British see my evidence they will change their minds about who is responsible. And change their minds about their Soviet allies.'

'You think that would be a good thing?'

'Of course. It is the truth.'

Ewa shakes her head. 'I would lay a bet that the British already know the truth but it suits them not to believe it.'

'But when the facts are presented to the world…'

Ewa snorts. 'It will make no difference. People will believe what they want to believe, regardless of inconvenient facts. Just ask the charming occupants of Guest House Hartman what they think they are fighting for.'

He turns to look directly at her and his voice has a hard edge. 'You saw the numbers marked on the envelopes. The numbering starts at one and goes up to more than four thousand. That's how many bodies were excavated this summer.'

'Who told you all this?'

'It doesn't matter. What matters is that I will be taking this evidence with me, back to England on the Dakota.' He looks away and picks at the short grass. 'Is the suitcase at the guest house?'

'No. The smell is too strong.'

'Where then?'

'Not far away.'

'Why won't you tell me where it is?'

'I don't want you going looking for it without me.' Irritation needles through her. 'Why did you not bring it here and hide it at the farm if you are so bothered about it?'

'I collected the case in the city and it's a hard thing to conceal, as you know. It is also best that Haller knows nothing about this plan until he absolutely has to.' Stefan's hand scatters the confetti of grass clippings. 'It may not be clear where everyone's loyalties really lie until they are tested.'

Ewa wishes suddenly that there was no copper band on her finger to complicate her indignation. She sighs and sinks back on to the field, throwing her arms above her head. Balls of white cloud dot the pale blue sky.

'Don't go, Stefan.'

'I'm right here.'

'I mean on the Dakota.'

'I have to, Ewa.'

He fumbles in his pocket for cigarettes and a lighter as Ewa props herself up on one elbow. Above, not far off, an aircraft engine wheedles.

'Are you going to fly the Dakota?'

'No, no. I'm not trained for heavy transport types.'

'What does it look like?'

'The Dakota?' His eyes narrow as he sucks on the cigarette. 'It looks like the future.'

She wonders what he means. 'Big, then?'

'Not too big to land on this field.'

'Here?'

He nods. She tries to picture this sunlit grassy expanse at night with the roar of a transport plane plunging down to land. But she cannot.

Above them a reedy engine whines. Stefan glances up, and then flings his cigarette away. Before Ewa quite realises what is happening, he has fallen on to her, his heaviness pushing the air out of her ribcage, his face covering hers.

'Lie still. Don't show your face.'

She can hardly speak for the weight of him. 'Why? What is it?'

Across his shoulder at the corner of her vision, something moves in the sky; long rounded wings, spindly bracing struts, toy-like wheels.

He whispers. 'A Storch.'

'They're not looking at us, surely?'

'They look at everything. Photograph everything.'

Both of them take quick shallow breaths. Ewa wonders if, from two hundred metres above, it must look as if they are making love even though it feels nothing like.

Stefan's eyes flicker. 'Can you see it? Is it circling?'

But when Ewa locates the outline in the sky, the plane is flying away. 'No, it's gone.'

Stefan rolls over onto the grass. Without meaning to, Ewa lets out a thin cry as his weight on her is replaced by a swirl of air.

He stares at the sky. 'Come with me, Ewa. On the Dakota.'

'What?'

'To England.'

'That's not funny.'

He turns on his side to look at her and the grass gives off a smell like the start of a summer morning.

'I'm not joking, Ewa. You just need to slip out of the guest house at the end of the Gauleiter's dinner and come to find us in the milk truck. I will drive into the city with Tomasz.'

'Jesus, Stefan.'

'I have to come to town anyway. For the suitcase.'

Ewa's stomach tightens. 'How can I go to England? My father…'

'There is nothing in any of this that would implicate your father.'

'I meant how can I leave him?'

Stefan sits up and takes hold of her shoulders. 'But think, Ewa. Think about Sunday morning. We could be in London by then, a newly married couple, looking for an apartment. A new life. We'd be together and safe. Your life would be normal.'

Her gut has contracted as if she is about to throw up. He is serious. Maybe this is what he has had planned all along.

'Don't even put thoughts like that into my head. It's not fair.'

'Just excuse yourself before the end of the Gauleiter's dinner. Look ill or something, and slip into the back alley. I'll be waiting there with Tomasz in the truck. We will pick up the suitcase and the Neptun receiver from the factory then drive here.'

Ewa pulls up her legs and puts her arms around them, resting her head on her knees. There is a look in Stefan's eye that she has not seen before and does not like.

'What is it you really want to pick up tomorrow night – me or the suitcase?'

'Both.'

'And if you had to choose?'

'I don't.'

'You will have to, Stefan, because neither me nor the suitcase will be going anywhere unless my father comes with us.'

Stefan stands up and runs both hands through his hair. 'There's a risk that the Dakota landing might go wrong. Or not happen at all.'

'I know that. I'm not stupid.'

'In fact, it's more likely to go wrong than right.' He thrusts his hands into his trouser pockets and turns away. 'That's why you must keep this with you at all times.'

He pulls one hand from his pocket. There is something red on the flat of his palm; a foil covered sweet with familiar dull red wrapping and *E Wedel* in curling gold letters. But Ewa's chest is thudding because she knows what is inside the chocolate.

She shakes her head. 'Haller gave me one of those before the last big action, but I flushed it down the officers' toilet. I could never bring myself to take it.'

Stefan kneels down beside Ewa and pushes the wrapped, deadly chocolate into her skirt pocket. 'They won't just beat you, you know, or burn you or try to drown you. That's what they'd do to a man.'

'What about you? Would you ever take one?'

'It depends.'

'On what?'

'On what I thought was coming next.'

She brushes grass clippings off her skirt and feels the lump of poison in her pocket. Perhaps this time, despite what she has said, she will not throw it away.

Her voice wavers. 'Anyway, I am praying to St Barbara for cloud on Saturday night. Then we can all stay here.'

'St Barbara gives protection from storms, so you're probably helping to keep the sky clear.' He stretches out his hand, pulling her up against him and whispers in her ear. 'That's why, my Ewa, we must make the most of today.'

The silk of her sleeve clings to his jacket as he takes her hand and guides her across the ditch. Stefan rights the bicycle and they walk, faster than a stroll, towards one of the neat stands of trees that border the long clover field. The copper band on her finger pinches where Stefan's hand grips hers.

In the distance, two dark figures are walking briskly at the edge of the field beside a stand of trees. One of them looks like Haller. The other might be Tomasz but she can't tell.

Ewa and Stefan step from the field edge into a dapple of shade beneath the trees. Ewa blinks as her eyes adjust to the light. Without a word, Stefan releases her hand and crouches down. He seems to be pulling up a wide swathe of the woodland floor. Then Ewa sees that it is a tarpaulin sheet camouflaged with leaves. Beneath it, oil cans and outdoor lamps are laid out in neat rows. A whiff of kerosene cuts through the wet soil dankness.

Stefan stares for a moment then adjusts the tarpaulin and re-secures the edge with a tent peg.

He wipes his hands on his trousers. 'Over there. Come on.'

Dense holly bushes fence off a tight circular clearing. Ewa follows Stefan in, pushing through the prickle of waxy leaves, before sinking down beside him so that they cannot be seen.

Lightly, Stefan strokes his fingertips along the curve of Ewa's cheek. 'My Ewa, my darling…'

Ewa takes his hand in hers and presses it to her lips. Then she whispers. 'Whatever happens, don't go back to that English girl, the pilot. Promise me.'

'Of course, my love. I am your husband now.' He pushes the hair from her eyes. 'And you... if any of the officers at the guest house...'

'There is no one but you, Stefan. Always. Always.'

'Ewa...'

His breath is hot on her face.

'Stefan...'

His hand slips from Ewa's waist to her thigh and already he is pushing up her skirt. Cool woodland air washes the bare skin above her stockings and heat rips through her. But she takes hold of Stefan's hand.

'Stefan... slow down.'

'What?'

'Slower, darling. Make it last. Who knows how long we will have to remember this...'

He groans and rolls over, pushing down on to her. Coppery fragments of dead leaves latch on to her hair. Stefan begins to cover her face in light, frantic kisses.

'Ewa, don't say that. Come with me on Saturday, please...'

'Stefan...' But then she presses a fingertip over his lips. 'Shhh...'

Because nearby in the wood, something is moving. And then Stefan hears it too. A cough. A man is close by. So close that he must have heard them.

Stefan turns over and sits up, fumbling his shirt back into his waistband. Ewa's hand slides away from his skin. For a second, she suspends the hand in air, not wanting it to touch, ever again, any surface except the smooth warmth of Stefan's back.

The moment though, has passed, and Ewa feels with a dull thud of certainty that they will not get another chance. She sits up and before she has even realised that she is crying, a teardrop leaves a dark trailing stain on the lilac silk of her blouse.

Stefan's head bobs up above the holly-leaf screen, before he again sinks down.

'It's just Tomasz. We should ignore him.'

But both of them know it is too late.

Ewa shakes her head and straightens her skirt as she stands. Not far off, Tomasz is leaning on a tree trunk and smoking a pipe. He is pretending that he has not yet seen them but is so close that this must be a ruse.

Stefan pushes through the thicket and as Ewa puts on her sweater, she hears him tell Tomasz that there are not enough oil lamps; there must be one for every eighty metres on both sides of the field. Tomasz replies that he will tell Haller and try to get some more. Stefan says that at least fifty men are needed to light and extinguish the lamps when given the commands. Then both men lower their voices and Ewa has the nasty feeling that she is being talked about. Her shoes stay unlaced as she strides towards them.

Tomasz waves. He is wearing a long brown shop-coat.

'Ah, the blushing bride!'

Ewa can only bear to meet his eye for a second. 'I must be going.'

She looks around for her bike as Stefan reaches over and pulls a flake of brown leaf from her hair.

'He says he will give you a lift, at least to the aircraft factory. Your bicycle is already on the back of his truck.'

'I…'

But she is suddenly unable to speak. If she says anything she will weep.

The milk-churn truck, with a rounded bonnet and planked wooden sides, is parked at the edge of the trees. Ewa does not touch Stefan again, hardly looks at him, before she climbs in. The cab smells of chicken shit and straw. Tomasz turns the ignition switch then lets the engine judder as he sucks a spark through the tobacco in his pipe. His cheeks bubble in and out as caramel pipe smoke suffocates the other smells in the cab. From the shadow of the wood, Stefan waves his arm slowly as the truck turns around. But Ewa does not wave back. She is reminded, horribly, of that other farewell beside a train leaving for Warsaw. Could this again be the start of a separation that will last for years? Or forever? Perhaps this time, if she waves back, it will break the spell of bad luck. But Stefan's outline has already melted into the shifting shadows of the trees.

Tomasz drives faster than seems safe on the pot-holed lane. He takes both hands off the steering wheel to change the double gears and Ewa has to hold on to the door as they turn on to the new highway. He revs the engine, pumping his foot on the clutch and flipping the two gear levers back and forth as the truck gains speed. The silhouettes of young poplar trees race across the windscreen. He is clearly trying to impress her. Conversation might at least slow him down, and stop her thinking about the choice she must make tomorrow.

'What do you do in the factory?'

'I'm not supposed to say.'

'As you like.'

'I'm the supervisor in the radio location workshop. That's how I'm able to obtain one of the Neptun receiver systems to send to the Allies. It's all top-secret stuff.'

She snorts, but the engine is probably too loud for him to hear. 'Big, is it? The Neptun?'

'Not especially.'

'Isn't it? I thought that's why the Dakota is coming, because the Neptun is too bulky to send overland with couriers?'

'Well, it's easier to send it by air, of course. But that's not the main reason for the plane coming.'

'What is the main reason?'

'For the passengers.'

She slides Tomasz a sideways glance. More than one passenger then. Has Stefan told him about his plan to take Ewa back to

England? For the first time, she lets herself imagine Stefan leading her by the hand past the whirring propellers of the cargo plane, up the stepladder and into the hold. But Stefan knows that she will not leave without her father.

'And how many passengers will there be?'

Tomasz shrugs, as if this is obvious. 'Apart from your husband, just one.'

Ewa looks out of the window so that he cannot see the flush of anger on her face. If Stefan believes that a copper band around her finger is all that is needed to control her life, he will be in for a shock tomorrow night.

'Ste.., I mean Anatol told you this, did he?'

'Well, I knew about the details of this action some time ago.'

'The action? You mean Operation Eagle?'

The truck is going faster than it should be. The loose bicycle clunks on the empty flatbed and the speedometer waggles uncertainly at the top of the dial.

'That as well.'

She turns to look at him. 'As well as what?'

But the long, low hangars of the aircraft factory have come into view and Tomasz is starting up another performance although in the opposite direction, with the clutch and the double gears. The truck jerks and bumps as it slows.

Then he speaks with the tobacco pipe clenched at one side of his mouth and only one hand on the wheel.

'I thought your husband would have told you by now.'

'Told me what, for God's sake?'

'About his going back on the Dakota.'

'Yes, yes, of course he has.'

'And about the other passenger.'

'Who do you think that person is?'

'I know who it is.'

'Who?'

'Gauleiter Greiser, of course.'

Ewa wills her face to stay blank but it has already gone rigid with horror. What is Tomasz talking about? Why, in God's name, would the most senior Reich officer in Wartheland want to travel to England? And if Greiser is the other passenger, what about Ewa?

Tomasz laughs. 'Ah, sorry! You didn't know.'

He slams his foot on the brake pedal and Ewa jerks forward as the truck comes to a stop by a cluster of birch trees that hides it from the factory gates. The engine ticks and whirrs.

A half-smile is fixed to his mouth. 'Don't worry, we have the action fully prepared.'

Ewa fights the urge to put her hands around his throat and shake him. She pushes on the handle and the door begins to creak open.

'For Christ's sake, either tell me what the nature of this *action* you are talking about is or shut up.'

The half-smile fades as Tomasz chews on the pipe stem.

'Well, I thought you would have been told. Maybe your husband thinks it safer for you not to know.'

'So, are you going to bloody well tell me or not?'

'Well, I suppose I have started now, so I should finish.' Tomasz takes the pipe from his mouth and sighs. 'On Saturday evening, whilst you are doing your best to get Gauleiter Greiser and his cronies drunk, your husband and I will come into your guest house yard and hide behind the toilet block. As soon as Greiser needs a piss we'll nab him, throw him in the back of this truck, and drive him to the landing ground. Then your husband will deliver him to the English on the Dakota. The best present that Mr Churchill has ever had!'

Ewa slides out of the truck and slams the door. And before Tomasz can come to help her, she has lifted her bike off the flatbed, mounted up and is pushing down on the pedals to hurry away. She picks up speed easily, standing up over the seat to ride faster.

Concrete whizzes under the wheels and her thoughts cannot

at first catch up. But it seems that by this time on Sunday, her life will have changed forever. She will either be with Stefan, emerging from the Dakota on to a drizzly airfield with a British intelligence officer asking who the hell she is, or she will be lying half-dead on the floor of a cell in Gestapo HQ. There seems no possibility in between. And Ewa cannot, for the life of her, imagine that either thing will ever really happen.

Posen, Greater German Reich
Saturday 9 October

The Gauleiter's spoon is suspended over a bowl of mushroom soup as he stares at Ewa's dress. Is he scrutinising the homemade cut of the Dirndl that she has copied from a magazine? She has never seen the real thing so the neckline frill and butter-yellow paisley pattern are probably not quite right; a Volksdeutsche attempt at real German. Ewa tries to look at Gauleiter Greiser's thinning hair and not meet his wide calculating eyes. With luck, he is simply admiring her breasts.

Raised voices and throaty laughter are starting to drown out the accordion whine from the gramophone. In the middle of the long crowded table a hand goes up. Ewa does not recognise the reddened face above a collar patch with four pips.

She goes over, smiling. 'Beer, Sturmbannführer?'

'Water. In a jug.'

'Are you sure? There is beer, pale and dark. Or wine?'

His eyes pin her. 'Water, I said.'

Her heart thumps. 'Yes, Sturmbannführer, of course.'

She leaves the dining room and hurries along the passageway into the kitchen, heart still pounding. The diners should have been in a celebratory mood tonight and there is no clear reason for their abruptness. Ewa shudders as the cold tap screeches into an earthenware jug. All of the glass pitchers are already full of beer that no one is drinking.

Outside, the old town hall clock strikes nine tinny chimes. Above the electric-lit yard, black gable-rimmed rooftops pattern the moon-pearl sky. There is no cloud at all. Nothing to stop the Dakota.

Perhaps Stefan and Tomasz are already out there behind the toilet block, waiting. Ewa tries to focus on the decision she must make. It will be the most important of her life; more momentous than choosing to go on the DV list, or to join the AK or even to marry Stefan. And, although he does not know it yet, Ewa's choice will be the turning point of her father's life too. But all that her brain can seem to consider is the state of the Schnitzels that are toughening in the stove whilst the Strudels turn soggy. Her mind would rather keep count of loaves and beer jugs than imagine how she will get herself and her father on to a transport plane to London in only three hours' time.

'Eva.'

Water splashes up from the rim of the jug, spattering her yellow bodice. She flinches but remembers to smile.

'Yes, Heinrich?'

'Could I trouble you for another basket of bread? The soup is delicious and some of the diners wish to wipe out their bowls.'

'Of course. I will bring it.'

'Shall I carry something for you?'

'No, no, please don't trouble yourself. But you are very kind.'

Her heart is beating too fast. She goes to the dresser, wraps a white linen cloth around the end of a dark brown loaf and cuts slices from it. Beck stands by the door, hands in the pockets of his wide trousers. His black jacket is buttoned right up to the metal cross at his collar.

'This is a big night for you, Eva.'

She keeps her eyes down. Does he know something? Has Stefan, God forbid, already told him where the smelly suitcase will be going and how it will get there? But that would be madness. She must assume that Beck knows nothing, and keep acting as though there is nothing to know.

The sharpened knife cuts dark bread into thin even slices.

'It is such an honour to host the Gauleiter's celebration. Do you think he is happy with the menu? And the surroundings?'

Beck nods. 'I heard him say how delightful the small German establishments in the city can be.'

Ewa puts the bread with its white cloth into a basket and takes the jug in her other hand. Beck lets her pass, clicking his heels softly as he moves out of her way.

In the dining room, Ewa stands against the wall watching men mop soup. The red-faced Sturmbannführer is loud and annoying. He bellows to his neighbour about the time he commandeered a newly assembled 190 from the Focke-Wulf factory here in Posen and made the test pilot fly to RHSA headquarters in Berlin, landing right on Prinz Albrecht Strasse. He laughs raucously but he is not drinking. No one is. Not even beer. Greiser sits with an untouched glass of Riesling.

Alenka, the liaison girl sent by Haller, stands awkwardly in a summer dress at the other side of room. Ewa signals to her to start clearing the bowls then follows her into the kitchen with a loaded tray. As they stack smeared crockery into the sink, Ewa lowers her voice into Polish.

'Alenka. When you serve the veal you must ask each man if he wants wine or beer.'

'Speak to them?'

'Yes. Say *Wein oder Bier*? Can you say that?'

'Wein... oder Bier.'

'Yes, that's right. And tell them we have Riesling.'

Alenka frowns. 'I don't know German, miss.'

'Try to say what I've told you. It's not hard.'

Alenka nods but her eyes are hostile. Ewa wonders why Haller could not have sent someone with even a smattering of the correct language.

Ewa picks up a platter of Schnitzels and tells Alenka to follow behind her with the bowl of steaming potatoes. At the door of the dining room, Ewa puts on her brightest smile and gestures for Alenka to do the same. As Ewa serves the Schnitzels, she asks each officer if he would care for beer or Riesling with his main course. All the answers are the same: *just water*.

Foreboding tightens Ewa's chest as she glances at the wall clock. Twenty past nine. The clock's hands are moving too quickly. She still has no clue what she should do, or even what she wants to happen next. So she goes on smiling, pouring water, listening. Conversations buzz through the room; compliments about the renovations on the Great Golden Hall of the castle and snide comments about Gauleiters from other parts of the Reich. There is a discussion about the wisdom of Reichsführer Himmler's recommendation to kidnap Aryan-looking children from Poles. But nothing is said about transport planes or insurgents.

Ewa sees her father squat beside the red-faced Sturmbannführer who says something into his ear. She hopes it is not a complaint about the food.

And still, no one touches the beer. Ewa cannot understand it. Even at breakfast most of the officers will have more than one glass each. She glances at Beck who is not eating or drinking, just smoking. He catches her eye and, oddly, he winks. This is not something she has seen him do before. Coldness runs down her back.

Then a short man in a checked suit stands up in front of Ewa, his blue eyes level with hers.

'Tell that Pole to shut up.'

Ewa's mouth goes dry. The hunting horns hanging crosswise on the wall seem to waver.

'I'm sorry?'

'Her bad German is annoying us.'

'Yes, of course. My apologies. Can I get you a drink?'

'No.'

Ewa feels suddenly sick. She hurries out to the kitchen and fills a beer tankard with water drinking the whole thing in one go as she stares at the empty sky. Then her father comes into the kitchen. Ewa turns to see him at the drop-down shelf of the dresser, slicing Strudel with a meat knife. A bloom of warm apple and pastry fills the air.

He looks up. 'Are you all right?'

Ewa wipes her mouth with the back of her hand and nods. 'You should use a serrated blade. That one will make the pastry crumble. Do they like it?'

'What?'

'The Schnitzel.'

'No complaints.' Oskar's cheeks are very red under the grey moustache. 'Take in the cognac. It's our last bottle. But put it on the table and let them help themselves.'

'They won't drink it. They haven't drunk anything.'

He shrugs. 'Let's have a last try. We won't make any profit on tonight if we can't charge for drinks.'

Another good reason to ply them with drink, as well as the stupid hope that they might not miss their most senior officer until he is airborne above their heads in a Dakota.

As Ewa goes back into the dining room, Greiser glances up and catches her eye. She forces a smile and places the Cognac bottle with a miniature glass in front of him on the table. He does not, as she thinks he might, tell her to take them away, but goes on cutting into his Schnitzel, chewing on veal, swallowing. He does not look her way again. Some of the other men have finished eating and are leaning back on their chairs, smoking or sipping glasses of water. Beck has disappeared.

As Greiser lays down his knife and fork, Ewa's heart skips a beat. Is he about to throw his napkin on to the table and head for the latrines? Perhaps she should try to stop him. Stefan and Tomasz may be in position but Ewa is not ready. Not ready to make her choice; not ready to leave her home. But the Gauleiter stays in his chair and takes the fat cigar offered by his neighbour, lighting it from a candle flame on the table.

Ewa clears dirty plates, piling one on top of another, squashing mashed potato, cabbage and gravy between the layers, feeling the weight of the mess. If she leaves on the Dakota, who will wash these dishes? Not her. Not tonight. Not ever again. She takes the plates to the kitchen and heaps them by the sink. Her father puts a hand on her shoulder.

'Go to bed as soon as they have gone. I'll wash up.'

A pain, like a punch, passes through her chest. 'Thank you, Papa. But I don't mind doing them in the morning. You should rest too.'

Her bed suddenly seems like the place in the world where she wants to be more than any other. If only time could stand still. If only Stefan had not come back.

Steam rises from cinnamon-laced apple in the shallow bowls that Ewa carries into the dining room on a tray. Around the long table, all collars are buttoned and ties still knotted. The cognac is untouched. And Beck is still not there. She imagines him in the latrine pissing, only inches away from Stefan who will have squeezed himself by now into the gap between the toilet block and the yard wall. Perhaps Stefan is watching Beck through a crack in the wood. The thought brings a clutch of panic to her chest.

At the sideboard, Alenka is struggling with a pile of plates. Ewa comes up behind her and whispers in Polish.

'Can you manage alone for a minute?'

'Not really. Where are you going?'

'Just to check the state of the toilet block in the yard.'

Alenka's eyes dart. 'Is everything all right? Anything I should know… about my work?'

Ewa gives a fleeting shake of her head. 'All is fine. Nothing of note to pass on. Don't forget the cream.'

In the light of the misshapen moon, the yard is colourless

except for a spill of yellow light from the toilet block. Cold air bites Ewa's bare throat as she stands and listens. A car engine accelerates on a nearby street, distant hooves click on cobbles, but the yard itself is silent. Is Stefan here? She cannot bring herself to look.

She goes to the half-open door of the toilet chalet and makes a fist to knock.

'Hallo? Hygiene service!' Her voice is a squeak. She coughs and tries again. 'Hygiene service!'

There is no reply. She steps inside. The toilet block is cold and clean and still smells of scouring powder. The bare bulb flickers above the urinal. Both cubicle doors are open far enough to reveal the high cisterns and handle chains. The chalet is empty as a mausoleum. And if Stefan and Tomasz are on the other side of the thin wooden wall they give no sign.

A shadow crosses the open door and hair rises on Ewa's neck. 'Eva.'

She goes to the doorway. 'Heinrich. You startled me.'

'Did I? Are you nervous about something?'

'Maybe a little stressed.'

'Don't worry. The evening has been a great success.'

'Has it?'

She steps out into the chill air and stands beside him. 'But hardly any beer has been drunk. And no wine or cognac.'

He shrugs and leans his shoulder against the chalet wall. 'I think some of the diners are feeling the effects of too many formal dinners this week. It is surprising that there is any beer left in the city.'

High above them, an unseen aeroplane thrums. Before she can stop herself, Ewa looks up.

Beck puts his head to one side. 'A big one is coming in, don't you think?'

Ewa's insides freeze. Sweet Jesus. Can he mean the Dakota?

He waves his hand into the plume of cigarette smoke from his mouth. 'You like aeroplanes, don't you, Eva?'

'I… yes.' Her smile should be brighter, but she cannot quite get her face under control. 'Why do you ask?'

'Your father told me that before the war you used to go to the Aero Club to watch the planes and meet the pilots.'

Ewa nods but her mouth is too dry to speak.

Beck sighs. 'I wish I could take you there still. Even though I am not a pilot.' He comes closer. His uniform is stiff with braid and metal badges. 'Would you come with me, Eva, if the club were to re-open?'

Ewa's heart drops a beat. 'Of course, Heinrich. But that is not likely, is it?'

'Who knows? At this moment in the war, everything seems so finely balanced. No one can say what the future might hold. Do you not think that too?'

He knows something. Ewa has no doubt, and she cannot bear to hear him say any more. She must stop him talking. She puts a ringless hand on his sleeve and squeezes it.

'I'm glad we have so much in common, Heinrich.'

He looks down at her hand and then into her eyes. An expression of pure joy crosses his face.

'Eva…'

Then his mouth comes towards hers, as she expected that it might, but it is too late to pull away. Beck folds himself over her, his lips warm and parted. His tongue touches hers and a thread of uncontrollable heat passes through her. Beck's thigh presses into the fold of yellow cotton between Ewa's legs. Without her quite knowing how it has happened, their bodies are entwined.

Beck's lips murmur against her ear. 'My God, Eva… you want it too.'

She starts to push him away. 'Later, Heinrich.'

'Yes, darling Eva.' He smiles and strokes a fingertip along her lips. 'Come to me later.'

Ewa knows then that she no longer has a choice. Tonight,

she must leave the only home she has ever known and she will probably never return.

But in that instant Beck's arm is wrenched away. A strap, looped around his throat, yanks back his head. He drops, and is dragged to the ground. Ewa stands stunned as dark figures with flat caps pulled down over their eyes tug at the writhing black uniform on the ground. Beck splutters but cannot speak. Arms flail as the men wrap rope around thrashing limbs.

One of the figures raises his fist and turns his face to the toilet block's yellow light. Stefan's cool eyes meet Ewa's. And, still looking into her eyes, his fist slams down in a single heavy punch to the middle of Beck's face.

Ewa sways. Her hand is clamped over her mouth. Now, Stefan and another figure are lugging Beck's limp body towards the yard gate. Beck's taste is still in Ewa's mouth. Nausea rises. She puts a hand to the chalet wall and bends over to spit a fat gob of saliva onto the asphalt. Before she can straighten, a hand has gripped her upper arm and is pulling her towards the gate.

Stefan's mouth is in her hair. 'The suitcase.'

She cannot speak.

'Where's the suitcase?'

She heaves her arm but his grip is firm.

'My father...'

'No. There's no time.'

By the back door, a man's laugh booms from inside the guest house, but Stefan has pulled Ewa almost to the gate.

'We can't leave Papa.' Her voice is louder. 'Please let me get Papa.'

'Then we'll all be dead.'

'Stefan, please.'

'Quiet!' He hisses at her. His grip is starting to hurt. 'Get in the truck.'

The milk-churn truck is not far from the back gate, engine running. The headlights are on but dimmed to slits with tape.

Stefan pushes Ewa into the cab then climbs in behind her so that she squashes up against Tomasz who is at the wheel. Tomasz heaves the handbrake free and the truck jerks forward. Ewa's bare knee scrapes against the metal dashboard. Wetness slips down her shin.

Tomasz drives slowly but keeps the gear high so that the truck feels quiet and loose. Ewa falls against him as they turn the corner. The cab reeks of petrol and sweat. Moonlight stipples the shuttered street.

'The suitcase.' Stefan's eyes flash in the half-light. 'Where is it?'

'We have to go back for my father.'

Ewa surprises herself with the calmness of her voice. But she is drained of feeling. Even her shin is numb.

'He'll be all right. Let's just get the case.'

'No, Stefan. Not unless we get Papa first.'

'Fuck, Ewa.' Stefan bangs the door hard with the side of his fist. 'Tell me where it is.'

'Not without my father.'

Brakes scream suddenly and Ewa braces her hand against the dashboard. The truck judders to a stop, engine pulsing. Tomasz drapes his arms over the steering wheel and stares at Stefan.

'What in Christ's name is going on?'

Stefan growls through his teeth. 'Keep driving, but slowly.'

'No. Not until you tell me what your wife is doing here when she should be plying the enemy with cognac and coffee. And why all that you two seem bothered about is who forgot the suitcase for your little vacation. While you're at it, you can tell me why we've got the wrong sodding Hitlerite.'

Stefan's eyes narrow. 'Pull off the street.'

Tomasz rolls his eyes but keeps the engine low as they turn into a narrow side street with high warehouse walls on each side. He glances in the side mirrors then lets the truck roll to a stop.

'What do you propose we do with lover-boy out there on the flatbed?'

Stefan's voice is taut. 'We'll take him with us.'

'To the landing field? The komendant will hit the roof.'

'We'll tell him what it was, a mistake. But one that does not really matter. SS-Obersturmführer is still a high rank.'

'You mean you want to put that joker on the Dakota, instead of Greiser?'

'Why not?'

'The AK would be a laughing stock. We can't go to all this trouble to send a nobody on our first air bridge.'

A shadow slithers across the moonlit cobbles and the cat's shriek gives Ewa a jolt of sudden certainty.

'You must kill him.'

Stefan and Tomasz both turn to look at her. She did not realise what she was about to say until the words formed in her mouth, but now she has no doubt that she is right. How else to prove to Stefan that her embrace with Beck meant nothing? How else to protect herself and her father now that Beck knows she is working for the AK?

Tomasz shakes his head but Ewa is fired with conviction.

'Why not? Shoot him now. Get rid of him. He's not worth taking to England. And if something goes wrong and the SS get him back alive, we're all finished.'

The firmness in her own voice startles her. She sees that this is also a test for Stefan to prove that he is not secretly conspiring with the SS-Obersturmführer.

Tomasz gives a slow whistle. 'She's right.'

But Stefan leans across Ewa, ignoring her, and points his finger into Tomasz's face. 'Listen, you fuck, I am the senior officer here. And I say no. Nothing will go wrong and I will take the Obersturmführer with me to England...' he turns to Ewa, 'instead of the suitcase.'

Lüssow, Greater German Reich
Saturday 9 October

As the truck slows to pass the railway station, the sky above the illuminated porticos seems caged by a grid of black tram wires. Ewa puts a disguising hand across her face when she sees the station guard but Tomasz gives him a thumbs-up and then they are out on to the new highway and speeding away from the city.

Stefan is rigid beside Ewa, his skin grey in the moonlight. Cold air seeps into the cab.

'You don't know what you've done, Ewa.'

'Don't I?' She bunches the thin cotton of the Dirndl into her fists. 'There's nothing in your precious suitcase that would change anyone's mind. Not if they have good reason to believe in a lie.'

'That is bullshit.'

His voice makes something icy take hold of Ewa's heart and twist it.

Tomasz bangs the steering wheel. 'What the hell is this suitcase? And why is Fritz out there a substitute for it?'

Stefan's voice is monotone. 'Just drive.'

Ewa thinks of Beck, lying bound and stiff with pain an arm's length away. Is he struggling to escape? And if he is not… why not? A sudden thought bleaches into her brain. Have Stefan and Beck planned this together from the start? Even the kiss in the yard that seemed to provoke Stefan's assault could have just been a way to hide their collusion. Ewa turns to look at Stefan's handsome profile in the grey light, but his face is blank.

The city is behind them. Thin headlight beams illuminate a wedge of road ahead as the truck picks up speed. Tomasz drives fast, not seeming to care that he can see almost nothing. Ewa keeps her eyes on her skirt but she feels Stefan's every breath.

A sick emptiness creeps into her stomach as she imagines what might be happening at the guest house. Have they noticed Beck missing from the dining room? Is her father wondering whether Ewa has already gone to bed? She cannot bring herself to imagine more. Neither can she let herself consider what might be about to happen at the landing ground.

The truck bumps off the highway and along a track between ever-darkening trees. Then it pulls to a shuddering stop. Headlights slice across a group of men with flat caps and hunting rifles. Then Haller is at the driver's door.

He shines his torch into Ewa's face. 'Mother of God. Get out. All of you!'

Ewa follows torchlight to the rear of the truck. Haller yanks open the tailgate and Tomasz grapples Beck to the edge of the flatbed. The torch shines across Beck's soiled black jacket with its red armband, and then on to his face. The skin is shiny and yellow; the eye folded into his cheek. A rope gags the mess of his mouth.

The torch beam goes to Stefan's face.

Haller's voice is quiet. 'So, start explaining.'

'We got the wrong one, unfortunately. But nothing else has changed. And the Neptun is here.'

Perhaps only Ewa can detect the fear in Stefan's voice.

'Nothing has changed? You really think that?' Haller's head jerks towards the men with rifles. 'Get this piece of horseshit out of my truck.'

Ewa jumps back as Beck, arms and legs bound, is dragged on to the mud. Nearby, metal jangles and a horse fidgets. Shadows waver between moonlit trees as Haller swipes torchlight over the unmoving body. Then he drills light on to the face.

'SS-Obersturmführer. Heinrich Beck. God in heaven.'

The shaft of light pivots up on to Stefan.

'What, in Christ's name, is going on?'

'A mistake, Komendant. Like I said. But what's the difference?

Taking either him or Greiser would be a propaganda victory. And I know for a fact that this one has secrets that will be valuable to Poland.'

Haller gives a dry laugh. 'Like the new names of streets in the Jewish Quarter?' Haller's beam glares onto Ewa. 'And her? Why is she here?'

Ewa winces but Stefan's flat tone does not change.

'She got caught up in the struggle in the yard. It wasn't safe for her to return into the guest house.'

'What a complete cock-up.'

Ewa hears herself speak. 'But now I am here, I can pass on my communication to you in person.'

'And what would that be?'

She does not miss a beat. 'The Dakota must not land.'

And as she says the words, Ewa realises that this is indeed the best solution. If the Dakota stays in the sky, the AK's reception party will melt back into the trees. Stefan will not go to England and, as long as Heinrich Beck is disposed of, Ewa will be able to return to the guest house as if almost nothing has happened.

Stefan goes up to Haller. 'Don't listen to her. She does not know what she is talking about.'

With a hard hand, Haller pushes him away. 'I will decide that.' He turns to Ewa. 'Young lady? Tell us what you know.'

She thinks back to the warm smoke-filled dining room, the smell of gravy, buzz of voices.

'Something is not right. Greiser and his party didn't drink.'

Haller pauses. 'None of them?'

'Not even beer.'

Close by, there is a sudden lash of water. Ewa jerks round and Haller's torch beam carves across the butter-yellow skirt and on to black trees. But it is just a horse pissing on mud.

'That's a worry, but not enough to call off the landing.'

Ewa steps closer to Haller. 'And SS-Obersturmführer Beck knows something.'

Stefan lurches towards her but Haller puts up a hand to stop him.

Ewa speaks with sudden confidence. 'He was listening for a plane, a big one he said, and looking at the sky.'

Haller stands silent for a moment and then nods. 'Someone put a jacket over this girl's dress. It's too bloody bright.' He takes a step towards the figure on the ground and then rams his farm boot into Beck's ear. *'Aufwachen!'*

Another thwack of boot on skull brings a flimsy groan from the ground. Then Haller kneels and speaks calmly into Beck's ear whilst roughly untying the rope from his mouth.

'What do you know about tonight? Why were they not drinking?'

His German is fluid with the sing-song lilt of the region. Beck does not reply.

'Answer me, Heinrich.' Haller moves the rope to Beck's neck. 'Or shall we try Polish eh, *Henryk? Odpowiedz mi!'*

Beck groans again and Haller looks up at Stefan. 'Well, comrade? Do you want to try?'

But Stefan is staring through the mesh of branches at the slate-grey sky. 'Listen.'

Then Ewa hears it – the distant hum of engines.

Stefan looks back at Haller. 'It's coming. You must give the order for the flare path, Komendant.'

For long seconds, Haller looks from Stefan to Ewa and then at the rumbling sky. At last, he turns and waves his rifle. A roaring flash of orange light rips through the darkness. The carthorse, squealing and rearing up in its traces, is silhouetted against the flames from a blazing oil drum. Colours slick over Beck's bruised skin like petrol on dirty water.

From the row of men with flat caps and moustaches, one comes to Haller, rifle in hand. Ewa hears some of the words murmured between them: *landing code, stable lamps, transmitter.* A jacket is draped around Ewa's shoulders. The sweet heavy smell of Mokri tobacco enfolds her. Someone pushes her to follow the rustle of Haller's footsteps to the edge of the trees. She must keep up, and she must think of a way to change Haller's mind and stop the Dakota from landing.

Beneath the sweep of the sky, grey grass stretches into the ashen distance. Ewa's neck is clammy inside the rough collar of the jacket but she has started shivering and cannot seem to stop. A harness jangles and hooves stamp but the distant engine-hum is deepening. It can only be the Dakota.

'It's coming.' Haller strides into the bouncing orange light, an oversized pistol in his hand. His voice cracks through the snarl of oil-drum flames. 'Action stations!'

One by one, stable lamps are set alight at exact intervals along the edge of the clover field. The grey grass mutates to an eerie nocturnal green.

The Dakota's engines are thundering now, almost overhead. The roar vibrates through Ewa's chest as the plane passes low over the trees, propeller-engines churning on the black wings. It is a very big plane, as big as any she has seen. A white light winks, again and again, from the bull-nosed cockpit.

Stefan comes up to Haller. 'And now you must give the order to start the Morse code signals.'

'Shut up, Bergel. Don't tell me what to do.'

Stefan's hand is on Haller's arm. 'Listen to me. The Dakota is about to make its landing circuit. The cockpit signaller is asking us for permission to turn on the lights. You must give the signal from the ground or the pilot will not make his approach.'

Still Haller does not move.

'For God's sake…' Stefan pulls his jacket back and tucks it behind something in his waistband. His hand hovers at his side, '…give the order.'

Haller turns to face him. 'Are you threatening me?'

He sounds unsurprised.

With a cold creep of certainty about what she must do, Ewa

feels herself moving forward until she is standing next to Haller. One side of his face is orange in the barrel's flame-light.

'Don't listen to my husband. The plane must not land.'

'Why? What do you know?'

'He and Obersturmführer Beck have been plotting something together. It's no mistake that Beck is here.'

'No! Ewa, you're wrong. That's bullshit.' Stefan's voice cracks. 'Jesus! The Dakota is ready to come down. For Christ's sake, Haller, give the order, tell them to land!'

Ewa's voice is firm. 'Don't trust what he says. Call it off.'

Stefan turns to her, pleading. 'Jesus, Ewa. Ewa!'

She does not look at him. It is for his good as much as hers that she is doing this. He might not think it at this moment, but he is much better off not returning to England. And, as long as Beck is out of the way for good, Ewa can return to the guest house tonight. She rubs her hands up her icy forearms. If only she had the strength and the imagination to kill Beck herself.

The Dakota's snub-nosed outline passes over the far grove of trees, engines growling. As it banks for a final circuit of the landing field, the plane's black outline pivots on its wingtip against the pearl sky. A pinprick of light in the cockpit winks.

Haller takes a stubby pistol from his belt and loads it with one fat round, then stretches his arm into the air as if about to start a race. In one swift movement, Stefan jumps forward grabbing Haller's arm, trying to push it down and point the flare gun at the ground. But with his left hand, Haller lands a punch on the underside of Stefan's chin. Stefan clutches his mouth with both hands and reels back.

A shot cracks. Red light threads up in to darkness. For a moment, the firework flare hangs high above the field in a chalky waft of powder. Haller stands, feet apart, and lowers his arm. He is looking, as everyone is, at the red-tinted sky. The Dakota's cockpit has gone black. The plane's nose turns slowly upwards towards the oval moon and the wheels fold gently back into the wings.

Ewa stands frozen in the flare's red light. Then, she looks round. Stefan has taken a step backwards, his right arm stiff at his side. His profile is sharp against the oil-drum flames; blood is smeared over his mouth, his eyes are unblinking. His pace quickens as he scuttles back to the edge of the trees where Beck lies still on the ground. Nearby, a sudden flash exposes Tomasz with his rifle raised.

Then, a shot, very close, rips through the stillness. And when Ewa looks across the landing field, Haller is, for some reason, sitting slumped on the grass with his legs stretched out in front of him. His hand, holding the flare gun, rests limply on the ground.

Ewa's eyes drift over the unnatural colours of the nighttime countryside as her mind tries to process what is happening. The open field is illuminated by the blazing oil drum and remnants of the red flare. And on the far side of the landing strip, inside another copse of trees, strange white lights are twinkling. These dots of whiteness begin to stretch and grow, becoming trails of burning light. Then, they blast out of the black branches, and are coming closer.

Ewa stands, paralysed, as quiet punches of air seem to surround her. The carthorse whinnies then screams. But Ewa still cannot move. Her eyes become transfixed by hunched grey figures in close-fitting helmets who are coming across the field towards her, running and firing. Something whistles past her neck leaving a breath of air. Shadows skitter.

'*Runter!*'

Get down! Did someone say it? Ewa drops to the ground.

Stefan, she is sure it is him, crouches as he runs across the grass. But she cannot tell whether he is heading towards the grey helmets or away from them.

Ewa lies flat, pressing her face into the damp earth. It smells mouldy and comforting. Blades of grass tickle her cheek and dew seeps through her skirt on to her knees. If the firing stops, just for a moment, she will look up and work out which way to run.

Gingerly, she rests her chin on the mud and her eye catches the bright egg of the moon. Beside it, the Dakota's dark outline stands upright on its tail as it climbs. Then Ewa's face is slammed against the ground. Her teeth bite into soil. She tries to cry out but her tongue is pushed against grass. Her arms rip backwards. Wire bites her wrists. Something inside her flattened nose goes pop.

A rough hand is on the back of her head, scooping up hair and jerking her head back. Tape is pressed over her eyes and mouth. And then her whole body seems to be pulled upright by the roots of her hair. Her feet stumble, shoeless as she struggles to balance. Hands grip her upper arms. Lips and warm breath brush her ear, and the voice that comes from them is vaguely familiar.

'Don't worry, Fräulein. I've got you.'

 ## Gestapo HQ Posen, Greater German Reich
Sunday 10 October

Window bars blacken against a blanching sky. In the corner of the cell, a bleary-eyed girl squats, swaying over a half-full bucket until her trickle becomes a drip. She wipes herself with a bare hand and dries it on her coat. Ewa knows it can't be long until she must go over there too. She closes her eyes.

Since the metal door slammed in the dark, she has been crouching motionless but awake against the wall. Every sound in the night – an engine revving, a drunken shout, the fizz of electricity, a woman's stifled sob – has brought with it a spasm of fear.

In the cell, five women are sleeping under greasy blankets

on two plank beds. They grumbled as Ewa was thrown in with them but soon went back to sleep. Even though Ewa saw nothing beyond the blindfold as she was brought into the building, she has no doubt about where she is. There were at least six flights of stairs, so this cell must be high enough for the window not to be opaqued with cement.

One of the women snorts but Ewa decides not to open her eyes. Now the others are waking, she will pretend to be asleep. All of her concentration should focus on her cover story which must be simple and stuck to no matter what. Perhaps if she rehearses the details over and over in her mind she will prepare herself for the ordeals ahead. Everyone knows what goes on inside this anonymous office block; cigarettes stubbed out on the soles of feet, fingernails pulled out one by one with pincers. And there must be plenty more tortures as yet unknown. Yes, she must concentrate. But she can think of nothing except last night.

The separate events have already fractured in her memory and their sequence is now unclear. There was certainly an ambush from the trees by troops well hidden and waiting, waiting no doubt for the Dakota to land before making their move. Could the Gestapo know, by now, that it was Ewa's words to Haller that stopped the plane from landing? Perhaps they had already been told that, by the same person who had tipped them off about the Dakota in the first place…

'Hey, you. Over there…'

Ewa opens one eye. The woman's hair is spiked with grips in the tangled remnant of an elaborate roll; the dress under her cheap coat is cut low across her large bosom.

'… what are you, then… some sort of *Volksdeutsche*?'

Ewa looks down. The butter-yellow skirt is ripped and smeared but she is still wearing her homemade Dirndl and frilly white blouse.

'I'm a waitress.'

The other occupants of the cell rub their eyes and prop

themselves up. The big-breasted woman looks Ewa over then folds her arms.

'And that's your uniform, is it?'

'Yes.'

'And very nicely it goes with your yellow hair.'

'It's peroxide.'

'Like I say, very nice.'

The woman glances at the others and smirks.

A scrawny girl on the smaller bed lifts her head like a deer in a trap. She whispers to a pock-marked woman next to her then sits up and reaches into her coat pocket.

'Here.'

She stretches out a hand to Ewa with a slice of dry black bread. Ewa blinks and takes it, but shakes her head at the chipped china cup that the big-breasted woman is holding out. The woman looks offended.

'What? Too dirty for you? Think you're going to catch something?'

Across the cell someone titters.

Ewa lifts one shoulder. 'I'm not thirsty.'

'Like hell you're not. Go on girl, drink some water, and eat a bit of bread. You're less likely to throw up if you do. And we've cleaned up enough vomit in this shithole.'

Ewa chews the sawdust bread and washes it down with a gulp of eggy water. She realises that her nostrils are getting used to the toilet stench of the piss bucket combined with unwashed bodies and menstrual blood. Perhaps it does not take long to get used to anything.

The big woman puts her hands on her hips. 'I'm Walentina.' Her head goes to one side as Ewa chews. 'Nice to meet you too, dearie.'

'Ewa.' She wipes her mouth with her hand then slides a look at Walentina. 'Have you been in here long?'

'Any time here is too long.'

'Why? What do they do to you?'

'Depends what you've done, sweetheart.' Walentina raises an eyebrow. 'What have you done?'

'I don't know.'

'Come on. You must know why they've picked you up.'

Ewa shakes her head. Stick to the story; don't change it, no matter what.

'I've done nothing.'

'Well then,' Walentina perches her large behind on the edge of the plank bed, 'I couldn't say what will happen.' She leans over and takes the cup out of Ewa's hand. 'But don't worry, darling. In that dress, you'll be right up their alley.'

She laughs and the others join in to a chorus of cackling and coughing so raucous that Ewa does not hear a key turn in the cell door. The guard's eyes scan the room but fix on the yellow Dirndl. Ewa flushes hot and then cold and cannot stand without leaning against the wall. It has started.

The guard leads her along a shiny linoleum corridor, and then another, to an office. The room is ordinary; a small modern window, a filing cabinet, two desks. Behind one of the desks is a man in field grey. It takes Ewa a moment to recognise him; his face looks less red under the neon glare. But as soon as he starts to speak, she remembers the same self-satisfied voice telling a story about an F-W190 landing on Prinz Albrecht Strasse, and the same voice, the same words even, in her ear at the landing ground.

'Don't worry, Fräulein.' The Sturmbannführer is smiling but his eyes are full of hate. 'There's no point lying. We know everything about you.'

Ewa wants to convince herself that he is bluffing, but she is suddenly without the strength to do anything for herself. Just staying upright in front of the desk takes all of her concentration. There is no chair in the room apart from his.

'Let's start at the beginning, shall we? September 1940. You joined the AK as a liaison girl...'

'I am a waitress.'

'And not a very good one. Please shut up until you are asked to speak.' He glances down at a paper on the desk. White flakes powder the shoulders of his jacket. 'So, at first you used to meet someone you knew as Marek from the aeroplane factory. Or at least, you walked past him on the bridge at dusk and he would pass you an envelope to put in your basket when no one was looking. That's right, isn't it?'

She feels herself start to sway. Concentrate on his shoulders. Count the flakes of dandruff.

'I don't know what you are talking about. I help my father run the Hartman guest house. That's all I've done since the war...'

His fist crashes onto the table. Papers flutter. Behind her, the guard takes a step closer. *One flake, two flakes, three...*

The Sturmbannführer sits back in his chair. 'And then you were promoted, given a noiseless typewriter and possibly a microfilm camera. Did you have a camera?'

Four flakes, five... His voice drifts underwater.

'Can I sit down?'

'No.'

He puts his elbows on the table and rests his chin on clasped hands. 'Not unless you stop this waitress crap. Stop denying things that we already know to be true.'

Somebody, obviously, has talked. Marek? But he disappeared months ago. Denial seems futile. They seem to know everything already. But if she confesses, will it make things better or worse? If only she could sit down she might be able to decide.

'So, tell me, were you given a microfilm camera?'

'No.'

'But you had a noiseless typewriter?'

'No.'

She does not see where the blow comes from, does not even feel it at first. Then pain drills into her body with such force that she cannot even cry out. Her teeth are clamped together, grinding. The guard steps away, thudding a short rubber truncheon against his palm. Then the ache bursts into the side of Ewa's head and water blurs her eyes. Her knees soften. She fastens her eyes on a black scuff mark on the white wall. Stand, don't fall.

The Sturmbannführer rolls his eyes. 'If you're pretending that you're about to faint it won't work. All of our methods have been scientifically tested. A sharp blow behind the ear delivers extreme pain without ever resulting in unconsciousness.'

Ewa tries to keep all of her weight in her feet, like one of those toys that always comes upright after being knocked over.

'So, I'll ask you again, and remember – we know the answer. Did you have a noiseless typewriter?'

Ewa licks her lips. The pain on the side of her head is easing. She can take it.

'No.'

'What was that?'

The Sturmbannführer scrapes back his chair and walks around the desk. His eyes are level with hers.

'What did you say?'

'No. I am just a waitress.'

Her voice is a whisper, but he hears it.

'This stubbornness will have serious consequences. Not just for yourself but for others also. You should know that your father is here awaiting interrogation.'

She rocks, one foot jerking back to steady herself, as dread descends. Her father. If she yells *he knows nothing!* that would only admit that there is something to know. And, in truth, Ewa has no idea what her father might already have guessed about the reasons for her comings and goings with a basket over her arm when there was no shopping to be done. Anything he suspects might be tortured out of him. Perhaps they will kill him. And it will be Ewa's fault.

The Sturmbannführer's fishy breath is in her face. He is close enough for each fleck of dandruff to take on its own distinctive shape.

'Tell me then, Fräulein Hartman, exactly what it was you were doing in a farmer's field at one in the morning without a coat?'

'Meeting my lover.'

Has she said it too quick? Does it sound too rehearsed?

'Your lover? You surprise me. I thought you were a girl with very high morals.' He steps backwards to perch on the desk. 'And who is he, your lover?'

'Jerzy.'

'Jerzy who?'

'I... I'm not sure of his second name.'

The Sturmbannführer looks genuinely shocked. 'You really do surprise me.'

'I... we hadn't known each other long.'

'But long enough to fuck him in a field?' He shakes his head and picks a half-smoked cigarette out of the ashtray. 'Why that field?'

'That's where we used to meet. He lives nearby with his brother.'

'And your coat, or rather the lack of one?'

Good question. She blinks and remembers Stefan's jacket amongst the leaf-shreds.

'I laid it on the ground for us.'

'For you... to copulate on?'

She nods and gulps down a retch in her throat. *Stefan. Stefan.* She wonders if she even says his name. But if Stefan had not dragged her from the yard, she might not even be here.

'Let me get this clear. You spend Saturday in the kitchen, working hard all day to prepare an admittedly decent meal for the Gauleiter. Then you wait on us all, more or less attentively. But before the dessert is fully served you become so consumed by an itch between your legs that you cycle fifteen kilometres through the night to fuck some Polish peasant in a field.' His eye twitches. 'Like a yelping bitch on heat.'

If she nods or speaks or even catches his eye she will throw up.

He lights the dead cigarette and sucks hard to revive it. 'And you and your lover just happened to be fornicating in the same field that had been prepared as a landing strip for the arrival of a Douglas Dakota C-47 that very same night.'

Slowly, with her hair falling over her eyes, she nods.

'What was that?'

'Yes.'

For a few seconds she is aware of his eyes searching her face. She keeps her own eyes open and focuses on his left shoulder. Suddenly, her arms are dragged behind her and wire cuts into her wrists. Her fists and eyes clench shut as she waits for the pain.

But the impact, when it comes, is no more than the light tap of a finger against her forehead. Through a squint, she sees the Sturmbannführer's knuckles hovering in front of her face. Again, he taps her brow.

'Hallo! Anybody at home?' He laughs and throws a wink at the guard. Then the Sturmbannführer's leer evaporates.

'Take her to the white room.'

 ## Gestapo HQ Posen, Greater German Reich
Sunday 10 October

Hard hands grip Ewa's arms and pull her, stumbling, along a well-lit corridor. She tries to weep, to scream. At each door she wants to cry out *Papa!* but her voice is gone. His poor broken body could be slumped behind any one of them. And yet it is just as likely that Oskar, at this very moment, is standing in the kitchen at the guest house wondering where Ewa has got to and what to cook the officers for their Sunday lunch.

The guard opens a steel-bound door and pushes Ewa forward. Wire bites into her wrists. Then the door slams shut. For a few seconds, the air thickens into blackness, and then the light is switched on. Ewa winces. The blaze is so bright that she cannot fully open her eyes. Every surface in the tiny room is white. No chair, no mattress; nothing but the blinding glare.

She flops on to the white tile floor, crouching forward, hands still wired behind her. Without warning, a prayer mumbles from her lips: *Ave Maria, gratia plena, Dominus tecum, benedicta tu...* The words flow like ointment through her brain. And if anything about her life is ever to be right again, she will need a miracle.

The cell's dazzle is magnified by a silver reflector around the floodlight. Her eyes cannot adjust to the light. There is a faint smell of burning. Ewa knows that if she had kept the cyanide sweet, this would be the time to take it, although, even now, she would be too cowardly. Stefan has perhaps already bitten into his own chocolate-covered glass phial. Unless, of course, the ambush, the arrests and the shootings were all part of Stefan's own plan...

Ewa tries to roll over then cries out with the pain from her bent and bound arm. There seem no edges to the room; ceiling, floor, walls meld into one. It is possible that everything Stefan has said and done this week has been a sham; the declarations of love, the wedding, the entreaty to board the Dakota, the sex. Because all he seemed to care about in the end was the suitcase. And Beck.

Ewa's eyelids screw into a tight black dazzle as she thinks of Beck's soft tongue in her mouth. She has to hope that the beating from Haller was enough, or the crossfire. But whichever way, please God, let him be dead. And then, for all of the Sturmbannführer's bluster, Ewa might still be in the clear. Only Beck saw what really happened and so, if he is alive, her own life is done for as surely as if she had bitten on a capsule of cyanide.

Ewa's shoulders throb and her wrists smart under the wire cuffs. Hydrogen-white light buzzes in the bulb and the brightness closes over her like chlorine-filled water. Even when she closes her eyes, white spots penetrate her retina.

She tries to fill her mind with a reason to live and recites without speaking, the oath she took in the back room of a bottle factory: '... *I pledge allegiance to the Republic of Poland. I promise to guard her honour and fight for her liberation with all of my strength, even sacrificing my life...*'

Perhaps they are all dead, not just Beck but Stefan and Tomasz too. About Haller there is no doubt. She saw him die in front of her before the real shooting started. The bullet that floored him seemed to come from the trees behind her; the trees where Tomasz had been standing with his rifle raised, and Stefan too, with a revolver...

Ave Maria... gratia plena... The prayer comes back, twirling through her mind in a simple intensifying plea. Let time rewind. Let everything be as it was yesterday. And then she would know not to be alone with Beck, not to have anything to do with him. Because if she had not kissed him... *Ave Maria... gratia plena...*

Time stretches and unspools. There is no night, no hunger, no sleep. Just whiteness.

Then the cell door opens. The guard's features are lost in a black blur. Fear quells pain as he grabs Ewa and drags her limply along corridors, down stairs, to a stark room. No windows, no desk. Just a metal chair and a ceiling light with a grille across it that throws black bars on to grey tiles. In the corner, oddly, there's a bathtub. Ewa has no idea whether it is night or day.

I am a waitress, I am German.

The guard takes off the wire cuffs and points at the chair. The act of flexing her arms and sitting down brings such relief that Ewa almost weeps. Perhaps they will be reasonable this time; listen to her story, believe her. But her story, she knows, is laughable. She puts her hands flat on her thighs. The scrapes on her wrists are flecked with blood; her nails are rimmed with black earth.

Behind her the door clicks. Footsteps circle. She keeps her eyes on her hands. *I am a waitress, I am German.* And then her chin is clamped by a hand, her head wrenched up.

'Hello again.'

The face in hers is not the Sturmbannführer but another she remembers from the dinner; the short man in the checked suit who sat next to Greiser. No suit now, just his shirtsleeves rolled up, and a black shiny apron covering his clothes. A waterproof apron. Why? Her gut is hollow with dread. His fingers press into her cheeks.

'Now then. You're not going to give me any of that *I'm a waitress* shit, are you? Because things will get much worse for you if you do. Just start telling me about the past three years – the work you have done for the AK, which of their thugs you know. And what was going to be loaded last night on to the Dakota.'

Checked-suit man lets go of her face. But she cannot speak, even if she wanted to. Her shoulders are shaking too hard. She opens her mouth.

'What's that?'

'I... am... a...'

'Hmmm.' He takes a step back then smiles and folds his arms. 'All right. We won't mess around. I'll tell you what it is that really interests me. You won't be surprised. I want to know more about an undercover British agent, Stefan Bergel, code name Anatol.'

At the sound of his name her heart drops in her chest. But, despite the terror, hope leaps. Does this mean that Stefan really is a British agent; that he is not working for Beck or for the Gestapo; that he did not betray the AK? That he is alive?

'I don't know anyone called...'

'Come on. Really? You don't know the name of your own husband?'

Blood ebbs from her head. 'I don't know anyone called Stefan...'

As he stares at her, she knows that she is going to faint. It's coming. There is lightness in her head, speckling at the edges of her vision. A nod passes from her interrogator to the guard then he adjusts the roll of his sleeves.

'I'll ask nicely one more time. But if that doesn't work we will have to try some other methods which, I'm afraid to say, are rather more brutal than those used by the Sturmbannführer.'

Sweet Jesus. What does that mean? Teeth ripped out, electrical shocks to her genitals? She clenches her jaw but her teeth will not stop chattering.

Then the door clicks as it closes and a grey uniform goes past her; the jacket draped over one shoulder, a sleeve dangling loose. She looks up and knows it is him before he turns to face her. Any strength she has left evaporates.

'Hello, Ewa.'

The wrong name in Beck's mouth hits her like a punch. He coughs gently, trying not to move his chest.

'I'm sorry it has come to this.'

His speech is slurred, his bottom lip bloated and stapled together with a thick black stitch.

He coughs again. 'Would you like a cigarette?'

She cannot move except to shiver. Nausea rises and then falls inside her stomach.

Wincing, Beck raises the white sling inside his open jacket and pulls out a yellow packet. He wedges a cigarette in his mouth and flicks the lighter with his good hand.

'Please don't lie any more. It will only result in distress.' The lit cigarette is wedged awkwardly between two fingers. 'But you will be pleased to know, I am sure, that Stefan is alive. We'd just like to know a little more about his activities in recent weeks.'

She looks down at her shaking hands. Vomit bites the back of her throat and the hot taste of it seeps into her mouth. 'I don't know... anyone called Stefan.'

Beck closes his good eye briefly. The other is sunk into a fold of puffy skin. He places the cigarette carefully on his lip next to the fissure sealed with black suture.

'It will be so much better if you tell us everything without delay.'

Ewa keeps her eyes down and her face blank as sick rises and falls in her throat. Oh God. If only she had the chocolate in its dull red foil. How eagerly she would put it into her mouth, right now, and crunch through glass into oblivion.

The man in the waterproof apron comes forward.

'Tell us what was going to be put on the Dakota. Stolen equipment? Escaped prisoners?'

His interest seems real. Maybe Stefan is alive, and is being interrogated in the room next to this one. Or perhaps he has escaped and is on the run. Perhaps he will even make it to England again. Yes. That is what will happen. Ewa feels it in her bones. Stefan will go back to his foreign lover. The English girl pilot will be the one to keep him in the end.

Ewa's fingernails dig into her leg. Self-inflicted pain is the only possible distraction. 'I... don't know... anyone... called Stefan.'

Beck groans. 'Come, Ewa. Or may I still call you Eva? It sounds so much nicer.' His voice is shaky. 'You have no reason to be loyal to him. Your husband did nothing to protect you last night when you came under attack.'

He winces and takes a drag on the cigarette. 'And shall I tell you a little more about your husband? Some things that you may not know?' He pauses. 'What if I tell you that, despite his military service for the Republic of Poland, and the Royal Air Force, and his activities with the AK, Stefan Bergel is a patriotic German? A certain incident in Russia when he was a prisoner of the Soviets has confirmed his loyalty to the Fatherland ever since.'

Don't listen, just breathe. One breath in, one breath out. But Ewa cannot ignore what Beck has said. *An incident in Russia?* What does he mean?

'That is why he has been so helpful.' Beck coughs and makes his voice louder. 'That is why he told us about the Dakota.'

Don't look up. Don't listen. He's lying.

'So you see, Eva, how little reason you have to help Stefan. You must instead help yourself and tell us what we want to know.'

Bile comes suddenly into her throat. As Ewa sits on the metal chair, hot salty vomit streams out of her mouth into her lap. The lumpy brown puddle begins seeping through her butter-yellow skirt on to her thighs. She hangs her head, retching and spitting the last foul particles from her mouth.

'Very well.' The man in the apron exhales. 'I suppose that's an answer of a sort.'

Ewa's mouth is raw with the aftertaste of stomach acid. Air swirls around her bare arms. Metal clunks against metal. There is a gush of water from a tap turned on at full blast. What are they going to do? Then the aproned man's face is in hers. She clamps her eyes shut but feels the waft of his sour breath and his spit on her cheek.

'Not very fragrant now, dear, are you? Do you want a bath?'

He lays his hands on Ewa's upper arms and pulls. All of the blood in her body seems to drop to her feet. She opens her mouth. *Yes sir, you're right, everything you said was right, I'll tell you all I know.* But she finds that she isn't saying anything, just gulping on air.

There's a clack and flip of rubber; a sound so unnerving that she can keep her eyes closed no longer. The aproned man is pulling on a pair of black rubber gloves. Something hot runs down the inside of her leg. Hands are on her, yanking, grasping, thrusting her towards the bath. Numbness paralyses Ewa's body but she understands, as if from a great distance, that she is about to be drowned in a bath of freezing water. For this, she is grateful. Her life no longer matters. And once submerged, no one will notice the piss and vomit trickling down her shins on to the slimy mess of her bare feet.

1945

Cirrus

Delicate high cloud formed of falling ice crystals. The milky formations appear stationary but they are in fact moving at great speed.

Only when Sonia asks if she wants to come to the parish hall does Vee remember that it is election day. She shrugs and says all right. A walk will be better than sitting brooding all afternoon in the school-dinner stuffiness of the mess. She wonders why any of them bothers coming here at all. ATA may still be paying their wages but hardly anyone gets to fly.

Despite the humid weather, Vee puts on her uniform jacket and fastens the belt. At least when she is wearing it, she can say that she is a pilot without raising a laugh. Sonia sets off in her jacket too but once they leave the aerodrome through the wicket gate and are on the path along the roadside verge, she takes it off. Vee does not even loosen her tie.

Sonia uses her jacket to wave away a bumble bee. 'Do you know, I think I might vote for Mr Attlee.'

'Really?'

'We're all grateful to Mr Churchill and so forth, but I imagine everyone could do with a change.'

'Mmm.'

Sonia throws Vee a sideways glance as she hooks her finger in the jacket's coat-loop and hoists it over her shoulder. 'I hear Frank Spratley is leaving.'

'Got a job, has he?'

'BOAC.'

Sonia sounds as if she might actually be pleased for him.

Vee sniffs. 'Thought so.'

Frank is about the fifth ATA pilot she has heard of to get a job with an airline. All of them men.

The hedgerows hum in the dull warm air and wood pigeons coo from the high elms.

'Do you have a plan, Vee, for when they finally give us our cards? It can't be long now, can it?'

'Well, I won't be working for BOAC, that's for sure.'

'You never know, it might be worth asking.'

Vee shoots her a look and Sonia shakes her head, chuckling. 'I know. But there could be other openings for you as a pilot. Aerial photography and such.'

'You mean where there are no passengers to see that their pilot is a lady?'

'Exactly.'

'But I'm not even going to get a job like that ahead of a demobbed RAF pilot who has a family to support.'

'Well, yes. I take your point. So what will you do?'

Vee shrugs. But she has little doubt that her path is leading back to the factory office, and it will be as if everything she has achieved in the past two and a half years never happened.

'How about you, Sonia?'

'Oh, I shall travel.'

Vee frowns for a moment as she imagines Sonia taking a series of buses and trains without going anywhere in particular.

Sonia's wry smile acknowledges her confusion. 'A cousin in the Argentine has invited me out to his ranch.'

'Goodness.'

'Yes. Should be a hoot.'

Sonia tries to rein in her smile and Vee wonders if the *cousin* might be rather more to Sonia than that.

'As soon as ATA bids me cheerio, I'll buy my passage. There's marvellous flying to be had down there, I believe.'

'That sounds grand.'

Sonia always does her best to imagine what it is like to live without much money, but she can never quite manage it. And Vee cannot properly explain to her how it feels to work all week in some airless office just to pay for a half-hour circuit around Surrey. Vee has already decided that if she cannot work as a pilot, she will not fly at all.

Sonia puts her hand to her brow to survey the grassy expanse of the landing ground. 'I doubt there's much more flying for us here.' Then she looks at Vee with her head to one side. 'You'd like to go out with a bang though, wouldn't you?'

'What do you mean?'

'Make the last flight one to remember?'

Vee shrugs with one shoulder. 'Any chits, such as they are, will go to people more senior than me.'

'Perhaps that won't be the case next week.'

'What do you mean?'

'Because there may be a very nice chit indeed with both of our names on it.'

'Are you sure? Where to?'

Sonia taps the side of her nose, conspiratorially. 'Let's just say that we'll be needing the reserve fuel tank on the Anson.'

'The Continent?'

Vee cannot believe that such a thing will happen. Everyone wants a crack at a foreign flight. How good it would look in their logbooks – not *Tangmere* or *Ringway* or *Cosford*, but *Brussels*, *Bordeaux* or *Berlin*.

'Only first officers have been on the foreign flights so far.'

'Well, I shall simply tell Captain Mills that Second Officer Katchatourian is by far the best placed to be my co-pilot because she has had all of the necessary inoculations: cholera, paratyphoid and what have you.'

'But I haven't.'

'Well, your name makes it sound as if you have visited exotic parts. And he won't dare disbelieve me if I put on my best voice when I tell him.'

Vee smiles but doubts Sonia has that much influence over Captain Mills. Despite the almost flawless record in Vee's logbook, she suspects that he still regards her as a reckless pilot. And he still hasn't got the hang of pronouncing her surname.

At the final perimeter of the landing ground, the afternoon bus from Maidenhead lumbers past and the red brick cottages of the village come into view. Vee's pace slows. She cannot imagine what she will do for the rest of the day let alone the rest of her life.

At the parish hall, a *POLLING STATION* sign hangs on the fence. Sonia goes on to the path lined by pink and yellow snapdragons that leads to the half-open door. But Vee stays by the road.

'Are you not going to vote?'

Vee shakes her head. 'I'm not sure that I have the right papers with me.'

'That shouldn't matter. Come in and speak to the clerk.'

'I think I'll pop back to my digs, to see if I can find the letter.'

'As you like.'

Sonia seems to suspect that Vee is lying and looks miffed. But Vee cannot bring herself to consider any part of the future. Even putting an *X* on the ballot paper is too much of a decision to make. The simple choice: *Conservative* or *Labour*, *Churchill* or *Attlee* requires more energy than she can muster.

Further down the road, the bus is pulling away from the stop. A few people have got off; women with headscarves knotted under their chins and a man in uniform. After the bus and the other passengers have departed, the man stands looking around. It is an RAF uniform – stripes on both sleeves and a side-cap. Something about the man's stance, as Vee walks towards him, makes her pulse quicken. Then he raises his hand and she stops dead.

Her legs want to move but cannot decide which way to go; to run towards him, or turn on her heel and scuttle away. Embarrassment still lingers. And she has been so certain that he was not coming back.

She decides to smile and walk on, to be cool and grown-up in the way Sonia might be.

'Hello there.'

She keeps her smile fixed.

'Hello, Vee.'

He has grown a moustache. Perhaps that is what makes his cheekbones seem more prominent. He is not gaunt exactly, but thinner. It could be ten years not two since she last saw him.

'What a surprise.' She tries to sound airy. 'It's like you've come back from the dead.'

'No, from Northolt.' Stefan's moustache twitches into a grin. 'Not quite so bad.'

He takes off his cap and looks more like the man she remembers even though the dark hair that used to fall over his brow is slicked flat and eroded at each side by his forehead. Vee wonders if they should kiss cheeks or shake hands or something. But he makes no move. She puts her hands in her pockets.

'So, you just happen to be passing this way, do you?'

'I come to see you, Vee, obviously.'

'Oh.'

She does not quite know what to say. Or what to feel. They stand, smiling stupidly at each other, until Vee cannot bear it any longer.

'I'm going this way, if you want to come for a walk.'

He nods and there is almost a click of heels, but maybe that is her imagination.

'How are you, Vee?'

'Oh, you know.'

As she indicates for them to turn on to the lane, she slides a look at him. His body seems shrunk inside the bulky belted jacket but his eyes are still the palest, fiercest blue she has ever seen.

There is no pavement and they walk alongside each other a pace or two apart on the asphalt.

'So...'

She cannot think what to say next. Even the safest question like *how are you?* or *where have you been?* could open up topics fraught with pain or embarrassment. The war has made small talk impossible.

'Do you mind me coming here to see you?'

'Of course not. I often wondered where you were.' The admission sounds pathetic and Vee feels herself colouring. 'I mean, at first, when they told me you had gone and I thought... well, I didn't know what to think.'

'You asked about me?'

'Only once. Northolt told me not to bother again.'

He snorts and shakes his head. 'It was all hush-hush then.'

'And is it still?'

'What?'

'Where you've been for the last two and a bit years?'

He sighs then gives a sardonic smile. 'Well, this year, I have been on a guided walking tour of central Europe. But the accommodation was third rate and the service terrible.'

It is coming back to her now, how he used jokes to side-step awkwardness.

'You were a prisoner?'

'Yes.'

He fiddles with the button of his top pocket and pulls out a pack of cigarettes. Vee shakes her head as he offers her one. His long fingers cup the yellow flame as he strokes it across the tip of the cigarette. His hands are trembling.

'And you, Vee? Still flying, I see.'

'I wish.'

He frowns, quizzical and Vee waves a hand.

'Well, it's all coming to an end, you see. Most of the air movements have gone to Transport Command. And there are too many RAF pilots idle for them to worry about giving any flights to ATA.'

They are almost at the railway bridge.

'But you still want to fly?'

She cuts a smile on to her mouth. 'More than anything.' They stop on the bridge and Vee leans her arms on the parapet. Iron tracks curve into the distance. 'I can't bear the thought that I might never see it all again.'

'What?'

'You know. The sun glinting off a Spitfire's windscreen and England spread out below me like a giant map.'

Her voice wavers and she blinks, irritated at the blur in her eyes

Stefan taps his cigarette on the edge of the bridge. 'You think you know what is in the future, but no one does.' White ash flutters towards the dark track. 'And was it only aeroplanes that you loved while I was gone?'

She laughs and turns to look at him. 'Cheeky bugger!'

There has, indeed, been no one else since Stefan disappeared. No one else quite measured up. But she will not yet give him the satisfaction of saying so.

In the distance, a train's clatter builds. Stefan drops the cigarette, stamping a thick sole on to the pavement.

'If you want me to go now, Vee, no problem. There is another bus in three hours.'

She laughs again and starts to say that it would be quicker to walk back to London along the train track, but then the bridge begins to shudder. In a sudden roar from below, coal-infused steam rushes up, engulfing them both. As the mist melts and the train thunders away, Stefan is closer; his grey-blue sleeve is almost touching her dark ATA navy. Without quite thinking, Vee leans in and Stefan's finger touches hers. Then he pulls her to him. Vee finds that she is wrapping herself around him and kissing him back. Even with the moustache, his lips, his mouth, his tongue, taste like a favourite half-forgotten treat. As they kiss, something inside her, something tense and fearful, seems to disconnect and lighten.

Vee pulls her head away and looks into the bluest of eyes. 'Three hours you say?'

'If the bus comes when it should.'

'That's more than enough to finish what we started last time.'

He takes a breath. 'Are you sure, Vee?'

She nods. She has never been surer of anything. 'My digs are over there. At the farm.'

The harvest is getting started so the house, as far as Vee can tell when they go in, is empty. Stefan follows her up the narrow stairs and strokes the edge of her hand. He has to stoop under the doorway to her bedroom. She turns the drooping key in the lock and unbuttons her jacket.

Stefan smiles, very wide and steps towards her. He looks down and touches the loose point of her tie. He starts to say something but before the word forms, their bodies fold into each other. Shirts, shoes, underthings, peel away. Vee does not think or speak but only feels – his skin, his lips, his tongue. He pulls her, quickly, roughly almost, on to the low bed. Her mouth stings from the scratch of his moustache.

He is on top of her and she knows that this time it will happen. His hand is under her spine, pushing her up and bringing her to the right place. He whispers.

'Is this all right, Vee?'

'Yes,' she says. 'Yes.'

He covers her mouth with his and swallows her cries. Vee has heard that everyone thinks the first time is no good. But they are wrong.

Afterwards, she and Stefan stay, hardly dressed, plaited together on the bed. When they were together before during the war, everything was rushed and breathless. She'd never imagined having a chance to spend long leisurely hours simply being with him. But perhaps now, that is not such an impossible idea.

Vee's gaze swims around the room – from the picture in a

frame, like a school photo, of herself and the other women pilots, to her winter greatcoat hanging on the back of the door. She wonders if the last two years would have been any different if she and Stefan had done this before, in the alleyway behind The 400 Club. The thought makes her feel as if she has lost forever something that should have been hers.

Stefan seems to read her thoughts and strokes a finger across her cheek. 'I am sorry, Vee, about before, in London.'

'What happened then, Stefan?'

He blinks slowly. 'I was not myself. It was that day we heard about the bodies. In the forest. Thousands of our Polish comrades shot by Soviets.'

She remembers vaguely a newsreel. Ragdoll corpses lifted from the soil as Nazis in long coats looked on. She has seen worse newsreels since.

'I thought the Germans were to blame for that.'

'Only if you believe what the British want you to believe.'

She flinches. He makes it sound like she is the enemy. She pulls away from him and sits upright on the bed. The candlewick bedspread is becoming threadbare and she pulls at a loose tuft of cotton.

'And it was this news that put you off, was it?'

'I suppose.' Sweat coats his brow. 'I felt... I felt useless. And so I was with you.' His body beside hers does not so much tense as become silent. 'I am sorry.'

'You don't need to apologise for that. It was the running away...'

'I know. There is no excuse.'

'Then I began to think maybe you couldn't contact me because you had been shot down. And I suppose at some point that became true...'

'No, I was not shot down.'

'So how did you end up as a prisoner of war?'

'Long story.'

Vee's finger circles a bare patch on the bedspread that looks like a blue cloud in a milky sky. Stefan shifts his weight on the bed and cool air rises between them. The silence is suddenly unbearable.

'Tell me, Stefan. We have time.'

He sighs. 'I went to Poland.'

'To fight?'

'Yes. And to find something and bring it back. But I failed. So I must go back and try again.'

He glances up at her from the pillow and holds her gaze. She senses then, with a jolt, why he is here.

'Please don't say you've come looking for a lift.'

His eyelids lower and she knows that she is right.

He raises himself on the bed and takes hold of her hand, entwining his fingers with hers. 'Listen, Vee, if you cannot help, it does not matter. But this thing I must find in Poland is something very important for my government. For my country.'

She stifles an urge to laugh. His excuse sounds so implausible that she cannot bring herself to ask what he means.

'There must be plenty of RAF flights from Northolt to the Continent. Can't you go back on one of those?'

He shakes his head. 'This is a private matter. Best RAF does not know.'

'Top secret, then?'

She hears a sneer in her voice but when she sees his face, regrets it. She thinks for a horrible second that he might weep. But his voice, though quiet, is steady.

'The truth, once proved, will change everything.'

'You sound very sure.'

'I am. Can you help me?'

Vee's finger traces the arc of his shoulder. 'I'll see.'

Berlin, British Sector
Friday 13 July

Sunlight drills into the cockpit as the Anson turns to the east. Vee squints at the dazzle, her hands clammy on the steering yoke. She bends her head from left to right, tendons crunching. The cockpit stinks of worn leather and greased metal. Engines drone.

Below, a sparse open landscape rolls past – unfenced fields, dark woodland, a scattering of towns. Some settlements are still red-roofed, others are pummelled grey as ash. Clouds cast giant shadows on the empty sunlit ground. It is nothing like England.

Sonia holds up the map to Vee and their bare forearms brush above the hydraulic levers. Vee follows Sonia's scarlet fingernail that is pointing out their position then glances down at the gap between propeller blur and wing. The same angle of railway line and river is reproduced on the ground. She gives Sonia a thumbs-up.

Then, in the hold, there is a clunk of metal on metal that makes them both look round. Sonia smiles and arches her dark eyebrows above her sunglasses. Vee is glad that the engine noise does not allow for much conversation. She glances again over her shoulder at the cargo bay crammed with crates and bales stacked around an iron lung. Stefan is kneeling beside it, tightening the straps that run over the top of the raised metal cylinder with glass portholes along each side and securing it to the hold. He glances up and his hair falls forward over one eye. Electricity needles through Vee's insides. That moustache suits him.

Sonia winks as she turns back to the map and Vee shakes her head but cannot help smiling. Sonia really has gone out of her way to be helpful. She did not seem to think it at all outlandish that Stefan wanted to hitch a free lift to Berlin but merely asked what the chances were of him getting away with it. Stefan had said, as if he knew the place well, that he would simply blend in with other uniforms at RAF Gatow. And anyway, he insisted, everyone would be too busy to ask him any questions because they would be staring at the beautiful lady pilots getting off an Anson. Sonia had laughed and called him a smooth-talker and had asked no more.

Vee swore to Sonia that she will take the full rap if they get into any hot water over it. But what, in fact, is the worst that ATA can do? Sack her? That is coming anyway. And a job reference for a pilot who also happens to be a woman is not worth the sheet of headed notepaper.

Sonia clearly assumes that Stefan and Vee are a couple now. But Vee has no sense of this herself. And it is possible that as soon as they land, he will say cheerio and she will never see him again. But Vee cannot imagine that really happening. Surely, so soon after returning, he would not disappear again.

Soon, open water flashes between forests and Sonia glances up from the map. She jabs a finger downward by the side window.

'Gatow,' she shouts.

There is a movement of air behind her and a whiff of shaving soap and bacon as Stefan leans forward between the seats, pointing.

'There, see.' A fat dirty cloud hangs near the horizon. 'Berlin.'

Sonia leans over to shout. 'Shall I take control, for landing?'

Vee's hands twitch on the yoke. She has the sense that once they leave it, she will never fly an aeroplane again. 'Would you mind if I... this may be my last chance.'

Sonia shrugs politely. 'All right.'

But Vee suddenly feels a little sick. On the ground, two parallel stripes of white concrete wedge into the dark trees. She turns the steering yoke and banks the Anson into a wide downward arc around a square control tower blasted with shell scars. The hangar roofs have caved in and most of the windows in the aerodrome's long, low barrack block are smashed, but the runways look smooth.

Staring at the engine speed indicator, Vee pulls back on the throttle and watches the needle drop below *100mph*. Then there is a hand on her shoulder and Stefan's mouth beside her ear.

'All right, Vee? You look white.'

'I'm fine. Really. Get strapped in.'

She throws a glance over her shoulder as he goes to the metal bench beneath the fuselage window. As she turns back to the instrument panel, dials and gauges swim below the blinding windscreen.

Then, Sonia is tapping the indicator lights. 'Undercarriage!'

Vee's stomach lurches and she reaches down to grab the handle at the base of her seat. With a whir of wheels lowering, the indicator lights turn green. But the Anson seems to have lost its line of approach.

'Vee! Speed!'

Sonia is tapping another dial. *85*. Yes. Still too fast. Concrete rushes up.

'Vee! Pull back! Pitch up!'

Red fingernails stretch out. Another hand is on the steering yoke. The drum of engines dips and slows. With a crack, the Anson hits the runway, then lists and bounces back into the air. The cockpit jerks and tips.

Now Sonia is pushing the yoke forward and pulling the throttle back as far as it will go. Another thump, a squeal of rubber on concrete, twin puffs of smoke. But the wheels are on the ground and seem to stay there.

Sonia lets go but Vee's hands are welded to the yoke as she steers the Anson gingerly across the concrete. She heads towards a bank of assorted aircraft, British and American, all wearing black and white invasion stripes on their wings and tails. She cannot bear to meet Sonia's eye. With a squeal, the plane comes to a sharp stop. The engines idle and then sink into silence.

Sonia leaps up, her head bent against the Perspex roof, her skin white and bathed in sweat.

'Good God, Vee! What happened there?'

'I… I must be a bit rusty.'

Sonia's dark eyes flash. 'A bit?'

'I'm sorry.'

Sonia puts a hand through her hair. 'No damage done, I suppose. Stefan, are you all right?'

'Fine!' He stands up, slapping at his trousers. 'How are you, Vee?'

She coughs, but says nothing.

Sonia is peering out of the side window towards the control tower. 'They'll all be watching.'

Stooping, Stefan comes forward and looks out of the window but takes care not to be seen. He whistles.

'Busy! Traffic coming in for the Peace Conference, I think.' He takes hold of a cargo strap hanging from the roof. 'So ladies, what is it to be in Berlin? A little sightseeing, a restaurant, maybe a show?'

'Very droll.' Sonia hardly smiles. 'There's nothing to see I believe but bombsites. And actually, I'm meeting an old friend of Tony's here.'

Stefan turns. 'Vee?'

She has no idea what he is talking about but knows that she cannot face an evening sitting between Sonia and one of her chaps.

'I don't suppose that the Anson will be needed for anything else today.'

He nods. 'I will wait at the front gate.'

In the Ops room, plywood is nailed over the broken window and fat flies circle the dangling bulb. Vee lets Sonia do the talking, and marvels at the effectiveness of her manner which is flirtatious but grandly remote. The awestruck flight sergeant cannot take his eyes off her. Vee hears him ask about the heavy landing but Sonia makes some plausible excuse about the almost empty fuel tanks and gives a radiant smile. Again, Vee owes her.

Stefan is right, of course, about his blending in. The aerodrome's reception area is crammed with uniformed men dozing or staring blankly at the once-white walls. In a fug of cigarette smoke and stale khaki, Vee picks her way between legs and kitbags. Outside, the humid air has undertones of pine trees and stagnant water.

Stefan is leaning against the wall. As he sees Vee, he smiles so broadly that her heart seems to somersault. He comes forward and puts an arm around her shoulder. Perhaps they are a couple now.

'Shall we?'

He nods at a dull green truck with canvas flaps tied back over the tailgate. They sit on crates in the back as it bumps over rickety bridges around a lake. Trees and scrubland give way to houses and then to dilapidated blocks of flats where empty windows leave black holes in the walls like dead faces.

Vee holds on to the tailgate as the truck swerves to avoid a slimy heap of grit. At the top of the heap, an old woman in a feather hat pokes the green shoot of a potato plant with a stick. The city's wreckage begins to unfold through the lorry's canvas arch like a newsreel.

Vee looks at Stefan. 'Is it far?'

'No. We will get off at Anhalter, the railway station.'

A railway station. Her stomach ripples. Why would he be going there except to leave?

A reek of bin-wagon threads through the heat. On the piles of rubble that have become embankments alongside the road, women in shorts or wrap-over aprons pass buckets of stone to each other up and down the mounds. Stefan stands up but looks only at Vee.

'Ready?'

Gears crunch and the lorry jerks forward before it comes to a stop by a ribcage of black girders looming across the hazy sky. In front of the station's shell-scarred arches is a sea of ragged figures – men and women, children and babies. Some sit on the ground, others move in slow lines. Despite the clammy heat, all are wearing winter coats.

Stefan puts out his hand to help Vee down from the truck. His grasp is firm. He bangs the tailgate shut and the truck crunches off.

Vee does not let go of his hand. 'Why are we here Stefan? Are you leaving?'

'No, no.'

'Then why are we at a station?'

'To find information...' he lets his fingers loosen from Vee's, '... about the person who knows where to find the thing I am looking for.'

Despite the heat, Vee shivers. 'A person?'

He nods. 'I will ask the Tracing Service.'

He puts on his side-cap and straightens his tie. Vee has suddenly no doubt that this someone is female.

A stench of second-hand clothes sours the air as Stefan leads the way through the people camped on the ground. Vee meets the stares of these *Displaced Persons* they are called now – a woman with red-blotched skin, a wizened old man in a flat cap, a blond boy chewing the end of an unlit cigarette. She is used to sidelong glances from strangers. Her dark-belted uniform with its embroidered gold wings often attracts envious looks or even gasps – *Goodness, a woman pilot!* But she is not used to looks like this.

Beneath the remains of the station roof, Stefan ignores the snaking queue of DPs and goes straight to a desk with a *UNRRA* banner. Vee stands awkwardly at his side. Once Stefan's back is turned, a gaunt woman in a shapeless raincoat hisses, *Zicke!* and Vee is glad she cannot understand. Despite the gloom, she takes her sunglasses from her jacket pocket and puts them on.

Stefan is talking quietly but very fast to a middle-aged woman in spectacles behind the desk. Vee tries to make out the words but Stefan is speaking German fluently and fast, like a native in fact. The sound of it makes Vee's pulse quicken. Then, the woman asks a question and Stefan stops. Does he look at Vee before he answers? His voice is quieter but Vee hears.

'*Meine Frau.*'

Her heart misses a beat. Surely that is German for *my wife*? What can he be saying? But *Frau* means woman as well as wife. Vee wishes she had paid more attention in Miss Twait's German lessons instead of staring out of the window every Friday afternoon hoping to see a passing aeroplane. Stefan must simply have said that he is looking for a woman, but his words leave a nasty taste in Vee's mouth.

The woman in spectacles is now showing Stefan a clipboard. His finger travels down a list and then stops. He nods, signs a slip of paper and takes Vee's arm as he turns away. His face is white.

'Stefan. What's wrong?'

'Come. Let's go.'

'Did you find out what you wanted?'

'Let's get away from these people.'

They leave the station by a different exit and head towards a mud-baked plain strewn with debris that shimmers into the distance. At the roadside, Stefan stoops to a figure hunched on the ground. The young man's face is gaunt and dirty but surprisingly shiny top-boots poke from his tattered overcoat. Stefan offers a cigarette then gives him the whole packet. He fires fast questions before listening intently to the young man's slow replies. German again but Vee cannot understand a single word.

Colour has come back into Stefan's face and he smiles at Vee as they link arms and move off. She feels the squeeze of his elbow through her jacket. He squeezes tighter, pulling her back from the roadway as a convoy of trucks clatters by. Vee does not like the way he seems to be controlling her movements and she tries to pull her arm free but Stefan stands frozen, his eyes trained on the passing trucks. Each one has a dusty red star on the door and a flatbed crammed with scrap metal – bicycles, railings, car bumpers. Engines rev and screech. A soldier with ammunition belts slung crosswise over his high-collared tunic rides alongside on a pony, a machine-gun balanced on the sheepskin saddle. He kicks with stirrups that stretch almost to the ground and the pony breaks into a canter on the cobbles.

Vee wonders suddenly what she is doing here, and feels a twitch of anger with Stefan. Why has he brought her to this ghastly place when he seems interested only in finding someone else?

'Actually, I think I should go back now, to Gatow.'

Stefan turns to her. 'Not yet, Vee.'

Her voice tightens. 'It's not very nice here, is it?'

'I must talk to you first. Come. Let us go to Tiergarten.'

'I don't...'

'Please, Vee.' He takes her hand. 'Just for a few minutes, so that I can explain.'

A ditch runs along the far side of road. The only bridge over it is a plank that bounces as Vee crosses the black water lumpy with half-hidden detritus. Not far off, a carved general in a cocked hat points his marble finger at the wasteland of blasted tree stumps and stagnant canals.

Stefan unbuttons his jacket and sits on a shattered stone column. He takes out a cigarette and lights it, blowing a long trail of smoke into the fetid air. Nearby, naked boys yell as they take turns to jump into an oily pond.

Vee sits beneath a cloud of green midges and feels a drip of sweat run into the seam of her brassiere. The fur-lined flying boots that seemed such a good idea on the chilly airfield this morning are coated in white dust. Her anger has dissolved into exhaustion. She feels that the moment is coming when he will say goodbye, and she wants more than anything to get it over with.

'I know you're leaving, Stefan. Just say whatever it is you want to say and then go.'

'Vee. Believe me. I did not think this would happen so quick.'

'What would?'

'I thought I would need to look much harder for Ewa.'

She bats away something buzzing by her ear. 'Forever? What do you mean?'

'No, no. You don't understand. That is her name, the person I am looking for. Ewa.'

Vee feels a stab. Ewa. That is her. His woman. The *Frau* he declared to the Tracing Service; the girl he could not get out of his mind in the alleyway behind The 400 Club. Vee can imagine her clearly now: Ewa in a thin summer frock, tall and suntanned, as she stands in a cornfield laughing and tossing her golden hair.

Vee's stomach knots. She snaps a blade of yellow grass and crumbles the dry seeds into her fist.

'And you are going to her now.'

It does not need to be a question.

Stefan sighs. 'It will not be easy. That Luftwaffe chap told me that everything is coming west. No one goes east. No one wants to.'

Vee presses two fingers to her brow. 'What do you mean? Luftwaffe?'

'I gave him cigarettes.' Stefan half smiles. 'Everyone now pretends to be someone they are not.'

Vee frowns. 'I don't.'

Suddenly, the air is split by a strangled, bellowing scream.

'What in hell was that?'

Vee gives a start and her gaze whips around the cratered wasteland. The remains of a triumphal arch poke at the colourless sky.

Stefan shrugs. 'Sounds like an elephant.'

'An elephant?'

'The zoo is near. An elephant must have survived the bombings.'

He stubs his cigarette into a bullet-hole on the stone.

Vee takes a long breath in and then out. Her nose fills with the stench of blocked drains.

'This Ewa… who is she?'

For a second Stefan's hand is still. Then he flings the cigarette stub away. A button on his shirt comes open to show a circle of white skin.

'I told you, Vee. What I am really looking for is evidence vital to the future of my country. Ewa is the only one who can tell me where it is.'

'All right, Stefan. You don't have to tell me.'

He reaches out to take both of Vee's hands in his and rubs his thumbs over her fingers. 'Listen, Vee, I must do this thing now. No one else can. After it is done, everything will be different.'

In the hazy white light, his eyes are black dots inside irises of arctic blue. Vee has not the faintest idea what he is trying to tell her, nor the slightest doubt that he is hiding the truth. But she realises that she does not care. All that matters is putting off the moment when they will say goodbye.

'Where is she then, this Ewa?'

Stefan blinks for a moment too long. 'Poznań.'

Berlin/Lusowo, Poland
Saturday 14 July

Vee and Sonia stand on the concrete, overnight bags at their feet and hands shading their eyes as they follow the slow circuit of a Dakota above the trees.

Sonia raises her voice above the blare of engines. 'There's all sorts of transports coming in today.'

'For the Peace Conference?'

Sonia nods. 'Everyone is saying that the PM is going to be on one of them.' She glances at Vee and smirks. 'Don't tell anyone that I didn't vote for him!'

The Dakota descends, wheels down, towards the concrete.

Vee picks up her bag. 'We had better get our flights out of their way.'

'Do you mind awfully, Vee? About my having the Spit?'

'Of course not.' Vee hopes she sounds convincing. 'My fault for not being here when they sorted out the chits.'

'They were rather odd about it actually. The Ops officer asked me if you were Russian.'

'Good God. What did you say?'

'I said no, Turkish.'

'Christ, Sonia! I'm English. You know that.'

'I know, but your name... everyone wonders about it.'

'But after all of the flying I've done for ATA, all of the hours and types in my logbook... do they not trust me?'

'He said he didn't want to be giving the photo-reconnaissance Spitfire to a Russki. It's sort of a spy-plane, and they seem very twitchy about the Soviets here. But he put you down for the Anson without any bother.'

Vee is too shocked to reply. When she thinks of all that she has done these past three years – the days spent freezing in open cockpits unable to see the ground for rain, the nights stuck out on hard camp beds, the friends lost to cloud cover...

'I wondered if you might prefer the Anson anyway, and get straight back in the saddle, so to speak. After a fall, it's always best to take the next fence at the gallop.'

Sonia beams as if this is a joke, but her dig about Vee's pancake landing feels like salt on a cut.

Vee can't quite manage a smile. 'Of course.'

'And it's a straightforward run down to Pilsen and back, I believe.'

If she had more energy, Vee would walk back to the Ops office and tell them to stuff their chit. But another way to repay their small-minded suspicions could be simply to alter the direction on the Anson's compass.

Sonia flashes her brightest smile and picks up her overnight bag. 'Jolly good.'

'So where are you going in the Spit?'

'Bari.'

'Where's that?'

'Heel of Italy.'

'My word.' Vee turns to her, blinking. 'How long will you be gone?'

'Couple of days I should think. Depends when I can hitch a lift back.' Sonia's dark eyes sparkle. 'I can't wait to get into a Spit again. It seems like an age. And they said this one was the perfect aeroplane for a lady.'

'What did they mean?'

Vee slides a sideways look at Sonia who has opened her silver compact and is drawing a scarlet O around her lips. No one would guess she is the same girl who two years ago was scraped off the locker room floor half-dead from grief and booze.

Sonia snaps the compact shut. 'I'll soon find out!' She waves as she strides off. 'Good luck with the Anson.'

Inside the Anson, yesterday's cargo has been unloaded and the hold restocked with exhaust pipes and lorry tyres. Vee stows her bag and goes to the pilot's seat. The choice is Stefan's now. She made no promises, but told him that if she had a flight and he could get on board unseen, she would do her best to get him closer to where he wants to go. She knows that this was just another way to put off the final goodbye.

If Stefan is still on the aerodrome, he will have seen this flight clearly marked on the movements board: *Avro Anson N5334 –*

RAF Gatow to Pilsen (ATA 2ⁿᵈ Off. V Katchatourian). Earlier, a harassed sergeant briefed Vee sketchily about route, signals and weather: *minimal risk of precipitation, hazy cloud at 8000 feet* and she has a map of three countries in her bag. The choice is now Stefan's.

And now that Vee is scanning the gauges and setting the altimeter to a hundred above sea level, the thought of flying wildly off course into the Soviet sector to help a not-quite boyfriend with some far-fetched quest seems increasingly absurd. In fact, the very thought of him, and of what they did on Vee's sagging farmhouse bed, is beginning to seem fantastical. Perhaps Stefan has again evaporated from her life. Perhaps he never really returned.

Luminous movement at the edge of the cockpit window makes Vee look up at a Mark Nine Spit that is being pushed across the strip. Black and white invasion stripes are painted around the wings but every other surface of the aeroplane is a delicate ice-cream pink. The Spit's airscrew turns hesitantly before spluttering into a blur. Then the engine roars, flames caressing the cowlings, and in the cockpit Sonia turns, beaming, to the ground crew who are balancing on the tail. The men bounce off and the Spit gathers speed before sliding into effortless flight. Wheels flip outwards into the wings, and the pink silhouette merges into the white distance. For a moment, Vee wishes more than anything in the world that she could be Sonia.

She folds the map on to the clipboard and with a sigh turns the compass dial to *S*. Stefan, it seems, is not coming. So she will fly the Anson alone today and she will make damned sure that her take-offs and landings are textbook perfect. This may be the last chance she gets.

Outside, a fitter is pulling a petrol bowser around the plane and shouting to his mate so Vee does not take any notice of the creak in the fuselage. Only when creaks become footsteps does her head turn.

Stefan smiles thinly and presses a forefinger to his moustache. Vee catches her breath. He is wearing a brown suit – well cut and sharp-shouldered with a white shirt open at the neck. She realises that she has never before seen him in anything but flying overalls or RAF blue. He is a different man in a suit – better looking, more relaxed, less trustworthy.

'I thought you must have changed your mind.'

She keeps her face blank and his smile drops.

'If you can't do this, Vee, I understand.'

But she shakes her head. 'In for a penny, in for a pound, I suppose.'

'What?'

'I mean, I have already brought you this far, and it's not much of a detour, is it?'

'No. Not much.'

But they both know that it is not the distance that matters but the direction.

Vee opens out the map. 'So show me exactly where we are going.'

Stefan stands behind the pilot's seat and looks down at the map with the air of a diver about to take a convoluted plunge off the top board.

'Here.'

His finger taps a town about a hundred and fifty miles east of Berlin.

Vee squints. 'I thought you said Poznań.'

'Yes.'

'It says *Posen.*'

'They are the same.'

She frowns but he must know. She must trust him.

'And where do we land?'

He points to green emptiness outside the city and a long thin lake, almost rectangular. 'Here.'

'All right.'

She puts out a hand to adjust the compass. The needle swings from *S* to *E*.

'Thank you, Vee.'

He puts a hand on her shoulder but unease twitches through her. The risks are considerable – not just from flying into the forbidden Soviet zone, but also the danger, greater probably, of landing a heavy-laden transport plane on a field. But she has made her choice, and her choice is Stefan. Vee flicks the magneto switches and the thunder of engines stifles the questions in her brain.

Once in the air, the haze around the aeroplane magnifies the morning glare and obscures the distant horizon. But soon the pulverised city is behind them and the air clarifies. For once, Vee is glad that the Anson has no radio. She need not lie to anyone about where she is going.

Stefan stares at the map and then out of the window. Soon, he points down for Vee to look too. A snaking brown river cuts between yellow fields. On both banks, roads fan towards the mangle of metal that was once a bridge. On the western side, a wide highway ribbons with traffic. Trucks, carts and people all moving at the same slow pace away from the river. On the eastern bank, the flow hardens to a stop at the crossing point. The only movement is a maggoty churn of people around stationary vehicles.

Stefan leans over and smiles. 'See? Much better to fly.'

Vee frowns. 'But how will you get back?'

He shrugs. Maybe he has no intention to return.

Vee grips harder to the steering yoke and a spot of pain pushes against her forehead. The engines have an odd whine to them. Perhaps Gatow fuel is too rich. She reaches out to adjust the mixture lever but is distracted by a mirror flash from the ground, and then another. A signal? The black and white stripes on the Anson's wings are as good as a target.

She glances at Stefan. 'Shall we go higher?'

But the sky above the roof is thickening. Whiteness has oozed over the last gaps of blue. Vee glances at the altimeter. Twelve hundred. Safe enough, at least where there are no hills.

Then Stefan points to a distant glint of water. As Vee looks, the lake takes on a distinctive narrow shape and that mirrors a clear strip of pale grass nearby. Thank goodness. They are almost there.

She glances at Stefan. 'Is that field long enough?'

'It was long enough for a Dakota.'

'Really?' There is nothing anywhere around except the empty farmland and a few sparse buildings. No sign of any aerodrome. 'A Dakota landed here?'

He does not answer and his face is unreadable. Perhaps he did not hear.

Vee checks the gauges and dips the nose. This will not be easy, especially with the Anson carrying so much weight. But she will prove that she can do it, to him and to herself. And the concentration required will put thoughts of their parting out of her mind.

She reaches for the undercarriage lever. Red light to green, flaps down, throttle forward, then, at the last minute, nose slightly up. The ground looms. Toy trees become real. Dark greens are flashing past and then yellow grass. She holds her breath. A bump. And another. But then they are on the ground and bouncing fast over the mown field with a slight sway to the left. Vee makes herself take a breath. But the Anson's speed drops obediently and with a forward lurch they slow to a stop.

Stefan squeezes her arm and raises his voice over the idling engines. 'Perfect!'

But Vee is already looking around, assessing the best line for a turn and a take-off. 'Where shall I turn?'

He points to a cut into a stand of trees where the field widens. There looks to be just enough space to spin the Anson on its tail-wheel. But as they move off, Stefan peers up at the sky. Cloud has rolled out into a thick darkening layer across the whole sky. At the far end of the landing field there is no clear divide between grass and air.

'So, you will be all right? To go over the top?'

'What? No.' He must remember that she can only fly using ground-contact navigation. 'I'll have to stay below the cloud.'

He shakes his head. 'It is getting lower.'

'What is the base at, do you think? Eleven hundred?'

'Nine.'

'Damn.'

Vee slumps back into the seat and runs a hand through the knots in her hair. She glances at Stefan. It would be convenient for him perhaps if she is stuck here. Then he can do what he needs to do and get a lift back on the Anson. She will not allow herself to consider whether this is what she wants too.

'Let's just wait here for a short time.' Stefan points to a pocket cut between the trees. 'Put the plane over there.'

The propellers slacken as Vee swerves the Anson across rough grass. As soon as walls of dark trees surround the plane on three sides, she cuts the engines.

Stefan's voice booms in the silence. 'Come, let's get some air and check the vis.'

Vee cranks open the door on to a rush of grassy air. Her legs jar against solid ground.

Stefan jumps out after her. He holds out a yellow packet. 'Cigarette?'

'All right.'

A suck of nicotine dulls the throb in Vee's head. The regulations are clear: *Forced landing due to bad weather: remain with aircraft at all times.* She hadn't always done that, of course. Aeroplanes had been left in fields before now, but those were fields in England.

Vee folds her arms across her stomach while keeping the end of the cigarette close to her mouth. Cloud quilts the sky.

'I'll have to stay with the Anson.'

'Then I will stay with you.'

'No. You have things to do. That's why we came here. I'll be all right.'

He sighs and puts his hand inside his jacket. 'Then take this.'

She stiffens at the heft of the revolver in his hand. 'Why? What do you think is going to happen?'

He shrugs. 'Nothing, I hope. But if someone comes and wants something, how else will you stop them?'

'I wouldn't be able to use it.' And as she says the words she realises that she no longer has any control over this journey. When she turned the compass dial, her fate was tied to Stefan. 'Perhaps I should come with you.'

He puts the gun back into his waistband but keeps his eyes fixed on Vee. Then steps forward on the dead grass. His hands are on her shoulders.

'Vee, believe me, I'm sorry. I did not mean for you to have a problem like this. But listen, it is not yet midday. There is time for the cloud to lift so that you can fly to Pilsen, unload and be back at Gatow before dark. What I have to do might take only a few hours.'

'And then we could fly back together?'

'I hope, yes.'

'What if you can't find what you are looking for?'

'Then we will come back here anyway. I promise. And you are right, you should come with me, Vee. It will be safer.' He comes closer and lightly kisses her cheek. She puts her arms around his waist but then senses a distance in his embrace that tightens the unease in her stomach.

Then, not far away, there is a bang of wood and a shout. Stefan looks round. Tucking the revolver under his jacket, he signals for Vee to stay still and goes to the edge of the clearing. The voice shouts again. Stefan replies with words Vee cannot make out, not even the language. She goes after him to the edge of the beech wood. Hazy air fills tree-trunk arches above a floor of dry leaves. The voice is coming from the other side of holly bushes in a dense circle. It is a man speaking Polish. Stefan's hand goes to his waistband.

Then in a swishing of feet, the man appears. He is youngish, wearing a grimy checked shirt and heavy workman's trousers. A rifle is slung over his shoulder. Stefan's expression is blank. The man stops then starts to run, straight towards them. Stefan shouts something but the man keeps running.

Vee's thoughts freeze. 'Stefan…'

'Get behind me.'

His arm goes out, shielding her. But the man is already there, in front of them. He grabs Stefan's shoulders, starts talking in low, hurried words. And then, the man buries his face in Stefan's neck, the shotgun swinging on his shoulder. Stefan circles his arms around the man, whispering fast sentences and then, still talking, he takes hold of the man's arms and pushes a gap between them. The man's eyes shine.

Stefan turns to Vee. 'This is Tomasz.'

The young man's smile droops at one side of his mouth and the new beard on his chin is a shade redder than his hair. Vee says *hello* and he replies. Gin something?

Again he gives a lop-sided smile. Vee feels stupid that she does not know a single word of Stefan's language.

Stefan touches her arm. 'We will go with him, for now.'

They walk out of the trees and on to a sandy track. On either side, grassland rolls to the wide horizon broken only by dark stands of trees. Greens of all shades seem unnaturally luminous in the milky light. The men's voices bounce with hard consonants and sliding vowels. *Nie, tak, nie wiem.* And then from Tomasz's mouth, comes a jolt of words Vee knows: *Avro Anson* and then *Dakota.* But Stefan's low canter of words does not change its tone. He could be saying anything. And it seems rude to interrupt.

The open field ends in a clump of spindly birch trees and a long barn. Vee keeps to the edge of the track, away from the dark slime in the core of each rut. The cart tracks deepen. Then with a crack through the still air something hard snaps. Vee jerks round. At the ridge of the barn roof, a big pile of sticks and loose straw is moving. The straw parts and a curved head bends back to show the black bead of an eye and a conical red beak. White wings spread wide; the red beak clatters. Vee has never seen a stork except in story books. Stefan and Tomasz do not give it a glance.

The track widens into a deserted village street of ragged thatch roofs and crumbling outbuildings. They go towards the only solid-looking house that has a row of tall windows and a tiled orange roof. Tomasz pulls a heavy key from his pocket.

'*Prosze, prosze.*'

He waves them inside a dusty hallway filled with a smell of paraffin. The rooms to each side are empty except for dirty linoleum and torn net curtains. Floorboards echo under their boots. In a kitchen at the back of the house, a ceramic stove radiates heat although the room is already sweltering. Tomasz takes the rifle from his shoulder and leans it against the wall then throws a log into the stove from the woodpile in the middle of the floor.

'*Prosze.*'

He is smiling and gesturing Vee towards an upturned wooden box. She sits on it warily. Sweat runs down her spine. Stefan is leaning against the wall, arms folded and his face blank. But clearly he knows this man and Vee suddenly has no doubt that Stefan has been expecting to meet him all along.

Tomasz pulls a small pan on to the cooking plate and throws Vee a crooked smile.

'*Kawa?*'

Stefan laughs and Vee looks round.

'What's he saying?'

271

'A joke. He asks if you want coffee.'

'Why is it funny?'

'You will see when you drink it.'

Tomasz clatters the pan then hands her a scratched enamel cup. The brown liquid tastes of school toilets and mud. Vee looks over the rim of the cup at Stefan who has moved to the window, hands in pockets. He fires short unintelligible questions at Tomasz and listens intently to the long replies. Their sentences have a new rhythm but the same word crops up again and again. *Ewa, Ewa, Ewa.* Vee looks away.

The walls of the bare kitchen are scuffed and spattered but at the top, near the ceiling, pink tulips with light green leaves have been stencilled around the room in a perfectly continuous line. Someone, a woman, must once have been proud of this place.

Abruptly, Stefan pulls back the ragged net from the window and peers through mud-speckled glass into a wide paved farmyard. Grass grows through the broken cobbles. White sky merges into rust-stained roofs.

Then Tomasz comes over to Vee so close that she smells his unwashed armpits. He is gesturing for her to stay where she is and briefly he presses his hands down on her shoulders to make his point. His grip is strong. Her scalp tightens.

'He wants me to stay here, I think.'

Perhaps she should. The thought of coming face to face with Ewa and her cornfield curls is unimaginable. Stefan turns to Vee with an easy smile but his words come back like bullets.

'Not a chance. We leave here together.'

'Where to?'

'To the city, or at least to the isolation hospital close by. I have already told him that we need two bikes.'

Poznań, Poland
Saturday 14 July

Men in brown coats lift the bed with Ewa still on it and carry her into the blinding outdoors. As the bed's metal legs are lowered on to dead grass, Ewa tries to smile at the grey-bearded face above her feet. But the orderly will not look at her. He must think a smile from the dying unlucky. Or perhaps Ewa's ravaged features are too repulsive to behold.

She turns her face to the light. Sunshine is supposed to be a cure. But the suffocating white air presses down on her like a pillow. Midges hover in a tang of creosote. Crows shriek. From the sweat on nearby faces, Ewa knows that the day must be sweltering but beneath the thin blankets her own sweat is icy. Breath bubbles through her lungs – in, in, in, and then damply, out. Exhausting as it is, she must concentrate on this process. She must not, above everything else, cough. She closes her eyes.

Then a hand is on hers, shaking. Did she sleep? She must have. Her eyes open. Not far off, women in blue aprons are carrying a stretcher along one of the meandering mud paths between the huts. Their load is covered with soiled tarpaulin. It does not look heavy.

Ewa's hand is shaken again and she moves her eyes to a face. A woman. One of the so-called nurses.

'Mrs, Mrs.' The woman has a thick Ukrainian accent and will not stop shaking Ewa's hand. If only she had the strength to pull it away. 'Your husband is here.'

Ewa cannot make sense of the words. What in God's name does the woman mean? But then, swimming in front of her, are Stefan's eyes. The rest of the face is hidden behind a white surgical mask looped over his ears. This is not how she usually sees him in her dreams. But the collar of his open-necked shirt is beautifully white so she knows it cannot be real.

'Ewa... Ewa.' The dream is speaking to her in Stefan's voice. 'Ewa... Ewa.'

The heart-stopping blue eyes travel, horrified, over her face. And a rubber-covered finger touches her cheek. The rubber is warm. Real. Perhaps this is not a dream. But Ewa clenches her teeth and turns her head away. She wishes, more than anything, that Stefan would remove his finger from her skin. Whether in a dream or real life, she cannot stand for any man to touch her now. Even her husband. A cold teardrop runs into her hair.

'Why are you here?'

He looks shocked. Is it the question or the language? She would prefer never to speak German again but the nurses are nearby. Even some of the patients have recovered enough to be nosy and she guesses that none of them speaks anything other than Polish.

'I've come for you, Ewa.'

One corner of her mouth smiles. 'Looking like this?'

'You will get better.'

'I will die.'

'No.'

It must be Stefan. He never listens. Even now he wants the last word.

Air irritates the stickiness in Ewa's lungs. But as he is here, there is a question she has been meaning to ask, one that will not go away.

'Was it you...?'

His eyes above the mask frown. 'Yes, Ewa, it's me, Stefan. I am here.'

'Was it you that killed Haller?'

'God, no! Ewa... what are you talking about?'

'I saw the shot, from the woods. You were there.'

Stefan's face is still for a moment and then he blinks. 'And you think I killed Haller?'

She does her best to shrug.

'And so you think that I am the traitor? That I told them about the Dakota?'

'Were you?'

He sighs. 'Ewa... how can you...?' His voice folds in on itself, and then something in his eye changes. 'Ewa, listen. Who else did you see beside me in the woods that night?'

She tries not to breathe too deeply. 'Robak?'

'Yes, Robak. Tomasz Puźniak. He is still there, at the farm. And he knows where you are.'

Again she tries to shrug but Stefan shakes his head.

'Maybe you don't know, Ewa, what is happening here. Everyone who ever had any connection to the AK is being picked off. By police arrest or straightforward murder. For some reason, though, Tomasz has escaped. You must be careful.'

Ewa cannot make sense of his reply, cannot quite remember the sequence of those long-ago betrayals. And if Robak wants to kill her, he will need to be quick. This thought makes her want to laugh but the spasm in her throat is horribly close to a cough.

Stefan strokes a rubberised finger along her hand. 'Ewa... I am here to finish what I started last time. If any of that evidence has survived, I must take it to the Peace Conference in Potsdam without delay.'

'The suitcase...'

'Yes, the suitcase. Ewa... is there any chance that the suitcase still exists?'

She turns her face away. 'You and Beck were in it together, weren't you?'

He sighs. 'Ewa, I have a chance now, perhaps the only chance there will be, to show the truth to the world.'

'And you think the world will care?'

'The truth is so terrible that it must. And once the Allies know the truth...'

'You still care about your dead comrades more than about me.'

'No, Ewa, no. Once this is done, I will come back to you, I promise.'

She whispers. 'You always say that.'

'And I always do, don't I?'

Tears gather in his eyes, but she turns her face away.

She has no energy left to think of anything else that Stefan says, only about what is happening inside her chest. He must go. He must leave her to her phlegm. Stefan and his suitcase mean nothing compared to the terror of a cough.

'Ladies' changing room. The grille behind the cubicle.'

He frowns for a moment then nods. 'The swimming pool… I will be quick and then I will come back and get you.' He leans closer and speaks slowly so that she can hear every word. 'And you should know, Ewa, that our marriage is registered with the Royal Air Force and the Polish government in London.'

She tries not to sigh too heavily. 'I was pregnant, you know.'

Her words come out as a gurgle of spit.

'What?'

She tries again. There may never be another chance.

'In the women's camp they took it out of me. Put it in a bucket. I heard it cry but they told me I was a silly bitch… how could it, at six months?'

He rips off the surgical mask. His face is thinner, older. He has a moustache. But his face makes sense. This, she realises, is how she should have been imagining him if she had allowed herself to believe that he might be alive.

'Ewa? What are you saying?'

But now she feels the horror starting in her chest and she must concentrate. She will need all of her energy to ensure that the cough expels an efficient volume of phlegm without causing her to shit herself or vomit in the process. She wishes that Stefan would just go away, but he keeps talking.

'Listen, you must believe me, Ewa. I swear it was not me who told them about the Dakota. Things went very wrong that night, but I had to try and safeguard the only proof we have about who slaughtered our countrymen.'

Stefan's face comes very close. She wishes she could tell him to take those piercing blue eyes away. Phlegm is starting to bubble and gather at the top of her lungs. She must focus on her breaths – in, in, in, out, out. This is so absorbing that for a moment Stefan's face disappears.

'Ewa... I swear...'

She makes her mouth and nose into a shrug. Spittle runs over her lips. She must ration her words. There are not many left.

'I'm sorry I called off the Dakota...'

'No, don't be sorry, you saved it by doing that.'

'And I never fucked Beck. I know you think I did. But I never fucked anyone except you. Not until the Russians came to the camp to liberate us.'

'What? Jesus Christ, Ewa...?'

But the bloody phlegm is gathering in her throat. She should stop talking. Calm herself, minimise the attack. The cough is wheezing and worsening. She turns her head away. And in that moment she sees a stranger's face appear at the corner of the hospital hut. It is a woman's face – a striking olive complexion and calm hazel eyes. She looks dependable and honest. She looks foreign.

Stefan turns to the woman and Ewa sees the recognition in his eye. Then Ewa knows. This is her. The English pilot. She is of average build and not especially pretty. But there is no mistaking her foreignness or her profession. The sheepskin flying boots give her away.

In a thwack of rubber, Stefan strips off the gloves and grabs Ewa's hand but she cannot move her eyes from the foreign girl. And in her shock, Ewa loses control of the cough.

Goo creeps from the top of her lungs into her throat. She retches. Then the spluttering begins. She claws at Stefan, trying to lean forward and he takes hold of her racking body, horror spreading across his face.

'*Schwester*,' he shouts, not realising at first that it was the wrong language. 'Nurse!'

Across the grass, a big woman in a blue apron is coming towards them with an enamel bowl. But by now, Ewa has decided what to do with the lethal spit swilling around in her mouth.

'Nurse!'

Stefan shouts again, but as he does so, Ewa tilts back her head and with careful aim, sends a stream of blood and fatty mucus into Stefan's eyes.

'*Scheisse!*'

He cannot help himself. At moments like this, his first language is always closest to the surface.

He stands up and steps back, letting the Ukrainian woman through with her bowl and her back-rubbing and her soothing words in a mongrel dialect. Ewa submits to the firm hands but in the corner of her vision, she sees Stefan wiping his face with a big white handkerchief and the foreign girl going up to him, her serious face perplexed. Then they turn to go.

A spasm grips Ewa's throat. What has she done? *Come back*, she wants to shout, *come back*. But the cough has her in its stranglehold, stifling her voice, suffocating her. She wants to reach her hand out to Stefan, to get up, to run after him but the cough convulses her body, pinning her to the bed. Every shred of effort she has left goes into holding limply on to the bowl.

He is about to turn the corner now and is almost out of sight. *Wait! Wait, Stefan, I love you! I will never love anyone but you!* The cough, though, swallows her words and then regurgitates them in an acid torrent of bile.

In the momentary lull of expectoration, Ewa snatches another glance at the corner of the hut. But there is only a black wood wall and the dead sky. Stefan is gone. And Ewa knows then, with an iron thump of certainty, that no matter how long she might live, she will never see her husband again.

Poznań, Poland
Saturday 14 July

The track is rutted so Vee has to push the bike away from the rows of black huts that now look more like a riverside scout camp than an isolation hospital. Stefan is beside her but they do not speak. And once they are beyond the sagging trees and through the chain-link fence on to asphalt, he mounts up and begins to ride.

The mounds of rubble grow taller and the winding gaps between them narrower as they cycle into the city. Vee stares at the way ahead thinking only of what she will say to Stefan – that she did not mean to spy on him, she had simply been strolling around the huts for something to do. That is what she is trying to tell herself too.

In truth, once he left her with the bikes and went to find Ewa, Vee could not keep still. She did not go looking for Stefan and Ewa. And she assumed that visitors would do their visiting inside. But at the end of a row of single beds lined up on the grass outside a hut, she saw them.

As Vee turned the corner, she saw that Stefan was not wearing the surgical mask they had given him and he was clutching the patient's hand without any gloves. The figure on the bed was so slight that she seemed part of the bedding. Then her hollow face turned and her sunken eyes fixed on Vee. In that look there could be no doubt that Ewa knew who she was.

Despite the rough road surface, Stefan is pedalling fast between piles of debris. Nothing in the city is undamaged. Apartments, offices, shops, have all collapsed and become cut-through ruins or heaps of rubble. There are plenty of people around though, all of them pushing or carrying something – handcarts piled with straw, brushes and shovels, suitcases. A few are smartly dressed with briefcases or with summer sandals and hats. Everyone is intent on where they are going next.

When she chanced on Stefan with Ewa, Vee had tried not to stare but her eyes refused to be polite. They had moved, magnetically, from Ewa's face to her hand and in particular to the plain metal band on her ring finger. The sight of it gave Vee a jolt and made her dart backwards and out of Ewa's view. But as Vee thinks of it now, the bad taste that was left by the sight of the ring lessens. Because the plain band was on Ewa's right hand and so it cannot be a wedding ring.

Stefan glances over his shoulder and makes a hand signal to turn to the left. Brakes squeal. The ground is strewn with glass, brick and scrap metal so the bikes must be pushed. Vee is at last glad to be wearing her flying boots.

They head for a thick-walled building that towers above the rubble embankments. Apart from shell-scars to the grey render, this is the first edifice that seems intact. Stefan leans his bike's handlebars against the wall and signals Vee to do the same.

'Wait here while I look around the other side.'

She nods, glad to postpone the discussion, unwanted yet irresistible, about what the dying woman in the isolation hospital may or may not mean to him.

Dust and drains infuse the heavy air. The pulverised street is deserted except for a woman in a halter-neck top and a man's cap who is painting a solitary door. Afternoon sun has perforated the haze and Vee puts her hand to her brow, squinting at the half-collapsed apartment block. The front wall is open like a dolls' house; one room is still decorated with flowered wallpaper, another furnished with a hefty sideboard. At the base of the block, the woman painter dips her brush into a pot of black paint.

Stefan returns and beckons Vee towards steel doors at the back of the sturdy-walled building. He pulls on a rusty chain, clanking the padlock. There is nothing else anywhere near worth locking up.

'Vee, have you a file, for nails?'

Has he never noticed her fingernails? She shakes her head.

'Or a hair pin?'

There is a kirby grip wedged into the seam of her trouser pocket. With a snap, Stefan breaks it in half and slides a look at the woman with the paintbrush, but she is engrossed in her work. As the woman picks up her pot and moves away from the door, she leaves a glistening black swastika and a single word: *świnia*. Stefan pushes the kirby grip into the lock.

'There.' The freed padlock is in Stefan's hand. He opens the doors. 'Bring the bikes inside.'

Before Vee enters the doorway, she sees that the woman painter has reached the corner of the street and is dragging a crate towards a spike of stone façade that is still upright. She is just able to reach the paintbrush high enough to daub the letters of *Becken Strasse* into a black smudge.

As the steel doors close, Vee's eyes adjust to the dim light. It is some sort of disused engine-room. Slatted shadows stripe the glass-strewn floor. Stefan moves to the louvered door and pushes it open. Tall windows bleed blue light into the cavernous vault beyond.

At first, Vee cannot make sense of what her eyes are seeing but it seems that the yawning void in the floor is a huge empty swimming pool. Turquoise paint peels from the plunging sides and the arched metal steps lead only into air. At the bottom of the deep end, broken chairs and crates litter a puddle of slimy black water. Above a broken diving board, the apex of the soaring dome is as blue as the skies behind a cold front.

Vee shakes her head. 'It's a very grand building for a swimming pool.'

'It was not a swimming pool until the war.'

'What was it before?'

'I don't know the English word. *Synagoga*. For Jews.'

'A synagogue?'

'Yes.'

Beneath the blue dome, the balcony is filled with rows of benches for spectators. A whiff of chlorine lingers.

'Why would anyone go to the bother of making it into a swimming baths? In wartime too?'

'To clean the stain of *Juden*. With water and chemicals.'

'What on earth...?'

But Stefan is picking through twisted metal and smashed wood below the spectator gallery and does not seem to hear. He tries one of the doors beneath the balcony and pushes against something heavy on the other side. The door scrapes ajar and Stefan squeezes himself into the slit then disappears.

Somewhere nearby, water drips. Vee sits at the edge of the deep end, legs dangling high above the murky puddle. *4.5m*, the mosaic tiles say, whatever that is in feet. How wonderful it would be if the pool were still full of cool water and she could immerse herself in its cleanness, floating on her back to stare up into the blue dome. Perhaps then she would be able to think straight.

Suddenly outside, not very far away, there is a boom. Vee flinches and looks up. A car backfiring? Or gunshot? Her heart tightens. Who would know? Her gaze falls back to the blue concrete void below her and she realises that she has inched a little closer to it. A little too close. What a stupid way that would be to die, after all of the other times she has come close – a fall from fifteen feet rather than five thousand. She stands up and moves away from the edge. It was a mistake, she can see that now, not to ask Stefan before they came here exactly what he was up to. It is a mistake to be here with him at all.

Another crack in the air makes her jump, but it is just Stefan yanking at the door below the balcony. He squeezes himself through then hauls something out behind him. It is a big dusty suitcase. Bringing it towards Vee, he clears a space in the debris beside the pool, then lays the case on the tiles. A sour smell wafts up. Vee's nose wrinkles.

'Is that what you've been searching for?'

Stefan nods and presses at the catches. With a click and a swirl of vinegary air, the suitcase lid flips open. Vee presses her finger to her nose but crammed inside are just envelopes, piles of bulging brown envelopes that are spotted with fatty stains. Can this really be what Stefan has gone to so much trouble to find?

'What is all this, then, Stefan?'

He does not reply but starts to rifle through the packages until he finds the one that he wants. It is marked *1001* in neat faded ink and the seal has already been opened. Stefan eases the contents on to the floor; a bronze badge in the shape of a swooping eagle, an ebony cigarette-holder, a rusted pen with lizard-skin markings.

Stefan stands up and steps back, still looking at the contents.

Vee gives a snort. 'Is this why we have come here? And put the Anson in harms way, as well as ourselves?'

Stefan's hand rasps back and forth across his chin.

'Well, is it, Stefan?'

He blinks up at the blue arc of the dome. His eyes are wet. And every part of him is trembling.

'Those things there, on the floor, they belonged to someone I killed.'

'What? When?'

'When I was a prisoner. The first time. In Russia.'

'When you were with the Polish forces?'

He nods. 'The first winter of the war... I never doubted that they would let us go.'

'And did they?'

Briefly, Stefan's eyes close, then they seem to open on to something very far away. Vee has seen that look once before, when she overheard her father talking about the horrors that made him leave his homeland.

Stefan slumps down on to the dusty tiles and Vee goes to sit beside him. When he begins to talk quietly, quickly, his words are as much addressed to the building around him as to Vee. She senses that he will not leave this place until he has confessed.

'I thought they were releasing us in April 1940. They took us from the prison camp and put us on a train and then buses. The bus windows were painted grey and my friend Henryk said that this was a very bad sign, but still I had hope. They took us to a large villa, a dacha they called it, in the forest. The guards here were different to those in the camp. They shouted at us and hit us with their guns and herded us into a barbed-wire pen behind the house.

We stayed in that pen as it got dark and colder. Everyone was asking: *Are we meant to stay out here all night?* Then we heard the noises. Muffled cracks. Coming from the house. At last, somebody said the thing we were all thinking. *Was that a pistol shot?* And then I smelt the cordite and I knew it was.'

Vee puts a hand on Stefan's arm but he does not seem to notice.

'My friend Henryk pulled me to a corner of the wire pen. We shared the last cigarette in his packet and he told me his plan. He, like me, grew up in Poland but speaking German. *Remember,* he said, *that you and I are citizens of the Reich.* I was so afraid that I could not think what he meant. Henryk's eyes were frightened but his certainty swept me along. He said we should insist to our captors that our families were always loyal to the Kingdom of Prussia and then to Germany, that we were forced to join the Polish armed forces but are now delighted that our home towns are German again. Henryk said he would tell them that his uncle held a senior position in Gauleiter Greiser's administration in Reichsgau Wartheland. Which was true.'

'And was it true, about you being loyal Germans?'

'Me? Never. I am Polish. Nationality is not just about language. A great nation like Poland should be more than a group of people who happen to say their prayers in the same tongue.'

Stefan looks down at the rusted fountain pen on the floor and touches it lightly with his finger. 'Henryk thought differently, I know. But as we stood listening to pistol shots in the darkness, I could only pray that his plan would work. I knew that the Soviets had let some prisoners go free from our prison camp when they insisted that they were German and had contacts at the German Embassy in Moscow. That was in the days when Hitler and Stalin were bosom pals. *Anyway*, I thought, as we shivered behind the barbed wire, *what harm can it do to try*?

It was not long before the guards took us in single file into the dacha. I stood in line behind Henryk in what seemed like a recreation room. A stout Russian officer at a card table was questioning the prisoners, in Polish, for their name, home town and date of birth. Then he told them to remove their coats and caps and to place their belongings on the table. We could all hear the thudding of gunshot but the men seemed in a kind of trance and went willingly, as they were directed, through a panelled door.

But when Henryk arrived at the card table, he broke the spell. The Russian officer was stunned to silence by his stream of angry German. Henryk's own family had links to the highest ranks of NSDAP, he said, and if we were not safely delivered into German hands, there would be a major diplomatic incident. The Russian officer then asked him his name. *Heinrich*, he replied.

The officer was irritated but replied in good German. *All right then. Go with that guard there.* Then he looked at me. *Are you a Fritz too?* he asked. I simply nodded and my fate was sealed.

I do not know how long Henryk and I sat on a bench in a side room waiting. I should have been thinking about my treachery, my betrayal of the solemn oath I had sworn to the Republic of Poland when I joined the Air Force. But all I could think was: *do not send me through that panelled door.*

When the stout officer burst into the side room he was wearing a stained leather apron, like a butcher. For a second, I thought, stupidly, that the troops must have been hunting in the forest and the stout officer had been butchering the game. Henryk began to shout something in German but the Russian wearily put up his hand. *Spare us the drama*, he said, or words to that effect. *We are happy to believe that both of you are Volksdeutsche, but you must prove your allegiance to Hitler. The Pole is an enemy both of the Reich and of the USSR. Now you must demonstrate to me that the Pole is your enemy too.*

At this point, he took a Walther pistol from behind his apron and placed one bullet from his pocket into the magazine. I glanced at Henryk but he was looking only at the gun. *Come with me*, the officer said. I was so afraid that I could hardly walk but I followed Henryk across the recreation room and through the panelled door.

We went down a short flight of concrete stairs and into a dim corridor. A generator was rumbling but I could still hear the shots. We came to a metal door that might once have been a meat larder. The stout officer waved the handgun at Henryk. *You first*, he said. Then he knocked on the metal door and Henryk disappeared inside.

As I waited by the door on my own, I wondered whether to run. Perhaps I could find an exit directly from the cellar to the outdoors. But even if, by some chance, I could get away from the building without being seen, how could I navigate the vast Russian forests and travel a thousand kilometres with no map or money and no hope of seeing a friendly face? And so, I stayed where I was.

Then, very close, there was a blast and Henryk came back out through the door. His face was grey. *You*, said the officer in the apron and he pointed the pistol at me. I went into the windowless room. It smelled like a butcher's shop with a blocked latrine. The bulb was dim and at first I could see nothing. The cellar walls were padded with sacks and in the corner beside another closed door was a guard who looked sweaty and possibly drunk.

Then I saw that someone was lying face down on the concrete

floor. Someone rather small in very wide trousers. Not moving. The hands were tied behind the back with wire and as I could not see a head, I wondered if the body had already been decapitated. But then I realised that the head was bent forward into a sort of manhole in the floor.

The stout officer thrust his gun into my hand. The Walther PPK is a small gun but quite heavy. *Let me show you the correct angle,* the officer said and pulled me by the elbow. He guided my arm towards the head in the manhole and angled my wrist so that the nozzle of the pistol rested on the nape of the prisoner's neck. *A little higher,* the officer said, *that's right.*

The prisoner's hair fell forward and exposed the neck. The hair was very thick and curly. Dark blonde. A lock of it fell on to the barrel of the PPK. I wondered who it was and if I could remember anyone from the camp who would let his hair grow so long. But all through the winter, we prisoners had kept our heads covered in balaclavas or scarves. Then I thought no more and I pulled the trigger.' Stefan lowers his head and for a while does not seem to breathe. 'After the blast, there was a sound in the manhole like air escaping from a tyre. And with that sound, I realised who it was that I had killed.'

During his story, Vee's eyes have not moved from Stefan's face. She squeezes his arm.

'And who was it?'

Stefan snorts. 'I understood then why the Soviets had agreed to Henryk's ridiculous demands. Even an officer of the NKVD might prefer not to place his pistol against the one head, amongst the hundreds to be blown apart, that was female.

'Female?'

Stefan does not seem to hear her. 'How convenient that a stupid Volksdeutscher in a Polish uniform was there to do the dirty work instead.'

Vee frowns. 'Were there women officers, then, in the Polish army?'

Stefan's face is deathly white. 'In the Air Force, yes.' His pale eyes turn at last to rest on Vee. 'The woman I murdered was a pilot. Like you.'

Lusowo, Poland
Saturday 14 July

'Up there. Checkpoint.'

Without braking, Stefan comes to a stop, one foot on the ground. The dusty suitcase is cradled between his forearms and balanced on the crossbar. Vee wonders if the peculiar load will draw curiosity from passers-by but no one in the crumbling streets pays any attention.

Stefan nods to the end of the street where a youth in a mismatched uniform is fiddling with the stock of a sub-machine gun. Stefan bends his head towards Vee.

'Don't speak and it will be all right.'

Shakily, he sets off, keeping one protective hand on the suitcase. Overhead, a thin spire teeters from the skeleton of a church.

As they get closer, the youth in uniform raises his arm, signalling them to stop. His other hand stays on the gun hanging around his neck.

Stefan dismounts and lifts the suitcase on to the ground. The stink of decay swirls. He starts talking; an easy stream of Polish through a wide smile. The youth replies in slow sullen syllables and raises his chin at the case. Stefan shrugs as he talks and holds out his hands. The tip of a roll of green banknotes is protruding from his fist.

The guard turns to Vee, eyes narrowed. She looks at the ground and holds her breath but Stefan does not stop talking. Then he seems to shake hands with the guard as if something is agreed. The guard steps back, one hand in his pocket and waves them on. Stefan clamps the suitcase between his forearms as he remounts the bike and begins to pedal.

The road widens. To each side, empty clearings are piled with debris amongst the warehouses and workshops that still stand. Children in rags wave and shout. A boy throws a stone. Despite his cargo, Stefan's speed does not let up. Vee follows, pedalling hard on the gearless bike until she is alongside him.

'What will you say about the suitcase, if anyone asks?'

'Like I told the boy with the gun. Medical supplies.'

'He believed you?'

'Of course not. He was just glad not to need a closer look. And to have some dollars.'

'What are you going to do with the suitcase when we get back to Berlin?'

'Take it to Potsdam.'

'And you think it will prove that the Soviets were to blame for the killings?'

'Yes.'

'But will anyone at the Peace Conference listen? Now they have seen what the Germans did in their concentration camps?'

A muscle in Stefan's cheek twitches. 'They must.'

On a cleared patch of pavement, someone has made a makeshift café with boxes and stools arranged around a tea urn. The warehouses and blocks of flats in this district are less damaged. A locksmith's merchandise is laid out on a tabletop outside a shop. Trains whistle. There are, at last, patches of blue in the sky.

Vee recognises the start of the tree-lined highway that brought them to the city. Behind a chain-link fence, a tattered windsock hangs by an open field and if Vee squints at the big curving sheds and distant factory buildings, the place could almost be the Hawker factory at Langley or Vickers-Armstrong at Castle Bromwich.

Once they are past the airfield, Stefan takes a different turn.

This track leads them to the field where the Anson landed without passing through the village. Vee's stomach hops as they approach, but the Anson is still there behind the elbow of trees, camouflaged by summer leaves. Vee skirts the wing and drops her bike to the ground. The white sky is mottled with blue. There is nothing now to stop them taking off.

She rolls her shoulders and her head thumps. The last thing she ate was a sausage roll for breakfast in Berlin. But inside the plane her chocolate ration is in the overnight bag. The orange squash in her Thermos might even still be cool.

Stefan has dismounted and is lifting the suitcase onto the Anson's wing. The aeroplane clanks and groans. Vee stoops to follow him through the open door.

'Everything all right?'

Stefan is in amongst the cargo finding a place to secure the case. Lorry tyres and crates are all still tied down with straps; the folded map is still clipped to the instrument panel in the cockpit. Vee goes to the niche beneath the metal bench for her bag, but the space is empty. For a second her thoughts freeze. She could swear that she put her bag there as usual, but perhaps in the strange commotion of setting off from Gatow she stowed it somewhere else.

'Can you see my overnight bag down there?'

Stefan looks up, frowning. His face is flushed. 'What?'

'I thought I left my bag here but I can't see it.'

He stands up, holding a coil of wire which he stuffs into his pocket.

Then he rubs his hands on his jacket. 'Come, Vee. Outside.'

'Why?'

He does not reply. She follows him out on to the wing and jumps to the grass. Before she can catch up, Stefan has righted the bike and is back in the saddle.

'Where are you going?'

'To return the bike.'

'Can't we just go now? Forget the bikes.'

'No.'

'What about mine, then? Shall I come with you?'

'No. Leave it in the trees over there. And you should stay in the trees too.'

'Why?'

'If I am not back thirty minutes from now start up the engines and leave.'

'Stefan, I can't just...'

'You must go, Vee. Promise me. Take the suitcase to the Americans at the Potsdam Peace Conference. That is most important. Thirty minutes only, yes?'

Her pulse quickens. 'Shall I keep the gun, then?'

'No. Just stay in the trees. If anyone comes, anyone at all, hide.'

Vee feels suddenly cold. 'Stefan... you are coming back, aren't you?'

'Yes.'

His eyes seem empty. She goes forward and touches his hand but his fingers grip the handlebars. Then he pushes down hard on the pedals. Vee watches him ride away across the yellow field and does not breathe until he has disappeared.

She stumbles to the shade of the trees and slumps down on the dead leaves. Everything makes sense now. His precious suitcase is safely stored on a transport plane with a love-struck woman pilot who will deposit it with the American delegation at Potsdam, leaving Stefan to nurse Ewa back to loveliness. Because he is doing more than returning the bike, that is for sure. And now that he has gone, it seems ridiculous to Vee that she ever imagined him coming back with her to Berlin.

She glances at her watch. Quarter past five, Berlin time. Perhaps she should just go now. Why should she wait half an hour when he is so obviously not coming back? But her hands are shaking. Unsteadily, she stands and goes to the Anson.

Everything might look clearer if only she could find that chocolate ration and flask.

Inside the plane, the fatty odour from the suitcase is already hanging in the air. Vee checks the space between the tubular struts under the second pilot's seat but the overnight bag is not there either. The dashboard clock has a hollow tick. Five twenty-three. Almost ten minutes he has been gone. It will take her fifteen to do the checks and warm up the engines. She will start the process any minute now.

She goes outside. The low sun has pierced a clear hole in the cloud and the field is bathed in dusty light. The vis looks all right to at least fifteen hundred. Vee flicks a strand of hair from her eyes and starts her walk-around checks – kicking the tyres to test their hardness, pulling on the rudder wires, running her hands along the cowlings. A tidemark of moisture makes her examine the fuel cap more carefully but it is probably just condensation. Nothing untoward. The flaps and tail-plane move freely, the airscrews are clean. Five thirty-eight. More than twenty minutes since he went. She wipes her hands on her trousers and takes a long breath of grass-scented air. A blackbird trills. It is time to start the engines.

Inside the open doorway, Vee puts up her hand against the glare of low sunlight. Is there a quiver of movement at the edge of the grass? Warm air crosses her face. But there is nothing to see except the empty field and the distant stripe of a sandy track across it. Cloud is rising, thinning, breaking up. She slams the door and turns the handle to *SHUT*. Stefan has gone. Gone back to Ewa as he must always have been intending that he would.

The sour smell of the suitcase catches at Vee's throat as she picks her way across canvas bracing straps to the cockpit. The thin padding of the pilot's seat still seems to hold her shape. As she sits, her hands go instinctively to the panel through the pattern of routine checks: *Hydraulics – DOWN, Flaps – UP, Fuel mixture – RICH, Column control – UNLOCKED*. And then she sets the compass to **W**. Numbers glow green on the panel clock. Quarter to six. She flicks the first ignition switch.

The seat shudders. There is a sound from the engine like the squeak of chamois leather on glass and petrol vapour needles through the cabin. Then the port-side propeller booms into the roots of Vee's hair. She flicks the second magneto switch and the thunder thrills through her from both sides.

For a second, her eyes close. She will tell them at Gatow that poor vis stopped her journey to Pilsen and she will have to try again tomorrow. But she can imagine the look they will give her. So this might be the last time that she will ever have control of a war plane, the last time that she will feel the elation and power of the cockpit, the last time that she will ever feel quite so alive.

The windscreen panels carve black lines on to the yellow field. Vee reaches behind her for the straps. And at the edge of her vision something dark drops. The straps fall loose as she stands to check both sides of the windscreen for one last time. But there is nothing. And then the Anson gives a lurch. The cabin door is still closed but the handle is moving. Someone is outside. Hairs stiffen on the back of her neck. Is it Stefan? Or Tomasz? Or someone else? On the instrument panel, the needles on the temperature and pressure gauges are hovering in the middle of the dials. The Anson is ready to go. Then the door bursts open.

'Stefan!'

He falls into the plane, his head lolling forward on to the dirty floor. Blood seeps from his jacket. He gives a low moan.

'My God, Stefan. What's happened?' She is on the floor beside him. Her hands are already covered in his blood. 'Are you all right?'

Stupid, stupid question. What is she saying? But the muscles in Stefan's face are moving as he tries to speak. His hot breath is on her cheek.

'Berlin…'

'Stefan, you need a doctor.'

His face is paper white but his eyes are clear.

'No. Berlin.'

'Stefan. I can't fly with you like this. I'll turn off the engines and get help.'

'No… fly, Vee, fly now.'

Her chest is pounding. What should she do? The nearest hospital must be in the city. But how can she move him? Perhaps in the village… but how can she even ask for help? She hasn't a single word. Her mind gallops. If she does fly, it is less than an hour to Gatow. There is a clinic there and RAF medics. Perhaps he is right.

She takes hold of his hand and shouts into his ear. 'All right, Stefan. I'm going to fly you to Gatow. Quick as I can. We just need somehow to stop the bleeding.'

Her boot slips on the wetness as she stands, eyes casting around the hold. And then she sees her overnight bag in the cargo area wedged between two tea chests. How did it get there, in a place that she would never have stowed it? And the clasps are open. The flask seems to be missing but her clean white shirt is still crisp with starch.

'Here.'

Folding her shirt into a pad, she pulls open Stefan's jacket. One side of his shirt is sopping red. The revolver is still tucked into his waistband and a sheen of blood reveals the cross-hatching on the grip. She puts two fingers on the sticky handle and pulls it free. Then she presses her clean shirt on to Stefan's wound as hard as she dares. Above the blare of engines, he yelps like an animal.

'Sorry, Stefan, I'm sorry. But I need to tie you in as well.'

Reaching out, she takes hold of a loose end of bracing strap and eases it under Stefan's spine. He groans but she pulls the strap tight around the improvised dressing. At least he is now bound, if loosely, to the fuselage. She must fly the Anson faster and more smoothly than she ever has.

Stefan's eyes are closed and he is not moving or making any sound. Only breathing. Vee takes the barrel of the gun in her fist and pushes up the safety lever with her thumb. Then she stands up, fastens the door handle and, with a gulp of sour air, scrambles back to the cockpit.

What has Stefan done? Is someone coming after him? If they are, the engines have been booming across open countryside for at least ten minutes. Everyone nearby must know that the plane is here. But nothing outside seems to move except the shimmer of leaves in the breeze. Vee places the revolver within her reach in the pouch beneath the side window.

She sits and fumbles with the seat straps, hands smeared with Stefan's blood. But the engines are warm and as soon as she touches the rudder pedals and opens the throttle, the Anson spins on its tail-wheel. The plane begins to bump over the grass. Vee's eyes flick across the instrument panel to the fuel gauge: *tail on ground – 25 gallons*. Had it not been less than that when they landed? Twenty-three gallons, she could have sworn. She puts her finger on the glass circle and taps on the dial. But the needle stays on *25*. The fuel level cannot have gone up. As with the overnight bag, she must be mistaken.

Vee puts the Anson in the furthest part of the field. Still no one is about. Behind her, Stefan is quiet, as if asleep. Ahead, the field looks flat and inviting. She pulls back the throttle. Is there a slight cough before the engine responds? But it does not matter, the Anson is gaining speed.

Wheels judder, wings vibrate. Faster now. Vee feels the slight tilt from behind as the tail-wheel leaves the ground. She glances at the speed. *85*. About right. Then the shaking in the cockpit ceases and the wings are still. The ground falls away. The trees start to do that thing that she loves, becoming miniature, like accessories for a model railway. *Undercarriage – UP*, red light on. Good. The plane seems to leap and lighten as the wheels fold themselves away.

Treetops blur and beyond them roofs appear. Vee can see the muddy main street of the village and a crowd of people gathered outside the biggest house with the orange roof. Tomasz's house. But then that too, shrinks. The cloud is well clear of the cockpit's glass roof. Vee glances at the compass. Time to bank now, and to get on the right course. West.

She turns to glance at Stefan. He is still, perhaps asleep. She must tell him, as soon as he wakes, that she has no doubt the Polish female pilot would have understood perfectly that Stefan had no choice about what he did. The poor woman would have certainly forgiven him just as Vee, in the same place, would too. She wouldn't think twice.

Vee turns the steering yoke and pulls back on the control column. As it always does on a turn, the Anson slows. But then there is a bang. It is loud, close, unfamiliar and it makes her flinch. Instinctively, she glances through the side windows at each propeller in turn, but they have not slowed. Already though, the Anson is losing height. Vee pulls back harder on the column, pushing up the throttle. She checks the gauges because she cannot think what else to do. The port wing is tilting now. Trees, fields, barn roofs are getting closer. She looks up to the sky. Not so long ago the cloud had been very close. Now it seems impossibly far away.

No matter. If one of the engines fails, she'll find a place to land. She can land without both engines at a push. She has done it before. Not in an Anson, mind you, but others have, and lived to tell the tale over a gin in the mess. It should not be too hard, should it? The fields are big here and some have been harvested. People are cutting the square cornfield directly below. The ground looks flat and hard. She can land somewhere near one of those hamlets. Maybe there will be someone there to help Stefan. He is losing blood after all and Berlin, on one engine, would be a stretch. Perhaps a forced landing will end up being for the best.

The Anson is still dropping and there is still no reason for it that Vee can understand. Each second seems to lengthen. Her eyes swivel across the instruments and the windows. Cornfields, dark woods, the lake. And yes, over there, to the north, an unfenced stubble field, not too rough. To the north. Turn towards it. Please turn. Treetops are just below. Sycamores and oaks and birch are all rising up. A branch brushes one of the wings. A birch branch. But that field is not far, over there, just beyond these trees. Not far. Almost there.

Poznań, Polish People's Republic
November 1945

Ewa has been boarded out on the wrong side of the river as the people there are less fussy about who they will take. The hospital doctor, a Russian woman, insisted to the wife in very bad Polish that Ewa was no longer infectious, if indeed she ever had been. It can't have been Tuberculosis, the doctor said, or Ewa would certainly be dead by now. The family are suspicious though. They have rigged up a curtain between Ewa's truckle bed and the grandfather's, and they will not let her cook any of her food in their pan. Ewa does her best not to let them hear her cough.

The hospital gives Ewa a small amount of light work in return for paying for her rent and board. It is nothing much – rolling bandages, sweeping the floors of the huts. She does not mind, although some days when she wakes and her chest feels bad, she wonders whether she will even have the strength to open her eyes.

Several times in the summer that cough nearly saw her off, but there is no doubt now that Ewa is getting better. Her recovery seemed to start, in fact, on the afternoon that her husband visited with the foreign girl. Before that, Ewa's world had shrunk to the size of her respiratory tract. Then, once they appeared, the horizon suddenly opened. Perhaps they re-ignited in her a spark of life. Who would have guessed that jealousy and rage could be so therapeutic?

Ewa often thinks about their visit as she makes her slow daily trek to the hospital. From the collapsed bridge she can see the corner of the hut where the girl-pilot appeared. Ewa remembers her standing there, shocked and staring, with her gaze aslant, as if Ewa were a letter containing very bad news. The girl looked mousy and reserved, she was English after all, but she seemed tough too. As soon as Ewa noticed the foreign girl's unseasonal sheepskin boots there could be no doubt about who she was.

The marshy plain beneath the squashed bridge is webbed with brown streams. A great weight from above seems to have pressed down and left the bridge undulating between its stone arches. Metal tramlines rise up and down across it like a roller-coaster track. But the makeshift wooden walkway laid across the dips is busy with people.

On her walks across the bridge, it is not long before Ewa sees someone she knows. Although it is November, the weather is not yet particularly cold but a young woman is clopping towards her in a fur coat. The coat has an old-fashioned cut but the richness of the sable is breathtaking. Ewa sees a twitch of the pencilled eyebrows and knows that the woman has recognised her too.

'Good day, Alenka.'

Ewa puts out a hand and it touches the fur sleeve as Alenka yanks her arm away. The feel of the coat makes Ewa gasp; its softness has an essence of luxury and beauty that she thought had evaporated from the world. Alenka does not look at Ewa as she clomps off but Ewa hears her parting words: *Niemiecka suka*.

Ewa keeps walking. She had thought herself numb to any insult after enduring so many in the women's camp at Ravensbrück, as if the receptors in her brain that used to convert words into pain had all been switched off. But here she is, on the collapsed bridge in her home town, feeling as if she might cry because a dolled-up liaison girl has called her a *German bitch*.

The tears are not for herself, of course. As soon as she could stand up from her hospital bed and insist that she had simply been suffering from a chest infection, Ewa had picked her way to the old town and found the corner of the square where there used to be a guest house. Now there is not even enough of it left for them to daub on abuse in black paint.

Ewa then went to the post office which was one of the places where people congregated to search for the missing. She blinked twice when she saw old Jabłoński still in a postman's uniform although one with all of the badges pulled off so she could not tell which government had issued it to him. Through everything, he continues to deliver the post in the old town. His knowledge of its crevices and alleyways has been as good as a bulletproof vest.

Jabłoński was reluctant to tell her, but she insisted. For her own safety, she said, she had to know. So he explained, perhaps leaving out some details, about how, when Ewa was arrested, the German occupiers had turfed her father out of the guest house. But otherwise they had left him alone. Some of the top brass must have been fond of him and had sympathy for an old soldier. He is dead now, though. In the end, Oskar Hartman's Polish neighbours delivered his punishment for speaking the language of his grandfather too well.

Ewa tried to press Jabłoński about what exactly had happened to her father but he would not say. And since then she has seen a corpse hanging from the lamp post outside the Hotel Bazar with a black swastika painted on its bloated belly. So she is glad that she does not know the whole truth. Alenka's insult, like the final clank of a key in a lock, confirms what Ewa already knows, that sometime soon she must leave the city that has been her only home and never come back.

Ewa cannot really argue with Alenka's description, though. She knows herself to be a bitch; just look at how she treated her husband when she last saw him. And anyone who knows the various names she has answered to can have no doubt about her ancestry. She sees now, and with complete clarity, that anything she fought for in the war, any sacrifice she made, will, in this newly named country, simply count against her. She also realises, and the thought provokes a nasty hacking laugh, that the German occupiers actually saved her life by sending her to their women's concentration camp. If she had been in Poznań when the war ended here in the spring, she would now be in the same place as her father.

After the unpleasantness with Alenka, Ewa keeps a scarf around her mouth and her head down when she goes to the market. The trestle stalls stand on the same spot as the flower market but the square is unrecognisable. At the centre of the wasteland, a wrecked tank points its long-range gun at the sky. The tank has become a fixed point in a city of shifting rubble. It is almost a source of gaiety with garish posters pasted over the gun turret – a dancing couple in evening dress, a rosy-cheeked baby, an advert for toothpaste.

Ewa stands in the potato queue wrapped in her scarf. The air is mild, though, which is just as well because she has no winter coat and no notion of how to get one. She shuffles forward and pushes the scarf back from her face, trying to see what is set out on the stall. The sparse produce is arranged in a diamond pattern. But one good potato will last her a couple of days. The woman in front of her in the queue has nothing on her head at all. And with a flutter of her stomach, Ewa recognises the outdated hairstyle.

Ewa stands for a moment wondering what to do. There is no doubt in her mind that saying anything to anyone about the AK is as good as buying a ticket to Siberia. But Ewa does not much care what happens to her next. Her desire to know what happened before is stronger. She taps Gertruda on the shoulder.

Gertruda turns hastily and Ewa sees that she has been recognised. She also understands the look on Gertruda's face; her nonchalance is masking terror.

'Hello there.' Ewa tries to keep her voice light. 'Shall I see you in church sometime? I still go to St Adalbert's.'

Gertruda nods. 'Saturday perhaps. For confession.'

Then Gertruda loses her place in the queue as she scuttles away.

The following Saturday, Ewa sits in the same pew for most of the morning. She does not mind. She has nothing else to do and compared to her room, the church feels quite warm.

As the priest is leaving for his lunch, Gertruda comes in, genuflecting more deeply than is really necessary. She catches Ewa's eye and beckons her to sit away from the altar where they will be in the shadows.

As soon as Ewa kneels beside her, Gretruda starts whispering into her clasped fingers like a prayer. 'We never found out who it was but there was a traitor in the AK that is for sure. The Germans had their raid so well planned there can be no doubt.'

Ewa bends her head and pretends also to pray. 'Who do you think it was?'

'Tomasz Puźniak.' Gertruda's words spit out. 'Pah! Robak. The worm!'

'Are you sure?'

'After the ambush, the Gestapo seemed to have no interest in him. And last February, when the Russians came, he ducked and dived then too. The NKVD picked off all of our old AK comrades except for him. They even gave him Haller's farm. He had learned how to suck up to whoever was in charge and tell them what they wanted to know. A born snitch. He was the only one who made it through the war.'

Except for you, old woman, Ewa thinks but does not say *and for me*.

'At least he got his justice in the end.' Gertruda continues.

'How?'

'Murdered. In July. Executed, in fact. His wrists were fastened behind his back with wire and there was a single bullet hole in the back of the head. Pah! Good riddance!'

'Did someone from the AK take revenge?'

'No, no. It was the British.'

'What? How do you know this?'

'I was told about it on very good authority by a woman from the village who used to work for Jan Haller and held him in the greatest respect. She and her daughter were harvesting a cornfield when they saw a British plane land near the village. Then, a few hours later, it took off again. And in that time, Robak had been killed. The women saw his body. Assassinated. For sure.'

A cold film of dread, such as she has not felt for many months, begins to wash down Ewa's spine.

'In July you say...'

'Yes. The British must have still been angry about the Dakota escapade. That's why they sent their secret agents to kill the worm.'

'What do you mean? Secret agents?'

'Two people. A man and a woman. Although they did not get away, more's the pity for them.'

Ewa's heart drops like lead. Her voice is hardly there. 'What happened to them?'

'A plane crash. The workers rushed from the cornfield when they saw the plane falling into the trees. But it was too late. There was no explosion, no fireball, so they found the bodies – a girl strapped into the cockpit, still warm. And a man, although you would hardly know that was what it was, they said. A bloody mess, he was.'

Ewa's fingers are so tightly clasped that she feels the ridges on her bones. *A bloody mess.* Gertruda does not notice a tear slip down Ewa's cheek.

'The police, or men who said they were police, came soon after, and shooed the farm workers away. No one found out who the dead couple were or what the plane had been doing in their village. But it was a British plane, there was no doubt about that.'

Ewa does not hear any more. She starts to mumble. Perhaps Gertruda thinks it is a prayer and not the words: *my poor darling, my poor darling*, repeated again and again. Ewa does not notice when Gertruda slopes off. No one in the church takes any notice of the thin woman weeping on to cold stone. Nowadays, everyone goes to church to cry. As soon as Ewa thinks she has no tears left, she stands and tries to make for the door. But her eyes go towards the entrance to the sacristy and then begin to stream all over again.

Later, as she stares from her bed at the stains on the ceiling, Ewa thinks about the girl-pilot and decides not to hold a grudge. Perhaps Stefan, in his own way and for reasons he thought to be good, was using the foreign girl for his own ends, just as he had used Ewa. And neither will Ewa blame the girl-pilot for the crash. She seemed like someone you could rely on in an emergency. She probably did her best.

Over the next days, the weather turns biting cold. Ewa wears every piece of clothing that she owns and still shivers. But she does not mind. The arctic air seems to bring clarity to her thoughts. She knows now that her life will be different to anything she ever imagined, but she will have a life, of that she is determined.

The men in the post office exchange shifty looks when she asks for a stamp on a letter to England. She sees them looking too when she comes in every day to check for a reply. But she has had a word with Jabłoński and the foreign post when it arrives, does not go astray.

It is not just a letter she receives, but a parcel. There is a letter inside it and a piece of stiff paper with numbers and words that have the look of money. Her own letter, addressed to: *Royal Air Force, London* was written in German which she guessed would be more likely than Polish to be understood. But the reply is in English, as are all of the other things in the parcel – a hardback book, a set of cigarette cards showing seaplanes, and a pilot's logbook with the initials *SB* embossed in gold.

She sits on her stale bed and presses the open logbook to her face, breathing as hard as her lungs will permit. And yes, she is sure, it gives off the very faintest smell of unfiltered cigarettes and shaving soap.

One of the orderlies at the isolation hospital used to boast, until the woman doctor gave him a very arched look, that he had once visited America. Ewa takes Stefan's things and the letter to show him. She gives him half a cabbage and makes him promise not to tell anyone about what he will translate.

The orderly's eyes light up. It is a postal money order, he says. For seven pounds. Ewa has no idea at all how much that is worth. The letter tells her that this is her widow's pension, backdated. The letter also says, although the orderly's English is not as good as he has led everyone to believe, that a travel pass would be available should she ever wish to visit Britain. He tells her that the hardback book is called *The Correct Word and How to Use It*. The seaplane facts on the cigarette cards Ewa can work out for herself.

And so, not long before Advent, Ewa stands beside a hand-painted platform sign at the railway station. She turns up the collar of her new second-hand coat. The air is sharp but deliciously clear; feathery cirrus clouds comb the turquoise sky. She will take trains and a boat and another train, and keep heading west. When the track runs out, she will get off the train and try not to go anywhere else ever again.

She will make a life for herself. Occasionally she might even persuade herself that she is in love. But the new name, *Mrs Eve Bergel*, which is written on her letter of safe passage, will be the last one she ever has.

Sometimes in the years to come Eve will wonder what might have happened on that sultry afternoon at the isolation hospital if she had not spat in Stefan's face. Was everything that followed after that her own fault? And if she had not told him where the suitcase was hidden, he might not have come to be inside the Avro Anson as it fell into woodland with an ashen-faced English girl at the controls.

Thoughts like this are pointless, she knows, but they keep her memory of Stefan alive. She will not waste time in imagining what became of the suitcase filled with relics from a war crime that no one wants to remember. For decades to come, the whole world will agree that this particular atrocity, somewhat awkward amongst the countless uncomplicated others, is best forgotten. She always knew that Stefan was deluded about the power of facts to change anyone's mind. But she will not blame him for trying.

And as she grows older, Eve will also do her best not to be too hard on the poor girl lying on a makeshift hospital bed, trying not to cough up her guts when her husband appears. How could that girl have possibly known, as Stefan ripped off the surgical mask, that she would never see his dear face again?

Instead, even as she lies, fading, on her kitchen floor, Eve will try to remember the best of her time with Stefan Bergel. She will think of him on that wide grassy airfield pointing up at the cirrus clouds, and perhaps, in her last moments, she will remember the cool brown water of the lake and sunlight slicing through reeds on to their bare limbs. This is what love can be, she will remind herself. This is what life can be.

1963

Aerogram

Sehr geehrte Frau Bergel,

I am sorry, I know I intrude upon your peace and I could not blame you for thinking that the reasons behind this letter are entirely selfish. I should have written it many years ago but I told myself there was no way of finding you, despite the fact that I never looked. A chance occurrence has, however, compelled me now to write.

My twin boys, you see, are nearing fourteen and they show a great aptitude for languages. Whilst looking for a summer school to help them improve their English, I came upon a brochure for The South Coast School of English. And in it, though I had thought never to have that joy again, I saw you.

The sight of your face stirred in me so many thoughts and memories that expressing them to you has become inevitable. Should you throw this letter away unopened, I would not bear the slightest reproach. However, should you read it and then have questions for which only I am left to provide an answer, please, dear lady, write back. I swear I will give you an honest reply to any question. My memory of those years, when I can bear to delve into it, remains clear.

Indeed, some memories have recently started to come unbidden. I find myself doing everyday tasks, like filling a watering can for my dahlias or watching a garage attendant pump fuel into my car, and I find my vision intruded by images from the war.

These appear to be real, earthly things. I have seen the charred body of an old man in my children's sandpit, a dead baby in my filing cabinet and last week a young woman in a yellow Dirndl apparently drowning in my freshly drawn bath. Good, you may say. And I myself, in a way, feel glad that I have not escaped entirely unscathed from my part in Germany's war.

Before I write of your husband let me first offer my sincere condolences for your loss. I know that he died many years ago and I see from your name that you have not remarried. I regret, sincerely, that my sympathies are so belated. Despite all that happened I still count your husband, above all, as my friend.

Did he ever give you an account of our time together as prisoners in Russia? He may not have burdened you with the story of how we escaped from the hell that this imprisonment became in the end and I will not inflict that story upon you now. Should you wish to know, you have only to ask. Suffice it to say that the massacre we avoided was more terrible than anyone now cares to believe. I wonder whether the full truth of this Polish tragedy will ever be known. Certainly, untold thousands of our best countrymen were slaughtered and no one, save their nearest loved ones, wants to remember them. These heroes have been betrayed by the whole world and this betrayal seems only compounded with the passing years. The real culprits behind this slaughter are no nearer justice and it is worse than pointless for someone like me to broadcast the truth. So I have kept quiet.

Posterity allows me to see the futility of your husband's quest for justice in respect of our murdered comrades, but in 1943 the situation appeared very differently to us both. When he first came to me, on a bright autumn morning as I was leaving the swimming pool, I had an uncanny intuition about what he was going to request.

This was the first time we had met since our ghastly release from Soviet captivity over three years before. I was shocked but also delighted to see him looking handsome and well dressed on your city's fine streets. In 1940, he had slipped away suddenly from the train that was carrying us out of the USSR and I often wondered what became of him.

Unlike me, Stefan's revulsion for what the Soviets had done to our compatriots did not drive him into the service of Germany. I may be deluded, but even now I do not blame myself for the choice I made in 1940. No one knew then the depths to which the German nation would sink, not even those who were about to set that horror in motion. It was only later in the war that I saw what a mistake I had made, but by then it was too late. In October 1943, standing there in the shadow of the new swimming pool, I was trying not to admit to myself that when Stefan told me about his escape from our Russian train and his daring journey through Rumania and France to England and the RAF, I was envious.

So here he was, perilously far behind enemy lines and throwing his trust wholly into the hands of a German officer. Stefan insisted that he was seeking a purely personal alliance with me to safeguard the truth. He knew about the documents that had been exhumed from the Katyn graves and the work of the Posen Forensic Institute to preserve and catalogue them. The Reich authorities always hoped that the proof of this war crime would drive a wedge between the Western Allies and the USSR.

Stefan knew too that I had been placed in charge of the project to preserve the relics. His plan was to transport some of this exhumed evidence into Allied hands without the prior knowledge of the British. He stressed that neither the Reich authorities nor even the AK, each of whom had their own agendas with regard to the massacre, should know anything of his plan. He and I alone would preserve a cache of evidence which, if the war went badly for Germany, would be the only remaining proof that the Soviets had, in 1940, massacred the whole military elite of the Republic of Poland.

I saw at once the sense in what your husband was proposing. By that time, the Red Army was pushing us back from the east and I sometimes seemed alone amongst my colleagues in realising that their direction of travel would be only one way. When they reached Posen, as I knew that they would, the Katyn grave goods would become one of their most valuable spoils of war, spoils which would instantly be thrown upon a bonfire.

So it made sense to me that some of the mass of relics that I had been in charge of preserving should be sent for safe-keeping in England. How the envelopes were to be transported to there, I never asked. And believe me, Frau Bergel, your husband never said. It was well known that the Polish underground had a network of couriers who ran clandestine supply lines through Slovakia and Hungary as well as the Baltic. So I assumed this to be the mode of transit to England. It was not until the morning of the fateful day that I learnt about the planned arrival of an Allied transport plane to our area. By then, the suitcase of evidence was already in your husband's possession and I was fully implicated in his plot.

And what of you in all this, dear Frau Bergel? I knew all along who you were. I remembered your name and your beautiful face from the letters and photographs that Stefan had showed me on his ragged bunk in our Russian prison citadel. So, three years later, when I arrived by happy accident in Posen and then came to the Guest House Hartman, I was already smitten.

Let me assure you, dear lady, that whilst we lived in the same house, I had no idea that you were involved with the AK. Once I knew that Stefan had returned, I suspected, of course, that you must be in touch with him in some way. But I did not understand the extent of your participation in the insurgency until I saw you with him and the others through the darkness at the partisans' landing ground. Later, in that horrible office block in the aftermath of the raid, my only concern was to spare you the police's more extreme forms of persuasion. This is why, in an attempt to produce a confession, I told you, to my shame, that your husband was a traitor.

In the years since then I have thought of you many times, wondering if you had survived the indignities of the women's camp and after the war, avoided the retributions that were meted out in our Polish homeland. Then, to my joy, I discovered The South Coast School of English. When I saw your face in the brochure, I have no shame in admitting that the sight of you made me break down and weep. Your elegance, your wisdom and your resilience shone from the page. You are, dearest Eva, even more lovely now than when I knew you in our youth.

I told you once, do you remember, that you would always be able to rely on me as a person? In this, as in many things in my life, I failed, but I do not seek your forgiveness. Even asking for it seems like an impertinence. All I hope is that you can remember what happened and that you can try to understand.

Mit besten Grüssen
Heinrich Beck

Author's Note

Amongst the fictional characters in this novel there is one very real person, the Polish Air Force officer, Janina Lewandowska (1908–1940). It was Janina's fate that provided me with the key to constructing my WWII story about women pilots and Polish resistance fighters which became *When We Fall*. Janina's remains were unearthed in the forest at Katyn, now in Russia, by occupying German forces in 1943. The occupiers found thousands of Polish prisoners of war who had been killed by the Soviets in 1940 and buried in mass graves. But Janina Lewandowska, a pioneering parachutist and pilot, was the only woman.

As part of my research for this novel, I had seen the charming wedding photograph that shows Janina Dowbor-Muśnicka, daughter of the famous general and Polish national hero, marrying her gliding instructor Mieczysław Lewandowski beside one of the gliders they both loved to fly. The date of this photo is poignant. It was taken in the summer of 1939, just a few months before the outbreak of war when the newlyweds, both Polish Air Force reservists, would be called up to their respective squadrons and never see each other again.

Shortly after the initial publication of *When We Fall*, Janina's wedding photograph suddenly became much more personal when I was contacted by relatives of the two people in it. Jo Dowbor-Muśnicka is the granddaughter of Janina's cousin and Jack Lewandowski is the grandson of Janina's husband, Mieczysław. They got in touch with me separately saying that they had heard about my novel and explaining their connection to Janina. Thus began a remarkable dialogue in which Jack and Jo both generously shared with me many details about their family histories. As I found out more about Janina and Mieczysław, as well the post-war stories of their relatives, the wedding photograph which had before seemed poignant, soon became almost unbearably sad.

I would like to thank Jo and Jack for their generosity and for their kind words about *When We Fall*. My portrait of Janina is of course fictionalised, but I hope that it will help spread the real story of a remarkable young woman who was murdered in prime of her life.

* The Institute of National Remembrance (IPN) is a historical department set up by the government of Poland to research, archive and disseminate information about crimes against the Polish people during the period 1917–1990. For more information, including about the Katyn massacres, go to www.ipn.gov.pl

Acknowledgements

When We Fall is my second novel to be published, but it is the one I started first. I had the idea for it in 2008 after reading an obituary for the wartime pilot Diana Barnato Walker. At that point, I had not written any fiction since I was a child but I had a sudden feeling that if I was ever going to write a novel, the story of the women pilots of world war two would be a good place to start. I thought it might take me about six weeks to write a presentable version of a novel, a few months at the most. Twelve years later, here it finally is.

So, after such a long time in the making, there are many people to thank for the fact that this story has finally become a published book and I, in the process, have become a writer.

The journey started with the women of Air Transport Auxiliary, none of whom are still alive, but their incredible feats live on in the memoirs that many of them wrote. I think I have read almost all of these vivid, funny and often heart-breaking accounts of wartime life in the air and without them I would not have had the confidence to write about the world of the 'Spitfire women'. I am also grateful to Richard Poad and Maidenhead Heritage Centre who helped get my ATA research journey underway.

As my reading about the second world war deepened, I knew that the dramatic heart of the story would have to be in Poland, and in particular, in the Katyn massacres that were hidden for five decades by powers on both sides of the cold war. For readers who want to know more about what happened, the best introduction to the horror and impact of the atrocity is to watch the astonishing film *Katyń* (2007) by Andrzej Wadja whose own father was a victim.

From the mass of incredible books about the war that I read over the course of a decade, it seems unfair to single out particular titles. But I hope that as a follow-up to the fictional story of *When We Fall*, readers might like to find out more about the book's historical background. The best starting point for the ATA women pilots is *Spitfire Women of World War II* by Giles Whittell, for the intriguing story of wartime Poznań, read *Model Nazi: Arthur Greiser and the Occupation of Western Poland* by Catherine Epstein and for an astonishing insight into the Polish resistance movement written by one of its true heroes, please seek out *Story of a Secret State* by Jan Karski.

Many writers and editors have given generously of their time and expertise to help with this novel and to shape me into a novelist. Jacqui Lofthouse was there at the beginning and only she really understands quite how far I have come. Thanks to Richard Skinner and the brilliant Faber Academy/ Truckles writers, and also to Sarah Savitt, Sam Copeland, Alison Hennessey, Sara Starbuck, Neema Shah, Fiona Erskine and Marcelle Perks. Special thanks to Gaynor Arnold whose razor sharp editorial notes helped move the book's final draft on to a completely new level.

Friends and family who read any of the many earlier versions of this story all contributed in some way to the book that has now been published. Thanks to Eileen Milner, Sally Kirby, Polly Milner, Emily Milner, Lynne Eadie, Caroline Fox, Lorna Gentry, Phil Laymon, Lynne Thoms, Jane Shillaker, Will Orr and Niki Orr. Vicky Jordan and the staff and volunteers of Woodcote library were a big help in the early days of research. Thanks too to Marcelle Perks and Ingo Ebeling for advice about German usage and to Asia Milner for help with Polish. The heart of this story would not really beat without the knowledge of Poland given me by my sister-in-law, Asia. I am hugely grateful to her and my brother Terence, and to the Lipowicz family for their hospitality. Thanks also to Tomasz Laskowski for an inspirational tour of second world war sites in the wonderful city of Poznań.

When We Fall would still be languishing in one of those unsuccessful earlier versions were it not for the faith shown in me by my agent Andrew Lownie and by my fabulous publisher No Exit Press. Love and thanks for everything to Ion, CQ, Claire, Lisa, and to Katherine Sunderland.

It goes without saying that I could not have become a novelist without the love and support of my family: my parents Peter and Eileen; my daughters and their menfolk Grace and Toby, and Eliza and Kye; my mother-in-law, Sally and most of all my husband, Paul. I'm so lucky to live with the most enthusiastic, astute and encouraging reader that any writer could wish for. And if I'd let you read this book a bit sooner, my love, it might not have taken me twelve years to write it.

For more about my books go to www.carolynkirby.com

Reading Group Questions

1. What was your favourite moment in the novel?

2. Did you prefer the chapters told from Vee's point of view, or from Ewa's?

3. If you could ask Carolyn Kirby a question about this book, what would it be?

4. Did your understanding of the part played by women in World War Two change as a result of reading this book?

5. Conflicts about national identity are at the heart of this novel. How do the characters' experience of a mixed cultural heritage compare with those of people today?

6. The role of female pilots in the Second World War was little known until recently. Why do you think there are still so few women working as pilots?

7. When did you begin to suspect the identity of the elderly woman who opens the novel?

8. Did your view of Stefan change when you found out what he had done at Katyn?

9. Do you think the experience of the character Beck is reflective of German people as a whole during the Second World War?

10. *When We Fall* explores the choices individuals make when pushed to their limits. Do you agree with the choices each character makes when they are most tested?

11. Why do you think the publishers chose the cover they did and what do you think of it?

12. What do you think might have happened to Vee, Ewa and Stefan if they had all survived into old age?

NO EXIT PRESS

More than just the usual suspects

'A very smart, independent publisher delivering the finest literary crime fiction' – *Big Issue*

MEET NO EXIT PRESS, the independent publisher bringing you the best in crime and noir fiction. From classic detective novels to page-turning spy thrillers and singular writing that just grabs the attention. Our books are carefully crafted by some of the world's finest writers and delivered to you by a small, but mighty, team.

In over 30 years of business, we have published award-winning fiction and non-fiction including the work of a Pulitzer Prize winner, the British Crime Book of the Year, numerous CWA Dagger Awards, a British million copy bestselling author, the winner of the Canadian Governor General's Award for Fiction and the Scotiabank Giller Prize, to name but a few. We are the home of many crime and noir legends from the USA whose work includes iconic film adaptations and TV sensations. We pride ourselves in uncovering the most exciting new or undiscovered talents. New and not so new – you know who you are!!

We are a proactive team committed to delivering the very best, both for our authors and our readers.

Want to join the conversation and find out more about what we do?

Catch us on social media or sign up to our newsletter for all the latest news from No Exit Press HQ.

f fb.me/noexitpress **𝕏** @noexitpress
noexit.co.uk/newsletter